In th

He pr

Will she succumb
pleasure he offers?

SOLD
to the
SHEIKH

**Three exotic novels from three
outstanding bestselling authors!**

SOLD
to the
SHEIKH

MIRANDA LEE
EMMA DARCY
KATE WALKER

*M&B™ and M&B™ with the Rose Device
are trademarks of the publisher.
Harlequin Mills & Boon Limited, Eton House,
18-24 Paradise Road, Richmond, Surrey TW9 1SR*

SOLD TO THE SHEIKH
© by Harlequin Enterprises II B.V./S.à.r.l. 2009

Love-Slave to the Sheikh © Miranda Lee 2006
Traded to the Sheikh © Emma Darcy 2005
At the Sheikh's Command © Kate Walker 2006

ISBN: 978 0 263 87519 5

027-0609

*Printed and bound in Spain
by Litografía Rosés S.A., Barcelona*

Love-Slave
to the Sheikh

MIRANDA LEE

Miranda Lee is Australian, living near Sydney. Born and raised in the bush, she was boarding-school educated and briefly pursued a career in classical music, before moving to Sydney and embracing the world of computers. Happily married, with three daughters, she began writing when family commitments kept her at home. She likes to create stories that are believable, modern, fast-paced and sexy. Her interests include meaty sagas, doing word puzzles, gambling and going to the movies.

PROLOGUE

'You do not need to couch your diagnosis in soft terms. Please tell me the reality of my situation.'

The neurosurgeon looked across his desk at his VIP patient. He did not doubt that Sheikh Bandar bin Saeed al Serkel meant his brave words. But he wondered if the Sheikh was really prepared to hear that his odds of surviving were the same as those the bookmakers were giving on the Sheikh's three-year-old colt winning the Derby?

Even money.

'You have a brain tumour,' the doctor told him. 'It is malignant,' he added, impressed when the dark eyes fixed on him did not flinch or even flicker.

People usually paled at such news. But this man was holding strong. Maybe it was the Arab way—their belief that their lives belonged to Allah. Maybe he was thinking that if it was Allah's will that he die, then so be it.

Yet the man was only thirty-four years old. To all outward intents and purposes he was a splendid physical specimen of manhood. No one would guess by looking at him that he had cancer. Or, for that matter, that he was a sheikh.

Not for him any form of Arab dress. Or facial hair. His tall, lean body was clothed in the best Savile Row suit. His long, leanly handsome face was clean shaven.

But a sheikh he was. The only son of an oil-rich zillionaire and a London socialite—both of whom had been tragically killed in a fire on board a luxury yacht—he was Oxford-educated and currently lived in England, where he owned an apartment in Kensington, a stable full of expensive racehorses at Newmarket, and a stud farm in Wales.

The doctor's impressed secretary had made it her business to discover all there was to know about her employer's most exotic and possibly most wealthy patient. She'd been going on about him for a whole week, especially about his playboy reputation. He not only owned fast horses, he drove fast cars and dated fast women. Fast and very beautiful women.

The surgeon hadn't been impressed. Till now.

'And?' the Sheikh prompted.

The surgeon gathered himself to deliver the final blow. 'If you do not have surgery you will be dead within a year. The surgery, however, is risky. Your chances of survival are about fifty-fifty. The decision is yours,' he finished, with a shrug of his shoulders.

The Sheikh smiled, his flashing teeth looking extra white against his olive skin.

'You make it sound like I have a choice in the matter. If I do nothing, I will surely die. So of course you must operate. Are you the best man for this job?'

The doctor drew himself up in his chair, his shoulders broadening. 'I am the best there is in the United Kingdom.'

The Sheikh nodded, his striking face serious once more. 'I have great faith in the British. They do not overestimate their abilities as some people do. And they are excellent under pressure. Schedule surgery for me for the last week in June.'

'But that's three weeks away. I would prefer to operate as soon as possible.'

'Will my chances of survival be much worse by waiting three weeks?'

The surgeon frowned. It was never good to wait with cancer. 'Possibly not a great deal worse,' he conceded. 'Still, I do not recommend it.'

This time the Sheikh's smile was wry. 'But I am assured of staying alive for at least those three weeks, am I not?'

'Your headaches will get worse.'

'Can you give me something for them?'

The surgeon sighed. 'I'll write you a prescription,' he agreed grudgingly. 'But I am still not happy about this delay. What is your reason for waiting that long?'

'I must go to Australia.'

'Australia! What on earth for?'

'Prince Ali of Dubar has asked me to look after his thoroughbred stud farm there whilst he goes home for his brother's coronation. You might have read that King Khaled passed away yesterday?'

The doctor hadn't. He avoided reading the news. When he wasn't working he preferred to do something relaxing, like play chess. But he knew where Dubar was, and how wealthy its royal family were.

'Surely Prince Ali could get someone else?'

'I must grant my good friend's request. Ali saved my life once when we were boys and has never asked anything of me in return. I cannot deny him this favour.'

'But if you told him of your medical condition…?'

'My medical condition is my own private and personal matter. I and I alone will deal with it.'

'You need the support of friends and family at a time like this.'

For the first time those dark eyes betrayed something. A moment of weakness. No, of bleakness.

'I have no family,' he stated brusquely.

'But you do have friends. This Prince Ali, for instance. You should tell him about the tumour.'

'Not till he returns to Australia from his commitments in Dubar.' The Arab stood up abruptly. 'Your secretary has my e-mail address. Have her send me the hospital arrangements. Till then…' He held his hand out across the desk.

The surgeon stood up and shook it. Such a strong hand. Such a strong man. He would do his best to save the Sheikh. But he could not perform miracles.

'Look after yourself,' he advised.

'Can I ride?'

The query startled the doctor. This was the first patient awaiting delicate brain surgery who'd asked him such a question. Usually they wrapped themselves in cotton wool. They didn't fly off to Australia and ride horses and do goodness knew what else.

Still, to be honest, riding horses was unlikely to kill the man. Unless he fell off and broke his neck. He had a tumour, not an aneurism.

'I suppose you can,' he said. 'If you must.'

The Sheikh smiled again. An enigmatic smile this time.

'I must.'

CHAPTER ONE

'WHAT a total waste of time,' Samantha muttered as she threw her bag onto the back seat of her four-wheel drive, then slammed the door shut.

'And a total waste of money,' she added to herself, after she'd climbed in behind the wheel and started the engine.

Her only consolation was that she didn't have a too-long drive in front of her. The distance from Williamstown airport to the upper Hunter Valley was considerably less than the journey from Sydney airport. Only a one-and-a-half-hour trip as opposed to at least three.

Still, as Samantha angled the vehicle out of the car park and headed for the highway, her sigh carried frustration and disappointment. She should never have listened to Cleo. A five-day package holiday at a Gold Coast resort—regardless of how hip-hopping the place was—had never been going to find her a boyfriend, either long term or short term.

The wildly romantic notion of meeting the love of her life at such a place was just that: a wildly romantic notion.

The possibility of having a holiday fling hadn't been

high on the chance meter, either. Samantha just wasn't the sort of girl to pick up some handsome hunk who'd treat her to a few nights of wining and dining, followed by the kind of sex women dreamt about but rarely enjoyed.

Oh, she was presentable enough to attract some male attention these days, especially after Cleo had dragged her off last week to a beauty salon in Newcastle to have her long mid-brown hair streaked blonde and her naturally thick eyebrows plucked into elegantly slender arches. It had also helped that she now owned a few attention-grabbing outfits which made the most of her tall, athletic figure; Cleo had taken her clothes-shopping as well.

Samantha had to admit she'd looked pretty good these past five days.

Several guys had approached her, both around the pool and at the restaurant bar every evening.

It was her manner, she knew, which had quickly put them off.

She'd never mastered the art of flirting. Or of idle chit-chat. Or of sucking up to male egos.

Over the years she'd been constantly told by her girlfriends that she was too blunt. Too opinionated. Too assertive.

The truth was she didn't know how to act all girlie. She'd never learned, never had a feminine role model during her formative years.

Samantha had grown up in an all-male household, with four brothers who'd taught her how to be one of the boys. She'd learned to play sport like a boy and stick up for herself like a boy—with her fists. She'd never learned to defer to the male sex. Oh, no. If she'd done that in the Nelson home she'd have spent all her days in tears, trodden into the ground by her highly competitive, testosterone-fuelled brothers.

So she'd competed with them, and often beat them.

Not smart, her girlfriends at school had often told her. Definitely not smart.

Samantha had come to agree by the time she graduated. She hadn't had a single date during her high school years, let alone a steady boyfriend. She'd had to be escorted to her graduation ball by one of her brothers.

Admittedly, back then she'd been rather gawky-looking. Very tall and skinny, with no bust to speak of. Her extra short hairdo hadn't helped, either. Neither had her lack of flair with clothes and make-up.

By the time Samantha had entered Sydney University to do a veterinary science degree she'd just about given up on getting herself a boyfriend. Her love of animals—horses in particular—had filled the empty space in her heart. She'd paid for her higher education by working as a stablehand at a nearby racing stables.

University, however, Samantha had soon discovered, had a different code of sexual behaviour from the rest of the world. Not too many girls—even the plain, nerdy ones—finished their degrees as virgins. Most of the male students treated sex as a challenge and a sport. The more notches on their belt, the better. They didn't much care what their conquests looked like, or how they acted.

Samantha had eventually supplied a couple of notches during her four-year stint at uni. She'd grown her hair long during that time, developed some breasts, and had actually begun to look more like a girl.

But neither of her experiences—both of which had

been disappointingly brief—had rivalled the earth-moving events she'd read about in books. Love had certainly eluded her.

After graduating from university she'd gone to work for a vet at Randwick who specialised in the treatment of racehorses. He'd been in his early forties, a nice-looking, charming man who was very married.

In the beginning there had been no attraction between them. But after a couple of years their long hours of working together and their mutual passion for horses had created an intimacy between them. They'd formed a friendship which Samantha had found both fulfilling and flattering. She still hadn't been having any success with the opposite sex—perhaps she shouldn't have stayed living at home—so it had been very nice to have a man enjoy her company. Very nice, too, to have her natural intelligence and strong opinions appreciated and not put down.

She hadn't fallen in love with Paul. But she had come to look forward to the time they spent together. He'd made her feel good. She had become only too ready to work increasingly long hours, and to accept his invitations for more cups of coffee than was perhaps wise.

A more sophisticated girl would have seen it coming, the evening when Paul had grabbed her and pulled her into his arms and kissed her. His declaration of love had been quite thrilling. Samantha hadn't heard such passionate words before. Not directed at her, anyway.

For one awful moment she'd been tempted to give in to that voice which said that maybe this man's love was all she would ever have. She'd been nearly twenty-five, still dateless and almost desperate. But at the last second she'd looked over Paul's shoulder and glimpsed the photo of his wife and children which he kept on his desk, and she'd instinctively known he wasn't about to leave them. She'd suspected that what he wanted from her was not love, but the excitement of an extra-marital affair. A very convenient one at that.

Only the previous weekend Samantha had seen a programme on television which had interviewed a series of 'other women'. Sam had been amazed to find that they weren't *femme fatale* types, but mostly women with poor self-esteem, ones who were willing to accept the crumbs from their married lovers' tables. Most seemed not to believe they would ever find that one special person who was free to love them as they deserved to be loved.

Samantha didn't want second best. She'd never settled for second best in any other area of her life. Why should she with love? She wanted a man who didn't belong to some other woman. She wanted her own man, one who could give her everything she secretly desired. His undying love. His ring on her finger. And his children.

So she'd left her job with Paul. Left Sydney and home as well, after applying for—and to her surprise securing—an advertised position to be a live-in vet at the Dubar Royal Stud Farm.

An avid racing fan, Samantha had already known this highly regarded stud was one of the biggest and best breeding establishments in Australia. Run by an extremely wealthy Arab prince, money was never any object: they had the best stallions standing there—some flown in for the Australian season from other parts of the world—they had the best broodmares money could buy, and presumably the best equine practitioners tending them.

Given her rather limited experience with the breeding side of racehorses, Samantha had been surprised when she'd got the job. Still, she was a quick learner, and she'd soon learned all she needed to know from the other live-in vet—a very overweight man in his late fifties named Gerald.

To be honest, however, Samantha wasn't sure that it was what she wanted to do for the rest of her life. At the time of accepting the position she'd just wanted to get away from the temptation of Paul.

Of course there'd also been the added lure of a country lifestyle. She'd hoped that maybe country men wouldn't be as picky as city guys. Maybe they wouldn't find her blunt manner quite so off-putting. Or her choice of career in any way odd. Surely they wouldn't mind her preference for a low-maintenance look most of the time? Country women weren't renowned for wearing scads of make-up or always appearing as if they'd just stepped out of the hairdressers.

Samantha sighed as she steered her four-by-four down the wide main street of yet another small country town.

Unfortunately, her personal life at the Dubar Royal Stud hadn't worked out much differently than it had back in Sydney. The truth was she intimidated country guys even more than city guys. Most of the younger men working at the stud hardly dared look at her, let alone speak to her. Only Jack, who was a sweetie but somewhat on the slow side, seemed to be able to deal with her.

Ali, of course, spoke to her, but frankly Samantha found *him* intimidating. His wife, too. The stunningly beautiful Charmaine was an ex-supermodel who spent quite a bit of time doing charity work in Sydney. They had two children, a darling little girl named Amanda and a boy, Bandar, who was one year old, and named after some life-long friend of the Prince's—an oil-rich, racehorse-owning sheikh who lived in London and had an even worse reputation with women than Ali had before he'd got married a few years back.

Samantha only knew all this because Cleo had told her. As the Prince's housekeeper, and part-time nanny to his children, Cleo was in a position to know quite a lot about the Prince and his family. She wasn't a malicious gossip—in fact she was a lovely lady—but she did like to talk. During the occasions when Ali and his family went to Sydney for the weekend Cleo would invite Samantha up to the main house for dinner and a board game afterwards, during which the two women would chat away about anything and everything. They'd got along really well right from the first day, despite Cleo being around fifty.

If it hadn't been for Cleo's bright company Samantha would have cut and run before. As it was, she knew she wouldn't be renewing her contract when it ran out at the end of June. The truth was she missed Sydney and city life. The peace and quiet of the countryside was very nice in theory, but Samantha found it far too lonely up here.

That was why she'd been so susceptible to Cleo's suggestion about the Gold Coast getaway. She'd been due some time off. But truly she should have known it would be a foolish and futile waste of time.

Still, at least going there had achieved one thing. It had made Samantha realise she *could* attract a man—physically. Cleo's makeover had worked wonders in that regard. What she needed to learn now was how to play the dating—and mating—game, *after* the initial contact had been made. Samantha wasn't sure exactly how she was going to learn this, or who would be best to teach her, but she knew if she was serious about getting married she simply would have to change.

As she drove along the highway on autopilot—her preoccupied mind not taking any notice of her surrounds—Samantha began to wonder if there were businesses in Sydney who ran that kind of course. What she needed, she decided, was a flirting coach, who gave lessons in what to say and how to act.

A few lessons in lovemaking might not be a bad idea, either! But she supposed there weren't too many of those schools around. Or teachers. What a pity the two guys she'd slept with at uni had been clueless. What she needed to find was an older man who only wanted her for one thing and knew a thing or two about sex.

An *unmarried* older man, she reminded herself when Paul's face jumped into her head.

'Darn it!' Samantha exclaimed when she realised she'd driven right past the entrance to the stud.

Braking, she pulled over to the side of the road, and the semi-trailer which had been tailgating her practically took her side window off as it roared past.

'Cowboy!' she yelled at him out of the window.

She took her time making a U-turn, her eyes scanning the nearby paddocks as she did so.

'Mmm. Must have rained while I was away,' she remarked aloud. There was a touch of green about them. At this time of year the frosts had usually browned the grass right off, and the horses were mainly hand fed.

Not that they needed rain. Unlike other parts of Australia, the Hunter Valley rarely seemed to be affected by drought. The land was rich and fertile, flat along the riverbanks, then gently undulating as the land rose towards the Great Dividing Range. Perfect for growing crops and raising thoroughbreds.

Samantha turned into the wide gravel driveway, stopping in front of the huge black iron gates which were as impressive as every part of the property. The Dubar royal insignia was built into the middle of both gates, outlined in gold to stand out against the black.

Samantha zapped the gates open with the remote control she'd been given when she started work here. As she drove through, she recalled how awed she'd been by this place that first day. The no-expense-spared budget was obvious, from the freshly painted white wooden fences which enclosed each horse paddock to the magnificently modern barns and stables.

But it was the main residence which drew the eye as you drove up the long, wide, grey gravel driveway. A huge white-stuccoed, single-storeyed building, the house stretched across the top of a hill, its position giving it the perfect view of the valley below.

Samantha thought it looked like an abbey from an ancient land, with its many Moroccan style archways and cloistered verandahs. It certainly didn't look like an Australian farmhouse.

But of course it wasn't an Australian farmhouse. It

was a mansion fit for a prince. An Arab prince, rich beyond most people's wildest dreams.

A hundred metres or so below and to the left of the house was a smaller hilltop which had been levelled to make way for a helipad, from which Ali would fly to Sydney every weekend. His private and personal helicopter was huge and black. An ex-army aircraft, the interior had been fitted out with every luxury and security device. Or so she'd been told by Cleo.

Samantha had never actually been in it.

The helicopter was sitting on the helipad now, its dark silhouette faintly ominous against the clear blue sky.

Samantha wondered momentarily what it was doing there on a Monday. Usually Ali sent it straight back to Sydney after he returned on a Sunday evening. Despite his wealth, he did not keep the helicopter here all the time: it, and its pilot, stayed in Sydney all week, so they could be available for charter and mercy flights.

No doubt she'd find out the reason for its presence when she spoke to Cleo. That woman knew everything about everyone around here. Samantha would give her a ring once she'd unpacked her things and had a cup of coffee. Which reminded her. She'd better turn her mobile phone back on once she reached the cottage. Her five-day retreat from real life was over.

The driveway forked after a while, the short straight road on the left leading to the stallion quarters and the breeding barn, the winding road on the right heading uphill to the helipad and the house. Samantha took the track in the middle, which followed the river and would eventually take her to the cottage where she lived.

The river flats were given mostly to growing feed for

the horses, oats and lucerne. Though not in the winter. It was also the site of the training track where the yearlings were broken in, and where some of the older racehorses were given light work after spelling on the property—the aim being to get some of the fat off them before they were sent back to their city stables.

As Samantha approached the training track, she frowned at a most unusual sight, slowing her speed to a crawl as she drove past. There was a horse on the track—odd for this time of day. The clock on the dash showed just after noon. It was a big grey horse, its bridle being held by a tall, dark-haired man wearing hip-hugging blue jeans and an open-necked white shirt with long, fullish sleeves.

Samantha didn't recognise the man, but she sure recognised the horse. Smoking Gun was a highly prized stallion, flown over from England to stand here at stud this year at some phenomenal service fee. He had arrived a couple of weeks ago, to rest up after his first season in the Northern Hemisphere. His owner was the playboy Sheikh after whom Ali's son had been named: Bandar. Ali had warned all the staff before the horse's arrival that they were to protect the Sheikh's horse with their lives.

The stallion had not settled all that well, and it required a lot of time in the exercise yard to stop him kicking holes in the walls of his stable. They'd moved him into a specially padded stall to prevent injury, but by the end of last week there'd been talk of sending for a particular groom back in England who was famous for handling difficult stallions. A gypsy, according to Cleo.

Samantha presumed that was who was launching

himself into the saddle at the moment. The man certainly looked like a gypsy, with his black collar-length hair and deeply olive skin.

Sam's stomach tightened when the stallion reared, then danced around in circles, fighting for his head. One part of her brain could see that a long, steady gallop around the track might be more settling than a short romp around an exercise yard. But what if the horse started racing at full speed? What if he broke a bone? The stallion was carrying a lot more weight than during his racing days. What if something unexpected happened, like a dog running onto the track or something? Smoking Gun might stumble, or veer off and run into the fence.

Samantha glanced worriedly around. There was no one else in sight. No one watching. Not a single soul.

That was even more odd.

Alarm bells began ringing in her head. Ali would not have sanctioned this idea, no matter how unsettled Smoking Gun had become. It suddenly became clear that this groom—this gypsy!—had taken it upon himself to do this without permission.

She had to stop him.

Jamming on the brakes, she was out of her vehicle in a flash. But before she could shout a warning, the gypsy gave the stallion his head. The grey took off, its mane and tail streaming back. By the time Samantha leapt up onto the fence the horse and rider were almost at the first corner of the track, the grey's big hooves sending up clouds of dust.

Sam's heart remained in her mouth as they thundered down the back straight. Too late to do anything now. If she started waving her arms around, or ran out onto the track in an attempt to stop them, she might cause the kind of accident she feared. She would have to wait till this idiot decided Smoking Gun had had enough exercise.

Then she would tell him what she thought of him.

Her blood began to boil when he completed not one, but three circuits of the track. The stallion's grey flanks were spotted with foam by the time the rider reined him in, not all that far from where Samantha was now gripping the top railing of the fence with white-knuckled fury.

'What in heaven's name did you think you were doing?' she threw at him, her voice literally shaking. 'Did you ask Prince Ali's permission to exercise Smoking Gun in such a reckless fashion?'

The rider trotted the sweating stallion over towards her.

'And who might you be?' he shot back at her in an upper-crust English accent. Far too upper-crust for a gypsy groom.

Unfortunately, when Samantha's temper was on the boil she had a tendency not to be too observant.

It was impossible, however, not to feel the impact of the man's sex appeal. For a split second she just stared at him. What eyes he had! And what skin! His body wasn't half bad, either.

Her momentary weakness annoyed her all the more.

'I'm Samantha Nelson,' she snapped. 'One of the resident vets here. I presume you're the supposedly expert horseman sent out from England? Look, I'm not saying you don't ride extremely well, but what you did just now was foolhardy. So I repeat: did you have the Prince's permission?'

'I did not,' he replied, his tone and manner so impossibly haughty that it took Samantha's breath away. 'I do not need his permission,' he added, then actually tossed his head at her, as if he was king of the castle and she the dirty rascal.

It finally sank into Samantha's momentarily addled brain that the man she was trying to tear strips off just might not be a groom, let alone a gypsy.

Her stomach contracted as she realised his looks were not dissimilar from Prince Ali's, though he wasn't quite as traditionally handsome as her employer. This man's face was longer and leaner, his cheekbones harder, his mouth the only soft thing about his face.

Yet she found him far more attractive than Ali. He was as spirited as the horse beneath him—which, even now, wouldn't stand still.

'Ali has returned to Dubar for his brother's coronation,' the Arab informed her, his right hand tugging sharply at the bridle before reaching up to rake his hair back from where it had fallen across his face. 'Ali has put me in charge here till his return.'

Samantha found herself floundering under this unexpected turn of events. Or was it this man's overwhelmingly disturbing presence which was causing her normally sharp brain to lose focus? Finally, she gathered herself enough to absorb the facts behind his news. Ali's father, the King of Dubar, must have died whilst she'd been away. Samantha also reasoned that this man could not possibly be a close relative—or one of the royal family—or he'd be back in Dubar as well.

He might be an Arab, but underneath his autocratic manner he was just another employee, like herself. A man too big for his boots in more ways than one. Samantha couldn't seem to help finding him physically attractive, but she didn't like him. And she wasn't about to let him ride roughshod over her.

'Well, perhaps he should have put someone with more sense in charge!'

His black eyes bored into her, his very elegant nostrils flaring in shock. 'You are a very impertinent woman.'

'So I have been told on countless occasions,' she countered, with a defiant head toss of her own newly streaked blonde hair. Samantha supposed he wasn't used to a woman challenging him, which made her want to challenge him all the more. 'But I meant what I said. What you did with that horse was reckless in the extreme. Just look at him. He's exhausted.' At last Smoking Gun had calmed down, and was standing sedately beneath his irritatingly cool rider.

The Arab cocked a dark brow at her. 'That was precisely the point. He needed an outlet for his testosterone. He's become used to servicing several mares a day. He's young, and has yet to adjust to his life at stud. He wants what he wants when he wants it—like most young male animals. In time, he will learn that all good things come to those who wait.'

'Maybe so. But you can hardly ride him like that every day till he learns to control his urges. Or till the next season starts. It's way too risky.'

'*I* will assess the risk, madam. Not you.'

'Put him in a larger exercise yard, if you must. Riding him full bore on this track, however, is out of the question. I'm sure Prince Ali would not approve.'

'Whether or not Prince Ali approves is immaterial to me.'

Samantha fumed some more. The arrogance of this man was unbelievable. 'I will contact the Prince,' she threatened, 'and tell him what you're doing.'

The Arab actually laughed at her. 'Do that, madam. Ali won't tell me to stop. Smoking Gun belongs to *me*. I own every inch of this horse and I can ride him to death if I want to. I might contact Ali about *you*, however. I might tell him that his lady vet is as foolish as she is fearless. No, no—do not argue with me any longer. The horse is tired, and so am I. You can argue with me over dinner tonight. Eight o'clock. Do not keep me waiting. My time is precious to me.'

With that, he whirled and trotted the weary horse to the track exit, not giving Samantha a backward glance as he headed back towards the stallion barn.

CHAPTER TWO

For the first time in her life, Samantha was left speechless by a man.

It took her a full minute to gather herself enough to make it back to the four-by-four, her normally excellent co-ordination in total tatters as she fumbled with the door handle, then banged her shin on her way up behind the wheel. Pride demanded she not look in the rear vision mirror, but her pride was in tatters too, it seemed. She sat there for simply ages, staring in the mirror, till Smoking Gun and his playboy sheikh owner were mere dots in the distance.

Only then did she pull her fatuous gaze away, telling herself it was surprise and nothing more which had robbed her of her usual composure.

Samantha began to fume once more during the short drive home. Who did this Bandar think he was, ordering her around like that? He might own Smoking Gun, but he didn't own *her*! He wasn't even her employer. Her contract was with Prince Ali, not him. She didn't have to have dinner with him if she didn't want to.

The trouble was, Samantha realised with considerable chagrin as she pulled up in front of the tiny weath-erboard cottage which she currently called home, she *did* want to.

The female in her—that part which could not deny he was the sexiest man she'd ever met—wanted to spend more time with him, wanted to look at him some more, wanted to argue with him some more.

Their encounter had left her angry, yes. But excited, too. Excited in a way she'd never experienced before. All her senses seemed heightened. Her skin tingled at the thought of being in his presence again, of having those gorgeous eyes on her once more.

A quiver ran down her spine at the memory of them, and the way they had looked at her.

Had he found *her* attractive? Dared she hope he'd invited her to dinner because she interested him as a woman?

A quick glance in the side mirror put paid to that little fantasy. It was a passable face these days. Having her eyebrows plucked had really opened up her eyes. But she wasn't about to grace the cover of any women's magazines just yet. Her chin was too square, her mouth too wide and her neck too long. She did have good teeth, though. She'd have passed muster if she'd been a horse.

'Heavens to Betsy!' she exclaimed irritatedly as she propelled herself out of the four-wheel drive. 'No wonder he called me foolish. I *am* a fool for ever thinking a man like that would fancy someone like me.'

Slamming the driver's door, she yanked open the back door and hauled out her bag. Everyone who'd ever read a gossip magazine knew that billionaire Arab sheikhs dated supermodels and socialites. Sometimes they even married them. You only had to look at Ali's beautiful blonde wife to see the type they went for.

Samantha had her job cut out for her attracting an ordinary guy. The Sheikh was way out of her league in more ways than one.

'Not that I really care,' she grumbled as she marched up the steps which led onto the rather rickety front verandah. 'The man's obviously a male chauvinist pig of the first order.'

She just wished he hadn't called her fearless. Wished those incredible eyes of his hadn't flashed at her as he'd said the word. There'd been admiration in that flash.

Or had it been amusement?

Samantha's top lip curled at this last thought. She didn't like the idea of being invited to dinner to amuse the Sheikh. But why else would he have invited her?

Her perverse mind—or was it her unquashable ego?—catapulted her back to the flattering notion that he just might have fancied her.

The chilly air inside the cottage swiftly brought Samantha back to reality. *And* the present. Lighting the combustion heater would have to take priority over indulging in more wildly romantic fantasies.

But by the time she'd walked into the front bedroom and dropped her bag by the bed, Samantha found herself wanting to hurry over to open the old wardrobe and take another look at herself—this time in the full-length mirror which hung on the back of the door.

Taking off her leather jacket, she tried to see herself as a man might see her, doing her level best to ignore her own preconceived ideas about herself. Her gaze started at the top, then worked slowly downwards. She turned sidewards, checking herself in profile, and then her bejeaned rear view, before remembering that the Sheikh hadn't seen her from behind.

Pity. She had a good rear view—especially in stretch jeans.

After five minutes, Samantha had a much more positive checklist about her overall appearance than the quick one she'd made back in the car.

Face. Not bad. Nice blue eyes. Clear skin. Great teeth.

Hair. Good. No, better than good. Sexy. She now had sexy hair, when it was out. Which it was at the moment.

Figure. Damned good. Provided a man didn't mind tall, with B-cup breasts. But she had great legs, a flat stomach and a tight butt.

Who knew? Maybe the Sheikh had grown bored with all his super-glamorous, super-sucking-up girl-friends and wanted to try something different. Like a six-foot-tall Aussie girl with an attitude problem and a suddenly over-inflated opinion of herself.

'Truly, you've begun to let Cleo's mini makeover go to your head,' Samantha muttered.

That's what I should do, Samantha decided sensibly after shutting the wardrobe door. Ring Cleo and find out exactly what's going on around here.

Samantha scooped her bag up off the floor, dumped it onto the plain white duvet which covered the double bed and unzipped one of the side pockets. Extracting her mobile phone, she turned it back on, ignoring the message bank ringtone which heralded missed messages, and called the number up at the main house.

'Norm, here. How can I help you?'

Samantha was momentarily taken aback. Norm was Cleo's husband. He worked for Prince Ali as well, as a general handyman and gardener around the house. But he never answered the phone.

'Norm?' she said. 'Hi. It's Samantha. Is Cleo there?'

'Hi, there, love. Yep, she's here—running around like a chook with her head cut off. You've no idea what's happened.'

'Er…what?' Samantha thought it best not to tell Norm about her run-in with the Sheikh.

'Ali's dad kicked the bucket last Thursday—the day after you left—and Ali's had to go home for the funeral, plus his brother's coronation. The whole family's gone for three weeks. Anyway, Ali asked this mate of his to keep an eye on the place whilst he's gone. He's the bloke they named little Bandar after: Sheikh Bandar bin Something-or-other. Cleo knows all about him. You can ask her later. Anyway, we thought he wasn't arriving here till tomorrow. He flew in from London last night and was supposed to rest up today in that hotel suite in Sydney that Ali owns. But it seems he was keen to get here and see to that horse of his. You know the one. He's been giving poor Ray a whole heap of trouble.'

Samantha knew the one all right. But he wouldn't be giving the stallion manager so much trouble after his three-mile gallop around the track today.

'Anyway, Cleo was a bit upset, because she didn't have the main guest suite ready for him,' Norm raved on, 'so that's what she's been doing. It's Samantha, love!' he called out, presumably to his wife. 'Yes, she's back. You are back, aren't you?' he directed at Samantha.

'Yes. I'm back.'

'She's back! Here's Cleo. She wants to talk to you.'

'Samantha. Why are you back so early? You weren't due home till late this afternoon.'

'I caught an earlier flight.'

'Oh-oh. That doesn't sound like the Gold Coast trip was a raging success.'

'It was a nice break.'

'You didn't get lucky, then?'

'Nope.'

'Never mind. It was worth a try. Did Norm tell you what's been going on here?'

'He sure did. Poor Ali. Was he upset about his dad dying?'

'Hardly. The old man had him exiled, after all. But he was glad for his brother. Said it was about time Dubar had a king who was more in touch with the real world. Have you heard about our very interesting temporary visitor?'

'Yep. Norm told me. Though he couldn't quite remember all his names. Only the Sheikh Bandar bit.'

Cleo laughed. 'Yes, I can't remember all his names, either. But he's a bit like Ali where names are concerned. Doesn't stand on too much ceremony. Likes to be called Bandar.'

'Really?'

'Yes, really. Doesn't let grass grow under his feet, either. Was off to see his horse as soon as he arrived. But not before asking me to put on a small dinner party tonight. Nothing grand, he said. He just wants a getting-to-know-everyone meal with the main management staff. I presume he means Ray and Trevor. Gerald, too, of course—which means you'll probably get an invitation as well.'

'He's already asked me,' Samantha confessed, feeling foolish indeed now over the fantasies she'd wound around the invitation. More than foolish. She felt like a balloon which had just been pricked.

'What? You've met Bandar already? Why didn't you say so?'

'Because it was just so embarrassing. I didn't realise he was who he was at first, Cleo,' Samantha said dispiritedly. 'I thought he was just a groom. And a gypsy to boot.'

'A gypsy! Well, he does look a bit like a gypsy, I suppose. With that hair and skin and eyes. But, Samantha, for pity's sake, he doesn't look or act anything like a groom! So tell me. What on earth happened?'

Samantha told her the horrible truth, though she didn't add the genuinely humiliating part about how she'd thought he might have fancied her.

'Oh, Samantha,' Cleo exclaimed, half-laughing, half-chiding. 'One day you'll have to learn to put your brain into gear before you open your mouth. Men hate aggressive women. That's your main problem, you know, love. You're way too aggressive.'

'I prefer to think of myself as assertive,' Samantha defended, though a bit more lamely than usual.

'Same thing. But not to worry. It's not as though you're trying to come on to the Sheikh. I mean, men like that…' Her voice trailed off knowingly.

'I'm well aware of the kind of women men like that go for, Cleo,' Samantha said drily.

'Unfortunately not short, plump, fifty-year-old married women having a bad hair day,' Cleo quipped back.

Now it was Samantha's turn to laugh. Cleo always made her laugh. She was going to miss her when she left.

Cleo sighed in that wistful way women had been sighing since time began. 'My, but he *is* very attractive, isn't he?'

'I suppose so. If you like male chauvinist pigs.'

'Samantha, truly, he's no such thing! He's just as charming as Ali. In fact, Bandar's much more charming than Ali was when he first came here. Must be all those years he's lived in London, mixing with the upper crust.'

'I can see he's charmed you all right. I'll bet the men don't think he's quite so charming.'

'You might be wrong about that. He was lovely to Jack. I measure a man's character by how he treats Jack. And how Jack responds to him. Animals and children can't be fooled.'

Women could be, though, Samantha thought privately. Give a man looks and wealth, and women seemed to become blind to their faults and flaws.

Samantha had always thought she was above such nonsense. But it seemed she wasn't. She suspected that if the Sheikh wanted to charm her, he probably could. Look at the way she'd been constantly thinking about him since their brief encounter.

She had to stop it.

'Is there anything I can do to help?' she offered. 'Norm mentioned you were pretty busy. And Gerald isn't expecting me back on the job till tomorrow morning.'

'No, I'm on top of things now. And I have Judy coming in later, to help with the cooking and serving.'

'What are you going to cook?'

'No idea yet. Nothing too flash or complicated. Roast lamb, probably. With home-baked bread. And some of my quince pie and cream afterwards. Ali loves that menu, so it should be all right. I'm not sure about an entrée. I might just put out some nibbles to have with drinks beforehand.'

'He won't drink if he's a Muslim,' Samantha pointed out.

'Gosh, you're right. I didn't think of that. I'll ask him when he gets back what his attitude to alcohol is. Ali always serves it, though he doesn't drink it himself. But the men will be expecting a beer or two. Especially Ray. Trevor, too. And Gerald loves wine with a meal. Look, I'm sure he won't mind the others having a drink. He's a sophisticated man, and he's lived in London most of his life. He must be used to the western world's drinking habits by now.'

'If he isn't, he soon will be out here,' Samantha said drily. Australian men loved their beer.

'Did Bandar give you a time to be up here?' Cleo asked.

'He said eight.'

'Oh, dear—that late? By the time everyone has a drink and a chat it'll be nearly nine before you all sit down to eat. I sure hope he doesn't expect me to serve up dinner at that ungodly hour *every* night. I know people who live in Europe eat late in the evenings, but we don't. Not up here in the country, anyway. Still, he's the boss, I guess. I'll just have to put up with it till Ali gets back. But I'm going to miss all my favourite TV shows. Oh-oh—I hear someone on the gravel outside. I think he's back. Gotta go, love. See you tonight.'

Tonight, Samantha thought with a shudder as she clicked off her phone.

Already she was looking forward to it. And dreading it.

'I'm a bloody fool!' she growled, just as her mobile phone rang.

'Yes?' she said sharply.

'Sam. It's me—Gerald. A little birdie told me you were back. Look, I could do with a hand. One of the weanlings has slipped in some mud near a gate and gashed its front leg. A colt, of course. I need someone to keep him calm while I stitch him up. Do you think you could come? You seem to have a special touch with colts.'

Samantha was only too glad to do something. The thought of sitting around the cottage, getting herself into a state about tonight, did not appeal.

'I'll be right there,' she said.

'Great! See you soon, then.'

Samantha slipped back into her leather jacket, her spirits lifting immediately. Working with horses always made her feel good. Because she was good at it. No one could ever take that away from her.

To hell with men, she thought as she headed for the door. Give me horses any day!

CHAPTER THREE

DARK fell long before eight o'clock. The days were short at this time of the year, with the temperature dropping sharply once the sun sank behind the mountain range, especially on nights like this, which were clear of cloud. A full moon hung low in the sky, bathing the valley in its silvery light and making the huge white house on the hill stand out even more.

Samantha left the cottage right on eight, knowing full well it would take her another couple of minutes to drive back to the fork in the road, then up the hill to the house. She was determined not to be right on time, as ordered by the Sheikh. But not late enough to be seriously rude.

She was also determined not to surrender to temptation and try to doll herself up for this dinner. The others there tonight would think it odd. They were used to the way she looked and dressed. Cleo might roll her eyes at her choice of clothes, but that was too bad.

Her boot-leg blue jeans were clean. So were her elastic-sided riding boots. Her black roll-neck was as good as new and not too warm. The house was well insulated, and air-conditioned, though she suspected that the fire-places would be lit tonight. Samantha had put on her black leather jacket for the drive up, but would remove it once she was inside.

She'd decided against make-up, despite now owning quite a bit and being able to apply all of it reasonably well. Cleo had left no stone unturned before sending her off last week on her mission impossible.

Samantha reasoned she hadn't been wearing any make-up earlier today, when she'd met the Sheikh, so she wasn't about to plaster any on tonight. Not even lipstick. The same thing with perfume. She had, however, freshly shampooed, conditioned and dried her hair—for fear it might smell of horses—but she'd pulled it back and fastened it at the nape of her neck with a black clip. No way did she want him thinking she was trying to look sexy for him by wearing her hair down.

She took her time driving up the hill, noting the now empty helipad with a mixture of surprise and irritation. That she'd missed hearing the helicopter's departure was an indictment on her distracted state of mind. The darn thing was horribly noisy. Admittedly she'd put her stereo on fairly loudly when she'd arrived back at the cottage around five. Possibly the helicopter had left during the time she was inside. Hopefully, it had. She didn't like to think she was totally losing it.

The other three staff members coming to the dinner had arrived by the time she pulled up her vehicle in the guest parking area to the side of the house. Gerald's very dusty four-wheel drive was parked between Trevor's battered ute and Ray's equally worse-for-wear blue truck.

Country men, Samantha had quickly come to realise last year, weren't as car-mad as city guys. All they required from a vehicle was that it did the job required. Both Ray and Trevor were dyed-in-the-wool bachelors in their late forties, not at all interested in attracting women, so their vehicles were even worse than most.

Samantha was very attached to her forest-green four-wheel drive, bought not long before she left Sydney. She liked to keep it clean and polished and performing well.

Samantha guided it smoothly to a halt on the gravel beside Trevor's ute, leaving the keys in the ignition when she alighted. No one was going to steal it here.

She carried no bag with her. There would be no titivating tonight—unlike last week, when she'd run off to the nearest powder room all the time, to check her make-up and hair. She knew *exactly* what she looked like tonight.

Her tomboy image was reflected in Cleo's exasperated expression when she answered the front door.

'I know I said there wasn't any point in batting your eyelashes at our VIP visitor,' Cleo muttered as she closed the door behind Samantha. 'But truly, girl, a little practice wouldn't go astray. On top of that, you're late. I don't think Bandar is pleased. He was just asking me where you were.'

Samantha liked the thought of the Sheikh not being pleased. But she didn't show it. She just shrugged in feigned indifference as she removed her leather jacket and hung it in the coat closet which came off the spacious foyer. 'I'm only a few minutes late. I presume everyone's in the front room?' She was well acquainted with the layout of the house, having traipsed around after Cleo on several occasions.

'Yes—so get yourself in there, pronto. I have a roast to attend to.' And Cleo was off, a bustling bundle of energy, dressed tonight in an emerald-green velour tracksuit.

Cleo was as far removed from a cliché housekeeper as one could get. No dreary black dresses for her, or severely scraped-back hair. Cleo's hair was very short, very spiky, and very red. Her lipstick tonight was just as bright.

Once alone, Samantha glanced to her right at the shut double doors. Like all the doors in the house, they were very grand, made of a rich cedar, carved in a middle eastern style, with huge brass doorknobs. Behind these, she knew, was a formal reception room, with brocade-covered sofas and chairs arranged around an enormous marble fireplace. The fire would be lit tonight, making the expensive furniture glow and the chandelier above gleam as only a crystal chandelier could.

Steeling herself, Samantha reached for the right door knob, turned it, and pushed the door open.

'Ah—here's Sam now,' Gerald announced as she walked in.

Samantha had heard stories about people in stressful circumstances imagining that everything around them seemed suddenly frozen, like a tableau. Maybe that was going too far, but her step definitely faltered. Her eyes swiftly bypassed Gerald, who was sitting in an armchair, holding a glass of sherry, before flicking over Trevor and Ray, both of whom were perched uncomfortably at either end of the main sofa, glasses of beer in their hands, and finally landing on the man standing to one side of the softly glowing fire, his left elbow leaning on the marble mantelpiece, a crystal brandy balloon cupped in his right hand.

If Samantha had thought the Sheikh sexy earlier today, she now found him devastatingly so. He looked simply superb, in slimline black trousers and a royal blue silk shirt, the design of which was not dissimilar in style from that of the white shirt he'd had on earlier. Open-necked, its long sleeves were fuller than a business shirt, gathered in at the cuffs. He still didn't look like a sheikh, but no longer like a gypsy. His black wavy hair was too well groomed, his face freshly shaved, his appearance immaculate.

He did still look exotic. And not quite of this world. Samantha could see him playing the part of a buccaneer—a very wealthy one, by the look of his jewellery.

Several large rings graced his elegantly long fingers. One had a black centre stone, the second a diamond, the third a huge blue sapphire. Undoubtedly all were real. A thick gold watch encircled his left wrist. A thinner but probably even more expensive gold chain hung around his neck, the end nestling in the wispy curls of chest hair exposed by the deep V of the shirt.

His head had turned at her entry, his black eyes raking over her from top to toe. They did not flash at her this time, either with admiration or amusement. But there was something in their depths which compelled her to keep staring at him. She literally could not take her eyes away from his, could not move.

But there was movement inside her. A hot rushing of blood. A feeling not of being frozen, but of melting.

'I was beginning to worry something might have happened to you,' he said, an impatient edge in his voice.

Ray made a sniggering sound. 'Not likely. Sam's not that kind of girl—are you, Sam?'

'And what kind of girl *am* I, Ray?' Samantha whipped back, irritated by the remark, yet grateful for the distraction. At last she managed to look away from the Sheikh, close the door behind her and walk further into the room.

'Not the kind who gets herself into trouble,' Ray said with a dry laugh.

'Any woman can get herself into trouble,' the Sheikh remarked, his softly delivered words drawing Samantha's eyes once more.

'Come,' he commanded. 'I'll get you a drink.' And he gestured for her to follow him over to the long sideboard under the front windows, where Cleo always put the drinks and the glasses.

Samantha was startled that he would personally be getting her a drink. Cleo had said he didn't stand on ceremony, but Samantha hadn't found the owner of Smoking Gun of an easygoing or casual nature earlier today. He'd been downright arrogant and autocratic in his manner towards her.

Possibly he was a chameleon of a male, depending on his mood and the occasion. She'd met plenty of moody men in her time. Her father was moody. So were a couple of her brothers. Moody, and occasionally mean. One good thing about coming to live in the country had been finally moving out of home. When she returned to Sydney she would buy a place of her own. She had plenty of savings—enough for a deposit on a house.

'What can I get you?' he asked, slanting a questioning glance over at her as she joined him by the side-board. 'Spirits? Wine? Or something *softer*?'

Was that a slight smirk she glimpsed in his eyes when he said the word *softer*?

'You don't have to serve me,' she returned stiffly. 'I am quite capable of getting myself a drink.'

Now he smiled. Definitely a smile of amusement.

'I am sure you are,' he said smoothly. 'But that is not the point. A gentleman always gets a lady her drink,' he added, and flashed her a warm smile.

Samantha gritted her teeth. He was determined to have his way, either by using his authority to order her around or by laying on the charm. Of course men like him were used to having their own way. Used to exercising their charm over women as well. Cleo had already fallen victim to it. Now *she* was in danger of following suit. The man was almost irresistible when he smiled like that.

And didn't he know it!

This last thought made Samantha resolve not to surrender to his charm. Different, perhaps, if he'd been an ordinary man. But swooning over a billionaire playboy sheikh not only went against her grain, it was a total waste of time. Much more so even than her getaway to the Gold Coast.

'A glass of white wine will do,' she said offhandedly, as though she didn't give a hoot what she drank, or who she drank with.

But as she watched him draw a bottle of Chardonnay out of the ice-bucket and pour the chilled wine into a glass, her treacherous body refused to obey her head. Standing this close to him was doing strange things to her.

Not only had her heart started racing, but all her senses seemed suddenly to be heightened. Never before had she been conscious of how a man smelled—perhaps because the men she was around mostly smelled of horses.

Bandar didn't smell of horses. Not in the slightest. The scent wafting from his body was as exotic as he was: something spicy, sensual and sexy. Oh, yes, very sexy.

'I am told this wine comes from an excellent local vineyard,' he said, as he held the glass out in her direction.

She turned to take it and their eyes met once more, his again flicking from her face to her feet, then back up again. Not with admiration this time, either. Curiosity, perhaps?

Samantha winced inside. She knew what he was thinking. What kind of woman was this, who cared nothing for her appearance?

Embarrassment besieged her, plus a perverse regret that she hadn't taken some trouble with her appearance tonight. Her tongue raced to her rescue, as it always did when she found herself feeling vulnerable in male company.

'I thought Muslims didn't drink,' she said sharply, when he picked up his brandy balloon again.

He took a sip before lowering the glass from his mouth. 'Some do,' he replied, eyeing her with curiosity. 'The world is full of imperfect people. But I am not Muslim.'

That took her aback. 'Oh. Sorry. I just presumed. Most of you are.'

His dark brows lifted. 'Most of *who* are?'

'Arabs.'

'Some Arabs are Christian,' he pointed out. 'Some

are Jewish. Some are even Buddhists and atheists. But I am not any of those, either.'

'Then what are you?' she threw at him.

'I am who I am.'

'Which is what?'

'Just a man named Bandar.'

'A *sheikh* named Bandar,' she corrected. Samantha hated false modesty. He was no ordinary man, this Bandar. He was a billionaire, for starters.

'Yes, I am a sheikh. But it is merely an inherited title. I prefer not to capitalise on it. Some people I mix with in London like to address me as Sheikh because it makes them feel important. I'm sure you are not one of those. So please…call me Bandar.'

'Suits me,' she said with a shrug. 'We call everyone by their first names here in Australia. Except perhaps the Prime Minister.'

'And what do you call him?'

'Depends on whether we're happy with his policies or not,' she quipped, feeling more comfortable with this kind of conversation. It was what she was used to being with men: slightly caustic, not in any way tongue-tied or vulnerable.

He stared at her, then shook his head. 'I think I have a lot to learn about Australians,' he said. 'It is a pity I will only be here for three weeks. I suspect it might take considerably longer to understand your very different culture.'

'A lot of people don't think Australians have *any* culture.'

He looked at her hard again. 'You are a most unusual woman. We will talk later. Over dinner. But for now there are a few things I must say to the others. Do sit down,' he ordered, before striding back towards the fireplace.

Samantha sat down. There was a time and place for outright rebellion and this was not it. Besides, she suddenly *needed* to sit down, her verbal sparring with Bandar having left her feeling oddly weak, as though she'd used up all her resistance to him.

Not that it really mattered.

Her capacity to resist this man was never going to be challenged. Or tested.

Nevertheless, her eyes followed him slavishly as he took his position at the mantelpiece once more.

'Thank you for coming to dine with me this evening,' he began, his manner now very formal and serious. 'Before we retire to the dining room for our meal I have a few things I wish to make clear. Firstly, I want to reassure you that Prince Ali has the fullest confidence in all his staff here, especially his stallion and mare managers,' he said, dipping his head slightly towards Ray and Trevor. 'He has not put me in charge to interfere with the general running of this establishment, but to be here to make decisions if decisions need to be made. Fortunately, it is not a busy time. Foaling in your country does not begin till August. But thoroughbreds are sensitive creatures, notorious for causing unexpected problems. If a problem arises, please refer it to me. I am a very experienced racehorse owner and breeder. There is nothing I do not know about this industry.'

Samantha tried not to look askance at this rather egotistical statement. She already knew that Bandar was arrogant. But, truly, was there anyone on the world who knew *everything* about horses?

'Having touched on the subject of my horseman-ship,' he continued. 'I know there was considerable dis-sention amongst you about my riding Smoking Gun on the track today. You, Raymond, expressed some reser-vations at the time. Gerald also. And Samantha—who happened to pass by the track at that particular time—was quite disturbed. She thought what I was doing was reckless and risky. And said so in no uncertain terms.'

Samantha straightened in her chair when her three colleagues swung round to give her looks which pro-claimed that she obviously didn't know which side her bread was buttered on. Naturally, she hadn't mentioned her run-in with Bandar when she'd been working with them this afternoon. But now that it was out in the open she wasn't about to back down.

'I still think exactly the same thing,' she said without hesitation. After all, what could he do to her? Have her fired? She was quitting soon, anyway.

'Why am I not surprised?' the Sheikh muttered, his dark eyes glittering at her. 'But you are wrong, madam. I know that horse inside out, and I know what he needs to make him behave himself. He has behaved since then, has he not?' he directed at the stallion manager.

'Been like a lamb,' Ray concurred.

'He will, however, not be so lamb-like in a few more days—at which point I will ride him again. I trust there will be no further objections. Now, do any of you have any questions?' he asked, his gaze settling back on Samantha.

She held his steady regard without visible squirm-ing, which was a minor miracle. She was certainly squirming inside.

'Ali was gunna go to a dispersal sale this Wednesday,' Trevor piped up in his broad Aussie accent. 'The owner of one of the local stud farms around here died six months ago. His wife is sellin' up everything and movin' back to the city. The mares are real quality. Some of 'em are in foal to top-line stallions. I know Ali was real keen to attend.'

'I see. I shall ring Ali tomorrow and talk to him about it. If he is agreeable, I will go to this sale in his stead. But I might need a driver for the day.'

'Sam could drive you,' Gerald suggested. 'She could check over any mares you might like the look of at the same time. Sam doesn't miss a trick, and she's got a good eye for a horse.'

Samantha's stomach flipped over when Bandar looked at her. 'Is that agreeable with you, Samantha?'

Goodness, what a question! It was *not* agreeable. It was breathtakingly exciting and extremely worrying. How could she function properly with him by her side for a whole day?

Somehow she gave a nonchalant shrug of her shoulders. 'You're the boss,' she said, as though the matter was of no consequence to her.

He smiled a small, enigmatic smile. 'I will let you know before tomorrow evening if I will require you on Wednesday. Now I think it is time for us to retire to the dining room.'

CHAPTER FOUR

THE table in the formal dining room was huge, capable of seating at least twenty people. Cleo had set only one end: her VIP visitor clearly expected to grace the head of the table, with two settings on either side of him. A huge bowl of fresh flowers sat in the middle of the long table, which meant it would be totally useless for hiding behind.

Samantha swiftly slipped into one of the chairs furthest from the end, grateful when Gerald sat down next to her, with Ray and Trevor taking up the two settings opposite. Bandar made himself comfortable at the head of the table, shooting her a sharp glance as he flicked out his serviette.

Ignoring him, she shook out her own serviette with slow, considered movements and placed it on her lap, her eyes fixed on the connecting door through which she hoped Cleo would soon come.

She did, carrying a tray laden with steaming bowls of soup.

'You decided to serve an entrée after all?' Samantha whispered, when Cleo placed her bowl in front of her.

'You should have known that by the arrangement of cutlery,' Cleo whispered back.

Samantha didn't like to tell her that the arrangement of cutlery had been the last thing she'd been thinking about when she'd sat down at this table.

'I hope the menu will be to your liking, Bandar,' Cleo said, when she returned to the dining room with a plateful of herb bread. 'It's one of Ali's favourite meals. Sweet potato and leek soup, followed by roast minted lamb, finished off with quince pie. Home-made too, of course. We have a lovely quince tree on the farm,' she added, pride in her voice.

'I can see why Ali never wants to travel,' the Sheikh replied. 'He is looked after too well here.'

'Oh, go on with you,' Cleo said, and actually gave him a playful nudge on his upper arm.

He looked momentarily shocked. Then amused.

'Oh, dear—I've forgotten the wine!' Cleo suddenly exclaimed. 'I'll go get it right now.'

'Make mine red,' Gerald called out to Cleo as she hurried back towards the door which led into the kitchen.

'I have both opened,' she returned over her shoulder. 'Never fear.'

'Ali told me his housekeeper was a treasure,' Bandar said warmly whilst Cleo was out of the room. 'I can see what he means. She is like a breath of fresh air. Under other circumstances, I might try to steal her away.'

'You wouldn't stand a chance of doing that under *any* circumstances,' Samantha jumped in, before she could think better of it. 'Cleo would never leave Ali, or his family. *Or* Australia.'

His dark eyes glittered at her like they had once before, when she'd challenged him over Smoking Gun.

'You would be amazed how such things become irrelevant with the right offer of money,' he said, that edge back in his voice.

Just then Cleo re-entered the room, carrying a bottle of white wine in an ice-bucket, plus a decanter filled with red wine. She placed them both on the table within easy reach of everyone.

'If I paid you a million dollars a year, Cleo,' Bandar said silkily, 'would you come with me back to London?'

'That depends as what,' she shot back with a cheeky smile.

'My personal chef.'

Cleo pulled a face. 'Sorry. Now, if you'd said mistress, I might have considered it.'

Everyone laughed, even Samantha. But not for long. Soon she was just sitting there, staring down blankly at the soup and wishing she could be more like Cleo. That woman was never rattled by anything. She was so good with people, and had the most delightful sense of humour. It was a shame that she and Norm had never had children. She'd have made a wonderful mother.

This last thought gave rise to her own aspirations about one day being a mum. Hopefully, that was possible. Samantha had known for some years that she might have some trouble conceiving. She was shockingly irregular when she wasn't on the Pill.

Even if she *did* have a baby one day, would she be a good mother? What if she had a girl? A girl needed a mother who was feminine, who could show her how to act like a girl. How could she do that when she couldn't do it herself?

Adult life, Samantha had discovered, was full of

many unexpected complications and pitfalls. Being a child was much simpler—though perhaps not so simple when you didn't have a mother yourself.

'Didn't you like my soup?'

Cleo's aggrieved question brought Samantha back to the real world, where she discovered that everyone had finished their soup but she was still sitting there, with hers hardly touched.

'Oh, sorry, Cleo. Yes, it's lovely,' she said, taking a hurried mouthful. 'I was daydreaming. Leave it with me. I'll finish it. I promise.'

'Nope,' Cleo said, whipping the bowl away. 'You've lost your chance. Judy has the next course ready to serve.'

Which she did, placing a dinner plate in front of Samantha before she could say boo. It looked and smelled delicious, but somewhere along the line Samantha had lost her appetite. She sighed as she picked up her knife and fork, knowing she would have to force some down or Cleo would be totally disgusted with her.

This dinner party was proving to be an even worse trial than she'd imagined it would be. And what of Wednesday? How would she cope if Bandar wanted her to go to that dispersal sale with him? She'd have to spend the whole day with him. Alone.

Samantha had been unhappy with herself for a long time. Around the Sheikh, however, she was close to de-spising herself. If Cleo had been twenty-six, single and in her position, she wouldn't have come here tonight dressed in jeans with her hair all scraped back from her un-made-up face. Cleo would have been done up to the nines. She'd have flattered the Sheikh, flirted with him, and had a great time. He'd have been totally charmed, and probably would have ended up taking her back to London with him. Or at least taking her to bed.

He'd be good in bed. No, Samantha amended ruefully in her mind. He'd be *very* good.

Not that you'll ever find out, girl.

But she supposed she could *think* about it. And think about him.

Her eyes drifted sidewards and up to where Bandar was sitting, at the head of table, chatting away with Gerald, who was doing most of the talking—asking the Sheikh about his racehorses in England. It seemed Bandar owned an obscene number of champions, which showed just how rich he was. He had started eating his lamb, his eyes dropping to his plate, though his head remained tipped slightly in Gerald's direction.

Her surreptitious gaze fastened on his mouth, her own mouth drying as she watched his lips open and close over the food. He was a slow, sensual eater, licking his lips occasionally, his facial expression when he swallowed one of immense satisfaction.

Samantha could have watched him eat all night.

'Did you buy Smoking Gun as a yearling?' Ray suddenly piped up.

When Bandar glanced up and caught her staring at him Samantha could have died on the spot. His eyes narrowed on her for a split second before he put down his knife and fork and looked over at Ray, leaving her feeling humiliated once more.

'No, I bred him. I breed most of my horses. That gives me a lot of satisfaction.'

'You must've started breeding pretty young,' Gerald

remarked. 'Smoking Gun is six, and you can't be more than thirty.'

'Thank you for the compliment, but I will turn thirty-five this year.'

Samantha wasn't surprised that he was older than he looked. His face *was* unlined, unlike the other weatherbeaten men at the table, but there was a wealth of experience in his eyes.

'I inherited my father's stud farm when I was only sixteen. So, yes, I started young.'

Samantha imagined he would have started *everything* young.

'Has he always been such a handful?' Ray asked. 'Smoking Gun I'm talking about.'

'Not at all. He was extremely tractable during his racing career. But his new life at stud has excited him somewhat. Still, we men can surely understand that. There is nothing more stimulating than that time in a young male's life when he first discovers the pleasures of the flesh. And Smoking Gun has suddenly gone from servicing several mares a day to total celibacy. A frustrating situation for any virile male animal,' he said, his dark eyes sliding back down the table to Samantha.

His gaze was not in any way provocative, yet she found her breath catching in her throat and her mind conjuring up hidden messages both in his words and his eyes. She started imagining he was talking about himself, not his horse. That he was telling her his sex life had suddenly gone from a feast to a famine and he wasn't any happier about it than his stallion.

'Come springtime he will be as good as gold,' he went on, releasing her gaze as he flashed a warm smile around the table. 'From what Ali has told me, he has a veritable harem of the finest broodmares awaiting him here.'

'He sure has,' Trevor confirmed. 'His book is chock-a-block.'

'Lucky horse,' Bandar murmured, those dark eyes slanting briefly Samantha's way before dropping back to his food.

Samantha reached for her glass of wine and took a big gulp, telling herself she was suffering from a seriously over-active imagination. There were no hidden messages in his eyes. He wasn't interested in her. He *couldn't* be. She was a fool.

And from that moment nothing the Sheikh said or did could have been even remotely misinterpreted as a come-on. In fact he ignored her, with any conversation directed entirely at the men.

Not that he made much conversation from that point on. To be honest, by the time dessert arrived he'd begun to look tired. His dark eyes had developed even darker hollows around them. A few times he rubbed at his temple, frowning in that way people did when they weren't feeling all that well, or when something was on their mind.

After he'd eaten less than half of Cleo's large serving of quince pie, he abruptly put his fork down and stood up.

'I must apologise,' he said, his voice as strained as his face. 'It seems that jet lag has suddenly caught up with me and I must retire. I'll speak to Cleo on my way out. Reassure her it was not her cooking. I bid you good night. I will see you all in the morning. *Insh'allah,*' he added, with a somewhat wry twist to his mouth.

And he was gone.

'Well!' Gerald exclaimed. 'That was a bit rude. It wouldn't have hurt him to last till coffee.'

'He didn't look well,' Samantha said defensively, annoyed with Gerald for being so unsympathetic. Couldn't he see the man was all done in? Jet lag was known to strike quickly. Not that she'd ever experienced any. She hadn't been out of Australia. Another matter she would address in the near future. They said travel broadened the mind. Hers could certainly do with some broadening. She'd actually got herself a passport last year, after she'd left her job with Paul, but wasn't quite sure what she was going to do.

'What was that Arab thing he said?' Trevor asked. '*Insha* somethin' or other?'

'Got no idea,' Gerald replied. 'Never heard Ali say it.'

'Ask him,' Trevor said to Gerald.

'*You* ask him,' Gerald shot back.

'Oh, for pity's sake—what does it matter?' Samantha said irritably. 'He'll be gone by the end of June. He's only staying three weeks.'

'Thank God,' Ray muttered. 'He's not a patch on Ali.'

Samantha almost opened her mouth to defend him again, but shut it just in time. She didn't want them thinking she fancied him.

Bad enough that she did.

Wednesday popped back into her mind as she drove back to the cottage a short time later. Did she still not want to go with him?

The answer came to her as she lay in her lonely bed that night and wound the most impossible fantasies about the man.

Despite fearing she might make a fool of herself if she was alone with him, Samantha *did* want to go—if only to keep feeling the things he could make her feel. And think the things he could make her think. Exciting things. Sexual things…

In her head, they were riding together—Bandar on a big grey stallion, she on a lovely chestnut mare with a white blaze on her chest. They stopped on a riverbank where he lifted her off her horse, holding her close whilst his eyes travelled all over her flushed face. He kissed her hungrily. Not once, but several times. She was breathless by the time his head lifted from her mouth. He reached for the buttons on her shirt and undid them, one at a time. She was naked underneath. He spoke no words as he stripped her to the waist. He just stared at her. Her nipples tightened under his gaze. She wanted him to touch her breasts but he didn't. He laid her down on the soft grass and removed the rest of her clothes. The day was sunny, but not warm. Yet she wasn't cold. Her shivers were those of desire. She called out his name and he told her not to speak. She stared up at him as he took his own clothes off. His body was beautiful. He lay down next to her on the grass and began to stroke her. She couldn't bear it. She wanted him inside her. She told him, and he smiled. He kept touching her…teasing her. She sobbed her frustration. She told him that she loved him…

'What a load of bunkum!' Samantha muttered as she sat up abruptly and gave her pillow a frustrated punch.

Okay, so Bandar was attractive and sexy and sophisticated and rich, and just about everything a fantasy lover should be.

But the feelings he evoked in her had nothing to do with love. Samantha might be personally inexperienced, but she was an intelligent girl, living in the twenty-first century. Just because she hadn't felt this level of sexual attraction before, it didn't mean she couldn't recognise it when it hit.

Lust was what was making her head spin and her heart race when she was around the Sheikh. Not love.

Samantha lay back down, satisfied that she'd got that straight.

But knowing what was ailing her didn't make it any easier to bear. Letting her head fill with silly fantasies wasn't helping, either. It just left her feeling restless and wretched.

The sooner that infernal man went back to London, the better. And the sooner *she* went back to Sydney, the better. She needed to get on with her life. Real life. Not this foolish fantasy she'd been indulging in tonight.

Till that happened, some pragmatism was called for. Plus some common sense and composure. There was no need to get all in a knot if she had to go with Bandar on Wednesday. All she had to do was do her job and keep her silly infatuated self in check.

Surely she could do that?

Meanwhile, tonight there would no more weaving of imaginary sexual scenarios involving herself and the Sheikh.

Samantha snapped on her bedside lamp and picked up the novel she usually read at bedtime. It was an involving and complicated thriller, full of assassins and government agents and impossible plot surprises. Best of all, there was not even a hint of romance in it.

Perfect.

She sat up, propped a couple of pillows behind her, and started to read.

CHAPTER FIVE

JUNE in eastern Australia was the first month of winter. At this time of year in the upper Hunter Valley the temperature at night often fell below zero, with a frost by the morning. But then the sun would come out and the temperature would rise, often to a very pleasant twenty degrees.

Wednesday promised to be just such a day.

Samantha woke early, when the frost was still on the ground and the sun not yet risen, and the immediate curling of her stomach reminded her that, yes, it was Wednesday. And, yes, she was going to spend the day with Bandar at the dispersal sale.

His absence around the stud the day before had provided her with some respite from his disturbing presence. But the moment he'd called her late yesterday afternoon, informing her that he *would* be going to the dispersal sale and she was to pick him up at the house at nine the next morning, all her pragmatic resolve had vanished and her world had tipped off its axis again.

She'd found it difficult to get to sleep. She'd read her

bedside book into the small hours of the morning and actually finished the darned thing before sheer exhaustion had done the trick. But here she was, awake again, and it was only five-thirty. Three and a half hours to go before she was due to pick Bandar up.

Samantha had a feeling they were going to be the longest three and a half hours of her life.

She was right. Not only were they the longest, but the most trying. Common sense demanded that she not make any drastic changes to her appearance. But what was common sense in the face of female vanity?

In the end, she simply *had* to make some changes. But not to her clothes. She just teamed her oldest and most comfortable blue jeans with a long-sleeved blue and red checked shirt which didn't show the dirt.

Her face, however, she gave considerable thought to. She wanted to look as natural as possible. But she still wanted to look as good as she could.

Instead of foundation—which might be obvious in the daylight—she smoothed on a tinted sunscreen-moisturiser, which the cosmetic salesgirl had claimed would soften and even out her skin tones, and stop her getting freckles at the same time.

Samantha was happy with the result.

Next came her eyes. She decided against eyeshadow for the same reason she'd discarded the idea of foundation. Too obvious in daylight. Mascara, however, would not be. So she applied a couple of coats till her normally fine eyelashes were thick and dark, bringing out the blue in her eyes.

Lipstick caused her a dilemma. She'd bought really bright ones for her getaway—deep pink, red and burgundy. What she needed was something closer to the colour of her lips. In the end, she rubbed a little Vaseline over them. Less was more. Or so they said.

She waffled for a while over perfume. Should she or shouldn't she spray on some of the designer-brand scent she'd also bought for her getaway?

'Maybe just a little,' Samantha told herself as she picked up the bottle and aimed some behind her ears.

Last came the decision about her hair. She'd already blowdried it straight, the cleverly cut layers making it surprisingly easy to style, and Samantha had to admit that it looked great down and around her face. More than great—it looked sexy.

That last thought did it. Up her hair went into a ponytail. It was one thing to look good today, quite another to try and be sexy. That was the way to further foolishness and humiliation.

The old wall clock in the kitchen finally pronounced it was time to leave. With butterflies already gathering in her stomach, Samantha picked up her trusty blue denim jacket—in case the weather turned nasty—and headed for the door. At five to nine she was pulling into the guest parking area beside the house on the hill.

Cleo didn't answer the front door, as Samantha expected. Instead Bandar stood there, carrying a picnic basket.

He didn't look tired any more. He looked refreshed and absolutely fabulous, in black jeans and a white polo-necked top. No rings graced his fingers, she noted, but he was wearing a stunning silver watch. His black wavy hair was faintly damp, giving rise to an image which Samantha tried to immediately banish, but couldn't.

Thinking of him naked, in the shower, was not conducive to calming the butterflies still crowding her stomach.

'Cleo said there will not be any food provided at the sale,' he explained, when Samantha stared down at the picnic basket. 'She packed us some lunch. She said our destination is a picturesque property, with lots of nice spots for a picnic.'

A feeling of panic joined Samantha's nerves. But she kept her expression poker-faced. 'Fine,' she said. 'Shall we go?'

'I am all yours,' he returned.

All hers. Now, wasn't that a laugh? He hadn't even looked at her properly. Just a cursory glance. All that fuss and bother for nothing!

Samantha whirled and strode back down the steps, marching across the gravel to the four-by-four, her temper barely in check. Not that she was angry with him. Mostly it was with herself.

'Better put that basket in the back,' she advised sharply as she climbed in behind the wheel and started the engine. 'Looks like Cleo has packed enough for an army.'

He did so, just making it into the passenger seat before she began reversing.

'Are we in a hurry?' he remarked drily as he clicked in his seat belt. 'The auction does not start till one this afternoon.'

'Trevor gave me a catalogue. He's marked the mares he thinks are worth buying. There's ten. A full inspection of ten mares will take me all morning.'

'*I* will decide which mares you will inspect,' Bandar said, with a return to that haughty manner he'd adopted at their first meeting. 'And which ones I will bid on.'

Samantha gritted her teeth. But inside she was grateful. When he acted like that she didn't find him at all attractive. All she wanted to do was smack him one, right in his super-white teeth.

Keep it up, buster.

'How far to this stud farm?' he asked when they reached the highway and Samantha steered her wheel to the left, heading towards Scone.

'About thirty minutes.'

'Have you been there before?'

'Nope.'

'But you do know the way?'

'Ray gave me directions.'

'Some women are not good with directions.'

'As opposed to most men?' she shot back, slanting him a savage glance.

The shock on his face swiftly gave way to a rueful laugh.

'Like I said the first time we met, you are a very impertinent woman. But I like you all the same,' he added.

'Am I supposed to be grateful for that?'

She could feel his eyes on her, but kept her own eyes fixed on the road ahead this time.

'I did not realise you disliked me so much.'

Samantha winced. Did she really want to go down this path again? She had resolved to get past this kind of stroppy and self-destructive behaviour. Okay, so Bandar was a fair way up himself. But she supposed most men would be if they'd been born a sheikh with pots of money and people grovelling to them all the time.

'I don't dislike you,' she said. 'I just…resent your attitude.'

'What attitude is that?'

'In my country, it's rude to ride roughshod over other people's opinions.'

'Ride roughshod?' he repeated thoughtfully. 'That is a good expression. I like it. But surely I have not done that. I have just asserted my authority. Ali asked me to represent him at this sale. I must do what *I* think is best.'

'Ali chose his staff for their expertise. He listens to them. With respect, Trevor knows more about Australian broodmares than you do. He'd be seriously put out if you totally ignored his advice.'

'I see. Yes, I see. In that case, I will look at what your mare manager has marked in the catalogue. But I will not bid on them if I do not personally like them.'

'Or if *I* find some physical defect in them,' Samantha added, somewhat mischievously.

'I would not dream of bidding on a mare that you do not pass as one hundred per cent perfect.'

'Then you won't be bidding on much. There aren't too many perfect broodmares around. You might have to settle for pretty good.'

'I will settle for whatever you recommend, Samantha. Is that fair?'

'More than fair. Okay—now, why don't you have a look at the catalogue on the way there? It's in the glove box. You can study what's listed and see if there's anything which interests you. Do you have an age that you prefer in a broodmare?'

'Young,' he said, opening the glove box and drawing out the catalogue. 'I like them young. And I like them to have performed on the track. That ensures they have the right temperament to pass on. A lot of unraced mares are timid, as well as unsound.'

'I agree with you. Nervous Nellies don't make the best mothers.'

'Nervous Nellies? I have never heard that saying before. You have a lot of interesting expressions in Australia.'

'You have no idea. Most don't bear repeating. I'm sure that you have some interesting sayings as well. In fact, you said something the other night which made us all curious. *Insha* something-or-other?'

'*Insh'allah.*'

'Yes, that's it. What does it mean?'

'It means Allah willing. God willing.'

'That sounds religious. You said you weren't religious?'

'I do not like man-made religions. But I believe in Allah. And in an after-life. If you don't, everything is so pointless. Living. Dying. Especially dying.'

'I know what you mean,' Samantha said. 'My mother died shortly after I was born. It would be sad to think she isn't somewhere, looking over me.' Her heart lurched as it did whenever she thought of the mother she'd never known who had died so very young. 'But let's not talk of death. It's a depressing subject. We have a lovely day ahead of us, doing what we both like doing best.

'Looking at horses,' she added, when he shot her a quizzical glance.

He smiled. 'Already you know me well.'

'I know horsemen. I'm sure they're all the same the whole world over, whether they are rich or poor.'

'Undoubtedly. To a horseman, horses are everything. I could not live without them.'

'With your money, you'd never have to.'

'True,' he said. 'The trick is to stay alive.'

'I can't see you dying any time soon. Unless you break your silly neck riding Smoking Gun.'

When he looked at her and laughed Samantha finally started to relax, the tightness in her stomach uncurling, her grip on the steering wheel lessening. Her view of the day ahead gradually changed from panic to one of pleasurable anticipation. It would be challenging, seeing if she could find the true gems amongst all the fool's gold offered today. Interesting to see, too, if Bandar was as knowledgeable about horses as he claimed to be.

At the same time she would try hard not to think of him as a devastatingly sexy man, but as just another horse-lover.

A very wealthy horse-lover, admittedly. But there were plenty of those around. She'd mixed with many multimillionaire racehorse owners back in Sydney. She'd never been attracted to any as she was attracted to Bandar, but she'd envied quite a few.

'You are so lucky, Bandar, to be able to afford to buy any horse you want. I hope you know that.'

He glanced up from where he'd been studying the catalogue. 'I have never really thought about it. A man is either born rich or poor. After that it is up to him to make of his life what he will. Since my father died I have increased my wealth considerably through my own endeavours. I feel I have earned the right to buy whatever I want.'

Samantha did not argue with him, but she considered it was surely an advantage to be born rich.

'One day,' she said, 'I'm going to go to a top yearling sale and buy myself a simply fabulous colt.'

'Not a filly?'

'Oh, no. I much prefer colts.' She always had—right from the time she'd first become interested in horses.

'Top colts command high prices,' Bandar warned her.

'I earn good money. And one day I'll have my own veterinary practice and earn a whole lot more.'

'You have ambition.'

'Girls are allowed to have ambition in this country,' she pointed out, somewhat tartly.

'Might I remind you that I live in England?'

'Maybe, but you are still an Arab sheikh, born into a vastly different culture. Not so long ago you'd have had a harem full of female love-slaves. And you wouldn't have thought it wrong.'

'You are so right. Having a harem of female love-slaves is a most attractive prospect. A man is not by nature monogamous. Muslims are still allowed up to four wives.'

'But you are not Muslim.'

'Not Muslim, and not married.'

'You have a girlfriend back home in England?'

'I have three lady-friends.'

'*Three!* And they're happy with that arrangement?'

'They have not complained.'

Samantha supposed he hadn't got his playboy reputation for nothing. But, brother, three girlfriends at once was going beyond the pale. It was positively disgusting!

'And what about you, Samantha? You have a boy-friend?'

'Not at the moment,' she bit out, her temper on the rise again.

'You do not like men much, I fear.'

'I like men fine.'

'But you like horses more.'

'That's the pot calling the kettle black. You like horses much more than women. If you liked women, you wouldn't be treating them so badly. Now, I think we should drop this subject before I get really mad with you. We have to spend the day together, so let's just stick to the subject of horses in future. Agreed?'

When she glanced over at him he looked totally non-plussed, as though he did not know what to make of her.

'Okay, so I'm not a run-of-the-mill female,' she raced on, before the situation got out of hand. 'I'm opinion-ated and downright difficult at times. But I'm also straightforward and honest, which I hope makes up for a lot of personality flaws. And I do like you, Bandar, despite your questionable morals. Any man who loves horses as much as you do has to have some good points, though I'm not sure yet what they are.'

By now he was fairly gaping at her.

'I promise to be on my best behaviour for the rest of the day if you promise not to tell me any more about your unsavoury lifestyle back home. Deal?'

He just shook his head at her, his expression one of total exasperation. 'You are impossible!'

'Yes, but I'm also driving. Deal?'

'I do not have an *unsavoury lifestyle* back home,' he argued.

'You are sleeping with three different women at the same time. Is that not true?'

'No. It is *not* true,' he said indignantly. 'I go to each of their beds on different nights. I do not have them in the same bed at the same time.'

'Oh, terrific. Glad we got that straight. That makes *all* the difference.'

He sighed with what sounded like satisfaction. 'I am glad we got that straight as well. I do not wish you to think I am some kind of roué.'

Samantha gave up at that point. The man *was* a roué—with the morals of an alley cat! He *had* been alluding to his own sex life the other night, when he'd been talking about going from a feast to a famine.

Who knew how he was coping out here, with no one to warm his bed at night? Unless he'd already seconded some of the girl grooms! She wouldn't put it past him. The man was sex on legs. He'd only have to crook his finger at any of them and they'd come running. Some of them weren't half bad looking, either.

This train of thought was not at all comforting.

Thank goodness the turn-off that led to Valleyview Farm had come. Some horsey distraction was called for. Anything to push out of her mind the image of Bandar going from one woman's bed to another's, and then to yet another's...

The road they'd turned onto was a dirt road, full of ruts and bumps.

'How can this stud farm be one of any quality?' Bandar soon complained. 'They cannot even afford to seal their roads.'

Samantha had to laugh. 'This isn't *their* road. This is a *public* road. Welcome to Australia!'

CHAPTER SIX

CLEO had been right about Valleyview Farm. It was a very picturesque place, with lovely lawns and gardens surrounding the main homestead, providing any number of spots for them to eat their picnic lunch.

And what a lovely lunch Cleo had provided: cold chicken, salad, freshly baked breadsticks and the most delicious carrot cake, along with two small bottles of chilled white wine which Samantha found nestled in the bottom of the cooler.

After three solid hours of inspecting all the mares marked in the catalogue, both Samantha and Bandar were more than ready to eat. They made short work of the food, enjoying it under a not-too-shady tree, with the dappled sunshine providing some very pleasant warmth.

Samantha tucked in whilst sitting cross-legged on one corner of the picnic blanket Cleo had also packed. Bandar sat with his back up against the trunk of the tree, his long legs stretched out before him.

'That was great,' Samantha said after she'd finished her cake, proud of herself for not staring at Bandar too much while he ate this time. 'I was so hungry I could have eaten a horse.'

'It is as well that Cleo packed us a substantial lunch, then,' Bandar replied, smiling at her over the rim of his glass. He still had an inch or two of wine left. 'Eating a horse around here could be a very expensive meal. Especially the ones *you* picked out for me this morning.'

'Oh, I don't know. We could be lucky and get some of them quite cheaply.'

'No,' he said, and swallowed the rest of his wine. 'I do not think so.'

'I appreciate they're all well-bred mares, some with very good performances on the track, but seriously, Bandar,' she said, her voice dropping to a conspiratorial whisper so that a group of people nearby didn't hear her, 'the turn-out today hasn't been wonderful. I suppose more buyers might still show up during the afternoon. But there were surprisingly few people here this morning inspecting the horses. There are going to be some bargains at this auction. Trust me.'

'We will not be here for the auction this afternoon,' he announced unexpectedly, putting his glass back on the blanket before getting to his feet.

Samantha scrambled to her feet also, confused by this unexpected turn of events. 'What do you mean? Why won't we be here for the auction?'

He took his time, brushing some grass from his black jeans before answering her. 'I have already bought the five mares we selected. I paid for them when you went back to the car to get the picnic basket.'

'Paid for them?' she repeated, totally thrown by this development. 'How much did you pay for them?'

'Two million dollars.'

'Two *million!*' she squawked, so loudly that the group of people turned to stare at them. But she didn't care. 'Two million—for five mares worth not more than a hundred thousand each! If that,' Samantha added, her hands finding her hips in total exasperation. The man had more money than sense!

He eyed her up and down with some exasperation of his own. 'Valleyview Farm has agreed to organise transport to Ali's stud farm as part of the deal,' he said coolly.

'No kidding? They'd probably have agreed to send the lot to Dubar for the price you paid!'

'Hush,' he commanded, his eyes flashing annoyance. 'This is not the time or the place for you to argue with me. Pack up the basket. We can discuss this back in the car.'

Samantha felt like informing Bandar that she was Prince Ali's vet, not *his* personal lackey. But he was already striding across the lawns towards the parking area and her vehicle. She had no option but to do what he ordered, or leave everything behind.

Samantha could just hear what Cleo would say to her if she did that.

So she fairly threw everything into the basket, cracking one of the wine glasses in the process. Stuffing the blanket on top, she snatched the basket up by the handles and stomped after Bandar. He was waiting for her by the passenger door, his face as thunderous as her own. They did not say a word to each other till they were both in their seats, Samantha being the first to speak.

'The reason you come to a dispersal sale,' she snapped, 'is to get a bargain! You do not pay upfront—

especially well above the market price. If you'd asked me, I could have told you what those mares were worth. I didn't realise you had no idea. I thought you knew *everything* about horses!'

He'd certainly shown a lot of expertise when he'd inspected the mares alongside her. She'd been fascinated at how calmly the horses had stood for him as he'd run his hands over them. He'd talked to them at the same time, in soft murmurings, telling them how lovely they were.

She suspected, by the furious look on his face, that she was not about to be subjected to any soft murmurings.

'My dear Samantha,' he ground out, with his jaw clenched so hard the veins were standing out in his neck. 'A bargain is only a bargain if you are in need of one. I can afford to pay more, and I did.'

'But you weren't using your own money,' she countered. 'You were buying those mares for Ali.'

'Do you think I would use Ali's money in making such a deal? I paid for them personally. They are to be gifts to my good friend.'

Samantha grimaced. 'Oh. I…I didn't know that. Sorry.'

'And so you should be,' he reprimanded. 'You are one of those women who speaks first and thinks later. I always have a good reason for what I do. For your enlightenment, Ali mentioned to me yesterday that the owner of Valleyview Farm is an elderly lady in severe financial difficulties. Her now deceased husband was not a good businessman. Two million is nothing to me, but could mean everything to a poor widow at this time in her life.'

'Oh.' Once again Samantha was taken aback, and also ashamed—both by her outburst and her rash judgement of him. 'Sorry,' she mumbled, before lifting her chin and shooting him an exasperated look. 'But you might have said that was your intention in the first place!'

'It was not my original intention. It was a spur-of-the-moment decision. I was going to stay and bid a more than fair price for those mares at the auction, but I changed my mind. If you insist on total honesty—and it seems you value honesty a lot—it was you who made me decide not to stay and attend the auction.'

'Me? What has your not staying for the auction got to do with me?'

'I think you know,' he said, his eyes locking with hers and holding them.

Samantha's heart began to race behind her ribs. 'I have no idea what you're talking about,' she claimed.

His eyes narrowed on her. 'I do not believe you. You are a highly intelligent girl. Does it embarrass you to admit the attraction between us?'

'*What?*' Her eyes flared wide with shock, her mouth dropping open.

'Do not deny it. The chemistry has been there from the first moment we met. Though you did make me doubt it when you showed up for dinner that evening looking like you were about to muck out some stables. What kind of woman is this, I thought to myself, who does not try to enhance her natural beauty?'

'Huh!' came her automatic reaction. 'I have no natural beauty to enhance.'

His hand cupped her chin firmly and brought her face closer to his.

'You think your eyes are not beautiful?' he asked, his own truly beautiful eyes caressing hers in a way which would make any woman melt.

Samantha melted, then overheated as outrage joined in.

She smacked his hand away, her cheeks going bright red whilst her heart did a tango within her chest. 'Don't you dare flatter me just to get me into bed! I know what's ailing you, Mr Moneybags. You've had to leave your playboy lifestyle behind and you're missing it like mad. You've been almost a week without one of your three girlfriends, and you're feeling like a bit on the side. Well, I'm not going to be that bit. For *your* enlightenment,' she threw back at him, using the same expression he'd used earlier, 'I'm not in the business of being used by men—especially arrogant, up-themselves sheikhs with more money than morals.'

Her tirade seemed to shake him almost as much as it shook her. Samantha could not believe she was doing what she was doing. Her fantasy man wanted to take her to bed and she was knocking him back! Not only knocking him back but insulting him so much that he was sure never to ask her again. How self-destructive could you get?

Samantha was trembling all through her body as she pushed open the driver's door and leapt out of the four-wheel drive. Knowing that she'd ruined everything once more only made her madder.

'I am going to the ladies',' she spat out. 'When I come back, I am going to drive us back home. When we get there, you can explain to the men why we didn't stay for the auction. I'm sure Trevor will be thrilled that you bought some of the horses he recommended and won't give a hoot if you paid scads for them. After dropping you off, I am going to go straight to my cottage. You can tell everyone I have an upset stomach. I'm sure they'll believe you. You're obviously an excellent liar!' she finished, whirling on the heels of her riding boots and stalking off.

Bandar gritted his teeth as he watched her stomp across the lawn, her arms swinging back and forth, her ponytail bouncing up and down.

Never in his life had he been spoken to in such a manner. No one would dare—certainly not a woman!

Why he wanted this impossible creature as much as he did was a complete mystery to him. Not only was Samantha Nelson *not* truly beautiful—she was right about that—she had a tongue laced with acid.

Right from their first meeting she had burned him with her words. Burned and challenged him.

A light suddenly snapped on in Bandar's head. Yes, of course! *That* was the reason behind his unlikely obsession with her. She challenged him.

Challenges had always compelled Bandar. Give him an unbreakable horse and he would go to any lengths to tame it, to have it welcome him as its rider, to have the animal eating out of his hand.

He had never actually found *any* woman a challenge before.

Up till now.

It galled Bandar that Samantha was his first failure with the opposite sex.

She came back into view in the side vision mirror, her body language still full of defiance and defensiveness.

He studied the stubborn set of her mouth, thinking to himself how satisfying it would be to have that mouth soften under his, to have it pleasure him as he liked to be pleasured.

His loins leapt at the image of her totally stripped of her defences as well as her clothes. She had a good body: high, firm breasts, a small waist, long, slender legs.

She would look good naked.

Bandar grimaced at the physical effect his thoughts were having on him. He would have to control his desires for now, or risk potential embarrassment.

But he was not done with this woman. She would be his. It was just a matter of finding out the right approach.

What a pity he had so little time. Less than three weeks and he would have to return to London. He might have to be ruthless.

Of course he was already rather ruthless where western women were concerned. Materialistic creatures, most of them. Always pretending they wanted you for yourself, when underneath it was really your money they wanted.

Was Samantha susceptible to money? he wondered as she wrenched open the door and climbed back into the driver's seat.

She did not look at him. Did not say a single word. Just stabbed the key into the ignition and got going.

The sexual chemistry was still there between them, regardless of how much she wanted to pretend it wasn't. Its pull sizzled through the airwaves, making Bandar suddenly aware of the perfume she was wearing.

She had not been wearing perfume the other night, he recalled. So why was she today?

Because she wanted him to smell it. Wanted him to be attracted to her.

So why had she rejected his advances?

Bandar considered the reasons behind her contrary behaviour all the way back to the stud, her ongoing silence giving him plenty of time to explore various possibilities. Nothing made sense—unless she was of a religious persuasion which precluded sex outside of marriage. That would also explain her outraged reaction to his having three lady-friends.

Somehow, however, having religious beliefs did not seem to match this girl with her acid tongue and prickly manner.

No, the reason had to be more personalised than that. Maybe she had been hurt by some man—some two-timing womaniser who had cheated on her and made her lose confidence in herself as a woman?

Horses who had been badly treated often became sour-tempered and contrary. Like Samantha was.

He was considering this idea when another possibility popped into Bandar's head.

What if she were still a virgin? What if the reality of sleeping with a man simply terrified her?

Bandar glanced across at Samantha's steely face and quickly dismissed this last notion.

No way was this girl terrified of *anything*.

Which left him with what?

He had no idea. All Bandar could be sure of was that she *was* attracted to him. He had felt it more than once.

On his part, he was more than attracted to her. Frankly, he could not think of anything else. Even when he'd been lying in bed the other day, suffering from the most excruciating headache, his mind had been filled with thoughts of her.

He wasn't suffering from a headache now. But his

body was aching. Aching with a need which had plagued mankind since the Garden of Eden.

At another time, in another place, he might have walked away. But not this time. By the end of this month he could very well be dead.

Such thoughts made a man prioritise. It also gave an urgency to his desires. Dead, he would never know what it felt like to hold this woman in his arms, to kiss her contrary mouth into compliance, then make love to her from dusk till dawn.

Bandar suspected that sleeping with this intriguing girl would be an experience such as he had never had before. An experience he wanted whilst he could still seize it.

He spent the rest of the drive home plotting and planning her seduction—a seduction which seemed as difficult as it was desired.

Patience, he told himself. Patience.

Facing imminent death, however, robbed a man of his patience, as well as his conscience. Samantha Nelson was going to become his, no matter what the cost!

CHAPTER SEVEN

TEARS trickled down Samantha's face. Slow, sad, self-disgusted tears.

She was curled up in the corner of the comfy lounge in her cottage, dressed in pink flannelette pyjamas and clasping a mug of hot chocolate in her hands.

The sun had set a couple of hours earlier. The night ahead promised to be chilly, but the combustion heater was pumping out plenty of heat. The television was on, but she wasn't watching it. She was sitting there, thinking what a pathetic creature she was. Full of bluster and bravado on the outside. But inside full of fear. Fear of making a fool of herself. Fear of the most important area of her life as a female.

Being with a man.

The drive home had been dreadful, with Bandar not saying a single word to her. And of course she had returned the favour, her tight-lipped pretence at being offended and outraged lasting till she'd dropped him off and gone straight to her cottage, as she'd said she would. There, she'd swept the phone off the hook, clicked her mobile off, then dived into bed, fully dressed, pulling the bedclothes up over her head in a vain attempt to shut out the world and the pain which had quickly flooded her.

She'd cried herself to sleep and not woken till it was nearly dark, at which point she'd risen, lit the fire, then taken herself into the bathroom for a very long bath and an even longer assessment of why she'd reacted so heatedly and adversely to Bandar's declaration that the attraction between them was mutual.

After all, it should have been welcome news, shouldn't it?

At first, she'd comforted herself with the excuse that what she'd said to him was spot-on. He *hadn't* been overcome with desire for her because she was anything special. He'd wanted sex, and she was the only game in town. No, that wasn't right. She wasn't the only game in town. She was, however, the easiest. Why? Because she'd made it perfectly obvious to this man-of-the-world that she fancied him. Hadn't he caught her practically drooling over him at the dinner table the other night?

And of course he must have noticed the changes she'd made in her appearance today. He'd have smelt her perfume, at least. That would have been very telling to a man of his experience.

Then there'd been her manner towards him during their inspection of the horses. She'd been all smiles and deferential questions. Maybe not sweet, but as close as she would ever get. By the time they'd had lunch together, she couldn't have blamed him for thinking she would be agreeable to a pass or two.

And what had she done?

Snapped and snarled at him like some rabid dog.

Truly, he must be thinking she was crazy!

Which she wasn't. Just a coward.

If only she could go back in time, she would do things differently.

The knock on the front door brought a grimace to Samantha's face. It would be Cleo, for sure. Dear, kind Cleo, worried that she was sick. Once before, when Samantha had been laid up in bed with a bout of flu, Cleo had come down every day with home-made soup and other tempting things to eat.

Samantha put down her mug of no-longer-hot chocolate and uncurled herself, hurriedly wiping her tears away with the back of her hands.

'I'm coming, Cleo,' she called out, when the knock came again on her way to the front door.

It wasn't till she was actually turning the doorknob that it occurred to Samantha that Cleo would have called out to her with her first knock. She would have said, *Hi! It's just me, love.*

Samantha's stomach scrunched into a tight knot when she saw who her caller was. Fate could not have planned a more humiliating scenario.

He was dressed in smart beige trousers and a pale blue crew-necked top, beige leather loafers on his feet, not a hair out of place, his face freshly shaven. And there she was in her bare feet and flannelette PJs, her hair all over the place and her eyes all puffy from crying.

'What…what are you doing here?' she stammered, both her hands coming up to clasp together just under her neck.

His eyes flicked over her from head to toe, their incredulous expression doing nothing to make her feel more comfortable.

'Cleo wanted to bring you some soup before she went into town,' he said, indicating the flask in his hand. 'She and her husband spend every Wednesday evening at some club, it seems. I told her I would do it. I explained that I wanted to personally check on how you were.'

'You walked all this way?' she said, before glancing over his shoulder and seeing the golf cart which Jack used to transport people and luggage from the helipad up to the house. 'Oh, I see,' she mumbled. 'You drove down in the buggy.'

Finding some composure—goodness knew how—she straightened, then reached to take the flask from his hand, holding it in front of her as if it was a protective shield.

'As you can see, I'm fine,' she said somewhat stiffly. 'If you recall, I wasn't really sick.'

He peered at her more closely, the low-wattage globe above the door not providing the best of light. 'You are not fine,' he said, sounding both concerned and surprised. 'You have been weeping.'

'If I have, it's none of your business.'

'I am making it my business,' he said firmly. 'I am coming inside and you are going to tell me why you are so upset.'

'You are *not* coming inside,' she said, denying him entry by standing in the middle of the doorway. Her pride would not let him humiliate her further.

His gaze was unflinching, his wide-legged stance and clenched fists reminding her of a street fighter about to do battle. 'I assure you that I am. If you do not move, I will pick you up and carry you inside with me.'

'You wouldn't dare!' she gasped, her head whirling at the thought.

'You will learn that I would dare to do of lot of things, Samantha,' he said, in a voice which sent shivers running down her spine. 'My time here is limited, and I refuse to waste it playing the gentleman. I know that you want me as much as I want you. I *know* it, Samantha,' he repeated, his eyes giving her no mercy. 'Your words might say one thing, but your eyes say another.'

'You're mad,' she snapped. But it was she who was mad. He was giving her a second chance and she was blowing it again.

'That won't work, Samantha. I can see through this façade you hide behind. It is nothing but a bluff. I am a very good poker player, and I know when my opponent is bluffing. In your heart of hearts, you want me to pick you up and carry you inside. You want me to make love to you till the dawn breaks. You are like an unbroken young horse who fears the saddle and makes a fuss if one is brought near. If I did not know better, I might think you were still a virgin.'

'A *virgin*!' she exclaimed, totally taken aback. 'Where on earth did you get that ridiculous idea?'

From the stupid way you're carrying on, that's where, came the rueful realisation.

But Samantha couldn't seem to stop. She'd been fighting with the opposite sex for far too long. Her bloody-minded attitude was deeply ingrained, and seemingly inescapable.

'*Not* a virgin,' he said, with satisfaction in his handsome face. 'That is good news. If you had been a virgin I would have had a dilemma on my hands. I do not sleep with virgins.'

'Oh, right. He doesn't sleep with virgins. Give the man a medal!'

He smiled. 'You have a saucy tongue. I will enjoy silencing it with mine.'

Samantha sucked in sharply. 'You really have tickets on yourself, don't you?'

He frowned. 'Tickets on myself? Aah, yes. I understand what you are saying. You are right. I do. But you, Samantha, do not have enough tickets on yourself. Yes, I can see the problem more clearly now. I should have seen it earlier. The clues were all there. You think you have no natural beauty, so you also think I could not possibly desire you. You think I just want to use you, like some streetwalker. But you are wrong. I find you incredibly desirable. You have aroused and intrigued me from the start. I want to make love to you more than I have wanted to make love to any woman. Ever!'

Samantha just stared at him, her heart thudding loudly in her chest, her head spinning at the passion in his highly seductive words. It might still be flattery—his claim that he wanted to make love to her more than any woman ever—but she thrilled to it all the same.

'I do not have time to play games,' he went on with fierce intent. 'I strongly suggest you say no *now* if you are still determined to reject me. Because once I touch you it will be way too late.'

She opened her mouth to say no, but nothing came out. It seemed her excited body had finally over-ridden her self-destructive brain.

When he reached to take the flask out of her hands she let him, watching with widening eyes as he tossed it

carelessly aside. When he swept her up into his arms she
let him do that too. Without struggle. Without protest.

With the decision to remain silent, all that silly defiance and pretence abandoned Samantha, to be replaced
by something she had never experienced before, but
which she found both delicious and intoxicating.

Surrender.

Her arms found a home around his neck, her head
nestling under his chin and a sigh escaping her lips just
before they pressed against his throat.

'That is better,' he growled as he carried her inside
and kicked the door shut behind them.

Yes, Samantha thought dazedly as she melted into
him. Much better.

He stopped in the middle of the hallway, his head
turning to the right to glance into her bedroom, then left
into the lounge room.

'Your bedroom is too small and cold,' he announced,
and headed into the larger, cosier room.

His lowering her to her feet on the rug in the middle
of the floor brought Samantha out of her daze somewhat. So did his fingers going to the top button on her
pyjamas.

'You should not wear your grandmother's night-
clothes,' he chided as his fingers worked their way down
the six buttons. 'You should wear satin or silk against
this lovely skin of yours.'

By the time he reached the last button, Samantha's
state of surrender had started receding, her thoughts
turning fearful once more. Okay, so she wasn't a virgin,
but she might as well be. She had no idea how to make
love. Or how to let herself be made love to. Certainly

not by a man as experienced as Bandar. What was she supposed to do? And say?

The truth. She had to tell him the truth.

'Bandar…'

His name came out in the smallest voice, one that vibrated with worry and tension.

He stopped and glanced up into her eyes.

'What is it?' His voice carried impatience. Maybe he thought she was going to tell him to stop.

'I'm not a virgin,' she told him tautly. 'But I'm not very experienced, either.'

He stared at her for a long moment, then smiled—a long, slow, sexy smile. 'Do not worry. I have enough experience for both of us.'

His hands abandoned her top, leaving it hanging undone whilst he cupped her face and brought his mouth down on hers. His kiss was as soft as his lips, sipping at hers till they gasped apart. When his head lifted, a low moan escaped her lungs. Her eyes searched his, awed that he could make her feel like this so quickly: as if she would die if he didn't kiss her again soon.

His mouth lowered once more, this time kissing her top lip only, wetting it with his tongue and nibbling at it with his teeth. He did the same with her bottom lip before his head lifted again. By then her whole mouth felt swollen, both her lips tingling, her body taut and expectant. Her nipples had peaked under her top; her belly and thighs were tight with tension.

His eyes held hers whilst his hands left her chin to trail down her throat, down into the valley between her breasts. Her nipples seemed to harden further in anticipation of being touched, or exposed, her heartbeat quickening further. His head lowered once more to her mouth, his tongue demanding full entry between her lips at the same time as his hands slid into the gaping top and covered her breasts.

Oh!

Being kissed by Bandar was exciting enough; having his palms rotate over her nipples at the same time was close to sensual overload! Her head spun, her back arched, another muffled moan echoed deep in her throat.

His head lifted, his hands dropping away.

'Wait here,' he commanded. 'Do not move. I will only be gone for a few moments.'

She did move, shivering and shaking as a violent shudder rippled all through her.

He was as quick as his promise, returning to the room with the duvet from her bed, spreading it out on the floor in front of the fire before straightening it and smiling ruefully over at her.

'Not the king-sized bed I would prefer,' he said. 'But we should be warm and comfortable enough.'

Samantha didn't think being warm was going to be a problem. She was already on fire.

'Come here,' he said, from where he was standing beside the duvet.

She walked towards him like a robot, her loose pyjama top moving with each step she took, bringing an acute awareness of her near-painful erect nipples. His black eyes raked over her as she approached, his gaze possessive and almost smug.

When she reached him, his hands lifted to stroke her hair back from where some had fallen around her face.

'I like your hair down,' he murmured, bending to kiss her lightly on the mouth once more. 'But I do not like these clothes you are wearing. I am going to remove them. Do not be afraid.'

Afraid? Was it fear sending her heartbeat wild? Or the most incredible excitement?

Samantha sucked in a deep breath when he peeled the top open, then paused to study her naked chest. His gaze was unreadable, giving her no indication if he liked what he was seeing. She had no reason to be ashamed of her body, but who was to say what Bandar liked or preferred? Maybe he was turned on by huge breasts and softly rounded bellies. Maybe he didn't like her well-toned stomach or her B-cup breasts?

After what felt like an eternity, he pushed the top back off her shoulders, releasing it so that it slid down her arms onto the floor. The pyjama pants followed suit, leaving her standing before him nude.

Her shoulders squared under his gaze, her chest rising and falling as he walked around her, looking her over as if she was a slave girl on an auction block.

Samantha found it hard to believe she was doing this. The old Samantha—the one she'd been less than a few minutes ago—would never have tolerated such a scenario. Not even in her fantasies.

This newly surrendered Samantha was totally enthralled with the feelings running through her. She could not get enough of his eyes on her. She would have stayed standing there all night if he'd commanded her to.

He shook his head at her after he'd encircled her for a third, exquisitely thrilling time.

'No natural beauty?' he muttered in dark tones. 'Do

you not own a mirror? If I had a harem, you would take pride of place in it. You are made for a man's pleasure, Samantha. For *my* pleasure,' he added as he swept her up into his arms and laid her down on the duvet, scooping her hair up from the back of her head and spreading it out like a halo.

'Do not move,' he commanded as he straightened. 'And do not close your eyes. I want you to watch me undress.'

She watched, wide-eyed and dry-mouthed, whilst he stripped his blue top up over his head, the action leaving him naked to the waist. He was as beautifully shaped as she had known he would be: broad shoulders tapered down to a slim waist and hips, his stomach was flat and hard, his arms rippled with the lean, strong muscles a rider needed. It was his skin, however, which drew Samantha's eyes the most. The colour of milk chocolate, and with surprisingly little body hair, it had the kind of smooth, silky texture which made you want to touch it.

Samantha wanted to touch it. She wanted to touch him. *All* of him.

She swallowed when his hands went to his trousers, unflicking the waistband. But he didn't undo his zipper, as she'd been anticipating. He stopped and sat down on the lounge, where he kicked off his shoes and pulled off his socks. When he stood up again, his hands hesitated once more on his zipper, his eyes thoughtful as they flicked over to her.

'I presume you are not on the Pill?' he said.

She shook her head. No way could she tell him that she was.

'No matter. I have come prepared,' he said, and pulled a foil rectangle from his trouser pocket.

His presumption that she would come across did not escape Samantha. But she refused to let it bother her. His arrogance and his confidence with women were exactly what she needed. Here was her older, more experienced lover: the one who would teach her all she needed to know. The one who'd force her not to fall back into bad habits.

Already he'd given her self-esteem a huge boost. If he'd seen evidence of her attraction for him in *her* eyes, then she'd seen genuine admiration for her body in his. The way he'd looked at her—was *still* looking at her—made her feel as if she was the most beautiful woman in the world.

It was *his* beauty, however, which soon distracted Samantha from any thought of herself. The removal of his last two items of clothing left him as naked as she was.

Samantha had grown up in a household of men; she had seen quite a few naked male bodies in her time. But she had never encountered one built quite like Bandar.

Perhaps it was his state of arousal which made him seem twice the size of a normal man. Samantha swallowed as she stared at him. He reminded her of a stallion, his impressive phallus rising from its nest of dark curls, reaching up beyond his waist. The head was glistening.

It was wet. As she was wet. She could feel the moisture between her legs, feel her body already preparing itself for him.

By the time he lay down next to her, protection in place, she was trembling.

'How many men have you been with?' he asked, whilst his hands started running up and down her body.

'Not many,' she returned huskily. 'And none like you.' No wonder he didn't sleep with virgins!

His smile reached his eyes. 'Do not flatter me just so you can get me into your bed.'

His wittiness made her smile. 'I never flatter men,' she countered, quite truthfully.

'I can believe that. But perhaps we should not talk. Not till afterwards.'

Samantha quickly realised why all those mares had stood so submissively for him. He had the hands of an angel… Or a devil.

Her body vibrated under his touch, the blood charging round her veins. Finally his head lowered, but not to her mouth this time—to her breasts.

A startled cry punched from her throat when his lips closed over her nipple.

This was something Samantha had never experienced. Her university bedmates hadn't bothered much with foreplay. But she'd often imagined how it might be to have a lover do this.

It was nothing like she'd imagined. Because Bandar seemed to be one of only a small number of men who could do two things at the same time. As he licked and sucked on her breast, his right hand slid between her legs, his thumbpad lightly caressing her, whilst his long fingers slipped inside her.

'Oh!' she cried out.

His head lifted from her breast to cover her mouth, smothering any further cries. His hand continued its delicious torment, his fingers and tongue moving in parallel penetration. His right leg pushed between her knees, easing her legs apart. She could feel his erection against her thigh, feel him begin to move his body rhythmically against hers. It excited her, his moving like that. Everything excited her. But especially his fingers and thumb. The pleasure they evoked became almost unbearable, her belly tightening and her thighs quivering. Suddenly she wanted to struggle, to scream out loud, to express her frustration.

His leg retreated abruptly. So did his mouth, and his hands rolled her over so that her back was to him. Before she could protest, a large palm splayed over her stomach, pressing her back into him, curving her spine and bringing her bottom upwards. She felt his hard body curve around hers, felt him move himself down between her buttocks till he reached where his fingers had been, sliding up inside her with surprising ease.

Samantha sucked in sharply when he rolled her face-down onto the duvet, then scooped her lower half up onto her knees. As she went to lift her upper body onto her hands, he pressed her shoulders back down, and her arms slid out in front of her and her head dropped.

'Keep your head down,' he commanded, when she went to lift it once more. 'You will like it like this. Trust me.'

Trust didn't come into it by that stage. She was his to command; his to position this way and that; his to take as he pleased.

The feeling of utter submission to his will excited Samantha. His hands grasped her hips, holding her firmly whilst he began to rock back and forth inside her, slowly at first, his flesh not withdrawing too far from her before he thrust forward again, burying himself in her to the hilt.

She could hear his heavy breathing. Or was that her own?

The moans were definitely hers.

He stopped at one stage, his hands releasing her hips to run up and down her spine. He bent over her, brushing aside her hair and kissing her neck. No, not kissing, exactly. More like sucking. She cried out when he began to bite her, shuddering with both pain and pleasure. She heard him mutter something she didn't understand.

He grabbed at her hips again and started to thrust, much more roughly. Samantha's nails scraped back and forth across the duvet as the sensations he was creating in her body began to build. Everything inside her grew tighter and tighter. Her muscles stiffened, squeezing Bandar, trying to hold him still. At the same time she craved for him to do it even faster, and harder. Anything to release her from this torment. Soon, she could not bear any more. Her mouth opened to plead, or to protest, when suddenly the first spasm struck.

Samantha had read about orgasms. But reading about them had not prepared her for the reality of the experience. Everything which had been building inside her simply burst, like a dam. The pleasure swept through her in waves, tidal in force to begin with. But gradually they lessened in impact, till the waves lapped quite gently at her, making her sigh with the most amazing feelings of satisfaction and content.

Only when her body become like a millpond did Samantha realise that all awareness of what had been happening with Bandar had ceased from the beginning of her own climax. She had no idea if he had come—had not felt anything but her own blinding pleasure.

His firm grip on her hips remained, but his body had stilled, his breathing heavy and ragged.

When he withdrew abruptly, her lower half collapsed onto the duvet like a house of cards. All her limbs had gone limp; her head was like lead. It took the most enormous effort to turn her face enough to glance over her shoulder at him. He was sitting back on his haunches, his hands gripping his knees. His eyes, when they connected with hers, seemed oddly frustrated.

Her stomach contracted. 'Did I do something wrong?' she asked, rolling over and pulling some of the duvet over her. Maybe he *hadn't* come? How would she know?

'Of course not,' he returned brusquely, his hands lifting to rake his hair back from his forehead. 'If I were a sheikh of the olden days I would buy you at once for my harem.'

'Really?'

'Absolutely. You have the makings of a perfect little love-slave. I want nothing more but to stay here with you for hours. Unfortunately, I have to go back to the house. I can feel a headache coming on. I must take my medication or I will be totally useless tomorrow—which I do not want to be,' he said, his eyes locking with hers. 'I will make love to you more than once next time, Samantha. I promise.'

She shivered under his glittering gaze. And the excitement of his promise.

'Have…have you always suffered from headaches?' she asked as he got to his feet and began scooping up his clothes.

'They are a recent development. I will be all right if I take my medication quickly enough. Now, point me to your bathroom. I must hurry.'

CHAPTER EIGHT

SAMANTHA stayed curled up in the duvet in front of the
fire after Bandar had gone. Her body felt totally relaxed,
but her mind did not take long to rev up again, finding
all sorts of complications.

Just when and where would their affair take place?
He could not keep coming down to her cottage. The staff
at the stud would cotton on. This was the country, not
the big, bad city. Things were quickly noticed here and
talked about. The men would lose respect for her and
her working life would become very difficult indeed.

Her intention to quit her position at the stud at the
end of June made no difference. The horsey world in
Australia was not that large. Everyone knew everyone.
A good reputation was important. At least it was to
Samantha. A lot of the girl grooms slept around, and
she'd heard what the men said about them. She couldn't
bear to have herself gossiped about that way.

Visiting Bandar up at the main house was out of the
question for the same reasons. Staff would see her car
parked outside late into the night and start asking questions.

Then there was the problem of Cleo.

Samantha supposed she could tell her about Bandar, and then have Cleo sneak her into Bandar's bedroom without anyone else finding out. But Samantha cringed at that idea. Perhaps because she knew Cleo could never keep a secret. Or probably because she just didn't want to see the incredulous look on Cleo's face.

She still felt somewhat incredulous herself. What was it about her which Bandar liked so much? He'd claimed she'd aroused and intrigued him from the start. Why was that?

The only thing she could think of was that she'd stood up to him a couple of times. Maybe strong women turned him on.

Not that she'd proved all that strong in the end. She'd been like putty in his hands tonight. Samantha shivered at the memory of her total subservience to his will. He'd ordered and she'd obeyed.

He was right. She did have the makings of a perfect little love-slave. For him, anyway. She would have to find some will-power before tomorrow, or she'd be agreeing to move into his bedroom and to hell with what everyone thought!

The morning found Samantha still curled up in the duvet. Great sex sure made a girl sleep soundly, she thought as she yawned and stretched. How fabulous did she feel! This was what she'd been missing all these years. This was what her girlfriends had often raved about.

And why, maybe, some women got mixed up with the wrong men.

Because they were good in bed.

Bandar wasn't just good in bed, Samantha conceded.

He was awesome. And she didn't mean just the way he was built. Though that was pretty fabulous, too.

She shivered at the memory of Bandar's hands. The way they'd touched her. She could not wait to have him touch her again. And look at her again. With no clothes on.

Her thoughts brought a swirling sensation to her head and a tightness to the pit of her stomach.

She was getting turned on, she recognised. 'Get up, girl,' she ordered herself, then immediately thought of Bandar again. He did like to order her around. And she liked to obey. Mindlessly. Blindly. Wantonly.

Her head swirled again, her belly tightening even further.

Her groan was full of frustration. Keeping her mind on her job today was going to be almost impossible. She'd be thinking of Bandar all the time. Looking out for him. Wanting him.

The wanting part would be the most trying. She hadn't realised how quickly desire could strike. One moment she'd been totally relaxed and content. The next, she'd been consumed with the need to be made love to again. She craved another climax. Craved Bandar inside her. Craved the soothing contentment of afterwards.

Jumping to her feet, Samantha swept the duvet up off the floor and hurried from the room.

'I can see you're still not feeling well.'

Samantha frowned as she glanced up at Gerald. They were halfway through worming the mares due to foal in August—an easy, though boring job. No real concentration was needed, and she'd been off on another planet the whole time.

But she could hardly tell Gerald what had been filling her mind. He'd be shocked to the core. Better to be keep Bandar's little white lie going. He'd apparently told them yesterday that she'd had an upset stomach.

'I'm not quite on top of things yet,' she said.

'Stomach still bothering you?'

'Mmm. My head, too.' And wasn't that the truth? Her head was her main problem. It simply would not give her any peace, constantly filling with images of her and Bandar last night.

'You should have the afternoon off,' Gerald advised. 'Have a lie-down.'

Samantha wanted to have a lie-down. But not alone.

Bandar's sudden appearance at the fence of the paddock they were working in startled her. She hadn't seen or heard him. The golf cart he was driving again today didn't make much noise on the gravel. It was the quietest of the vehicles used around the stud.

'Good morning,' he said as he stepped up onto the wooden railing.

Her nerves were instantly ajangle, her nipples hardening under her jumper just at the sight of him.

He was wearing stonewashed grey jeans and a fleecy black top with a zipper down the front. The day was cooler than yesterday, the sun not providing much warmth.

Samantha looked at him and he looked right back, his dark eyes not reflecting anything which had happened between them. Oh, but he was a cool customer!

But then he was a playboy, wasn't he? He had three girlfriends back home. What was she but another little bit on the side? A fill-in. Nothing all that special, despite his flattering words last night. Just someone slightly different to help him pass the time in what he was probably finding quite a dull place to live.

She had to be careful, and not let herself get carried away with this man. He was perfect as a fantasy lover. To actually fall in love with him would be very foolish indeed. She had to keep him in the role of fantasy lover in her head and in her heart. She had to learn everything she could from him, then wave him off at the end of his stay without a single second thought or regret.

Because that was what he would be doing with her. Hadn't he mentioned more than once that his time here was limited?

At the same time, Samantha could not deny that the next three weeks promised to be the most exciting time of her life. It was difficult to keep her head—or her feet—on the ground, the moment she got within calling distance of him.

'How are you feeling today, Samantha?' he asked matter-of-factly.

'She's not too good at all,' Gerald answered for her. 'Her stomach's still upset. I told her to take the afternoon off. Have a lie-down.'

'That sounds like an excellent suggestion. I have just the thing to settle that stomach of yours up at the house,' he said.

His voice and eyes were betraying nothing. But Samantha could hear the wicked irony behind his clever play on words. He was a devil all right: a sexy, devious, conscienceless devil.

'There is also a nice daybed out on the back patio, where it's warm but shady. The perfect place for you to lie down. That cottage Samantha lives in is in a cold spot,' he directed at Gerald. 'I visited her last night, to see how she was, and thought she would be better off up in one of the guestrooms at the main house. But I dared not suggest it.'

Gerald laughed. 'Very wise move. Our Samantha does not take kindly to male suggestions—do you, Sam?'

Samantha's smile was forced. 'That depends on what they're suggesting,' she bit out.

'Now, don't go getting stroppy,' Gerald said. 'Bandar's just being kind. Be a sensible girl and go up to the house with him—get that medicine into you. Then stay and have a rest. Cleo will be there to look after you.'

'Actually, Cleo will not be there to look after you,' Bandar murmured the moment she was seated beside him in the golf cart and Gerald was out of earshot. 'Thursday is her shopping day in town. She has just left. I made sure Norman went with her, so we will have the house to ourselves for at least three hours.'

'You're very sure of yourself, aren't you?' she threw at him. And of me, she added ruefully to herself.

His head turned to frown over at her. 'We are not back to square one, are we, Samantha?'

'No,' she said. 'But please don't presume I will always be at your beck and call. I have my pride, you know.'

He stopped driving, his eyes whipping round to bore into hers. 'You want me to make love to you again, do you not?'

'Yes,' she said.

'Then do not speak to me of pride. Pride is just an excuse for you not to be what you want to be.'

'And what is that?'

'A woman who has finally discovered the pleasures of the flesh and who wants more. Do not deny it,' he swept on before she could say a word. 'I know what I know. Pretence and pride will be your downfall, Samantha, if you let them: It is time to face the truth.'

'The truth?'

'You are a spirited girl, with a good brain and a strong personality. But you like to be controlled in the bedroom. That is nothing to be ashamed of. There are many women who need that kind of liberation before they can truly enjoy sex.'

'But how can being controlled be a liberation?' she asked, confused by his assessment of her sexual preferences. And yet he could possibly be right. She had liked it last night when he'd ordered her around, when he'd directed all the action.

'If you totally surrender yourself to your lover, it frees you of all responsibility for what happens. You don't have to concentrate, or compete. You just lie back and enjoy. If your lover is a good lover—and by that I mean skilled in the erotic arts, but not in any way depraved or cruel—your experiences can be out of this world. You just like your lover to be masterful.'

'What I would like is for you to stop talking about distracting things and start driving again.'

'You want me to get to the house in a hurry?'

'Yes,' she said, shuddering as she accepted she was now even more excited. There was no doubt he was totally corrupting her.

'Then I will go slower,' he said, and reached over to cover her knee with one hand. 'You must learn patience, Samantha. I give the orders; you simply obey. Do I make myself clear?'

'Perfectly.'

'You will do as I say? Always?'

She picked up his hand and put it right back on the wheel. 'In your dreams, Bandar. Last night was fantastic, but I do still have a mind of my own.' Though she suspected it might grow weaker with each passing day in this man's company.

He pursed his lips in disapproval of her defiance. 'I see you have not yet been broken in properly. But it is early days yet.'

'I am not a horse!'

'That is a pity. Horses cannot talk back. We are here,' he said, stopping right in front of the steps. 'Time for your medicine.'

'You are a truly wicked man,' Samantha said as she climbed out. For inside she was literally quaking with desire.

'You bring out my darker side,' he muttered, striding round the cart to where she was standing. 'Come.' He took her hand and drew her up the steps onto the cloistered verandah. The front doors were unlocked, and Bandar led her quickly through the foyer and down the wide hallway of the wing which contained all the bedrooms.

Samantha had been in the main guest suite. Once. Cleo had been cleaning it in preparation for visitors at Christmas time. Samantha had been helping her—not because she'd had to, but because she'd been lonely.

There were three rooms: a bedroom, sitting room and

en-suite bathroom. All were spacious, filled with good-quality country-style furniture and five-star luxuries—from the king-sized bed and the flatscreen television, hooked up to the satellite, to the corner spa bath with its eighteen-carat-gold-plated taps.

'I shall run a bath,' Bandar said, after he'd steered her into the sitting room and left her standing by an elegantly striped sofa.

Samantha winced. 'I smell of horses, I suppose?'

'I like the smell of horses,' he returned smoothly. 'One day we will make love on a horse.'

'Oh…' she said, her mind immediately forming an image of Bandar riding a horse and her, naked, sitting astride his lap, her back to him.

Her hands were holding the reins, because his hands were busy on her bare breasts. He was naked, too, and buried deep inside her, as he'd been last night. The horse was galloping and—

'But not today,' he went on, breaking the spell of her fantasy. 'Today I wish to bathe with you. Then make love to you in a proper bed.'

'Oh,' she said, for a second time. Was there no end to the erotic scenarios he would propose, which he had obviously experienced before?

A black jealousy claimed Samantha as she thought of Bandar bathing with other women, not to mention making love to them on galloping horses, and hard floors, and soft beds, and probably countless other places and positions.

'You've done these things with other women, have you?' she blurted out.

'What? Oh…*other* women.' His dark eyes narrowed, his brows drawing together as he considered his answer.

Samantha's heart grew tight in her chest. She didn't want him to admit it. And what if he said he had? What would she do? Would she have the courage to walk away?

'I have known many women. In fact, I have moved in a very different world to you, Samantha,' he said at last, 'where obscene wealth brings out the worst in men. *And* women. I have witnessed many scenes—most recently at a private party I attended not that long ago—but I was revolted. I enjoy playing erotic games, but lovemaking, for me, is a private and very personal activity. I do confess to preferring a partner who likes me to be master in the bedroom. I am not one of those inadequate men who needs the woman on top, so to speak. It is I who does the riding. I who does the binding.'

'The *binding*?'

'You will like being bound,' he stated, with shocking confidence.

'How can you be sure?' she asked, but breathlessly. The idea was already exciting her, bringing all kinds of questions into her head. How would he tie her up? Where? And for how long?

'I am sure,' he stated firmly, his eyes fixing on her parted lips. 'There are tea and coffee-making facilities over there,' he went on, nodding towards the built-in wall unit, the long wooden doors cleverly concealing everything a person would require to make a drink or a snack. On the day Samantha had been helping Cleo clean, her job had been to fill the small fridge with wine and soft drinks.

'You might like to make us something hot to drink whilst I run that bath.'

'No,' she replied, frustrated by his coolness and his control. 'I don't want a drink. I want you to kiss me. I *need* you to kiss me, Bandar. Right now.'

Bandar was taken aback by her passionate rebellion. But also stirred by it.

This was what had bewitched him about her from the start. Her headstrong spirit. And, yes, her passion. Having her blindly obey him last night had been extremely satisfying, but when she was like this—her blue eyes blazing and that saucy mouth of hers spitting defiance— he wanted to rip the clothes from her body and ravage her on the spot.

'If I kiss you, I might not be able to wait,' he admitted, feeling some alarm at the way he was suddenly feeling—like a volcano about to erupt.

'You're the one talking too much now,' she said. 'Why don't you just shut up and kiss me?'

Bandar's already precarious control snapped.

He covered the ground between them in a split second, crushing her against him and plundering her lips as he had never plundered a woman's mouth before. She more than matched him with her own hunger, her hands grabbing him by his top and yanking him even harder against her.

Bandar knew he could not last much longer, a situation which was quite shocking to him. He prided himself on his skill as a lover. To come prematurely would be mortifying in the extreme.

In desperation, he grabbed her ponytail and yanked her away. Their mouths burst apart, and Bandar stared down into her wildly dilated eyes before he suddenly fell to ripping off her clothes.

To hell with his pride. To hell with everything!

She helped him with the shedding of her jumper over her head, and then with her bra. Her jeans were a temporary stumbling block when the zipper caught in the fraying denim halfway down. He tipped her back onto the nearby sofa and dragged them down her legs, taking her elastic-sided riding boots with them. Her panties followed—unsexy cotton briefs which Bandar vowed to burn.

Once totally naked, she actually jumped to her feet and attacked *his* clothes. Bandar was too stunned—and too turned on—to stop her. She was like a wild animal, ripping and clawing at him. By the time he stood naked also he was once again perilously close to the point of no return.

She should not have touched him—should not have caressed him like that!

He took her standing up, lifting her onto her toes as he rammed up into her. Once anchored deep inside her, he carried her across the room and pushed her up against the wall unit, taking her wrists and pinning her arms wide against the wood, holding her solidly captive whilst he started pounding into her. He heard her cry out, and didn't know if it was a cry of pain or pleasure. He didn't care. He had totally lost it.

Bandar came with a speed unknown to him. Barely ten seconds after penetration he ejaculated, groaning and shuddering like some horny teenager with no control at all. His not using protection made him groan for a different reason. Yet how delicious it felt without anything between them. Bandar wallowed in the sensation of his seed flooding her womb. More satisfaction followed when she came, his physical pleasure heightened as her avid flesh milked him.

True regret was slow in coming. But when it did Bandar squeezed his eyes tightly shut, his lungs expanding then deflating in a deeply troubled breath.

Samantha was going to be furious with him. And rightly so. Though, damn it all, her behaviour had not helped. How could she expect a man to control himself in such a situation?

But you always have before, Bandar, came a rueful voice from deep inside. You never lose control. Never, ever.

Why are you so different with this girl?

A sound escaped her lips: half-sigh, half-sob.

He opened his eyes to find that hers were half closed, her head turned to one side. He got the impression she would sink to the floor if he wasn't still holding her arms up against the wall.

'Are you all right?' he asked, not daring to let her go.

Her eyelids opened slowly. Her smile was just as slow.

'Lovely, thanks,' she murmured.

'I did not use protection,' he said, becoming more perturbed by his reckless stupidity with each passing moment.

He did not want a child—especially not now, when he might not be here to protect it. Material provision could always be made, but having money was not the answer to everything, no matter what some people thought. A child needed his father to be there for him during his growing up years.

'Yes,' she said. 'I did notice that.'

How calm she sounded. *Too* calm. Bandar's gut crunched down hard, his concerns suddenly changing direction. Surely he hadn't just fallen for the oldest trick in the book? Was this what she'd planned all along? To seduce him and trap him with a child?

She would not be the first woman to try this tactic, not by a long shot. He had been almost caught once before, and his close call had made him very careful. This incident was the first slip-up he had made in fifteen years.

Bandar searched her unmade-up face, trying to see the truth behind her seemingly ingenuous persona.

Usually, Bandar could spot a fortune-hunter a mile off. He found it hard to believe Samantha was of that ilk, but no one knew better than he that some women would stop at nothing to get their greedy hands on his family's fortune.

'Why did you not stop me?' he ground out.

Samantha was startled by the anger in his voice. Then annoyed.

'*You* could have stopped,' she pointed out. 'No one forced you to do what you just did.'

His abrupt dropping of her arms and his equally abrupt withdrawal from her body brought a startled cry to her lips.

His eyes narrowed on her till they were cold slits of black ice. 'You are not inexperienced at all, are you? You have deceived me.'

'I have never deceived you,' she declared, but then pulled a face when she thought of her one small deception.

'I can see the guilt in your face.'

His accusatory tone made her mad. 'Just one wretched little white lie,' she threw at him. 'One which should please you.'

'Tell me.'

'I *am* on the Pill. I just didn't want to say.'

Funny. He didn't look pleased.

'I do not believe you,' he said coldly.

'What?' she said, her back straightening as her shoulders pressed against the wall unit.

'You heard me.'

'Yes. I certainly did. It just took a moment or two for the insult to sink in. Now that it has, I have one thing to say to you, Sheikh Bandar bin Bastard. Go to hell. Go straight to hell. And do not under any circumstances ever speak to me again!'

Samantha pushed him out of the way as she lurched away from the wall. 'Unfortunately I have to use your bathroom before I can leave,' she said angrily as she scooped up her clothes. 'Aside from the fact I desperately need to pee, I intend making sure I wash as much of you from me as I can,' she declared. She held her clothes in front of her, her knuckles white with fury. 'Not because there's any possibility of my having your child, you unspeakable excuse for a man, but because I could not bear to walk around with a single reminder that I once gave myself so totally to a man who had no respect for me whatsoever. But then, you don't respect any woman, do you, Bandar?' she finished up, whirling on her heels and stomping off to the bathroom.

CHAPTER NINE

BANDAR sat in thoughtful silence on the sofa, sipping a mug of tea and waiting for Samantha to emerge. She'd been in there for several minutes, during which the shower had been running for some considerable time. He didn't doubt the bathroom door was locked, so he hadn't bothered trying it. There was no point in talking to her whilst she was in such a fury.

Instead, he'd dressed, made some tea, spooned in several spoonfuls of sugar and sat down to drink it.

Her tirade had disturbed him. Had made him question himself in a way that no one had ever made him question himself—especially over his treatment and opinion of women.

His cynicism about the opposite sex, Bandar realised as he sipped, was so deep that it was bordering on paranoid. He understood why that was so. He had just cause for his attitude. But did that make it right?

Not every female in this world was a cold-blooded fortune-hunter, he conceded. Meeting him, however, and finding out he had billions at his disposal invariably brought out the greed in a person. He had seen the women he'd dated change once they realised just how wealthy he was. Suddenly they were willing to do anything for him. That private party he'd been invited to had been thrown by a woman who'd thought he could be seduced by such goings-on. She'd mistakenly imagined he might part with a lot of money to enjoy depravity on a regular basis.

Bandar had stormed out and never spoken to her again.

The three lady-friends he'd told Samantha about were nothing like that. They were, however, exceptions to the rule—all extremely wealthy in their own right, independent and successful women, who had goals other than trapping a rich man into marriage.

His relationships with them were casual and strictly sexual. Samantha seemed to think that was disgusting. But he had never promised or pretended to any of them that she was the only female in his life. They did not seem to mind that they were not exclusive. And they certainly were not in love with him. He provided them with company and sex, and vice versa. If he did not survive his operation next month they would not grieve for too long, if at all.

No one, Bandar had finally accepted, would truly grieve for him. He had no close family, no wife, no children.

Perhaps Ali would grieve a little. But not for too long, either. His life was full and busy, with his wife and children, and this beautiful place. In time, Ali would hardly remember that a man called Bandar had ever existed.

No, that was not true. Ali's son carried his name. He would never be truly forgotten.

This thought actually gave Bandar a jab of pleasure,

and made him see why men set such store by having a child to live on after them.

After them…

Bandar's hands tightened around the mug of tea as another realisation struck.

He did not want to die. Not any more.

Not that he had ever really *wanted* to die. But there had been a part of him which had not been devastated when the English doctor had delivered his dire news, a part of him which had said *yes*, finally an escape from the loneliness of his life, deliverance from the wretched feelings which swamped him every morning on wakening.

Feelings, Bandar conceded with some surprise, which had been strangely absent since his arrival here in Australia.

Was it because of his sexual obsession with this girl? Or the whole change of scene?

'Well, just look at him!'

Bandar's head jerked up at Samantha's strident voice. She was standing there in the doorway which led from the sitting room to the bedroom, her hands on her hips, glowering at him once more. She was fully dressed, her damp hair scraped back from her scrubbed face into a tight ponytail, her blue eyes still sparking at him.

'Oh, please don't get up,' she went on scathingly when he put down his cup. 'Drink your tea. I'm sure I can find my own way back. A good long walk is always excellent for the constitution. And for making decisions—though I've already made the most important one. When you next contact Ali, please tell him that I have quit. I will waive any severance pay for the right to be out of here in the morning.'

Bandar's first reaction was close to panic—a most unusual state of affairs. He never panicked.

Let her go, his brain told him. She is becoming a complication you can do without.

His body, however, felt differently. It still wanted her.

Gradually, his brain began to argue his body's point of view.

If you let her go, how will you get through these next three weeks? She will keep your mind from thinking of death. She will keep you very much in the land of the living.

He had already made plans to take her to Sydney with him for the weekend. Plans which, he finally accepted, he had no intention of changing.

She watched him rise slowly to his feet, saw the wheels already turning in his head. He was going to try and persuade her to stay. She could feel it.

Her hands dropped to her sides and curled into tight fists.

'There is no need for you to do this, Samantha,' he said, in that silky smooth voice of his.

'I can't stay working here,' she told him. 'Not after this. I was going to quit, anyway, at the end of June. I'm just bringing my exit forward.'

'You do not like working here?'

'No. I preferred working in Sydney. But I am not going to tell you why. I know what you're doing. You're trying to get me talking. You think you can change my mind.'

'I hope that I can,' he said softly. 'I hope you will accept my apology. I was wrong not to believe you.'

His saying sorry startled her. For it sounded genuine. He even *looked* sorry.

'My only excuse is that I have long been the target of unscrupulous women. I have developed a suspicious nature. But I have had time to think whilst you were in the bathroom, and I do not believe you had any secret agenda where I am concerned.'

Why, oh, why, did she have to look guilty?

He saw it. She knew he saw it. For he stiffened, his broad shoulders squaring, his black eyes narrowing.

'Are you now admitting to a secret agenda?' he demanded. 'Is that why you're leaving? Because your goal has already been achieved?'

She shook her head violently, annoyed with herself for letting her emotions show in her face. 'No. My goal has *not* been achieved. Look, I didn't really have a secret agenda where you're concerned. Not the kind you're thinking of, anyway.'

'Then what kind *did* you have?'

Samantha groaned. 'Oh, don't make me embarrass myself.'

'You must tell me,' he insisted.

'Look, I wanted you to teach me everything about sex—all right?' she threw at him, her confession sending his eyebrows ceilingwards.

'Not at first,' she raced on. 'At first I just secretly fancied you. You're very fanciable. Surely you must realise that? But I had no idea you fancied me back. I mean…men don't fancy me on the whole. Last night was…well, it was a shock. And a real eye-opener, I can tell you. I'd never had an orgasm before and… Oh, please, don't look at me like that. It's true. I did warn you I was inexperienced. I don't lie, Bandar. Well, not about most things. And you can't blame me for not telling you I was on the Pill. You *do* have a reputation as a playboy, and you openly admitted to having three girlfriends back home. How was I to know what I might have been risking by sleeping with you?'

'Nothing, I can assure you,' he ground out. 'I had a very thorough medical check just before leaving England and it was all clear. Except for a small problem with headaches.'

'Well, that's a relief. And I promise you there won't be any consequences to what happened here today in any way, shape or form.'

'Why are you on the Pill?'

'What?'

'It is a simple question. If you have not been having a regular sex life, why go on the Pill?'

'It's a long story.'

'I am all ears.'

'You still don't believe me, do you?'

Not entirely, Bandar was forced to admit to himself. But that was probably just his cynicism talking.

He was certainly intrigued by her story. Not only intrigued, but excited. She could not have confessed to a better secret agenda. It fitted very well with his plans, and his desires.

At the same time, he could not help feeling a little sceptical. Last night had been her first orgasm? And she was, what? Twenty-six, Cleo had told him. That seemed highly unlikely.

But perhaps it was true.

'I do believe you,' he said, thinking of his own secret agenda. 'I just want to know the reason.'

'Well, that's too bad, because I'm not going to explain myself any further. I'm going now, Bandar. Goodbye.'

'I don't want you to go,' he said, striding round the coffee table to place himself between her and the door.

'What you want no longer matters to me. Now, get out of my way.'

'No.'

'I'll scream.'

He smiled. 'No one will hear you.'

She crossed her arms and glared at him. 'You don't frighten me.'

'Yes. I do.' He came towards her, his hands reaching out to curl over her shoulders. But he did not draw her close. He kept her at an arm's distance, his eyes searching hers. 'Is this what you always do when a man shows interest in you, Samantha? Find some reason to fight with him and then run away? I have apologised. I *do* believe that you are on the Pill. And you do not have to tell me why if you do not want to.'

'I don't want to,' she muttered, but her arms uncrossed and dropped down by her sides.

Clearly her defences were on the wane. Bandar knew it would not be long before she would surrender to him once more. The prospect brought a sense of triumph and a dark pleasure, sending hot blood rushing round his veins. This was what he wanted. What he needed. Craving her constantly made him feel alive.

All he had to do was take control of that craving and everything would be all right.

'But you do still want me to teach you everything I know about sex, do you not?' he asked in a soft, seductive voice.

Her body stiffened, but her eyes showed she was tempted.

'Come now, forget your pride and be honest.'

'I suppose so,' she admitted grudgingly. 'But I don't like all this sneaking around. It makes me tense.'

'I agree. It is not conducive to total relaxation. Which is why I have already ordered Ali's helicopter. It will arrive tomorrow afternoon to take us to Sydney for the weekend. Ali has put his suite at the Regency Hotel at my disposal. I can teach you a lot in a weekend, Samantha. By Sunday you will not be the same girl. You certainly will not want to fight with me.'

Samantha groaned. The devil himself could not have tempted her more powerfully. To be alone with him for a whole weekend in some fancy hotel suite. Talk about fantasies coming true!

'But what am I going to tell everyone? I…I don't want them to know that you and I are…are…you know.'

'We will invent some excuse. You can say you need to go to Sydney to see your family doctor. Hint at some woman's problem that is too private to discuss. You did say you came from Sydney, did you not? Your father and your four brothers live there.'

Samantha frowned. She could not remember telling him that. But maybe she had. 'Yes, they all live in Sydney,' she admitted.

'That is the perfect solution, then. No one will know you are spending the weekend with me. They will think

I am just being kind in giving you a lift. Everyone will assume you are going to stay with your family.'

Samantha could not believe that he had already ordered the helicopter. He'd just presumed—again—that she would go along with whatever he wanted.

'Like I said before,' she said, with exasperation in her voice but adrenaline rocketing through her body, 'you're a wicked man.'

'Not wicked. Determined.'

'Do you always get what you want in life?'

'No,' he said, and smiled a wry smile. 'There are some things you cannot buy.'

'Are you talking about love?'

'Not at all. I can buy love, Samantha.'

'No, you can't. You can buy sex, but not love.'

'You may be right. But I do not want love, and I never have to buy sex. I get it for free.'

'I'm sure you do.'

He laughed, then drew her to him and kissed her, long and hard. By the time his head lifted Samantha had forgotten that she'd resolved less than a few minutes before not to have anything further to do with him. She could fight *him*, but she could not fight the desires he evoked in her—the needs, the all-consuming cravings.

'What time is it?' she asked, her voice husky.

'Just after one.'

'When will—?'

'Cleo and her husband will not be back till three at the earliest.'

'Then we can—'

'Do you really want to learn *everything* about sex,

Samantha? Not just various positions and physical techniques, but the more sophisticated aspects?'

'I guess so,' she said, not sure what he was referring to.

'Remember how I told you on the way up here that you should learn patience? We are about to go away together for the whole weekend, when we will indulge ourselves to the maximum. If we abstain from any further lovemaking today, your pleasure will be all the greater, your orgasms much more intense. The brain is the sexiest organ in the body. Just thinking about sex is sometimes the best foreplay. Do you think about sex much, Samantha?'

'Since I met you, all the time.'

His smile was oh, so sexy. 'I will take that as a compliment. And what do you think about?'

Her face flamed. 'I can't tell you that!'

'But you must. Talking about sex with your lover is even more arousing than thinking about it. Have you ever had phone sex?'

'Bandar, before I met you I'd hardly had sex at all.'

'I still find that amazing. A girl as passionate as you are.'

'My sarcastic tongue puts men off. That's another thing I'd like you to teach me. How to flirt.'

'Flirting is not something that can be taught. It will, however, come more naturally to you once you become confident in the bedroom. Your tongue will soften as your body softens. Come. Sit down on that sofa. I will get you a glass of wine and we will talk.'

'Just talk?' she choked out.

'I might play with you a little,' he said as he walked over to the wall unit and retrieved a half-bottle of wine from the small fridge.

'Oh, no,' she protested. 'No, don't do that. I couldn't stand it.' She plonked herself down on the sofa—a necessary move, given her legs had suddenly gone to jelly.

'You would have to stand it if you were bound.'

Her heart took off at the thought. 'You're not going to do that, are you?'

'No. Not today. But I want you to think about how it would feel to be bound naked to a bed, or a chair, or to whatever piece of furniture was suitable. Of course you would only do this with a lover you totally trusted,' he went on as he opened the wine bottle and poured some into a glass.

'But why would I do it at all?' she asked, somewhat breathlessly. 'I mean…why do you think I would like it?'

'Try to imagine the scenario. Once bound, you are forcibly rendered into a state of delicious helplessness. You cannot stop your lover from touching you. Or from taking you. Or from forcing you to wait. Sometimes he will make you come and come till you have dissolved with desire. At another time, if he is sufficiently skilled, he can take you to the edge of a climax and keep you balanced there for hours. Which one of those scenarios do you prefer, Samantha?' he said, sitting down next to her and holding the glass to her lips.

By now Samantha's mouth felt like parchment and her head was in a total haze. When he tipped the glass, she gulped down a mouthful of the wine, her eyes never leaving his.

He took the glass away, then bent to kiss her.

'Which one?' he whispered against her lips.

'Both,' she returned with a shudder. 'Both.'

* * *

Yes! Bandar thought triumphantly at her admission. She was his.

'You will be my perfect little love-slave for the entire weekend,' he purred as he held the wine glass to her lips once more.

She swallowed another mouthful, her eyes widening on him.

'You won't hurt me, will you?'

'Never!' he exclaimed, shocked that she would even think it. 'If you give me your body, I will give it nothing but pleasure. But you must trust me implicitly.'

He kissed her between mouthfuls of wine till she looked dazed and he was so cruelly aroused he wondered how he would last till the following day himself. Yet his male ego demanded that he did. Hadn't he claimed to her that a good lover was patient and skilled?

'Don't make me wait, Bandar,' she suddenly whispered. 'Take me to bed now. I promise to be your perfect little love-slave for the whole weekend in Sydney. But I can't wait that long. I need you now. I don't know what's wrong with me, but I…I have to have you inside me.'

He groaned. He could not help it. 'You should not say such things to a man.'

'You don't understand. It's like an addiction, this feeling. This longing. Tell me, will it ever go away?'

'Do you want it to go away?' he asked thickly as he scooped her up in his arms and carried her quickly towards the bedroom.

'Yes. No. I don't know. I can't think straight. I just want you to do it to me all the time.'

'I will do my best,' he said, thinking he wasn't much better.

'How long do we have before Cleo gets back?' she asked hoarsely as he lowered her to the bed and began to undress her.

Not long enough, Bandar suspected. 'About an hour and a half.'

'Hurry, then, Bandar,' she urged him. 'Hurry.'

CHAPTER TEN

'YOU know, Samantha, I think Bandar likes you.'

Samantha took a moment to school her face into a perfectly bland mask before looking up from her coffee. 'Oh, come now, Cleo, don't be silly.'

After Cleo had returned from her shopping excursion into town, Bandar had obviously relayed their agreed story, and a worried Cleo had come bolting down to the cottage to see if there was anything seriously wrong. Samantha had allayed her friend's fears by saying she was just having some women's troubles and wanted to see her own lady doctor back in Sydney, claiming that she didn't feel comfortable going to the old fuddy-duddy male doctor in the local town. She'd also added for good measure that it was high time she visited her family.

It had been Cleo who'd insisted on making them both some coffee, clearly because she wanted to sit down and have a good gossip. All Samantha wanted to do was be by herself.

'I'm not being silly,' Cleo insisted. 'I know when a man is interested in a girl. He keeps asking me questions about you.'

Samantha frowned. 'What kind of questions?'

'About your background. Your family.'

'What did you tell him?'

'Nothing much. Just the bare facts about your mum dying when you were born, and how you'd been brought up in a family of blokes.'

'I see,' Samantha said. Which she did. That was how Bandar had found out about her brothers. And probably quite a bit more. Cleo never stopped at just the bare facts.

'He was very concerned about you the other night. Which reminds me, did you like my soup?'

'It was lovely.' Samantha had found it out on the front lawn the following morning, and had it for breakfast. 'Thank you. You're a kind person, Cleo.'

'I try to be.'

'Not many people are these days. It's become a selfish world.'

'Bandar's a kind man.'

'You think so?' Samantha wouldn't have put kindness at the forefront of Bandar's virtues. His kindnesses usually had an ulterior motive.

'Look what he did for Martha Higgins.'

'Who on earth is Martha Higgins?'

'The woman who owns Valleyview Farm. Bandar didn't need to pay her all that money for those mares. Norm was speaking to Trevor, and he said they weren't worth near that much.'

'How on earth did Trevor find out what Bandar paid for them? Did Bandar tell him?'

'Heavens, no. Trevor heard on the grapevine. You know what it's like up here, love. Can't keep a secret in the country. So I asked Bandar about it, and he said that

Ali had told him about Martha's circumstances and he thought she might need a helping hand.'

'He can afford it,' Samantha said, thinking how easy it was for a billionaire to impress people. Bandar only had to start throwing a few million around and everyone thought he was the ant's pants.

'Lots of other wealthy people can afford charitable gestures, too,' Cleo pointed out. 'But they still wouldn't have done what Bandar did. He didn't have to offer you a lift to Sydney either, madam. Stop being so critical of the man. Truly, Samantha, there I was, thinking you liked him.'

'I do like him,' she admitted. 'But that doesn't mean I have to kiss his backside for giving me a ride.'

Cleo laughed. 'Can't imagine you kissing *any* man's backside.'

Samantha smiled a brittle smile. Oh, Cleo. If only you knew. I've already kissed every part of his body! I can't get enough of him, and it's beginning to worry me. What I imagined would be a bold but positive experience is rapidly becoming a dangerous obsession. I've already become his love-slave. No, not his love-slave. Love has nothing to do with what he's doing to me. More his sex-slave.

'Are you excited about going in Ali's helicopter?' Cleo asked.

Samantha had been trying desperately not to think about tomorrow. Because whenever she did she started thinking about what was going to happen, and then other things started happening.

Bandar had been so right when he'd said thinking about sex was one of the best kinds of foreplay. Every time her mind went in that direction her nipples would go hard and she'd get a tight, crampy feeling in the pit of her stomach.

She had it now.

Samantha knew she would toss and turn all night.

'You wouldn't happen to have some sleeping tablets, would you, Cleo?'

'Oh, dear, you really mustn't be feeling well if you want one of those. But, yes, I do have some. Got a script when I was having a bout of insomnia last year. The menopause can do that to you,' she added, and pulled a face. 'What we women have to put up with. Men sure are the lucky ones. But, as they say, it's a man's world.'

Samantha couldn't have agreed more. Even more so if the man was handsome and rich and used to getting everything he wanted. For some weird and wonderful reason Bandar wanted *her* at the moment. Maybe he just couldn't go too long without sex. Or maybe he fancied himself as an erotic tutor. She could see that such a role would appeal to a man who liked the kind of sex that Bandar obviously liked.

The trouble was, she liked the same thing. She'd revelled in his masterful display in the bedroom this afternoon. He'd made mad, passionate love to her at first, face to face, satisfying her need to have him inside her. Afterwards he'd carried her into the shower, where he'd washed her all over, then carried her back to the bed and made love to her with his mouth till she'd been reduced to total mush. Finally, he'd demanded she do the same to him.

Samantha had read about oral sex. But she had never imagined herself doing it. Or liking it so much.

But she could not imagine doing it to any other man. That was the part which was beginning to trouble her. The fact that she couldn't see herself even *wanting* any other man. Not after Bandar.

Samantha hoped this was just because he was such an amazing lover and not anything deeper. The last thing she needed was to fall irrevocably in love with her erotic tutor.

'I suppose you wouldn't want to come up for dinner tonight, would you?' Cleo suggested. 'I'm sure Bandar wouldn't mind.'

Actually, Samantha was pretty sure he *would* mind. He'd stated quite firmly when they'd parted this afternoon that they should not see each other till the helicopter flight the next day.

'You know, I sometimes think that man is lonely,' Cleo added.

This observation struck a raw nerve with Samantha. Because it confirmed what she already knew. Of course Bandar was lonely out here in Australia. He'd had to leave his three girlfriends behind in London, hadn't he? Necessitating his having to find a substitute for his suddenly empty bed. Namely, *her*.

She was just a fill-in. An amusement to alleviate his boredom.

But knowing the truth about Bandar didn't make it any easier for her to resist him. Or to risk disobeying him.

'Thanks for the offer, Cleo, but I think I'd better not eat too much today. Not if I have to go in that helicopter tomorrow. I'll just have some Vegemite toast for tea. But I'll follow you back up to the house right now and get that sleeping tablet.' She stood up immediately.

Cleo got to her feet rather reluctantly.

'Will Bandar be there?' Samantha asked as both women walked out to their respective vehicles.

'Nope. He's out riding that mad stallion of his again. He said he'd have to ride him again tomorrow morning to make sure he behaves over the weekend. Ray told Norm that he's a right handful, that one. They've tried him in a bigger paddock, but he's still full of beans. Ray says he's one of those stallions who doesn't settle properly unless he's going to the breeding barn every day.'

Like his owner, came the rueful thought.

'He'll be right soon, then,' Samantha said drily. 'He's got a full book for the season. Come late August he'll be popping off to the barn several times a day for weeks on end.'

'You know, the way those stallions can keep going like that truly amazes me,' Cleo said as she pulled open her car door. 'Horses are obviously a lot different to humans. In my experience, most men are oncers. Once a month,' she added with a slightly raucous laugh. 'But maybe that's just my poor Norm. I dare say a stud like Bandar can do a bit better than that. See you up at the house, love,' she said, and was off.

Samantha grimaced as she climbed in behind her wheel and turned on the engine.

Cleo was understating things. Bandar could do a *lot* better than once a month; once an hour was more like it. No way was he going to wait till they arrived in Sydney before the sex started again. It would begin in the helicopter. She knew it would. He'd already told her what she was to wear for the flight down. And what not to wear.

She would obey him, of course. That was what sex-slaves did.

They obeyed their masters.

A skirt, he'd ordered. And no underwear. None at all. Not a stitch.

She trembled at the thought.

She could hardly wait!

If Bandar had had a whip he might have given the horse under him a sharp crack. He wanted the stallion to gallop faster. And faster still.

Just as well he didn't have one, Bandar realised, because Smoking Gun had never liked the whip.

He knew it was his own emotions getting the better of him. He was trying to rid himself of *his* testosterone, not the horse's.

The situation with Samantha was getting out of hand. The more he had the girl, the more he wanted her. He kept having to fight for control of his body. Twice this afternoon he'd lost the battle.

He had lost control, and Bandar did not like that.

Hence his mad ride around the racetrack this afternoon. But it didn't seem to be working.

He had to stay away from her for a while.

He would attend to himself, *by* himself, in the shower. Tonight and tomorrow morning. The thought was distasteful, but necessary.

By the time Samantha joined him on that helicopter tomorrow Bandar aimed to have his wayward flesh under control. For how could he enjoy controlling her if he could not control himself?

And that was the name of the game this weekend,

wasn't it? He was the master and she was his eager little love-slave.

His mind filled with the images of all he was planning to show her and do to her.

His groan sounded tortured. But it was a torture born of promised pleasure. His, and hers. Oh, yes, she would enjoy herself this weekend.

He would make sure of that.

CHAPTER ELEVEN

'YOU look beautiful,' he complimented her as soon as they were alone in the helicopter.

Not as beautiful as you, Samantha wanted to say. But she was having trouble finding her tongue at that moment.

He was dressed in a black suit—not a business suit, or a tuxedo. Far more casual than that. The jacket was single-breasted, with only one button, the trousers loosely but elegantly cut, their waistband slung low on his hips. He'd teamed the suit with a pale grey rollneck which highlighted his dark colouring. The rings were back on his fingers, but not the gold chain he usually wore around his neck. His hair looked longer than on the day they'd first met, falling in glossy waves almost to his shoulders.

She could not take her eyes off him.

He seemed to be similarly taken with her appearance.

Samantha had to confess that she looked her very best, which was only to be expected since her preparations for this weekend had taken her several hours last night and all this morning.

Her hair. Her face. Her body. They had all been

primped and preened over, plucked and perfumed, till she was as perfect as she could be. Her nails were painted, her bikini line ruthlessly waxed to almost nothing, her skin moisturised and her make-up immaculate.

Her clothes had presented a small problem, since her wardrobe consisted mainly of jeans. She'd bought a couple of skirts and dresses for her Gold Coast getaway, but they were all resort-wear, chosen for the warmer climate of Queensland: light, flowery things which didn't have the sophistication she was looking for.

The only skirt in her wardrobe which would remotely do was calf-length and black, with a split up the front to her knee. She'd teamed it with a pair of black knee-high boots she'd had for years but which never really went out of fashion, and a top she *had* bought for her getaway, a soft silky burgundy number, with three-quarter sleeves and a deep cross-over neckline.

She'd thrown her good black leather jacket over her shoulders for the drive up to the heliport and the short walk from where she'd parked her four-by-four on to the helicopter. Even so, she knew she looked very different from what she usually looked like. Cleo's eyes would have popped out of her head if she'd seen her.

Fortunately, Cleo was not there to see her off. Clever Bandar had given her and Norm the weekend off, and they'd left early this morning to go to Port Macquarie and visit Norm's elderly mother. There was only the pilot, and he was a virtual stranger to her.

Bandar had been waiting for her in the helicopter. The pilot had been the one to take her overnight bag, then help her up the steps, and she'd been terrified for a moment that a wind would come and somehow blow up her skirt and he would see she was naked underneath.

But that hadn't happened, and soon she'd been safely inside.

Safe, but instantly intimidated and terrified.

This could not be her, Samantha Nelson, with this stunningly gorgeous man in these amazing surroundings. The interior of Ali's helicopter was fitted out like a luxury loungeroom in an English gentleman's residence, with wood-panelled walls, plush leather seating arrangements and the thickest carpet on the floor.

But it *was* her, standing there without her pants on, breathlessly waiting for Bandar to do wicked things to her.

'I see you have done what I asked,' he murmured, his eyes not leaving hers as he walked slowly towards her.

'How do you know?' she choked out. She still had her leather jacket on.

'A woman moves differently when she is naked underneath her clothes.'

'Yes. Very carefully.'

The hint of a smile played around his sensual mouth. 'But you like it.'

'I can't say that I do. It makes me feel too vulnerable.'

'But deliciously aroused.'

She could not deny it.

'You will be more comfortable without the jacket,' he suggested smoothly.

She winced as he removed her last defence.

Samantha did not have to glance down to know what she looked like. She could feel her breasts swell further, her erect nipples pressing almost painfully against the softness of the silky material.

He took his time draping her jacket over the back of

a chair, each second like an eternity to Samantha. At last he returned to take her arm, his touch sending an electric charge ricocheting throughout her body, making her feel faint with excitement.

'Come,' he invited, and led her over to two cream leather armchairs sitting side by side. They had a small table between them, on which sat two glasses of champagne, plus a long-stemmed crystal vase carrying a single red rose the like of which Samantha had never seen. Its petals were huge and velvety, the red graduating from scarlet to almost black.

'What an unusual rose,' she said as she lowered herself almost gingerly into the first armchair, trying to hold the slit in her skirt together at the same time.

'It is called Carmen,' he replied. 'Named after the character in the opera.'

'It's very…um…'

'Sensual,' he supplied, before she could think of the right word. 'You will note that your chair has seat belts fitted. Here. Take your glass of champagne and I will fasten you in.'

She almost dropped the glass he handed her, her whole body stiffening when he pulled the belt quite firmly across her waist and clicked it in.

'Not too tight?' he murmured, his dark eyes boring into hers.

Samantha swallowed, then shook her head.

For a moment she could have sworn he was going to kiss her. But he didn't. He straightened, then moved over to sit down in the adjacent chair, belting himself in swiftly before picking up a nearby phone and telling the pilot they were ready to leave. Only then did he pick up his own glass of champagne.

'I forgot to ask if you liked champagne,' he said after they'd both had a few sips. 'Do you?'

'I like *this* champagne,' she replied, and took a deeper swallow. Getting tipsy suddenly seemed like a good idea.

'You should. It is the best. Drink up.'

Samantha was doing as she was told when she felt the floor beneath her begin to rise. Her hands automatically tightened around the delicate glass, but their take-off was remarkably smooth, and stunningly silent.

'I can't believe how quiet it is in here,' she said.

'Everything is very well insulated,' Bandar explained. 'And as you can see, there are no windows.'

She hadn't noticed the lack of windows till he said it.

'What a pity. The view from up here today would be magnificent.'

Bandar pressed a switch in the panel built into his chair's armrest and the large television on the adjacent wall immediately came on, showing a news channel. Another flick of a switch and the screen filled with a panoramic view of the countryside below.

'Channel Six is connected to a camera on the underside of the helicopter,' Bandar told her.

'It *is* a good view, but I can't watch it for long or I'll get motion sickness.'

'I do not want you to watch it,' he said, and switched it off. 'I wish to talk to you.'

Samantha could not believe that he was suggesting that again. Didn't he know how she was feeling? How she'd been feeling since she'd woken this morning?

As if she could hardly breathe for wanting him again. Her life had been turned upside down by the cravings which continually washed through her. She wanted to kneel before him right now and take him into her mouth. She wanted to shamelessly lift her skirt. She wanted him to look at her and touch her. She wanted him to ravage her body till she found some peace once more.

She'd become a slave—not to him so much, but to her own increasingly dark desires.

'I understand you do not want to talk,' he said. 'You want me to make love to you. And I will, I promise.'

Her face flamed, her body moving restlessly in the chair.

'But first I wish to explain something.'

She did not—could not—speak. She just stared over at him.

'When I was a young man,' he told her, 'I became addicted to sex. I was like a child in a sweet shop, stuffing myself all the time. I had to have release morning, noon and night. When I was around twenty I took an older woman to bed and was promptly told that whilst I was built well I had no idea how to please a woman. I was accused of having no more finesse than a rutting ram.'

Samantha went on staring at him. Why was he telling her this? What did it have to do with the here and now? He had obviously learned plenty of finesse since then. He was the complete fantasy lover. She didn't want him to talk, damn it. She wanted some action!

But it seemed he was determined on telling his story.

'Stung by her criticism, I made it my business to read everything I could on sex and sexual techniques. The *Kama Sutra* was particularly enlightening. I had never thought of such positions before. Have you read it?'

She shook her head.

'I will give you a copy. But even more educational were other, more obscure erotic journals I discovered, written mostly by the Chinese. Chinese husbands understand that satisfying their wives is as important as satisfying themselves. They have become experts in the art of delay. With practise and mind control they can make love to their wives every night for a week without allowing their bodies release. When they do finally allow themselves release, their own pleasure is said to be enhanced a thousandfold.'

He smiled into her stunned face.

'I do not claim to practise that extreme version. But a few hours' delay, I have found, is well worth the effort. It is also an effective technique where one's female partner is concerned—something I discovered when first using bondage on a woman. If I do not touch you till we arrive at the hotel suite in Sydney, by then you will want me to make love to you with a much greater intensity. You will scream in ecstasy when you finally come. Would you not like that, Samantha?'

Samantha just stared at him. Didn't he realise she was at screaming point right now?

'Well, yes, I suppose so. But, no—not really. I mean...it sounds all very well in theory, but I'm not as sophisticated as you are, Bandar. When I said I wanted you to teach me everything about sex, I never imagined this type of way-out thing. Not that it isn't exciting, mind. I'm really looking forward to being your love-slave for the weekend. And I will happily practise this art of delay at some later date. But please, Bandar, if you make me wait right now, I think I will go crazy.'

His low laugh carried both amusement and satisfaction. 'Just as well I anticipated this reaction. You are far too passionate and headstrong for me to totally control just yet. But that is part of your appeal. Very well,' he said, unsnapping his seat belt and standing up. 'But the lovemaking will be of my choosing. I have no intention of undressing. Or of letting you out of that chair. You promised to obey me for the weekend. Are you ready to follow through on that promise?'

'Yes...'

What was he going to do to her? She began to shake inside with nervous anticipation.

He removed the half-empty champagne glass from her numbed hand and then undressed her. Where she sat. First her boots, each one removed slowly as he knelt at her feet. Then came her top, eased out from under the seat belt and then lifted up over her head. And finally her skirt, wriggled down over her hips whilst she raised her bottom an inch or two.

At last she was totally nude, the leather chair feeling cool yet cruelly sensual against her heated skin. The seat belt was snug around her naked waist, keeping her captive in the chair—except of course she could undo it if she wanted to.

But she didn't.

'You're not cold, are you?' he murmured when she shivered.

'No,' she admitted, the word coming out on a choked whisper.

He moved the table between the chairs aside, then walked around the chair as he'd walked around her at the cottage, looking at her, making her cheeks burn and her flesh tingle. He flicked the lever which leant the chair right back, then walked around her again, stopping behind her to finger-comb her hair back over the chair, after which he walked round to the front, where he eased her knees further apart.

Her hands clenched the armrests more tightly when he looked at her down there. She knew she had to be horribly wet. Knew he could see how excited she was.

The feelings which rushed through her at this realisation excited her even more. He would surely touch her there soon. Maybe he would even use his mouth, as he had the previous day. Oh, but he was so good at that.

But he didn't touch her there. Or kiss her there. Instead, he extracted the rose from the vase and started touching her with it, trailing the petals lightly over her skin.

At first just her arms, with long, light, sensual strokes, running from the backs of her hands up to her shoulders.

Several times violent shudders ran all through her.

Her legs were the next objects of his attention, that tormenting rose travelling from her toes to the tops of her thighs, before skimming lightly over the melting flesh in between.

The air became thick around her. Her eyes grew wide. Her mouth fell open.

Right when she thought she might start begging, he moved on to her breasts, trailing the rose back and forth across them. Her spine stiffened against the leather chair, her breasts lifting and her belly tightening. How was she going to bear it?

Not quietly. She gasped every time the rose contacted an aching nipple, then moaned when it didn't. The pleasure of the petals became a two-edged sword.

Because it wasn't enough. She needed more. Quite desperately.

'Bandar…' His name sounded like a plea. Which it was.

He did not reply, just bent to press the whole rose there, right where she wanted him to, crushing the petals against her most sensitive spot.

She splintered apart instantly, her mouth gasping even wider, her knuckles whitening as her back arched and her bottom twisted and turned against the chair. She squeezed her eyes tightly shut as spasm after spasm gripped her flesh, her orgasm more intense and lasting longer than any she'd had so far.

She did not become aware of Bandar not being with her any longer till she finally opened her eyes and found he was gone.

For a few moments her befuddled brain succumbed to panic.

Gone *where*?

But as her breathing slowed down and her mind began to clear she noticed that there were a couple of doors in the wood-panelled walls. Presumably one led to a bathroom. Maybe he was in there.

She was struggling with her seat belt when he emerged from one of the doors, and a wave of embarrassment swept through her when she glanced down and saw the scattering of blood-red petals between her legs. The rest of the rose was nowhere in sight. He had to have taken it with him.

Her fingers fumbled even more at his approach. She could not believe she had just done that, or that Bandar could do what he had without being turned on himself.

Yet he didn't look in any way aroused as he walked towards her. He looked totally in control, of himself and of her.

'Here. Let me,' he said gently, and helped her with the belt. Helped her get dressed as well.

When she was fully clothed he took her into his arms and kissed her, then held her close, stroking her hair at the same time.

'Do not feel embarrassed,' he murmured. 'This is what you have come with me to learn. Embrace the part you have promised to play this weekend, Samantha, and you will discover a side to yourself which you have kept hidden. You have spent far too many years dressing and acting without femininity. It is time to throw off that façade and become the woman you secretly want to be.'

Samantha could not help but find the nonsense in his arguments, glancing up at him with some exasperation in her face.

'Being a love-slave is hardly being a real woman, Bandar. This is all fantasy stuff. You know, I don't think you live in the real world. You are too used to women doing your bidding.'

'And you are too used to doing the arguing,' he returned quite sharply. 'You agreed to obey me this weekend. Are you going back on that agreement?'

'Can I reserve the right to rebel if things get too kinky?'

'I do not do kinky,' he growled.

'You have to be kidding. What do you think that was just now?'

'You think that was kinky?'

'Too right it was.'

'In that case maybe I *do* do kinky,' he conceded.

She swallowed. 'Just not *too* kinky, all right?'

'You have my word.'

Samantha sighed, feeling comforted by his assurance. Although a playboy in his personal life, Bandar still came across as a man of honour. He evoked a lot of terrifying feelings in her, but none of them was fear itself. She believed him when he said he would never hurt her. And she'd believed him when he'd given his word just now. He might not be a saint, but he was a long way from being a devil.

'So what do love-slaves do, besides lie back and enjoy?' she asked with a devilish smile of her own.

'They do everything their lord and master tells them to do. Without question, without hesitation, and *without* argument.'

'Are we talking just sexual things, here, or everything else as well?'

'Absolutely everything. I do realise that will be difficult for you, but I think you will learn a lot from it.'

'And what will *you* learn?'

Her counter-question clearly startled him at first. But then he smiled. 'I will learn to listen to my first instincts in future.'

'Meaning?'

'I knew you were trouble from the first moment we met. I told myself to walk away, but fate conspired against me.'

'How come?'

'No more questions, Love-slave. The weekend has begun in earnest. Sit down and fasten your seat belt. We are about to land.'

CHAPTER TWELVE

BANDAR stood inside the spacious sitting room of Ali's presidential suite and watched her out on the balcony, looking around with an almost naïve delight on her face. Anyone would think she had never been in a hotel before. Or seen Sydney Harbour.

Admittedly, Ali's suite was splendid, even by the most exacting standards. And the view was second to none, enhanced at that moment by the setting sun, its golden rays slanting off the Opera House and highlighting Sydney's famous harbour bridge.

She ran inside and grabbed him by the arm. 'You have to come out here, Bandar, and look at the view. It's absolutely gorgeous!'

'I have seen it before,' he replied, resisting the pull of her hand. Resisting the pull on his heart as well.

'When?' she asked, tipping her head on one side as she glanced up at him.

'A few years back. I stayed here with Ali one weekend. We went to the races together. Which reminds me. We will be going to the races at Randwick tomorrow afternoon. I will take you shopping in the morning for a suitable outfit. And for some other things.'

'What other things?' she asked excitedly.

He adopted a stony face. 'Do not ask questions, Love-slave. Now, go and run us a bath whilst I order some food from Room Service.'

'Shall I unpack your clothes as well?' she asked, doing her best to act and look subservient, but Bandar could see the mischievous gleam in her lovely blue eyes.

'The butler has already done that,' he replied brusquely.

'Oh, yes. The bowing and scraping Antoine. No wonder you're spoilt, Bandar. Having this kind of service all the time. And living in such glamorous surroundings. Just look at this place. I've never stayed in anything as fancy as this.'

'It is acceptable.'

'Acceptable! My goodness, I've never seen furniture like it. Or lamps, or rugs. And what about those paintings on the wall? They're absolutely stunning.'

'They are not originals,' he informed her, glancing at the well-known Renoirs and Picassos.

'Who cares? They still look great.'

He sighed. 'I do not think the role of love-slave suits you, Samantha. Perhaps mistress would be better. Mistresses are allowed to have opinions. And argue with their lovers.'

'Can't I be both?'

Bandar rolled his eyes. 'How can you be both?'

'I could be your mistress out of the bedroom and your love-slave *in* the bedroom. That way you can dress me in designer clothes and shower me with diamonds in public, but still order me around in private.'

'You wish me to shower you with diamonds?' he asked rather coldly. So! It was beginning already—the changing. An hour or two of sharing his lifestyle and she was thinking about diamonds!

'Why not? You could give me a racehorse or two while you're at it. I don't come cheap, you know.'

His teeth clenched down hard in his jaw, his facial muscles stiffening with disapproval and disappointment. He had honestly thought she was different. He should have known better.

Her laugh startled him. 'Oh, Bandar, you should see the look on your face.'

He frowned. 'You were only jesting?'

'What do you think?' she said, still smiling. 'I like to buy my own things, Bandar. And earn my own money. With my brains. Not flat on my back. I told you. This weekend is just fantasy stuff. For me, anyway. You might do this kind of thing all the time, but it's way out of my league.'

His relief was still tinged with irritation. He did not like the way she was always judging him, and making him feel he had to defend himself. 'I do not do this kind of thing all the time,' he stated curtly. In fact he could not remember the last time he'd taken a woman away with him for the weekend.

She grinned at him. 'Yeah, right. You've got all the moves down pat, Bandar. That speaks for itself. I'm not complaining, mind. I love your hoity-toity lord-and-master routine. It's going to be fun—and you're right. Quite good for me. I already feel different. More confident, in a weird way. Is a love-slave allowed to feel confident?' she added, with the most bewitching smile.

His heart lurched in a most alien fashion. This was not good. Not good at all. She was supposed to be a distraction, not an addiction. Or an obsession.

'Go run that bath,' he ordered sharply. 'Then get in. I will be along shortly.'

'Yes, Master,' she said, her lips twitching. 'Whatever you say, Master.'

The room felt very empty once she was not in it.

Just as your life will be empty when she is not in it.

Bandar scowled. What life? He'd probably be dead soon.

She is better off without you, so don't start complicating things. Besides, you are nothing to her but her sexual tutor. Her fantasy master. She might like you making love to her, but she does not really *like* you, or respect you.

This last thought truly rankled. His male ego was not at all happy with such a thought. He was used to respect.

No, you're used to being bowed and scraped to all the time, like she said. That is not true respect. That is just your money talking.

Sometimes Bandar hated his money. In his recently made will, he'd left all his racehorses to Ali and the rest of his estate to cancer research. But what if he lived? Maybe he should give it all away. Then perhaps he should come back to Australia.

It had been a challenge to win Samantha Nelson's body. It would be a much greater challenge to win her heart. And her respect.

Meanwhile, he could do little to change the present situation.

She wanted him to teach her everything this weekend? That was another challenge. Was he up to it?

Bandar's hand lifted to rub the slight ache which had gathered behind his eyes. In truth, he was not so sure. Suddenly he was feeling very tired.

* * *

Samantha hummed happily as she poured some fragrant bubble bath into the simply huge corner spa.

She'd decided the second she'd stepped out of that incredible helicopter onto the roof of the equally incredible Regency Hotel to put aside any doubts about this weekend and treat it exactly as it was: the fantasy of a lifetime and a simply fabulous adventure.

Everything that had happened so far only confirmed that decision. The personal security man who'd escorted them to this hotel suite. The personal butler who'd been there to greet them. And the suite itself: superstar luxury and then some, including complimentary flowers and fruit and chocolates and champagne—and who knew what else?

If she started taking any of this seriously she'd end up in some funny farm somewhere.

If there was one last lingering fear it was that she might never find this kind of sexual happiness with another man. But Samantha appreciated that sexual happiness wasn't everything in life—though it was difficult to appreciate it right at this moment.

With the bath rapidly filling, Samantha set about stripping off her clothes and trying not to think that shortly she would be lying back, naked, in that water with an equally naked Bandar. She felt thankful for the coverage the bubbles would supply, which was crazy considering that episode on the helicopter.

What did it matter if he could see her body through the water?

Perhaps it had been too long since he'd touched her, she decided as she scooped her hair up with both hands and wrapped it into a knot on top of her head. There was no doubt that once Bandar started making love to her all sense of embarrassment swiftly fled her mind, replaced by a delicious feeling of abandonment.

The bath was finally full, the temperature of the water just right. As Samantha lowered herself down into the fragrant bubbles she wondered just how many other women had run Bandar's bath for him. And obeyed his every command.

A lot, she forced herself to accept. So don't start imagining that you're anything special in his eyes. You are here just for his amusement and entertainment.

'Excellent,' he said as he walked briskly in, taking off his jacket and draping it over one of the many rails in the ultra-spacious bathroom. 'Our evening meal will be delivered in two hours. That gives us time to bathe and relax together before it arrives.'

'Relax together?' she echoed. 'Er…what does that mean?'

'You are asking questions again.' He stripped with amazing speed before slipping down into the water and settling back in the corner opposite her. The spa bath was so huge not even their feet touched. He leant back into the corner, sighing rather wearily, Samantha thought, as he stretched his arms along the sides of the bath.

'You sound tired,' she said.

Her observation brought forth another sigh. 'A little,' he admitted. 'Perhaps I should not have ridden that horse of mine so hard this morning.'

'Why don't I give you a massage after our bath?' she suggested. 'That will make you really relax. You might drift off for a while.'

He laughed. 'Do you really think so? I rather doubt

it. But you tempt me. Do you know how to give a
proper massage?'

'I've had enough of them myself to be able to make
a good attempt. I used to have a remedial massage once
a week during my soccer-playing days.'

'You played *soccer*?'

'Soccer, cricket, and Australian rules football. I had
four older brothers and a father who were right into
sport. If I hadn't done what they did, I would have been
left home alone all the time. No way was my dad ever
going to take me to dancing lessons.'

'I see,' he said.

'That's the reason I went on the Pill.'

'Pardon? I do not understand.'

'All that sport and training stripped every ounce of
fat from my body. I was so skinny that I was late going into puberty. Even then I only had a period every
six months or so. By the time I went to university
things had improved somewhat, but I was shockingly
irregular. When I did get my period it was very heavy.
Too heavy sometimes. After a few embarrassing epi-
sodes I went on the Pill. And I've never come off. The
doctor said it was good for me. He said that with my
physical lifestyle I needed to put some extra oestro-
gen into my system, so that I don't get osteoporosis
when I'm older. A pleasing side effect was that I
finally got myself some decent boobs. Decent enough
for me, anyway.'

'Your breasts are lovely,' he complimented. 'Your
whole body is lovely.'

Why did she blush? He couldn't even see her body.

'That is not flattery, either,' he added. 'I cannot seriously believe that other men have not found you as attractive as I do.'

'There was this man once,' she confessed. 'A man I worked with here in Sydney.'

'And?'

'He said he loved me.'

'And?'

'He was married.'

His eyes darkened. 'Did you sleep with him?'

'No. I told you. Before you, I hadn't had sex in years.'

'Did you want to sleep with him?'

'For a moment or two. But I didn't.'

'Why?'

'I…I didn't believe he really loved me, and I didn't want to be used.'

'Did you love him?'

'I liked him. We'd worked together for some years and we'd become close. But. no, I did not love him.'

'But he was the reason you left Sydney and went to the country to work?' Bandar said, startling her with his intuitive conclusion.

'Well, yes. Yes, you're right. Paul *is* the reason I left Sydney.'

And the reason she wanted to go back?

Bandar stared at her, but she was off in another world, her eyes not registering him. She was thinking about this man, this married man she claimed not to love. He did not believe her.

'How old is he?' he asked, trying not to sound as though he cared.

'Who? Paul? I'm not sure. In his forties, I guess.'

An older man. Possibly very experienced. Did she want to learn all about sex so that she could please this Paul in bed? Had she run away from him because she had no confidence in herself and in her femininity?

'Is he handsome?'

She shrugged her shoulders. 'He's not unattractive.'

So! He *was* handsome!

Bandar had never been jealous of a man before. But he was jealous of this Paul. Blackly, insanely jealous.

'You are not to contact him when you come back to Sydney,' he declared. 'You are not to sleep with him.'

Her head shot up. She was clearly taken aback by his demands. 'I have no intention of doing so.'

'You are not lying to me?'

She blinked, then smiled. 'Would I lie to my lord and master?'

'You are not taking your role seriously,' he snapped. 'You will get out of this bath immediately and have towels ready for me. You are to dry every inch of me. Very thoroughly. Do I make myself clear?'

She nodded.

'You will wear no robe. You will stay naked, and wet. And you will not speak. Is that also clear?'

She opened her mouth, then closed it again before standing up a little shakily and climbing out of the bath.

The dark triumph which washed through Bandar went some way to soothing his jealousy. And his ego.

This Paul might have her respect. But *he* had her obedience.

CHAPTER THIRTEEN

'COME,' he said, and held out his hand to her.

Samantha took it, and Bandar helped her from the taxi onto her feet.

They had come to the races at Randwick racecourse, as he'd said they would. But he had not taken her clothes-shopping this morning; they hadn't woken early enough.

Samantha liked the feel of Bandar's hand around hers. It was such a simple intimacy compared to those they had shared last night, yet it sent tingles running up and down her arm.

'You are very quiet today,' he said as he drew her towards the members' entry gate. 'Is there something wrong?'

Wrong?

That depended on his definition of the word. Was it wrong the way he made her feel, the things he made her do? Was it wrong that she had surrendered herself to him to the extent that she would do even more if he asked her? Was it wrong that the strong-minded, feisty girl she'd always been seemed to have disappeared?

Images flashed into her head: massaging Bandar all

over, kissing him all over, going down on him. She'd fed him afterwards, her own satisfaction deliberately delayed. Then finally he'd made love to her, spoon-fashion, making her cry out loud. Then afterwards he'd used the ties of the complementary bathrobes to secure her hands behind *his* back, keeping her body bound to his whilst he slept.

But she hadn't slept. She hadn't been able to. She'd waited breathlessly for him to wake, her body wanting him instantly when he did. He'd brought her release with his hands this time, making her beg him to untie her. Which he had, eventually. But only to bind her in other ways. Her favourite had been with her wrists wrapped together, then stretched high over her head and attached to the bedhead.

Bandar had been so right. She'd loved the delicious feeling of helplessness, of having no control.

Light had begun to break over the city when she'd finally fallen asleep, not waking till nearly noon.

And now here they were, at the races, with Samantha already wishing that they hadn't come. Usually she loved the races, but the trouble was she loved being alone with Bandar more—much more.

'I'm a little tired,' she told him. A lie. She had never felt more alive.

His laugh was low. 'I can imagine. But I thought we needed a break. At least, I did. Now, let us go inside and see if we can pick a winner.'

He paid their entry, then took her hand again, leading her through the crowds of people and over to the mounting yard, where the runners for the third race were already being saddled up. The horses' coats gleamed in the winter sunshine, testimony to the good work of their grooms. Samantha tried to show an interest in picking out a potential winner, but she could not think of anything but the man by her side.

Did she love him?

Probably.

There had been far too many moments last night when her emotions had been engaged as well as her body. When she'd been massaging him, for instance. She'd felt almost maternal towards him, very caring and protective, which was crazy: he did not need protecting. *She* was the one who needed protection—from him.

Bandar's hand tightening around hers brought her sharply back to the present.

'That man over there is staring at you,' he ground out. 'Do you know him?'

She glanced over and almost died.

'My goodness, it's Paul!' she blurted out.

Bandar's fingers tightened even further around hers. 'The man who loves you?'

'He doesn't,' she denied. 'Not really.'

'He is coming over.'

She had no option but to say hello, then introduce Paul to Bandar. But how?'

'This is…er…Sheikh Bandar,' she told Paul, who was still staring at her in a most embarrassing fashion. 'He's a friend of Prince Ali—Prince Ali of Dubar. My boss,' she added unnecessarily. Because Paul knew where she'd gone to work, Samantha having had to let him know a forwarding address for tax reasons. He'd even written to her there once, warning her of Prince Ali's reputation with women.

'I have heard of the Sheikh,' Paul said stiffly, and held out his hand towards Bandar, his eyes finally leaving Samantha.

Bandar did not let Samantha's hand go, and Paul's hand dropped back to his side.

'And I have heard of you,' Bandar returned, in that haughty manner he could so easily adopt.

'You've changed your hair,' Paul said to Samantha, ignoring Bandar, who was looking more furious with each passing second. 'Being blonde suits you. It's a lot softer.'

'I like it,' she said.

Seeing the two men together brought home to Samantha why she was so besotted with Bandar. Paul was an attractive man. But Bandar was a man amongst men. A superb male animal in every way. Beautiful and fit and proud, and if she wasn't mistaken he was something else at that moment which made her heart sing.

He was jealous!

'Actually, I've never seen you looking so good,' Paul went on, his eyes raking over Samantha again from top to toe.

Still, his staring pleased her. Because it wasn't pleasing Bandar.

'Are you staying in Sydney for the weekend?' Paul continued. 'Maybe we could meet up for a drink somewhere.'

'Samantha is with me,' Bandar snapped.

Paul looked flustered. 'Hey, I didn't mean anything by it. We're just old friends, aren't we, Samantha? No harm in having a drink together.'

'I beg to differ,' Bandar growled. 'Come, Samantha.'

Samantha threw Paul a slightly apologetic smile over

her shoulder as Bandar practically dragged her away in the direction of the grandstand. One part of her found his proprietorial attitude flattering. But there was still enough of the old Samantha left to resent such high-handed behaviour.

'Hey, cut out the caveman stuff!' she said, wrenching her hand away from his bruising fingers. 'You're hurting me. I seem to recall you said you would never hurt me.'

He swung round and glared at her. 'When a woman is with me, she does not try to organise assignations with other men. You can at least wait until I go back to London. Then you can come back to Sydney and sleep with that fool all you like.'

'What's got into you? Have you lost your brains? I told you. I do *not* love Paul and he doesn't love me.'

'He wants you. I can see it in his eyes.'

'Half the women here today want *you*, Bandar. Do you see me carrying on like some jealous idiot? I am with you because I choose to be with you. If I'd wanted to be with Paul, I could have chosen him. But I didn't.'

That shut him up.

His hands lifted to rake through his hair, his eyes showing genuine regret. And something else which evoked a worried response from her.

The penny dropped. It was pain she'd glimpsed—physical pain.

'Do you have one of your headaches coming on?'

Her question clearly surprised him. 'How did you know?'

'I saw it in your eyes. Do you have some of your tablets with you.'

'No,' he admitted with a grimace.

'Then we'll have to go back to the hotel.'

'*I* will have to go back. You can stay if you want to.'

'I don't want to stay. Come on,' she said, and this time it was Samantha who took *his* hand, Samantha who did the ordering and he the obeying.

Possibly it was the pain which made him so compliant. He did not say a word during the taxi ride, but she knew he was suffering. Once back in the hotel suite, she undressed him down to his underpants, then sat him on the side of the bed whilst she went to get a glass of water. He was fumbling with his bottle of tablets when she returned.

'How many?' she asked as she took the bottle from him.

'Two,' he replied with a shaky sigh.

She took two out, handing them to him along with the glass of water, before putting the bottle back on the bedside chest.

He winced as he swallowed them, a muffled moan escaping his lips as he lay back on the bed and closed his eyes. She hurried over and drew the heavy curtains, then closed the doors so that the room was almost dark. Kicking off her boots, she lay down next to him and stroked his head softly till finally, after an interminable period of time, he drifted off to sleep.

Only then did she take the bottle of tablets out into the light of the sitting room and really look at them.

'Good God,' she gasped. 'Morphine!'

What idiot doctor had prescribed *morphine* for migraines?

Unless it wasn't migraines Bandar was suffering from.

Samantha's heart stopped. No, it wasn't possible. He couldn't have anything more serious wrong with him. He was way too healthy-looking, too strong and too virile.

Look at the way he had ridden Smoking Gun around that track. Would a sick man do that? Okay, so it had made him tired. She'd be tired, too.

And yet what about that first night over dinner? Had it just been jet lag he'd been suffering from? Or had he been suddenly struck down by one of these simply appalling headaches?

He'd had another one on Wednesday night, too. Now another, only a few days later.

She knew migraines could be very bad, but usually not this frequent. And why have morphine to treat them?

She tiptoed back into the bedroom, placing the bottle of tablets by the bed before lying back down next to Bandar. He was breathing deeply now, his face free from pain. He did not stir when she kissed him lightly on the forehead, did not see the tears which filled her eyes and trickled down her cheeks.

'You have to be all right,' she whispered. 'You *have* to be.'

Bandar woke to find Samantha sound asleep by his side, fully clothed. His head still felt thick, but that was probably the after-effect of the tablets. He picked up her hand, which was lying across his chest, lifted it to his mouth and kissed it.

She stirred immediately, her eyelids fluttering open.

'You're awake,' she said, and he smiled over at her.

'So are you.'

'How do you feel?' she asked, her eyes searching his face.

'Much better, thanks to you,' he said, sucking one of her fingertips into his mouth, then turning her hand over and licking the centre of the palm. She gasped and tried to pull her hand away, but he grabbed her wrist with his other hand and she stopped struggling.

'You make almost as good a nurse as a love-slave,' he murmured, then licked her palm again.

Keep it light, Bandar, he told himself, and sexy. This is all she wants from you for now.

But he had hopes for the future. If he *had* a future.

'Bandar…'

'What?'

'You don't have a brain tumour, do you?'

He could not help it. Surprise stopped him in mid-lick, his head jerking up to meet her far too intelligent eyes.

'Do not lie to me,' she said almost sternly.

What did she think he was? A total fool? If he told her the truth then this was over, right now. He *had* to lie. Because he could not leave her just yet. He loved her too much.

At the same time, Bandar accepted that it was insane to delay his operation much longer. For one thing, he could not bear any more of these headaches. They were crippling; only his male pride had stopped him from screaming with pain this afternoon. He would contact Ali by e-mail later this evening and explain the situation. He'd brought his laptop with him. He'd e-mail his surgeon's office as well. And then he would book a seat on a flight to London for tomorrow night.

The next twenty-four hours, however, were going to be his. With the woman he loved.

'Where on earth did you get that idea?' he said.

'The tablets—they're morphine. You don't take

morphine for migraines. You do, however, take them for cancer.'

'Cancer!' He'd never actually thought of his brain tumour in that way. But it *was* cancer, of course.

The word was sobering. It was also very effective at making people look at you differently. If he confessed he had cancer she would be too afraid to have him make love to her.

'Do I look like I have cancer?'

'No…'

'I suffer from headaches,' he said. 'Flying always brings them on. I have found morphine to be the most effective medication. Those tablets are not strong ones, I assure you. I am not an addict. The only thing I am addicted to is you, my darling. Now, where was I?' he murmured, and returned to licking her hand.

She stopped questioning him, her eyes gradually glazing over.

He undressed her slowly, tenderly, taking his time to kiss every part of her body, to imprint the memory of her sighs on his mind. She would be the last thing he would think of before he went into that operating theatre. If he died, he would go with a smile on his face and love in his heart.

CHAPTER FOURTEEN

SAMANTHA didn't want to go back. As the time for their departure approached, her joy began to dim and her mood darkened.

So, it seemed, did Bandar's.

At four, neither of them made any move to get up and get dressed. Yet the helicopter was booked to leave at five, so that they could get home before dark.

Not that the stud felt like home any more to Samantha. *This* was where she was at home: in bed with Bandar.

'Don't go,' she said when he finally went to rise, her hands reaching out to clasp his arm.

When he turned, his face was grim. 'We cannot stay here for ever, Samantha. As much as I would like to.'

'Would you really?'

He bent to kiss her lightly on the lips. 'Of course I would. But life goes on. I have things I must do.'

'But you're not really needed back at the stud,' she argued. 'And neither am I. I could quit. We could go away together somewhere. Or we could stay here. For a while at least.'

His smile was strangely sad. 'You must not tempt me. Like I said, I have things I must do. And they aren't back at Ali's stud. There has been an emergency at home. I have to return to London tonight.'

Her stomach felt as if it had suddenly fallen into an abyss. 'You're going back to London?'

'I have to.'

'But...but why?'

'It is a private matter.'

'Take me with you,' she begged, panic spreading through her whole body.

'I am sorry, but I cannot.'

Her panic gave way to desolation... Desolation and desperation.

'But I can't live without you,' she sobbed. 'Don't you know that? I...I need you. You must take me with you. I won't be a bother, I promise. You can have those other women if you want, as long as you have me as well. Oh!' she cried, her whole mind shattering apart at the humiliating reality of what she'd just said.

She buried her face in her hands and wept.

His arms around her were gentle. 'I am not going back to those other women,' he said softly as he cradled her against his chest. 'I will come back to you as soon as I can.'

His amazing words brought some hope to her heart. Her eyes lifted, still glistening with tears. 'You mean that? You'll come back?'

He smiled and kissed her on the forehead. 'Would I abandon my perfect little love-slave?'

'When? When will you come back?'

'As soon as I can.'

'But when is that?'

'I'm not sure how long it will take to attend to this emergency. Be assured, I will not delay my return. If and when everything is fixed.'

'You don't sound sure that this problem can be fixed. Is it money? Have you run into trouble with some investments? Look, I don't care if you're poor. Please don't ever think that. I don't give a hoot about your money. I have money. I can pay for you to come back. I can support you.'

He stroked her hair and smiled so sweetly at her. 'This is not a matter of money. Now, do not upset yourself further. Go back in the helicopter and I will be in contact shortly. I will take your phone number with me.'

'You promise?'

'I promise.'

'When?'

'Give me a few days.'

Bandar could see she was not happy with that. But he could not risk talking to her when his emotions would be fragile. He had to stay strong for his operation. Had to change his will as well. In a few days she would be contacted. Either by him or his lawyer. For he aimed to leave her everything he owned, this woman who loved him for himself and not his money.

'I love you, Bandar,' she choked out, and it almost broke him.

'I'm sure you think you do,' he returned, hating the hurt look on her face but knowing he was doing the right thing.

'You don't believe in love, do you?' she threw at him. 'If and when you come back, it'll just be for the sex.'

He had to harden his heart. Had to find the steel to leave her.

'Would you rather I did not return?'

Suddenly she was back, the angry woman he'd first met, her spirit undaunted, her fire unextinguished.

'Please yourself,' she snapped. 'You always do.'

He smiled. 'I am glad to see that you have not changed. You still have more character than any woman I have ever known. You will see me again, Samantha, *insh'allah.*'

Samantha cried the whole way back in the helicopter. Character? She didn't have any character. She was a total mess!

She was still crying as she stumbled down the steps of the helicopter and threw herself into the arms of the red-haired woman standing at the bottom of the ladder.

'What's this all about?' Cleo asked, obviously perplexed. 'What's happened? Dear heavens, there's not anything seriously wrong with you, is there?'

'I...I can't tell you here.'

'Okay. I'll get your case and we'll go to the house. But where's Bandar?'

'On his way to London, the bastard,' Samantha blurted out.

Cleo's eyebrows shot up, but she didn't say anything, wise woman that she was. She waited till they were alone in the kitchen of the main house, with a cup of soothing coffee sitting in front of Samantha. The helicopter had long gone, and everything was very quiet.

'You've been sleeping with him, haven't you?' Cleo said, straight out.

Samantha was way past denying it, so she just nodded.

'When did all this start?'

'Last Wednesday night,' Samantha said with a weary sigh. Now that she'd stopped crying she just felt terribly tired. Though it was more an emotional than a physical tiredness.

'Mmm. The night I gave him that soup to bring to you. He's a fast mover; I'll give him that. And of course you haven't been sick, have you? That was all an invention.'

'I'm sorry, Cleo.'

'Don't be. I'd probably have done the same thing in your boots. Hard to knock back a man like that. I knew he liked you. I told you. By the way, why's he gone back to London?'

'He said there was some sort of emergency. He wouldn't tell me what. It sounded a bit suspect to me. He said he'd e-mailed Ali and explained the situation.'

'I'll give Ali a call later. He'll tell me what's up. So what's our playboy like in bed? Devastatingly good, by the look of you.'

'I can't begin to describe it.' If she did, Cleo would probably faint dead away.

'I suppose you've fallen in love with him?'

'Unfortunately.'

'Oh, I don't know about that. Sometimes it's better to have loved and lost than never to have loved at all.'

'That's crap, Cleo, and you know it.'

'But at least you've experienced the very best. Not a lot of women have, you know.'

'He was a fantasy come true. Maybe I should have kept remembering the fantasy part, then I might have kept my head.'

'He's one sexy man, all right.'

'He said he'd come back.'

'Really? You forgot to mention that bit.'

Samantha pulled a face. 'I don't believe him. He's gone and he's never coming back. He just said that to shut me up.'

'Really? Bandar doesn't strike me as a liar. I think I'll go and give Ali that call—see what I can find out about this so-called emergency back in London. Wait here.'

'I'm not going anywhere,' Samantha said wretchedly.

Cleo was gone quite a while, leaving Samantha too much time by herself to think, and to relive that last incredible night with Bandar. He'd been so different with her—not at all dominating or demanding, but a tender lover. She'd adored him that way perhaps even more than she had when he'd been doing his lord and master act. They'd talked, too: not about sex, but horses, mostly, and their mutual passion for them.

They hadn't spent every second in bed, either. They'd relaxed over a lovely meal at the dining table, then sat together out on the balcony with a glass of cognac afterwards, soaking up the glorious view and each other's company. She'd felt so happy. So…loved?

'I can't believe it,' Cleo said as she hurried back into the kitchen, snapping Samantha out of her dreaming. 'He looked so well.'

Samantha's stomach contracted fiercely.

'Oh, no!' she exclaimed as she jumped to her feet. 'He *has* got a brain tumour, hasn't he?'

She saw the horrific truth in Cleo's eyes. 'How on earth did you know?'

Samantha dashed for the nearest toilet, where she retched into the bowl. Retched and retched.

By the time she emerged she felt totally drained, but she'd come to a decision.

'Tell me what Ali said,' she demanded of Cleo. 'Tell me everything.'

Everything was not much. Men were not the world's greatest communicators. Bandar had a malignant brain tumour—operable, but highly risky. He'd delayed his operation to come out to Australia because Ali had asked him to. He'd felt obligated because Ali had once saved his life. It was an Arab thing. Not that Ali had agreed with him.

'Apparently, Ali told him a couple of nights back to get his butt back to London, *pronto*,' Cleo continued. 'Before things got worse. Because everyone knows things always get worse with cancer.'

'A couple of nights ago?' Samantha queried. 'Not yesterday?'

'No. Ali said Saturday.'

Samantha could have cried with both joy and despair. Bandar had stayed with her another night. He hadn't wanted to leave her. He loved her. He must! Why else would he not have told her the truth? He was protecting her. Or was it that he just didn't believe she truly loved him?

What did it matter *what* he believed? She had to go to him. Be with him. Show him how much she cared.

But maybe it was already too late.

'When is this operation due, do you know?'

'As soon as it can be scheduled. That's all Ali knows. What are you going to do?'

'I'm flying to England. I'll go get my passport, then drive to Sydney tonight and catch the first plane available. Can you get some information from Ali for me? I need to know Bandar's address in London, and the hospital where he's being treated. Don't let him tell Bandar. I'll ring you from the airport.' She was already up and off, adrenaline revving up her energy level.

Dear God, please don't let Bandar die, she prayed as she ran for the door. Allah, save him!

'Are you sure you want to do this, Samantha?' Cleo called out as she ran after her.

'Absolutely!'

CHAPTER FIFTEEN

SHE was too late.

She could not get a seat on a plane bound for London that night, or the next morning. The first available flight was the following afternoon, and even then she had to pay a business class fare.

By the time the plane touched down at Heathrow Airport, Bandar was already being prepared for surgery. Not that Samantha knew that at that precise moment. She didn't find out till she reached the hospital, the name of which Ali had supplied to Cleo.

The Sheikh *was* a patient, she was told by the woman on the reception desk. But he was currently in surgery.

Samantha would have asked more questions if she hadn't promptly fainted.

Consciousness returned and she found someone dressed mainly in white hovering over her. Not a nurse or a doctor, but a dark-eyed, olive-skinned man with a solicitous look on his handsome face and wearing a *kaffiah*, the traditional Arab headdress.

Her employer: Prince Ali of Dubar.

'Ali!' she gasped, and sat up abruptly from where she'd been lying on a lounge in someone's office.

He pressed her firmly but gently back down into a prone position. 'Not a good idea to get up too quickly after fainting,' he said. 'One of the nurses is bringing you some tea and biscuits.'

'But…but what are you doing here?' she asked. 'You're supposed to be in Dubar, attending your brother's coronation.'

'The official coronation day is not till tomorrow. By then I will be back in Dubar and no one will be any the wiser. I decided that today my place was with my friend. Unfortunately I was too late to see Bandar before his operation. I gather the same applies to you.'

The reality of why Samantha had fainted rushed back to her, turning her stomach over and making her chest feel tight.

'Oh, Ali, what if he dies?' she cried.

'Then he dies,' Ali returned, far too pragmatically for Samantha. 'What is written is written.'

'I can't stand it when people say things like that. There is no such thing as fate, or destiny. What is written is what you make happen yourself.' She sat up abruptly, not able to lie down any longer.

'He did not give himself the cancer,' Ali pointed out.

'How do you know? Cleo said Bandar is a lonely man. Loneliness can sometimes weaken the immune system. I've read about it.'

'Why would you read about such a subject? Because *you* are lonely?'

'Yes. Yes, I'm lonely,' she said, levering herself up onto her feet. 'I've always been lonely. Or I was till I met Bandar. I love him, Ali, more than words can say. And I think he loves me.'

'I am sure he does. Do you know he has left you everything in his will?'

Shock and grief made her angry. 'Good grief, I don't want his damned money! I just want him alive and well.'

'He knows that.'

'How long does this operation go on for?' she asked despairingly as she began to pace around the room.

'Not much longer, I am told. I asked that the surgeon visit us here as soon as it is over. Ahh, here is the tea…'

A nurse bustled in with a tray. Ali waved her off when she started fussing, saying he would attend to the pouring.

Which he did.

A watery smile broke through Samantha's misery as she accepted the mug of tea he fixed for her. He was just like Bandar. So sure of himself. So much in command of things.

But was she right? Did Bandar's surface confidence hide an inner loneliness?

'Tell me about Bandar, Ali. I need to know everything.'

Ali's laugh was rueful. 'You sound just like my wife, Charmaine. She has to know everything.'

'Tell me.'

'I can only tell you what I know. There will be some things only Bandar knows. Men always have their little secrets, some best kept from the women in their lives.'

'If you mean the three lady-friends he has been entertaining of late, then I know all about them. They're irrelevant.'

Ali's eyebrows lifted. 'I see you *do* understand Bandar. But be assured that those ladies meant nothing to him. No woman has meant anything to Bandar. Till you came along. Not even his own mother.'

'He did not love his mother?' What kind of child did not love their mother?

'She did not love him. He was a ticket to the good life, that is all. She met Bandar's father when he was most susceptible to her kind of beauty and bedroom skills. His first wife—a woman from his own culture—had not long died whilst pregnant with their first child. He'd taken it hard. It had been a true love-match. He went crazy with grief, using his money to try to forget. He went to London to live, and started mixing with a very fast crowd. Bandar's mother was a good-time girl, though the media kindly called her a socialite. She was little better than a whore, selling herself to whatever man could afford to pay for her very expensive habits.'

'She took drugs?'

'She was not an addict. But she used designer drugs to enhance her promiscuous lifestyle, and to seduce men like Bandar's father, who was not used to such women. Naturally he married her when she announced she was pregnant. By then he was obsessed with the woman. She continued to hold sway over him after Bandar was born. The boy was left to the care of others whilst they swanned off to the world's pleasure spots, spending money at casinos and on racehorses, sinking further and further into depravity. If Bandar's father had not had a continuous stream of money from the oil wells he'd inherited from his Bedouin father, he would have been bankrupt many times over. Bandar's parents were never there for him. They were killed in a fire on a yacht on Bandar's sixteenth birthday. He was at school in London. They were in the Caribbean.'

'What a terrible story. Poor Bandar.'

'Yes. Poor Bandar.'

'How long have you known him? I heard you were friends as children.'

'I first met Bandar when we were sent to the same school in Dubar. I was fourteen. He was a couple of years younger than me. A shy child, if you can believe that.'

Yes. She could. He'd not been wanted any more than she had been. Samantha knew only too well how that affected a child. But he probably hadn't been shy so much as introverted, relying on himself for company, not trusting others.

'The other boys at school knew about his mother. They taunted him about her. Called her a whore. He took it for a while, then one day he fought back. Unfortunately, he chose the wrong group of boys to fight. They were much bigger, and meaner. One was carrying a knife. Bandar had already been stabbed before when I intervened. Fortunately, his wound was not life threatening. After that, his father shipped him off to a Christian school in England. You can imagine what that move was like for Bandar. For a long time he was like a fish out of water. Spurned and isolated by the English boys. Eventually, however, he was assimilated into their world, though he credits his money for finally gaining him acceptance.'

'He's a cynic about his money,' Samantha said.

'Yes,' Ali agreed. 'But he has just cause. You do not know what it is like to be an extremely wealthy man, Samantha.'

'Bandar told me women target him all the time.'

'Some will lie and cheat to unbelievable levels. When Bandar was around nineteen he was seduced by a very beautiful and very clever woman. When she claimed she was pregnant, Bandar was beside himself. She did not want marriage, just money. Lots of it. Bandar, however, did not like to think of any child of his being raised without a father to protect it. Luckily, he spoke to me about the situation, and I had the woman investigated. It turned out she was already married. It was clearly all a scam to get money. I advised Bandar to get a court order demanding she have a DNA test after the baby was born, and suddenly there was no baby. Though there had been one. Whose it was, we will never know.'

'Bandar must have been devastated.'

'He learned a very valuable lesson. From then on he was very careful.'

Samantha could understand Bandar's cynicism, and his wariness, but in the end you had to have some faith in people or life wasn't worth living.

'If Bandar was sent to England to school and to live, Ali,' she asked, trying to piece things together, 'then how did you keep up your friendship?'

'Through horses. We didn't see each other for some years, but met up again when I was sent to my father's stables in England for a short time.'

'I see.'

It was good to finally understand the man she loved. But what good was understanding him if he died? Emotion welled up in her chest, tears filling her eyes. She put down her mug of tea and surreptitiously wiped them away, not wanting to cry in front of Ali.

'It is all right to cry,' he said gently. 'Charmaine cries all the time.'

'Oh, Ali…' She sank into his outstretched arms and wept and wept.

Her tears had subsided to just the occasional sob when the door opened and Bandar's surgeon entered. He was an extremely tall man, with a pleasant face and receding brown hair. He looked tired, but pleased.

'Everything went very well,' he announced straight away, and Samantha burst into tears again.

'His fiancée,' she heard Ali say, by way of explanation.

'But he said he had no one!'

'He kept his condition a secret from Samantha so that she would not worry.'

'Aah. I did wonder. Such an impressive man. My secretary will be devastated. She was charmed by the Sheikh when he came to me for his consultation. But back to the matter at hand: I was able to get all the cancer. It will not come back. His brain is fine, and no nerves were damaged. There will not be any after-effects. I did a brilliant job, if I say so myself.'

'I thank you,' Ali said sincerely. 'And so will Samantha. When she can.'

Overhearing this conversation forced Samantha to pull herself together.

'I can't thank you enough,' she said, grabbing the surgeon's hands and shaking them vigorously. 'You are more than brilliant.'

The man's smile showed some smugness. But he had a right to be smug, in Samantha's opinion. How brave they were, brain surgeons. Brave *and* brilliant.

'Your fiancé is in Recovery, young lady,' he said,

patting her hands. 'He'll be groggy for quite a while. Take it easy with him today. Don't tire him with too much chatter. Or too many kisses,' he added with a cheeky wink. 'We don't want him to expire from too much excitement too soon, do we? Now, I must go. I need to go home and sleep. I am exhausted.'

'Do you wish to see Bandar by yourself first?' Ali asked when the surgeon had gone.

Samantha grimaced at the thought of what Bandar would say when he saw her. 'I don't know, Ali. I was feeling so happy, but now I feel sick with nerves. Bandar won't think I've come after him for his money, will he?'

Ali shook his head at her, his expression exasperated. 'Women!' he said, and took her arm in much the same way Bandar always did, brooking no nonsense and no protest. 'They can be so blind. The man is besotted with you.'

'Besotted?' she echoed as Ali steered her from the room and along the hospital corridor.

'He left you all his prized racehorses, including the favourite to win the Derby. *That* is besotted!'

CHAPTER SIXTEEN

BANDAR came back to consciousness slowly, dazedly. He could hear things going on around him but could not seem to open his eyes. He mumbled something and a female voice asked him his name. He swore, and she laughed. He eventually pried his eyelids open to see a nurse bending over him, smiling.

'I see you've returned to the land of the living,' she said.

Bandar's foggy brain suddenly cleared. He had not died on the operating table. He was alive!

But for how long?

'How did the operation go?' he rasped, his throat like sandpaper.

'Very well indeed. Mr Pring got it all.'

Tears welled up in his eyes. Bandar turned his face away so that the nurse would not see.

'Just rest,' she said, and pressed a gentle hand to his shoulder.

He drifted off again. For how long he did not know. When he opened his eyes he was in a different room. And it wasn't a nurse standing by his bed but Ali, dressed in traditional Arab robes.

'Ali?' he said, and went to lift his head. But it seemed too heavy. He groaned with the effort, then gave up.

'You should lie still,' Ali advised. 'Here. The nurse left you some ice to suck. She said you might want it.' And he popped a couple of small pieces into Bandar's mouth.

'Do not complain about my being here,' Ali went on, just as Bandar was about to. 'I will not be staying long, now that I know you are all right. That infernal coronation starts tomorrow, or I would not leave at all.'

'You cannot let your brother down,' Bandar whispered.

'The royal jet is waiting for me at Heathrow. I will be back in time.'

'Thank you for coming,' Bandar said, his friend's kindness bringing a lump to his throat.

'My pleasure. But there is someone else here far more suited than I to holding your hand and feeding you ice.'

Bandar sighed. 'You have not hired me a private nurse, have you?' It was the sort of thing Ali would do.

'No. I was speaking of your fiancée.'

'My *fiancée*?'

'Fiancée gets Samantha more rights than calling her your Australian girlfriend.'

'Samantha is here?'

'She was here when I arrived; she'd fainted dead away on the floor in the hospital foyer.'

This time Bandar's bandaged head shot up from the bed. 'She is all right?'

'Apparently she fainted when she found out you were already in Theatre. Now she is worried sick that your cynicism will make you think things that are not true. She keeps talking about your obsession with secret agendas.'

'Where is she?'

'Outside, pacing up and down the corridor. Shall I go and send her in?'

Bandar could not believe it. She was here. She had come after him.

'How did she find out about my operation?'

'Do not ask foolish questions like that. She is a woman. All you need to know is that she loves you, Bandar. Never doubt that.'

'It is hard not to doubt when you have spent a life-time doubting. But I decided if I came through this operation I would put doubt aside where Samantha is concerned. I am going to marry her, Ali. If she will have me.'

'But you have only known each other a week,' Ali said, frowning.

'Some weeks are longer than others. Besides, when you have been to the brink of death, you realise there is no time to waste. I have made up my mind. Send her in. Then get yourself to Dubar.'

Ali nodded. 'You always were a stubborn boy. And often unwise in your choice of lady-friends. But you have picked well this time. You must come visit us in Australia when you feel up to the trip.'

'I will.'

'I presume I will have to hire myself another vet?' Ali said drily.

'I hope so.'

'You will owe me another favour.'

'When you get home you will see I have repaid you well already. There are five excellent broodmares in your stables which have not cost you a single cent.'

'Ahh, yes, I heard about them from Cleo. But I presumed *I* was up for the two million, since I was the one who told you to be generous to the Widow Higgins.'

'They are gifts, my friend.'

'In that case, I am in your debt. Till next time, Bandar…' A quick bow, a sweeping wave of his hand, and he was gone.

With Ali's departure, Bandar's heartbeat quickened, his eyes fixed on the door through which Samantha would come.

And suddenly there she was, looking terribly nervous as she came into the room and walked slowly towards his bed. She was wearing a skirt, a long flowery thing which showed off her slender figure. The top was pink, and rather low cut, definitely enhancing her natural beauty. Her face showed traces of recent weeping: her eyes were puffy and still glistening. Her hair was down, though a little messy—as it had looked that last morning, after they'd spent many hours in bed together.

'Please don't be angry at me for coming,' she choked out before he could say a word.

Bandar's heart flipped over.

Angry? He could never be angry with her. She was his life now. His future. His reason for living.

Nothing else mattered.

He reached out his hand and she came closer.

'Sit,' he said, and patted the side of his bed.

She sat.

He reached up and laid his palm against her cheek. She tilted her head into it, her eyes closing on a sigh.

'You will marry me, won't you?' he said softly.

Her head jerked up, her eyes flying open.

'No arguments now, little Love-slave. You must do as your lord and master commands.'

Samantha took his hand in hers, then shook her head at him. 'Australian girls never promise to obey their husbands, Bandar. Marriage is a partnership, made with love and respect for each other.'

Bandar smiled. She was not going to fall in with his wishes easily. But then, would he want her to?

'I don't like it when you smile like that,' she said stiffly.

'Smile like what?'

'Like you're keeping secrets from me. There are to be no more secrets between us. I will never marry a man who keeps secrets.'

'Very well. I love you, Samantha Nelson. I love everything about you, but mostly your contrariness and your courage and your character. But if you want the total truth, I did not always love you. I set out to seduce you because you were the ultimate challenge to my male ego. Plus the perfect distraction for my state of mind. Your secret agenda gave me the opportunity to have my wicked way with you without complications or consequences. I did not mean to fall in love with you. But I did.'

'I didn't mean to fall in love with you, either. You were to be just a fantasy lover. But sometimes, what is written is written.'

Bandar frowned at her. 'You have been talking to Ali.'

Her smile was slightly sheepish. 'He told me quite a lot about you while we were waiting for your operation to be over.'

He scowled. 'I will kill him.'

Samantha laughed. 'No, you won't. You owe him your life. You cannot kill him. Besides, you love him.'

'I love *you*,' he said passionately, pulling her hand over to his mouth to kiss it.

Tears rushed back into Samantha's eyes. Tears not just of happiness but wonder. He loved her. And he wanted to marry her. Which meant he trusted her.

Samantha knew it had to be incredibly hard for Bandar to trust a woman. He must truly love her.

But no more than she loved him.

She put her head down onto his chest and sighed. 'You must never leave me again,' she whispered. 'Not for a single minute.'

'Nor you me,' he returned, his hand stroking her hair. 'We will have another bed put in here till I am allowed home. And we will be married as soon as it can be arranged. Do I have to ask your father for your hand in marriage? Is that not your custom in Australia?'

The thought rather amused Samantha. She lifted her head and smiled at him. 'Yes, indeed. That is the custom in Australia.'

'Then it will be done.'

And so it was done.

Samantha would never forget the look on her father's face when Bandar asked him for her hand in marriage. The looks on her brothers' faces at their wedding were just as priceless. Ali refused to let them have some small civil service in the city. They were married at the Royal Dubar stud—the ceremony taking place in the magnificent pavilion by the pool, the reception held in a marquee which only a billionaire sheikh could afford.

Samantha listed that day as one of the happiest days of her life. Though none could really compare with the day Bandar asked her to marry him in that London hospital room. Or the day, less than two months after their wedding, that she told Ali she was pregnant. Amazingly, when she stopped taking the Pill, Samantha had no trouble conceiving at all.

Bandar had been in awe of his child growing in her belly right from the start, becoming impatient towards the end of her pregnancy to see his son. They'd known it was a boy from the ultrasound.

The joy and wonder which lit up Bandar's face when she handed him little Ali straight after the birth would remain imprinted on Samantha's memory for ever. The look of total love he'd given her was pretty memorable as well.

Oh, yes, that was the happiest day of all. For with the beginning of their family, Samantha realised that neither of them would ever be lonely again.

Traded to
the Sheikh

EMMA DARCY

Initially a French/English teacher, **Emma Darcy** changed careers to computer programming before the happy demands of marriage and motherhood. Very much a people person, and always interested in relationships, she finds the world of romantic fiction a thrilling one and the challenge of creating her own cast of characters very addictive.

CHAPTER ONE

SHEIKH ZAGEO bin Sultan Al Farrahn was not amused. Not only had there been criminal trespassing in the walled grounds of this family property—his mother's pleasure palace on the legendary spice island of Zanzibar—but also criminal use of the private harbour by a drug-running French yachtsman who was actually offering him a woman to warm his bed in exchange for letting him go.

Did the sleazy low-life think he was speaking to the kind of man who'd indulge in indiscriminate sex?

'She's very special,' the drug-dealer pleaded with all the oiliness of a practised pimp. 'A genuine strawberry-blonde. Hair like rippling silk, falling to the pit of her back. Beautiful, bright, blue eyes. Lush breasts...' His hands shaped an hourglass figure. 'Fantastic legs, long and...'

'A virgin, as well?' Zageo cut in mockingly, despising the man for thinking he could trade his whore for his own freedom, for thinking the trade could even be an acceptable possibility.

'Completely untouched,' Jacques Arnault instantly replied, a consummate liar, not so much as a flicker of an eyelash nor the twitch of a facial muscle to betray any unease with the question, despite the impossibility of there being anything virginal about a woman who had to be his partner in crime.

'And where is this precious pearl?' Zageo drawled, barely holding back his contempt for a man who was prepared to sell flesh to save his own skin.

'On my yacht. If you get your security people—' he glanced nervously at the guards who'd caught him '—to take me out to it, they can fetch her back to you.'

While he silently sailed away in one hell of a hurry!

Zageo gave him a blast of scepticism. 'On your yacht? You've managed to sail from the Red Sea, down half the east coast of Africa to this island, without being tempted to touch this fabulous jewel of femininity?'

The Frenchman shrugged. 'Stupid to spoil top merchandise.'

'And where did you get this *top merchandise*?'

'Picked her up from one of the resorts where she was working with a dive team. She agreed to help crew the yacht for free passage to Zanzibar.' His mouth curved into a cynical smile. 'A drifting traveller who could go missing indefinitely.'

'A fool to trust you with her life.'

'Women are fools. Particularly those with an innocent turn of mind.'

Zageo arched a challenging eyebrow. 'You take me for a fool, as well?'

'I'm being completely straight with you,' came the swift and strongly assertive assurance. 'You can have her. No problems.' His gaze flicked around the lavishly rich and exotic Versace furnishings in the huge central atrium which had always served as the most public reception area. 'With all you have to offer, I doubt you'd even have to force her. Unless you enjoy force, of course,' he quickly added on second thoughts.

Anger burned. 'You are breaking another law, monsieur. The slave trade was abolished in Zanzibar over a century ago.'

'But a man of your standing and influence…who's to question what you do with a woman no one knows? Even if she runs away from you…'

'Enough!' Zageo gestured to his security guards. 'Put him in a holding room. Have his yacht searched for a woman. If there is one onboard, bring her to me.'

Arnault looked alarmed as two of the guards flanked him to escort him elsewhere. He spoke quickly in anxious protest. 'You'll see. She's everything I said she is. Once you're satisfied…'

'Oh, I will be satisfied, monsieur, one way or another,' Zageo silkily assured him, waving his men to proceed with the execution of his orders.

Zageo doubted the woman existed, certainly not with all the attributes ascribed to her by Jacques Arnault. He suspected the Frenchman had been dangling what he thought would be a tempting sexual fantasy in the hope of getting back to his yacht and somehow ditching the men escorting him. Even though the security guards carried guns, a surprise attack might have won him time to escape.

However, if there was a female accomplice, she had to be brought in and handed over to the appropriate authorities. While she might not have been actively involved in drug-dealing, there was no way she couldn't know about it and would surely be able to supply useful information.

He relaxed back on the thronelike sofa, reached over the elaborately rolled armrest to pick up the mango cocktail he'd previously set down on the entwined monkeys table, and sipped the refreshing drink slowly as the anger stirred by the Frenchman's attempt to use sexual currency turned onto Veronique, who had declined the invitation to accompany him on this trip.

'Your mind will be on business, *cheri*,' she had prettily complained. 'It will not be fun.'

Was the amount of *fun* to be had the measure of their relationship? His three-month tour of checking the hotel chain he'd established throughout Africa could not be called a hardship on anyone's agenda—luxurious resorts in exotic locations. How much *fun* did she need to feel happy and satisfied?

He understood that for the much-in-demand French-Morrocan model, pleasure was inextricably linked with exciting leisure and being taken shopping. He understood that what he provided in this context was the trade-off for having her as his mistress. He had not understood that Veronique was only prepared to give him her company on her own totally self-indulgent terms.

Intolerable!

He had indulged her far too much. It wasn't enough recompense that the sex was good. It wasn't enough that Veronique was invariably a splendid ornament on his arm, superbly dressed to complement her dark-skinned exotic beauty. He found it deeply insulting that she had so little respect for *his* wishes.

His father was right. It was time he ended this too long fascination with women of different cultures and found one of his own kind to marry. He was thirty-five years old and should be thinking of settling down, having a family. He would cut his connection with Veronique and start considering more suitable candidates for a lifelong commitment—well-educated women from other powerful families in Dubai, women whose background ensured they would share his life, not just his bed and his spending power.

None of them would have strawberry-blond hair, blue eyes and fair skin, but such factors were hardly prime requirements for marriage. They weren't even factors to inspire a lustful dalliance. Right now the idea of trading in sex was particularly abhorrent, and Zageo found himself actually relishing the opportunity to hammer this home to Jacques Arnault's female yachting companion.

He hoped she did exist.

He hoped his men would find her on board the illicit yacht in the private harbour that served this private palace.

He hoped she actually measured up to the Frenchman's selling spiel.

It would give him considerable satisfaction to demonstrate that regardless of how attractive her physical assets were, they were worth nothing to him.

Absolutely nothing!

CHAPTER TWO

'I WILL get out of this! I will!' Emily Ross kept reciting as she struggled through the mangrove swamp.

These mutterings of fierce determination were interspersed with bursts of self-castigation. 'What a fool I've been! A gullible idiot to be taken in by Jacques. I should have just paid the money to fly here. No hassle about arriving in time. All safe and sound...'

Talking blocked out the fear of having made another wrong step, of putting her life in hopeless hazard this time. Yet reason insisted that the Frenchman could not have been trusted to keep his word about anything. The only sure way of staying in Zanzibar and getting to Stone Town to meet Hannah was to jump ship while Jacques was still off in his dinghy doing his drug-running.

So, okay...she'd done the swim from the yacht to shore, dragging all her essentials in a waterproof bag behind her. No shark or fish had attacked. Her feet had not been cut to ribbons by shells or coral or sharp rocks. Now she just had to find her way out of the mangrove swamp that seemed to cover the peninsula she'd swum to.

'It's not going to beat me. I *will* get out of it.'

And she did, finally emerging from the mud and tangled tree roots onto a wide mound of firmer ground which turned out to be an embankment above a small creek. More water! But beyond it was definitely proof of civilisation—what looked like the well kept grounds of some big property. No more swamp. The worst was over.

Emily's legs shook from sheer exhaustion. Now, with the fear of being swallowed up by the swamp receding and much easier travelling in sight, she felt like collapsing on the bank and weeping with relief at having made it this far. Nevertheless, the need to cling to some self-control persisted. She might be out of the woods but this was still far from the end of her journey.

She sat herself down on the bank and did some deep breathing, hoping to lessen the load of stress—the huge mental, emotional and physical stress attached to her decision not to cling to the relative safety of Jacques Arnault's yacht, not to remain captive to any further devious plan he might make.

Free...

The thought gathered its own momentum, finding a burst of positive achievement.

Free of him. Free of the swamp. Free to go where I want in my own time.

It helped calm her enough to get on with assessing her current position. A high stone wall ran back into distant darkness on the other side of the creek. It gave rise to the hope it might lead to a public road.

'If nothing else, it should give me cover until I'm right away from Jacques and his dirty business,' she muttered, trying to whip up the energy to move again.

Through sheer force of will, Emily drove her mind into forward planning as she heaved herself onto her feet and trudged along the bank of the creek until the stone wall was directly opposite her. Once across this last body of water, she could clean herself up and dress respectably in the skirt and T-shirt she'd placed at the top of the waterproof bag. Wearing a bikini at this time of night was hardly appropriate for meeting local people and sooner or later she had to confront someone in order to ask directions to Stone Town.

Waist-deep in water and hating every second of wading through it, Emily was concentrating on her footing when a commanding voice rang out.

'*Arretez!*'

The French verb to stop certainly stopped her!

She almost tripped in sheer shock.

Her heart jerked into a fearful hammering as her gaze whipped up to fix on two men pointing highly menacing rifles at her. They wore white shirts and trousers with black gun-belts, giving them more the appearance of official policemen than drug-running gangsters, but Emily wasn't sure if this was a good thing or a bad thing. If they'd caught Jacques and were connecting her to his criminal activities—which the use of French language suggested—she might end up in prison.

One of the men clapped a small mobile telephone to his ear and spoke at speed in what sounded like Arabic. The other motioned her to continue moving to their side of the creek bank. Having a rifle waved at her did not incline Emily towards disobedience. She could only hope these people were representatives of the law on this island and that the law would be reasonable in listening to her.

A giant fig tree on her left had obviously provided an effective hiding place for them to watch for her emergence from the mangroves. She wondered if other patrols were out looking for her. Certainly her appearance was being reported to someone. As she scrambled up their side of the creek bank, one of the men came forward and snatched the waterproof bag out of her grasp.

'Now hold on a moment! I've got my life in there!' Emily cried in panicky protest.

Having her passport, money and clothes taken from her was a very scary situation. Thinking the men might believe the bag contained contraband, she tried persuading them to check its contents.

'Look for yourself.' Her hands flew out in a gesture of open-palmed innocence. 'It's just personal stuff.'

No response. The men completely ignored her frantic attempt to communicate with them both in English and in her very limited tourist French. She was grabbed at the elbows and briskly marched across quite an expanse of mown grass to a path which eventually led to a massive three-storey white building.

At least it didn't look like a prison, Emily thought,

desperately trying to calm her wildly leaping apprehension. The many columned verandahs on each level,
with their elaborate wrought-iron lace balustrades, gave
the impression of British colonial architecture serving
some important government purpose.

Maybe a courthouse?

But why on earth would Jacques do his drug-running
right under the nose of legal officialdom?

Could it be terribly corrupt officialdom?

This thought frayed her strung-out nerves even further. She was a lone foreign woman, scantily dressed,
and her only tool of protection was her passport which
she no longer had in her possession. It took all her will-
power not to give way to absolute panic when she was
escorted up the steps to the front verandah and was
faced with horribly intimidating entrance doors.

These were about four metres high, ominously black,
intricately carved around the edges, and featuring rows
of big pointed brass studs. They were definitely the
kind of doors that would deter anyone from gate-crash-
ing a party. As they were slowly swung open Emily instinctively decided that a bowed head and downcast
eyes might get her into less trouble in this place.

The first sight she had of the huge foyer was of a gorgeous *Tree of Life* Persian rug dominating a dark
wooden floor. As she was forced forward onto this carpet her side vision picked up the kind of splendid urns
one might see in an art museum, which suggested this
could be a *safe* environment.

A burst of hope prodded her into lifting her gaze to

check out where she was being taken. Her mind absolutely boggled at the scene rolling out in vivid Technicolor right in front of her. She was being led straight towards a huge central atrium, richly and exotically furnished in the style of a palatial reception area.

A walkway to the rest of the rooms on the ground floor surrounded the two-steps-down sunken floor of this incredible area, which was also overlooked by the balconies which ran around the second and third floors. Above it was a domed roof and from the circumference of the dome hung fantastic chandeliers of multicoloured glass that cascaded down in wonderful shapes and sizes.

As amazing as all this was, Emily's gaze almost instantly zeroed in on the man who was certainly the focal centrepiece of this totally decadent and fabulous luxury. He rose with majestic dignity from a thronelike sofa which was upholstered in red and gold. His clothes—a long white undertunic and a sleeveless overrobe in royal purple edged in gold braid—seemed to embrace Arabian culture but he didn't look like an Arab, more aristocratic Spanish. What wasn't in any doubt was that Emily was faced with the most stunningly beautiful man she had ever seen in her life.

Beautiful...

Strange word to apply to a man yet handsome somehow wasn't enough. The cast of his features was perfectly boned and balanced as though he was the creation of a mastor sculptor. A thick mane of straight black hair was swept back from his forehead, falling in shaggy layers to below his ears but not to shoulder-length. It was a bold and dramatic frame for a face that comprised brows which kicked up at a wicked angle, lending an emphatic effect to riveting dark eyes; a classically straight nose ending in a flare of nostrils that suggested a passionate temperament; a mouth whose upper lip was rather thin and sharply delineated while the lower lip was full and sensual.

The man fascinated, mesmerised, and although she thought of him as beautiful, there was an innate arrogant *maleness* to him that kicked a stream of primal fear through her highly agitated bloodstream. He was fabulous but also very foreign, and he was unmistakably assessing her female assets as he strolled forward, apparently for a closer examination.

Because he was at a lower floor level, Emily had the weird sense of catapulting back in time to the days when Zanzibar was the largest slave trading centre of the world, with herself being held captive on a platform for the buyers' appraisal.

He lifted a hand to seemingly flick a hair back from his forehead as he spoke in Arabic to one of the guards holding her. The scarf she'd tied around her head was suddenly snatched away, the rough movement dislodging the pins which had kept her hair in a twisted coil around her crown. The sheer weight of the untethered mass brought it tumbling down, spilling over her shoulders and down her back.

'Hey!' Emily cried in frightened protest, her imagination rioting towards being stripped of her bikini, as well. She was suddenly feeling extremely vulnerable, terrified of what his next command might be.

A burst of fluent French came from the Spaniard/Arab. It was accompanied by a cynical flash of his eyes and finished with a sardonic curl of his mouth. While Emily had picked up a smattering of quite a few languages on her travels, she was not up to comprehending this rush of foreign words and she didn't care for the expression that went with them, either.

'Look, I'm not French. Okay?' she pleaded. 'Any chance you speak English?'

'So—' one black eyebrow lifted in sceptical challenge '—you are English?'

'Well, no actually. I'm Australian. My name is Emily Ross.' She nodded to the waterproof bag still being held by one of her guards. 'My passport will prove…'

'Nothing of pertinent interest, madamoiselle,' he cut in drily.

Emily took a deep breath, pulling her wits together enough to address the *real* situation here. 'Then may I ask what *is* of pertinent interest to you, monsieur?'

He made an oddly graceful gesture suggesting a rather careless bit of interest he was just as happy to dismiss. 'Jacques Arnault gave a description of you which I find surprisingly accurate.' He spoke in a slow drawl, laced with irony, his eyes definitely mocking as he added, 'This has piqued my curiosity enough to inquire if he spoke more truth than I anticipated.'

'What did he claim?' Emily asked, her teeth clenching as she anticipated hearing a string of lies.

'That you are a virgin.'

A virgin!

Emily shut her eyes as her mind exploded with the shocking implications behind *her promised virginity*.

It could mean only one thing.

Jacques Arnault…who couldn't lie straight in bed at night even if he tried, the consummate con artist who'd tricked her into crewing on his yacht, the sneaky drug-runner who had no conscience about anything, whose mind was completely bent on doing whatever served his best interests…had obviously come up with a deal to save his own skin.

She was to be traded off as a sex slave!

'No!' she almost spat in fierce indignation, her eyes flying open to glare at the prospective buyer. 'Absolutely not!'

'I did not believe it,' he said with a dismissive shrug, the tone of his voice a very cold contrast to her heat. 'Since the evidence points to your being a professional belly-dancer, I'm sure you've had many patrons.'

'A professional belly-dancer?' Emily's voice climbed incredulously at this further off-the-wall claim.

He gave her an impatient look. 'Your costumes were found onboard Arnault's yacht, along with the other luggage you abandoned in fleeing from being associated with the Frenchman's criminal activities. Avoiding capture.'

Capture!

So Jacques had definitely been nabbed doing his drug-dealing, and his yacht subsequently searched, leading this man to think she'd twigged that the game was up and had taken to the water to escape being caught up in the mess.

'I was not fleeing from capture tonight, monsieur. I was fleeing from being a captive on that boat since it set sail from the Red Sea.'

'Jacques Arnault was holding you against your will?'

'Yes. And any belly-dancing costumes your search turned up do not belong to me, I assure you,' she stated heatedly, resenting the implied tag of being a professional whore, as well.

The heat in her voice slid right down her entire body as he observed in mocking detail every curve of her femininity; the voluptuous fullness of her breasts, the smallness of her waist, the broad sweep of her hips, the smooth flow and shape of her thighs, calves, ankles...

'Your physique suggests otherwise, Miss Ross,' he commented very dryly.

Emily burned. Her arms, released by the guards who were still flanking her, flew up to fold themselves protectively across her chest. Her chin lifted in belligerent pride as she stated, 'I'm a professional diving instructor. I have a certificate to prove it amongst my papers in the bag your men took from me.'

Her inquisitor smiled, showing a flash of very white teeth, but something about that smile told Emily he was relishing the prospect of tearing her into tasty morsels and chewing on them. 'It's my experience that people can be many things,' he remarked with taunting ease.

'Yes. Well, you're not wrong about that,' she

snapped. 'Jacques Arnault is a prime example. And I think it's time you told me who you are and what right you have to detain me like this.'

Emily was steaming with the need to challenge him, having been put so much on the spot herself. The idea of bowed head and downcast eyes was long gone. She kept a very direct gaze on his, refusing to back down from her demands.

'You were caught trespassing on property that belongs to my family and you are closely linked to a man who was engaged in criminal activity on this same property,' he clipped out as though her complaint was completely untenable—a total waste of time and breath.

'You have no evidence that *I* was engaged in criminal activity,' Emily swiftly defended.

He rolled his eyes derisively.

'I swear to you I wasn't,' she insisted. 'In fact, the costumes you found probably belong to the woman who posed as Jacques Arnault's wife when I was tricked into becoming the only crew member on his yacht.'

'Tricked, Miss Ross?'

'I needed to get to Zanzibar. Jacques said he was sailing for Madagascar and would drop me off here if I helped…'

'With his drug-running?'

'No. With sailing the yacht,' she cried in exasperation. 'I didn't know about the drug angle until after I woke up onboard and at sea, having been drugged myself.'

'So…' He paused, his expression one of weighing up her account of the situation. He lifted a hand to stroke his chin as though in thoughtful consideration. But there was something simmering in his eyes that sent a warning tingle through Emily's taut nerves as he concluded, '…you claim to be an innocent victim.'

'I *am* an innocent victim,' Emily pounced, swiftly asserting, 'The deal was for me to be company for his wife as well as being another crew-member for the duration of the trip.'

One wickedly derisive eyebrow arched. 'Where is the wife?'

Emily heaved a fretful sigh. Probably her story did sound unbelievable but it was the truth. She had nothing else to offer. 'I don't know. She was gone when I woke up the morning after I'd gone onboard.'

'Gone,' he repeated, as though underlining how convenient that was. 'Without taking her belly-dancing costumes with her?' he added pointedly.

Emily frantically cast around for a reason that might be credible. 'Maybe she had to abandon them to get away from Jacques. I left quite a lot of my things behind on the yacht…'

'In *your* bid to escape.'

'Yes.'

'To escape what, Miss Ross?' he asked silkily. 'You must admit Arnault has kept to the bargain you made with him, bringing you to Zanzibar, as agreed.'

'Not to the public harbour at Stone Town, monsieur.'

'This private harbour is along the way. He was on course to Stone Town.'

'I couldn't trust him to take me there. After doing his

business at this location, he might have set sail for Madagascar, keeping me on as his crew.'

'So you chose to commit yourself to a formidable swim in unknown waters, then brave facing a mangrove swamp in the darkness. This is the act of a desperate person, Miss Ross.'

'A determined person,' she corrected, though she was beginning to feel deeply desperate in the face of this prolonged cross-examination.

'The kind of desperate person who will do anything to avoid facing prison,' he went on with an air of ruthless logic. 'A guilty person…'

'I haven't done anything wrong!' she yelled, cracking under the pressure of his disbelief in her testimony. 'I promised my sister I'd be in Stone Town for her and I wasn't sure Jacques would take me there.'

'Your sister. Who is your sister?'

'Who are *you*?' she whipped back, so frustrated by his incessant questioning of *her* position, the urge to attack *his* completely dismissed caution. 'My sister and I have important private business. I'm not going to tell a stranger what it is.'

Her defiant stance earned a glance that told her she was being utterly ridiculous in his opinion, but Emily didn't care. She wanted some answers, too.

'You are addressing Sheikh Zageo bin Sultan Al Farrahn,' he stated loftily.

A sheikh! Or was it a Sultan? He'd spoken both titles and either one made instant sense of this amazing place. But did he have any jurisdiction here?

'I thought Sultan rule was long gone from Zanzibar and the island is now under the government of Tanzania,' she threw back at him.

'While it has become part of Tanzania, Zanzibar maintains its own government,' he sharply corrected her. 'And I command considerable respect and influence here. Instead of fighting me, Miss Ross, you would do well in these circumstances to seek my favour.'

'And what does seeking your favour entail?'

Fiery contempt blazed from her eyes. Her nerves were wound up so tightly, she felt like a compressed spring about to explode from its compression. If he dared suggest a *sexual* favour…if he dared even lower his gaze to survey her curves again…Emily knew she'd completely lose it and start fighting like a feral cat.

Fortunately she was not dealing with a stupid man. 'Perhaps you need time to consider your position, Miss Ross,' he said in a reasoning tone. 'Time to appreciate the importance of giving appropriate information so you can be helped.'

Emily's mind slid from attack mode and groped towards wondering if she'd taken a self-defeating angle throughout this interview.

Her questioner lifted his arms into a wide, open-handed gesture. 'Let us continue this conversation when you are feeling more comfortable. A warm bath, a change of clothes, some refreshment…'

She almost sagged at the heavenly thought.

'I'll have my men escort you to the women's quarters.'

Right at this moment, Emily didn't care if the

women's quarters was a harem full of wives and concubines. It would be good to be amongst *females* again, great to sink into a warm bath and get cleaned up, and a huge relief to be dressed in clothes that provided some sense of protection from the far too *male* gaze of Sheikh Zageo bin Sultan Al Farrahn.

CHAPTER THREE

ZAGEO glanced over the contents of the waterproof bag, now emptied onto a side table in his private sitting room and divided into categories for his perusal. He picked up the passport. If it was a genuine document, Emily Ross was an Australian citizen, born in Cairns. Her date of birth placed her as currently twenty-eight years old.

'You have looked up this place…Cairns?' he asked his highly reliable aide-de-camp, Abdul Haji.

'A city on the east coast of far north Queensland, which is the second largest state in Australia,' Abdul informed, once again proving his efficiency in supplying whatever Zageo did or might require. 'The paper certifying Miss Ross as a diving instructor,' he went on, gesturing to a sheaf of documents on the table, 'is attached to various references by employers who have apparently used her services, catering for tourists at The Great Barrier Reef. They are not immediately checkable because of the different time zone, but in a few hours…'

Zageo picked up the papers. The certificate was

dated six years ago so Emily Ross had apparently been plying this profession since she was twenty-two. 'The resort on the Red Sea where Arnault supposedly picked up this woman...'

'Is renowned for its diving around magnificent coral reefs,' Abdul instantly slid in. 'However, it also employs belly-dancers for nightly entertainment.'

Zageo flashed him a sardonic smile. 'We will soon see if that picture fits.' He waved to the meagre bundle of clothes. 'This appears to be survival kit only.'

'One can easily replenish lost clothes by purchasing them very cheaply at the markets.'

Zageo picked up a small bundle of American dollars and flicked through them to check their value. 'There's not much cash money here.'

'True. No doubt Miss Ross was counting on using her credit card.'

Which was also laid out on the table—a Visa card, acceptable currency in most hotels. All the same, transactions and movements could be traced from a credit card, which didn't exactly tally with criminal activities.

'Surely there should be more ready cash if she is involved in the drug-running,' Zageo observed.

Abdul shrugged. 'We have no direct evidence of her complicity. I am inclined to believe she did make a deal with Arnault—free passage to wherever she wanted to go in return for crewing on his yacht...'

'And sharing his bunk.'

The cynical deduction evoked a frown that weighed

other factors. 'Curiously the search of Arnault's yacht indicated separate sleeping quarters.'

'Perhaps the man snores.'

'There does not appear to be any love lost between them,' Abdul pointed out. 'Arnault is eager to trade Miss Ross for his freedom and…'

'She jumps overboard rather than be caught with him. As you say, no love lost between them but sex can certainly be used as a currency by both parties.'

'Then why would Miss Ross not use her very blatant sex appeal to win your favour?'

It was a good question.

In fact, she should have done. It was what Zageo was used to from the women he'd met in western society. For Emily Ross to be an exception to the rule made no sense whatsoever. It was a totally perverse situation for her to look furious at his taking note of her feminine attributes, and to try blocking his appreciation of the perfectly proportioned curves by folding her arms. Women who wanted to win his interest invariably flaunted every charming asset they had. It was the oldest currency in the world for getting where they wanted to be. So why was Emily Ross denying it?

By her own admission she was not an innocent virgin.

Nor was she too young to know the score when it came to dealings between men and women.

Many things about this woman did not add up to a logical answer. The way she had spoken to him—actually daring to challenge him—had verged on disrespect, yet there had been a quick and lively intelligence behind everything she'd said. Those amazingly vivid blue eyes could have played flirtatious games with him, but no, they had burned with the strongly defiant sense of her own individuality, denying *him* any power over her, showing contempt for his authority.

'That woman needs to be put in her place,' Zageo muttered, determined to do it before the night was very much older.

Abdul's brow furrowed into another frown of uncertainty. He started stroking his beard, a sure sign of some perturbation of mind. 'If she *is* Australian…'

'Yes?' Zageo prompted impatiently.

'Perhaps it is because they are from a country which is detached from everywhere else…I have found Australians to be strangely independent in how they think and act. They are not from an authoritarian society and they think they have the right to question anything. In fact, those who have been in our employ at Dubai have bluntly stated we will get a better result if we let them perform in their own way.'

Zageo waved dismissively. 'You are talking of men. Men who have gained some eminence in their fields.'

'Yes, but I'm thinking this may be an endemic attitude amongst both men and women from Australia.'

'You are advising me that this woman may not be in the habit of bowing to any authority?'

Abdul grimaced an apologetic appeal to soften any offence as he explained, 'I'm saying Miss Ross may not have the mindset to bend to your will. It is merely something to be considered when taking in the whole.'

'Thank you, Abdul. I will give more thought to the problem of Miss Ross. However, until such time as you have checked the references from her previous employers, we will pursue the course I have laid down. Please ensure that my instructions are followed.'

Abdul bowed his way out.

His aide always understood authority.

To Zageo's mind it was utterly intolerable for Emily Ross not to bend to his will. At the very least the woman was guilty of trespassing. It was unreasonable of her to keep defying all he stood for.

She had to bend.

He would make her bend!

Emily's bikini had been taken away while she was relaxing in a luxurious spa bath, enjoying the warm bursts of water on tired, stiff muscles and the aromatic mixture of lavender and sandalwood oils rising out of the bubbles. She'd been invited to wear a wraparound silk robe during the subsequent pampering—a manicure and pedicure while her hair was shampooed and blow-dried. Five star service in these women's quarters, Emily thought, until it came time to discard the robe and dress for her next meeting with the sheikh.

She was ushered into a sumptuous bedroom where there was only one outfit on offer. It had not come from her waterproof bag. It had not come from the luggage she'd chosen to leave behind on the yacht. It did not belong to her but Emily knew instantly what it represented. Sheikh Zageo bin Sultan Al Farrahn wanted to see how well she fitted the contentious belly-dancing role. Without a doubt this was one of the costumes he'd accused her of owning.

The skirt seemed to be a concoction of chiffon scarves with colours ranging from deep violet, through many shades of blue to turquoise. These layers were attached to a wide hip band encrusted with royal-blue and gold and silver sequins with a border of dangling gold medallions. Violet lycra hipster panties came with the skirt. The cups and straps of the accompanying turquoise bra were also exotically patterned with sequins and beads.

Clearly this was not a cheap dress-up outfit.

It was an intricably fashioned professional costume.

Emily felt a twinge of concern for the woman to whom it did belong. What had happened to her? What was the story behind the storage of these specialty clothes on the yacht?

'I can't wear that,' she protested to Heba, the oldest of the attendants who'd been looking after her. 'It's not mine,' she insisted.

'I have been instructed it is for you,' came the inarguable reply. 'His Excellency, the sheikh, has commanded that you wear it. There is no other choice.'

Emily gritted her teeth. Clearly His Excellency's word was law in this household. He'd allowed her the leeway of cleaning up and feeling more comfortable, although most probably this indulgence was a premeditated softening up process and Emily was highly suspicious of the motive behind it.

Was the sexual trade-off still being considered?

Had she just been prepared for the sheikh's bed?

It had been so easy to accept all the pampering but now came the crunch!

She could either dig in her heels and remain naked under the flimsy and all too revealing silk robe—not a good option—or don the belly-dancing costume which was probably less sexually provocative and would definitely leave her less physically accessible.

Given there would be no avoiding facing the sheikh again tonight—he'd have her hauled into his presence if she tried disobeying his instructions—Heba was right. No choice. It had to be the belly-dancing costume.

Emily quelled a flood of futile rebellion and grudgingly accepted the inevitable, thinking that with any luck, these blatantly sexy clothes wouldn't fit and *that* would show him she'd been telling the truth.

Naturally the lycra panties proved nothing, stretching to accommodate her derriere. No problem. Annoyingly the skirt sat snugly on the curve of her hips—not too loose, not too tight. Emily eyed the bra balefully as she discarded the silk robe. It looked about right, but hopefully it wouldn't comfortably reach around her back.

To her intense frustration, the straps were perfectly positioned for her shape, the hooks and eyes met with no trouble at all, and the wired cups designed to uplift breasts and emphasise cleavage made her look so voluptuous it was positively embarrassing. Okay, her breasts were not small, but they weren't this *prominent*.

The belly-dancing costume actually made her feel more self-conscious of her body than the swamp-soiled bikini which had been whisked away the moment she'd discarded it to step into the spa bath. The skimpy two-piece had been a far more natural thing for her to wear. It hadn't been exotic and erotic, aimed at titillating a man's mind. It had simply been an off-the-peg garment for swimming.

However, there was no point in asking for it back.

Heba had her orders and clearly disobeying the sheikh was unthinkable.

Emily argued to herself that although she might *feel* caught up in a scene from *The Arabian Nights*, it couldn't be true, not in today's world. Even Heba was now using a very modern slimline mobile phone, undoubtedly reporting the state of play.

This forcing her to wear the belly-dancing costume had to be a pressure tactic, wanting her to feel more exposed, more vulnerable in the next interview about her activities. It couldn't have anything to do with a sexual trade-off. Not really.

Two security guards and a bearded man whom they clearly regarded as a higher authority arrived to escort her elsewhere. The women's quarters were on the second floor. Emily expected to be taken all the way down to the opulent atrium but she was led to a door on the first floor, which instantly evoked a wild wave of apprehension. At least the hugely open atrium had been like a public arena, overlooked by anyone on the ground or upper floors. She hoped, quite desperately, that some kind of official office was behind this door.

It wasn't.

The bearded man ushered her into what was undoubtedly a private sitting room, richly furnished and sensually seductive with its many cushioned couches surrounding a low circular table which held a tempting display of food and drink. It was occupied by only one person who instantly proceeded to dismiss her usher.

'Thank you, Abdul.'

The bearded man backed out of the room and closed the door, leaving Emily absolutely alone with a sheikh who apparently believed the only law that had to be respected was his own!

He strolled forward, intent on gaining an unencumbered view of her from head to foot—front view, side view and back view—in the costume he'd chosen for her to wear. Emily gritted her teeth and stood as still as a statue, determined not to betray her inner quaking and hoping that with her head held high, she looked as though she disdained any interpretation he took from how well the skirt and bra fitted her.

He moved behind her. Her spine crawled with an awareness of how close he was. Within an arm's reach. And he did not move on. His out-of-sight stillness played havoc with her pulse, making her temples throb with acute anxiety. What was he doing? What was he thinking? Was she imagining it or had he touched her hair, sliding fingers around a tress, lifting it away from the rest?

'You must fetch a very high price…as a dancer.'

The comment was spoken slowly, consideringly, his voice thick with a sensuality that raised goose-bumps all over her skin.

Emily swallowed hard to work some moisture into a very dry mouth. Her inner agitation had bolted beyond any control. Remaining still was beyond her. She swung around, catching sight of a swathe of her hair sliding out between the thumb and fingers of a hand that had been raised to his mouth. Or nose. The idea of him taking the intimate liberty of tasting it, smelling it, created total havoc in Emily's mind.

'You're making a big mistake about me,' she cried, struggling to find some defence to how he was making her feel.

'That was meant as a compliment, Miss Ross,' he answered, his mouth still curved in a look of sensual pleasure. 'There is no need for you to bristle.'

He didn't have the right to touch her without her permission. Emily wanted to say so but she sensed he would only laugh at the objection. Right now he had the power to do anything he wanted with her. All she could do was try to change his view of who and what she was.

'It sounded as though you thought I was a…a call-girl,' she protested.

His smile tilted with irony. 'I think it more a case of your choosing whom you'll take as a lover…as it suits you.'

Emily wasn't sure she liked the sound of that, either. She had the weird sensation of being silently enticed to

choose *him* as her next lover. Or was he setting a test—
a trap—for her?

'Come—' he waved her forward to one of the
couches close to the circular table '—you must be hungry after the rigours of your escape from Jacques
Arnault.'

Her stomach was empty—so empty it kept convuls-
ing with nervous energy. 'Does this mean you believe
I was escaping from him and not involved in the drug-
running?' she asked, not yet ready to take a step in any
direction.

He swept her an open-handed, graceful gesture.
'Until we reach a time and place of complete enlightenment, I would prefer you to consider yourself more
my guest than my prisoner.'

'You mean you *are* actually checking me out,' Emily
pursued the point, hoping for some sense of relief from
his false assumptions about her.

'Different time zones do not permit that process at
the moment but rest assured nothing will be taken for
granted. In the meantime…'

'I am hungry,' she admitted, thinking she'd feel safer
sitting down, safer keeping her mouth busy with eating
if she could make her stomach cooperate with an intake
of food.

Again he waved her forward. 'Please…seat yourself comfortably, relax, and help yourself to whatever
you'd like.'

No way in the world could she ever relax in this
man's company, but putting a table between them

seemed like a good defensive move. 'Thank you,' she said, forcing her feet to walk slowly, waiting for him to indicate where he would sit so she could settle as far away from him as possible.

Apparently he wanted to be face-to-face with her so she didn't have to manoeuvre for a position opposite to his. He took it himself. Nevertheless, there was still a disturbing sense of intimacy, just in their being seated at the same table. The couches around it were curved, linking with each other so there was no real sense of separation.

'What would you like to drink?' he asked, as though she truly were a guest. 'You have a choice of mango, pineapple and hibiscus juices, coconut milk…'

'Hibiscus juice?' She'd heard of the flower but hadn't known a drink could be made from it.

'Sweet, light and refreshing.' He reached for a jug of hand-painted pottery depicting a red hibiscus. 'Want to try it?'

'No, thanks. I've always loved mango.' Which she was long familiar with since it was such a prolific fruit tree around her home city of Cairns.

His dark eyes danced with mocking amusement over her suspicious refusal of the hibiscus jug. 'Where has your adventurous spirit gone, Miss Ross?'

The light taunt goaded her into shooting some straight truth right back at him. 'I feel like having some familiar comfort right now, Your Excellency.'

He picked up another pottery jug and poured mango juice into a beautiful crystal goblet. 'The familiar is safe,' he observed, a glittering challenge in his eyes as he replaced the jug and watched her pick up the goblet. 'A woman who plays safe would never have boarded Arnault's yacht. She would have taken a far more conventional, more protected route to Zanzibar.'

Emily fervently wished she had. Never more so than now. Dealing with this sheikh and his attitude towards her was undermining her self-confidence. She didn't know how to even set about *getting out of this*. Telling the truth didn't seem to be winning her anything, but what else could she do?

'I've crewed on yachts many times around the Australian coast. I was looking for a way to save the cost of plane fares.'

'You took a risk with a stranger.'

'I thought I could handle it.'

'And when you woke up and found there was no wife…how did you handle it then, Miss Ross?'

'Oh, then it came down to the rules of survival at sea. We needed each other to sail the yacht so agreements had to be reached and kept. Jacques only tried to cross the line once.' Her eyes hardened with the contempt she felt for the Frenchman. 'I think he found it too painful to repeat that particular error in judgment.'

The sheikh's mouth twitched into a sardonic little smile. 'Perhaps this contributed to Arnault's belief you were a virgin, Miss Ross, fighting for your virtue.'

She rolled her eyes. 'One doesn't have to be a virgin to not want a scumbag sharing your bed.'

'A scumbag…'

'The lowest of the low,' she drily explained.

'Ah!' One eyebrow arched in wicked challenge. 'And what of the highest of the high, Miss Ross? Where does your measure start for a man to be accepted into your bed?'

The highest of the high…

Emily's heart catapulted around her chest.

He was speaking of himself. Had to be. Which made this question far too dangerous to answer. If he actually did want to be accepted into her bed…the speculative look in his eyes was making her toes curl.

Emily quickly reached out to pick up some tasty tidbit from the table to stuff in her mouth.

Eating was safe.

Speaking was dangerous.

She was suddenly heart-thumpingly sure that a desire for sexual satisfaction was more on Sheikh Zageo bin Sultan Al Farrahn's mind than a desire for truth, and what he wanted from her was capitulation, vindicating everything he thought about her.

No way.

Never, she thought fiercely.

But what if he kept her here until she did give him the satisfaction he expected from her? She might never get to Stone Town for the meeting with her sister!

CHAPTER FOUR

ZAGEO watched Emily Ross eat. The consumption of an array of finger food was done with such single-minded focus, she could well have been absolutely alone in the room. *He* rated no visible attention whatsoever.

In any other woman's company he would find this behaviour unforgivably rude. In fact, he couldn't recall such a situation ever happening before. Emily Ross was proving to be an intriguing enigma on many levels, and perversely enough, her constantly challenging attitude was exciting more than just an intellectual interest in her. Mind-games with a woman were always sexy.

He suspected if he made some comment about her concentration on the food, she would lift those incredibly vivid blue eyes and state very reasonably, 'You invited me to help myself. Do you now have some problem with me doing it?'

What reply could he make to that without sounding *un*reasonable?

The plain truth was he felt peeved by her refusal to

show more awareness of him. It pricked his male ego. But he could wait. Time was on his side. Let her satisfy this hunger. If she was using it as an evasive tactic, it would come to an end soon enough and she'd be forced to acknowledge him again.

Besides, the Frenchman had not been wrong in his assessment of this woman's physical attractions. She was intensely watchable. Her hair alone was a visual delight—not just one block of colour but an intriguing meld of many variations in shades of blond and copper. The description of 'strawberry-blonde' had suggested red hair and pale skin, but there was more of an overall warm glow in Emily Ross's colouring. Her skin did not have the fairness that freckled. It was lightly tanned to a golden-honey shade.

Copper and gold, he thought. A woman of the sun with eyes the colour of a clear, sun-kissed sky. But her body belonged to Mother Earth, the fullness of her breasts and the width of her hips promising an easy fertility and a natural ability to nurture that Zageo was finding extremely appealing.

Perhaps it was the contrast to Veronique's chic model thinness that had him so…fascinated…by this woman's more opulent femininity. The lavish untamed hair denied any skilful styling by a fashionable hairdresser. The lavish flesh of her body—not fat, just well covered, superbly covered—allowed no bones to protrude anywhere, and would undoubtedly provide a soft cushioning for anyone lying with her—man or child.

She was a creature of nature, not the creation of diet

and designer wear, and Zageo found himself wanting to lie with her, wanting to sink into her softness and wanting to feel her heat envelop him and suck him in to the deepest part of her where secrets melted and intimacy reigned. That was when she would surrender to him. Utterly and completely.

Zageo relished the thought of Emily Ross's ultimate submission as he watched her eat. He was inclined to believe the Frenchman had not managed to get that satisfaction from her. Arnault's sexual frustration would have primed his readiness to try selling her on, demonstrating a total lack of perception about Zageo's character and the woman's. Emily Ross was of the mettle to play her own game by her own rules.

Nevertheless, Zageo had no doubt she could be bought, just like everyone else.

It was always a matter of striking the right trade.

The challenge was in finding out what buttons to press for the door of opportunity to open.

'Where were you aiming to meet your sister in Stone Town?' he asked.

Important private business—if Emily Ross had spoken the truth about her motive for coming to Zanzibar— invariably provided leverage.

Emily chewed over that question as she finished a tasty egg and asparagus tartlet and sipped some more mango juice. She didn't like the past tense he'd used, suggesting she wasn't going to be allowed to keep her appointment with Hannah.

Her gaze targeted his, projecting very direct intent. 'I still aim to meet her. She's counting on my meeting her. I left the yacht and swam for it because I didn't want to let my sister down.'

'Is she in trouble?'

The quick injection of concern almost tripped Emily into spilling her own worries about Hannah's situation. Caution clamped onto her tongue before it ran loose with information that was better kept private. Being an Australian, she was in the habit of assuming the world around her was safe unless it was proved otherwise. She had just been learning—the hard way—that she trusted too easily. Blithely believing that most people were of goodwill could land her in very nasty places.

'It's just a family meeting. I said I'd come. She'll be expecting me,' Emily stated, trying to sound matter-of-fact rather than anxious.

'Miss Ross, if I am to believe you were not in league with Arnault and his drug-running…' He paused to give emphasis to his line of argument. 'If I am to believe in your determination to meet your sister in Stone Town…there must be a designated place—be it hotel, shop, or private residence—and a name that can be checked there, giving credence to your story.'

Okay, she could see there was a credibility gap here that had to be crossed or her guest/prisoner status would remain as long as the sheikh cared to keep it in place. On the other hand, from the way he'd been eyeing her over, Emily had the distinctly uneasy feeling that not even credibility would earn her release from his custody. Still, she had to offer some proof that she was on a completely separate mission to Jacques Arnault's.

'The Salamander Inn. I don't know if Hannah has booked ahead. Unlikely, I'd think, since she was unsure of when she'd make it to Zanzibar. But that's our meeting place.'

'The Salamander Inn is a boutique hotel. It offers the best and coincidentally the most expensive accommodation of all the hotels on this island. I know this.' He smiled with an arrogance that somehow implied she'd just been very stupid. 'I own it.'

Oh, great! The chance of escaping from this man anywhere on Zanzibar looked increasingly dim!

'Fine!' she said on an exasperated sigh. 'Then you can easily check if Hannah has arrived or not.'

'Her full name?'

'Hannah Coleman.'

'Not Ross?'

'Coleman is her married name.'

'So your sister is not likely to book under the family name of Ross?'

'Hardly. Ross is *my* married name.'

That information ripped him out of his languid pose against the heaps of satin cushions on his couch. His body jerked forward, his loose robes suddenly pasted to a tautly muscled physique that seemed to bristle with assault readiness. Yet he spoke with a soft silky contempt which crawled straight under Emily's skin, priming her into retaliation mode.

'Where is your husband, Madame Ross?'

'His ashes were thrown to a breeze out at sea…as he'd once said he'd prefer to being buried,' Emily grated out, hanging firmly to being matter-of-fact so that she wasn't embarrassed by one of the waves of grief which could still sweep up and overwhelm her when she thought of Brian's death.

They'd been school sweethearts, rarely parted during all the years they'd spent sharing almost everything in each other's company. Then to have him taken from her so abruptly…being left behind…alone…cheated of a future together… *No, no, no, don't go there, Emily!*

She concentrated on watching her antagonist digest the news of her widowhood, the withdrawal of all expression from his face, the slow emergence of more sympathetic inquiry in his dynamic dark eyes.

'How long ago?' he asked quietly.

'About two years.'

'He was young?'

'Two years older than me.'

'How did he die?'

'Brian was with a rescue team during a cyclone.' She grimaced. 'He died trying to save an old lady's pet dog. A panel of flying roof hit him.'

'A brave man then,' came the thoughtful observation.

She managed an ironic smile. 'I don't think fear ever had any influence on Brian's actions. He just did whatever he set out to do. We used to go adventuring a lot, working our way around Australia.'

'You do not have children?'

She shook her head. 'We weren't ready to settle

down with a family. In fact, we were getting ready to set off on a world trip…'

'When the cyclone happened,' he finished for her.

'Yes,' she muttered, frowning at the realisation that she'd spoken more of Brian in the past two minutes than in the entire two years since her departure from Australia.

You have to move on, she'd told herself, and move on she had, a long slow trip across Asia, more or less going wherever the wind blew her on her travels, not wanting to face making any long-term decisions about her life—a life without the man who'd always coloured it.

She'd attached herself to other groups of people from time to time, working with them, listening to their experiences, soaking up interesting pieces of information, but what was highly personal and private to her had remained in her own head and heart.

So why had she opened up to this man?

Her mind zapped back the answer in no time flat.

Because *he* was getting to her in a highly primitive male/female way and she'd instinctively brought up the one man she'd loved as a shield against these unwelcome feelings. Her marriage to Brian was a defence against other things, as well, like the idea she was a belly-dancer with indulgent sugar-daddies on the side.

She was, in fact, a perfectly respectable widow who hadn't even been tempted into a sexual dalliance by the many gorgeous eye-candy guys who'd offered to share their beds and bodies while they were ships passing on

their separate journeys. Sex without emotional involvement hadn't appealed, and it didn't appeal now, either,
she fiercely told herself, willing her body to stop responding in this embarrassingly *animal* fashion to a
very foreign sheikh who wanted to treat her as a whore.

Having worked up a head of defensive steam, Emily
lifted her gaze to the man in the ruling seat and noted
that his disturbingly handsome head was cocked to one
side as though viewing her from an angle he hadn't
considered before, and the heart-thumping power of
those brilliant dark eyes was thankfully narrowed into
thoughtful slits.

'So what is *your* marital status?' she bluntly demanded.

His head snapped upright, eyes opening wide with a
flash of astonishment at her temerity. 'I beg your pardon?'

'Fair's fair!' Emily argued. 'If you have the right to
ask about mine, I have just as much right to ask about
yours.'

If he had a string of wives and a bevy of concubines,
perhaps he would cease to be so attractive!

His face clearly said she was being incredibly impertinent but Emily didn't care. 'After all, what do I know
about you?' she pointed out. 'I'll accept you're Sheikh
Zageo…whatever…whatever…and you own this place
as well as The Salamander Inn, which obviously means
you're terribly wealthy and probably influential, but—'

'Zageo bin Sultan Al Farrahn,' he broke in haughtily,
supplying all the names she'd forgotten in her current
fraught state.

'Right! Quite a mouthful to remember,' she excused. 'Though if it's a big issue to you, I'll try to hold it in my mind.'

'Rather than test your mind too far,' he drawled in a mocking tone that once more raised Emily's hackles. 'You may call me Zageo in my private rooms.'

'Well, thank you very much. It was really sticking in my craw, having to address you as Your Excellency,' she tossed at him. 'I mean honestly… how do you keep a straight face when people call you that? Though I suppose if you actually believe it fits you…' She paused to look at him in arch inquiry, then testingly ask, 'Do you consider yourself totally excellent?'

His jawline tightened. Emily sensed that pride was warring with his own intelligence which had to concede the presence of a few little flaws. No man—nor woman—was perfect.

'It is simply the customary form of address to any sheikh in my culture,' he stated tersely. 'I doubt Her Majesty, the queen of England, considers herself majestic. Nor think herself the highest of the high when addressed as Your Highness.'

'Okay. Point made,' Emily granted, smiling to show she hadn't meant to give any offence, though secretly she felt very pleased at levelling the playing field, if only a little bit. 'If I'm allowed to call you Zageo, you needn't keep on with Miss Ross. Emily will do just fine. It's actually what I'm more used to. We're not big on titles back home in Australia.'

And he needn't think she was overly impressed by his!

'Thank you, Emily.'

He smiled, instantly driving her mind into a jangling loop that screamed *Danger! Danger! Danger!* He'd just made her name sound like an intimate caress, sending a sensual little shiver down her spine. As for his smile…it was definitely projecting a pleasurable triumph in having won this concession from her, interpreting it as a dropping of hostility and bringing a much closer meeting ground between them.

She had a mental image of him storming the ramparts of her castle and it seemed like a good idea to pull up the drawbridge and shut the gate. 'So let's get back to *your* marital status,' she said, needing back-up support to hold the barriers in place.

'I have not yet taken a wife,' Zageo answered, undermining Emily's defensive plan.

Feeling decidedly miffed by this, she remarked, 'I thought sheikhs could take as many wives as they liked. You're a late starter aren't you?'

'I believe the right choice of wife in any culture deserves deep and serious consideration, given the intention of a lifelong commitment and the resulting alliance with another family.'

'Nothing to do with love, of course,' she tossed off flippantly.

'On the contrary, I have observed that compatibility tends to breed a more lasting love than the rather fickle chemistry of *being in love*.'

She pounced on what seemed like a beacon of relief from any sexual pressure from him. 'So you don't think giving in to chemistry is a good idea.'

'It is not something I would base a marriage on, Emily, but for a time of pure pleasure—' his eyes positively glittered with white-hot sexual invitation '—I think giving in to chemistry is a very sweet and satisfying self-indulgence, to be treasured as something uniquely special to the man and woman involved.'

Emily had to suck in a quick breath to stop an imminent meltdown in her bones, brain and other body parts she didn't want to think about. 'I take it you're not a virgin then,' she shot at him, mocking the value that had apparently been put on *her* virginity.

At least it temporarily interrupted the bolt of heat from his eyes, making him blink, then triggering a rippling peal of laughter, lessening the scary tension in the room and leaving Emily feeling slightly safer.

'I have not foresworn the pleasures of the flesh…no,' he eventually drawled, his eyes dancing an all too overt anticipation of pleasures *she* might provide, which did away with any sense of relaxation.

Emily drew in a deep breath and expelled it in a long, slow sigh, desperate to reduce the seesawing inner apprehension which made thinking nimbly very difficult. She felt stripped of any clothing armour and he'd just ripped off the mental armour she'd tried to put in place. Somehow she had to keep her mind at battle readiness because the fight for freedom would probably be lost if she let herself be distracted by this man's insidious promise of pleasures, which his eyes said were hers for the taking if she co-operated with what he wanted.

The big problem was he was the kind of man who'd tempt any woman into wondering how it might be with him…if, indeed, he would deliver amazing pleasure. Probably it was *The Arabian Nights* thing again, messing with her mind, making her think of Omar Khayyam's poetry expressing regret for the fleeting sweetness of life and love, which, in turn, tapped into the lingering emptiness of missing Brian, all contributing to her feeling of *why not experience this man*?

A harsh strain of common sense insisted it would compromise her whole situation if she did. 'I have to be here for Hannah,' she muttered, savagely reminding herself of her prime motivation.

'There cannot be any urgency about this meeting with your sister or you would not have chosen to come by yacht,' Zageo pointed out.

'Even by sailing, I figured I'd make it here by about the same time as Hannah. And I preferred to save my money.'

His mouth curled into a mocking little smile. 'Staying at The Salamander Inn does not equate with *saving money*, Emily.'

He was still doubting her story.

'I didn't say *I* was going to stay there,' she reminded him.

'Where did you plan to stay?'

'If Hannah wasn't here already, I intended to find a place that suited my budget while I waited for her.'

'Then you should have no problem with accepting my hospitality while you wait for your sister's arrival in Zanzibar,' he said silkily. 'That would undoubtedly suit your budget best. No cost whatsoever.'

'Oh, right!' Emily mocked back before she could stop her tongue from cutting loose on him. 'And I suppose you'll expect me to belly-dance for you every night!'

His elegant hands performed their graceful invitational gesture. 'If you feel you should recompense me in some way, by all means…'

'What if Hannah is at the inn already?' Emily cut in, hating the sense of being helplessly cornered, and feeling that Sheikh Zageo bin Sultan Al Farrahn was enjoying himself far too much at her expense!

'That can be checked immediately.'

He leaned forward and picked up a mobile telephone from the table. The modern means of communication again struck Emily as odd in this setting but the evidence of its use all around the palace assured her that life in the twenty-first century was not excluded here. Unfortunately most of the one-sided conversation she subsequently listened to was not in English. Of all the words spoken, only the name, Hannah Coleman, was recognisable.

Emily literally sat on the edge of her seat as she waited, hoping for news that would validate her story, as well as assure her of Hannah's safe arrival. 'Well?' she prompted anxiously, once the call connection had been ended.

The dark eyes targeted hers with riveting intensity. 'Your sister is not at the inn. Nor has there been a booking in her name.'

Disappointment warred with doubt as to the truth of what she was being told. 'How do I know you're not lying?' burst from her tongue.

His face tightened forbiddingly. 'Why would I lie?'

Even to her overstrained mind, *to get me into your bed* sounded absurd, given his extraordinary good looks and incredibly wealthy resources.

Zageo's dark eyes blazed with angry suspicion as he pointed out, 'It is you, Emily Ross, who has cause to concoct many lies in order to paint yourself as an innocent victim.'

'I swear to you on any amount of bibles or Korans or whatever carries weight in both our worlds, I've told you nothing but the truth.'

One black eyebrow arched in sceptical challenge. 'Where is your sister coming from?'

'Zimbabwe.' Realising she now had to explain more, Emily offered, 'You must know about the political problems in that country. It's world news. Everyone knows. Hannah's husband is trying to hang onto his farm, but he wants her and the children out while he…'

'Children?'

'They have two young daughters. The plan was for Hannah to bring them by road into Botswana when they thought it was safe enough for her to do so, then…' A helpful link suddenly leapt into Emily's mind. 'Hannah and her husband, Malcolm, spent a vacation at The

Salamander Inn five years ago. That's why she picked it as a meeting place. She knew it and thought it was somewhere safe for both of us to get to. Since you own the inn, surely you can have a check run on the records...'

'Not at this time of night.'

'Then first thing tomorrow morning.' Emily jumped to her feet, seeing a chance to end this highly unsettling encounter with him. 'In fact, by tomorrow morning I'm sure you have the power and facilities to have lots of things about me checked, so talking any more right now is really inefficient, isn't it? I'm terribly tired and if you'd just have me taken back to the women's quarters, I'm very happy to accept your hospitality for the night and...'

He rose from his couch, choking off Emily's speech with the formidable force of energy that rose with him. For several fraught moments, his gaze locked onto hers, telegraphing a strong and ruthless promise that if she was playing him for a fool she would pay for it.

Dearly.

But he did dismiss her from his presence.

'Until tomorrow morning,' he said in sardonic agreement with her timeline.

Pretend as she might about accepting an offer of hospitality for tonight, Emily found nothing remotely hospitable about the security guards who escorted her back to the women's quarters.

She was not Sheikh Zageo bin Sultan Al Farrahn's guest.

She was his prisoner.

CHAPTER FIVE

ZAGEO paced around his sitting room, incensed by the outrageous impertinence of Emily Ross, taking her leave of him as though she had every right to do as she pleased. This woman, who had to know she was a trespasser on his goodwill, had treated him in the same intolerable manner as Veronique. Which reminded him…

With a heightened sense of deadly purpose he moved to pick up the telephone and call the Paris apartment. He had bought it to accommodate the relationship with Veronique and she had recently taken to using it as her main residence. Zageo decided it would be a suitable parting gift as he waited impatiently for her to come on line.

'Ah, *cheri*! What a lovely surprise,' she responded with a gush of pleasure when he announced himself. 'Are you missing me?'

If she wanted some proof of her pulling power she was testing the wrong man. 'Veronique, we are at an end, you and I,' he stated matter-of-factly.

'What?' Shock. Then anxiety. 'What do you mean, Zageo?'

'I mean our relationship has run its course. You were happy to remain in Paris…and I now find myself attracted to another woman.'

'You are leaving *me* for another woman?' she screeched into his ear.

A sobering lesson for taking him for granted.

'I will sign over the apartment to you—a memento of our time together and one I'm sure you'll appreciate.'

'I don't want the apartment without you in it,' she cried wildly. 'I want you, Zageo.'

A claim that left him completely cold. If she wanted him so much, she would be with him. Clearly Veronique had thought she could have her cake without supplying the ingredients that made it desirable for him, too. A deal was a deal and as far as Zageo was concerned, she hadn't lived up to her end of it. Nevertheless, he was prepared to be generous.

'Please have the grace to accept it's over, Veronique. There is nothing more to be gained by carrying on. It cannot serve any good purpose. I promise you will have the apartment. I'll put the legalities in train tomorrow.'

'You've found another woman?' Her voice shook with hysterical incredulity.

An unforgiveable wound to her pride?

'I'm sure you'll find another man,' he drawled, aware there were many ready to slide into the place he'd just vacated.

'You can't do this to me. I won't let you—'

'Move on, Veronique,' Zageo cut in ruthlessly. 'I have. Let us meet in future as old friends who still hold some affection for each other. As always, I wish you well.'

He ended the connection before she could pour out any further futile protests. It was far better to part with a sense of mutual respect than with a tirade of mutual grievances. He hoped Veronique would be pragmatic enough to accept what would not be changed and count herself fortunate to have profited so handsomely from their relationship. The gifted apartment in Paris would undoubtedly provide balm to wounded pride.

The burning question now was…how to deal with Emily Ross?

She was showing no signs whatsoever of bending to his will. Quite the contrary. Despite the fact she had to realise her immediate fate was in his hands and it would serve her well to win his favour, she was flouting his authority at every turn.

If Abdul was right about this kind of attitude being common amongst Australians, perhaps it was not meant to be so offensive. On the other hand, Zageo did not care to accept it from a woman. Of course, he could turn her in to the local authorities, move her straight out of his life, and that was certainly the most sensible path to take, given that he'd decided to find himself a suitable wife.

Emily Ross was a distraction from what he should be doing. On the other hand, for the duration of this business trip through Africa, he would very much enjoy having her in his bed and teaching her who was master of the situation.

Tomorrow he would know more about her.

Knowledge was power, especially when it came to dealing with people.

However, when tomorrow came, enlightenment did not come with it.

'Government offices are not open in Australia on Saturdays and Sundays,' Abdul reported. 'We cannot check a marriage certificate or a death certificate until Monday.'

More frustration!

Having finished eating his breakfast, Zageo took a long deliberate moment to savour the aroma of his Kenyan coffee, wanting at least one of his senses satisfied. Then he once again considered the challenging and highly vexing enigma of Emily Ross. Investigating her was like chasing evaporating smoke—no substance to be found anywhere.

Abdul had already informed him that the Australian employers who had written her references were no longer at the same place of business. Reef Wonderland Tours had changed management eighteen months ago and Whitsundays Diving Specialists was now a defunct company. As for the Red Sea resort where she had supposedly been working with a dive team, no-one admitted to knowing anything about her, which raised questions about what profession she had plied there since her name was not on any record books.

Had she spun a complete tissue of lies last night?

Was anything about her self-presentation genuine?

'The belly-dancing costume fitted her perfectly,' he remarked drily.

'Indeed, it did, Your Excellency,' Abdul agreed.

Zageo frowned over the form of address all his staff customarily used with him. Normally he just took *Your Excellency* for granted, barely hearing it, but in real terms the title *was* ridiculous, as that highly perverse and provocative creature had pointed out.

'The authorities have come from Stone Town to take Jacques Arnault and his Zanzibar connections into custody,' Abdul ran on when no further comment came from Zageo. 'A decision should be made whether or not to include Miss Ross in this criminal group.'

'Not.' The answer was swift and emphatic. He would feel…*defeated*…by Emily Ross if he washed his hands of her before coming to grips with who and what she really was. 'We have no absolute proof of involvement,' he added. 'I'm inclined to allow her the benefit of the doubt, given how very difficult it is to undo an injustice once it has been committed.'

'Do you wish to keep her here or set her free to go about her own business?'

'Since Miss Ross has no prearranged accommodation, I shall hold her here as my guest. At least until Monday.' He gave Abdul a look that conveyed his determination to pursue more background information. 'As to her business, clearly it is not urgent since a

Hannah Coleman has not, as yet, booked into The Salamander Inn. If, indeed, there is a sister to be met.'

'A search of the five-year-old records at the inn did turn up a Mr and Mrs M. Coleman.'

Zageo shrugged, unconvinced by a name that could belong to any number of people. 'One wonders if that is confirmation of my new guest's story or mere coincidence,' he drawled derisively. 'I think I shall amuse myself by doing a little more testing today, Abdul.'

His chief advisor and confidante took several moments to absorb and interpret this comment. He then cleared his throat and tentatively inquired, 'Has the…uh…affair with Veronique run its course, Your Excellency? Are there some…arrangements…you'd like me to make?'

'No. It's done. I made the call and the arrangements last night. The decision had nothing whatsoever to do with Miss Ross, Abdul. It was made beforehand.'

Although Emily Ross featured highly as a replacement for Veronique in his life, having completely obliterated his former mistress from his mind.

'I've given her the Paris apartment,' he went on. 'Ownership will need to be transferred into her name. You'll see to it?'

Abdul nodded. 'Speaking of names, the Coleman name *was* attached to an address in Zimbabwe. Do you wish me to make inquiries in that direction?'

'It could be fruitful. One might well ask why hasn't the sister turned up? Yes…' Zageo smiled to himself. 'Pursuing this question presents a nice little demonstration of concern for those whom Miss Ross apparently holds dear to her heart.'

A weapon in the war, he thought, feeling an extraordinary zing of anticipation in the plan he would soon put into operation.

CHAPTER SIX

EMILY had to concede that being a prisoner in this astounding place was not hard to take. Her physical needs were wonderfully pampered. She'd slept in a heavenly bed. Of course, after the bunk on the yacht, almost any normal bed would have been heavenly but the lovely soft mattress and pillows and the amazing curtain of mosquito netting that had been pulled all around the bed to protect her from any possible bites had definitely made her feel as though she was sleeping on clouds.

Then to wake up and find her own clothes restored to her—even those she'd had to leave behind on Jacques's yacht—all washed, ironed, and either hanging up or set on shelves in the dressing room adjoining the bedroom…well, surely this was evidence that her real life had been verified and everything was moving back to normal. The fears generated by the grotesque situation last night seemed rather incredible this morning.

She'd happily dressed in a favourite skirt made of a

pink, blue and green floral fabric that swirled freely around her legs—lovely and cool for what was shaping up to be a hot day on the island. A blue top with little sleeves and a scooped neckline completed what she considered a fairly modest outfit, definitely not overtly sexy, just…pretty…and feminine. If there was to be another face-to-face encounter with the sheikh, hopefully he wouldn't have any grounds for viewing her in a morally questionable light again.

Breakfast on the verandah outside her suite in the women's quarters became quite a social affair. As well as Heba serving her a very tasty array of fruit and croissants, her two other attendants from last night's grooming session, Jasmine and Soleila, fluttered around, eager to please Emily in any way they could.

A selection of magazines were brought for her to flick through as she finished the meal with absolutely divine coffee. Heba, herself, opened a copy of *Vogue* to show photographs of celebrities at some big premiere in Paris.

'See?' she pointed out proudly. 'Here he is with Veronique!'

Emily felt a weird catch in her heart as she stared at the stunningly beautiful Sheikh Zageo bin Sultan Al Farrahn in a formal black dinner suit, accompanied by the stunningly beautiful world-famous model, the highly unique Veronique, who was wearing a fabulous evening gown of floating ostrich feathers that only she could have carried off so magnificently.

This photograph was not a slice of fantasy out of *The*

Arabian Nights. It was real life on the international scene, the jet-setting, ultra-wealthy beautiful people doing what they do, connecting with each other for fabulous affairs—social and personal.

Feeling considerably flattened, Emily realised that her imagination must have been in an extremely feverish state last night, running hot with the idea of being seen as a desirable woman to this man. Why on earth would he want her when such an exotic and classy model was available to him?

'Have they been a couple of long standing?' she asked Heba.

A shrug. 'Almost two years.'

Two years comprised a fairly solid attachment. Emily now felt thoroughly confused over why the sheikh was bothering with her when she could have been simply passed along to the local authorities for them to sort out her association with Jacques Arnault. Why had he taken such a *sexual* interest in her? Was it only a titillated interest because the Frenchman had tried to trade her for his freedom?

'But Heba, Veronique did not come with him this time,' Jasmine pointed out, giving Emily an archly knowing look as though it was obvious to her who was being singled out to fill the sheikh's empty bed.

'Perhaps her professional commitments didn't allow it,' Emily reasoned, unable to feel the least bit flattered by the idea of being *taken* as a temporary replacement. Totally repulsed by it, in fact.

'This could be so,' Heba agreed. 'The sheikh will be

travelling through Africa for some months. Veronique may join him somewhere else on his tour of the Al Farrahn hotels.'

The Salamander Inn was obviously one of many such places, Emily thought, more proof of fabulous family wealth. Not that she needed it. What she did need was to plant her feet firmly on the ground and find a way to walk out of the hothouse atmosphere of this palace and get back to normal life, no matter how difficult her normal life could be at times. At least it was real, she told herself, and she knew how to deal with it, more or less.

'Am I allowed to leave?' she asked Heba. 'I need to get to Stone Town.'

'You must wait for a summons from His Excellency,' came the firm reply.

There was no budging the women from that position and without inside help, any chance of just walking out of the palace was zero. The only way down to the ground floor was by the balconies overlooking the central atrium and security guards were posted at the foot of each staircase. It was impossible, wearing her own clothes, to get past them without being seen and apprehended.

No doubt about it.

She was stuck in this gilded prison until Sheikh Zageo etc etc decided to release her from it.

As the morning wore on, Emily felt more and more on edge about being kept here at his leisure. What was happening? Why couldn't he make up his mind about her innocence in regard to Jacques's activities? When the summons finally came, she was bursting with impatience to be led to the man who ruled her current fate, her mind fizzing with persuasive arguments to win her freedom.

It wasn't acceptable to be either his prisoner or his guest. Now that she knew about his relationship with Veronique, any further offer of hospitality from him would have to be viewed as highly dubious. Besides, it was better all around to put this whole stressful episode behind her as fast as possible.

She did not expect to be escorted right out of the palace, transported to the harbour she had swum out of last night, and ferried to another boat!

Jacques's yacht was gone.

This was a sleek and very expensive looking motor cruiser.

Emily did not want to get out of the small outboard motorboat and climb up the ladder to the deck of a cruiser that was capable of whisking her right away from Zanzibar. Rebellion surged through her veins. She looked at the water. Was swimming away an option this time?

'It would be wasted effort, Emily,' came the sardonic remark from above.

Her stomach contracted at the sound of that voice. Her heart fluttered in a panicky fashion. All the prepared arguments in her mind started crumbling as they were hit by a sudden sense of futility. She knew with instinctive certainty that until this sheikh willed an end to the *hospitality* he was extending to her, there would be no end.

All the same, her natural independence would not roll over into abject submission. Her chin tilted defiantly as her gaze lifted to his. 'Why am I here?' she demanded. 'I thought you were going to have me checked out.'

'Unfortunately the weekend is not a good time for reaching sources of information.'

'When will be a good time?' she challenged, though mentally conceding that what he said was probably true.

He shrugged. 'Perhaps Monday.'

Monday. Two more days of living under a cloud and forced to endure the sheikh's company whenever he commanded it.

'Be my guest, come onboard,' he urged.

They were orders, not invitations. Emily heaved a fretful sigh as she rose to her feet and stepped up to the ladder. 'Some guest,' she darkly muttered. 'A considerate host would care about where I want to be and it's not on another boat.'

'But this is a pleasure boat which is fully crewed. No work at all for you,' he assured her in the silky tone that made her skin prickle with an acute sense of danger lurking.

'It's still on the water,' she grumbled.

'What a strange complaint from someone who is supposed to be a professional dive specialist!'

'Diving is something else,' she insisted.

'We shall see.'

There was something ominous in those words but

Emily was hopelessly distracted from pursuing that thought. He offered his hand to help steady her as she stepped down onto the deck and it was so startling to find him very informally clothed, wearing only a white T-shirt and casual shorts, she accepted it, and the strong fingers suddenly encompassing hers gave her a further jolt of physical awareness.

She tried not to look down at his bare legs, specifically his thighs, a glimpse of which had felt far too erotic for comfort. On a powerful male scale, they added immeasurably to his sex appeal, as did his taut cheeky butt when he turned to give instructions to a crew member.

In an instinctive need to get a grip on herself, Emily wriggled her hand out of his grasp and folded her arms across her rib cage. Then she ended up flushing horribly when he swung back to her and observed that her block-out body language had inadvertently pushed up her breasts.

'Relax, Emily,' he advised with a quirky little smile and wickedly challenging eyes. 'We're simply going for a ride to Pemba Island where the water is crystal clear and the coral reef provides superb diving.'

'How far away is it?' she asked sharply.

'Not far. People travel to it by ferry from Zanzibar.'

Ferry! Well, if she got marooned there, Emily reasoned, at least there was some form of public transport to get her back to Stone Town.

'Come.' He urged her towards the door leading to the cabin. 'We will sit in the saloon for the crossing.'

The saloon on this boat was a far cry from the cramped cabin on Jaques's yacht. Not only did it contain an elegant dining table that could seat ten people, the lounging area was also sumptuous; cream leather couches running along underneath the windows, plus a cosier conversational area with a grouping of chairs and sofas around a low table to allow the serving of light refreshments.

Emily chose to sit by the windows, her arm resting along the padded backrest of the couch as she looked out at the harbour Jacques had sailed into last night. She felt the vibration of the cruiser's big engines being revved up and knew they were about to power this motorboat out to sea.

Her *host* moved past her, seating himself on the same couch about a metre away but turned towards her, his arm hooking over the backrest, his hand dangling within easy reach of hers. Although she was acutely aware of his close presence, Emily resolutely ignored it, watching the mangrove swamp being left behind as the boat carved through the water towards the exit from the harbour.

'Do not be disturbed. We shall return,' Zageo assured her, apparently not insensitive to her inner tension.

'Why are you taking me with you to Pemba Island?' she asked, still not looking at him, afraid of revealing just how vulnerable he made her feel.

'The reefs around it are largely in a pristine condition, unspoilt coral gardens supporting a vast array of marine life,' he informed her. 'As a professional diver yourself, you may well have heard that this area is an underwater naturalist's dream.'

'No. I hadn't heard.'

'I am surprised,' he drawled. 'Pemba is now listed as one of the top dive spots in the world.'

The taunt over her ignorance of this fact goaded Emily into locking eyes with him. 'I didn't come to Zanzibar for diving,' she stated belligerently, resenting his forceful interruption of her personal mission. 'Why don't you just let me go to get about my own business?'

'What is there for you to do?' he retorted reasonably. 'Your sister has not yet checked in at The Salamander Inn. I have instructed the management there to notify me the moment Hannah Coleman arrives and identifies herself. In the meantime, what better way for you to spend today than taking up a superb diving opportunity?'

His logic was difficult to fault, yet undermining it was the undeniable fact she had been given no choice. 'You don't believe me, do you? You still think I'm a drug-running belly-dancer. And this—' she waved an arm at her luxurious surroundings '—is just another gilded prison.'

The hand lying close to hers on the backrest of the couch moved in a lazy dismissive gesture. 'I believe that most things reveal themselves, given enough time, Emily.' His eyes glinted a very direct challenge. 'If you are a professional diver, for example, I should have no doubt whatsoever about it after our visit to Pemba.'

'You want me to prove myself to you?'

His smile was slow in forming and caused her pulse to quicken. 'Perhaps I simply want to share a pleasure with you,' he suggested seductively, stirring a whole hornets's nest of hormones that buzzed their insistent message that he wanted more than an *underwater* pleasure with her.

Emily jumped to her feet, too agitated to remain seated beside him. 'Why are you doing this?' Her hands flapped in wild incomprehension of his motivation as she directly confronted him. 'I'm nobody to you. Just a passing blip on your radar screen. Totally insignificant. Why put your personal time into…?'

He surged to his feet, seeming to tower over her, causing her throat to close up, cutting off her ability to communicate by speech. He took her waving hands and planted them palm flat against his chest, holding them still with his, forcing to feel the heat of his body through the thin cotton of his T-shirt, feel the strong beat of his heart, feel the rise and fall of his breathing, which all made her feel a terribly, terribly intimate connection with this man.

'An accident of fate?' he finished for her, though it wasn't what she'd meant to say.

Emily couldn't remember what she'd meant to say. She found herself staring at his mouth as it shaped more words—soft, silky words that slid into her ears and infiltrated her mind, somehow deactivating her own thought processes.

'Sometimes things happen for a reason—a time, a

place, a meeting which no one can foresee—and it is a huge mistake to deny it any significance. It may not be random factors driving the seemingly accidental collision, but forces of nature which we would do well to ride, Emily, because they were meant to be…meant to gain a result that would not be achieved otherwise.'

What result?

How could anything significant come from this… this mad attraction?

He slid her hands up to his shoulders and even though he released them, did she pluck them away from the tensile strength of the muscles supporting the breadth of those extremely masculine shoulders? No, she didn't! Her hands were stuck in self-indulgent mode, wanting to feel what he'd silently commanded her to feel.

And the mouth she was staring at was coming closer, still shaping words but she no longer heard them. Her heart was thundering in her ears. A wild wantonness gripped her mind and rippled through her entire body, urging an eagerness to experience whatever was about to come her way.

His lips brushed hers, the softest possible contact yet it started an electric tingling that begged for a continuation of the exciting sensation. Emily didn't move away from it. She closed her eyes and concentrated on her response to what was barely a kiss, yet it was sparking some volatile chemistry which was surprising, stunning, mesmerising.

Another brushing.

A slow glide of the tip of his tongue, sensually persuasive in parting her lips, caressing the soft inner tissues.

She felt him move, stepping closer to her, hands sliding around her waist, arms drawing her into a full body contact embrace. One part of her mind warned that she shouldn't be allowing this, but the clamouring need to feel and know the full extent of her response to him overrode any niggling sense of caution.

All her nerve ends seemed to be humming in vibrant anticipation of more and more stimulation. To deny the desire he stirred was impossible and she couldn't find a strong enough reason to fight it. The sheer, dizzying maleness of him called to her female instincts to revel in his strength, exult in his desire for her, savour the potency of the sexual chemistry that obliterated the differences between them—the differences that should keep them apart.

His mouth took possession of hers, no longer seductively intent, but ruthlessly confident of kissing her in whatever way he willed, smashing any inhibitions Emily might have, arousing mind-blowing excitement, inciting highly erotic passion that shot quivers of need through her entire body—a thrilling need, an aching need, a rampant all-consuming need.

She felt his fingers entangling themselves in her hair, tugging her head in whatever direction his mouth wanted to take in kissing her, felt his other hand tracing the curve of her back, reaching the pit of it, applying the pressure to mould the softness of her stomach around the hard thrust of his erection.

His sexual domination of her was so strong, Emily barely registered that she was perilously close to letting the situation reach a point of no return. She forced her mind out of its whirl of sensation long enough to consider what the outcome might be from having sex with this man.

She didn't know.

Couldn't even begin to guess.

And the sense of losing all control of her life was suddenly very frightening.

CHAPTER SEVEN

ZAGEO was so acutely attuned to the flow of mutual sexual desire between them, he instantly felt the sudden jolt of resistance that spelled imminent change. Emily's pliant body started to stiffen, muscles tightening up, shrinking from contact with him. She jerked her head back from his, shock on her face, panic in her eyes. Fight would come next, he realised, if he didn't act to soothe the fear and calm her agitation.

'Enough?' he asked, forcing his mouth into a whimsical little smile, even as his gut twisted painfully at the necessity to reclaim control of the extremely basic need she'd ignited in him.

Her lovely long throat moved convulsively as she struggled to get her thoughts in order and make a sensible reply. The vivid blue circles of her irises were diminished by huge black pupils, yet to return to normal size. She licked her lips, as though desperate to wipe the taste of his from them. But there could be no denial of her complicity in what they'd just shared. He had given her time enough to reject a kiss. She had not rejected it. Nor any other move he'd made on her up until now.

'This is not a good idea!' she pushed out emphatically, then scooped in a deep breath to deliver more oxygen to a brain which was probably feeling even more heated than his.

'On the contrary, the most beneficial existence comes from having one's mind in harmony with one's body. Mentally fighting what comes naturally is the bad idea, Emily,' he asserted.

'Right!' Another deep breath as she collected her wits, belatedly plucking her hands off his shoulders and spreading out her palms in an appeal for understanding. 'Well, just so you know, Zageo, my mind was off in la-la land and my body took a turn all on its own, which doesn't come under the heading of *harmony*!'

'And if your mind had not been in la-la land, what might it have thought?' he swiftly challenged, needing an insight into what drove her behaviour.

She eased her lower body back from his and he dropped his hands from her waist, letting her move to whatever she considered a *safe* distance.

'I'm sure you're well aware of being attractive to the opposite sex,' came the quick chiding, her eyes already deriding any protest on that score.

'You are not without attractions yourself,' he pointed out.

A tide of hot embarrassment swept up her throat and into her cheeks. 'Sometimes it's definitely better to ignore all that stuff because it's a distraction from really important things,' she argued. 'Getting personally involved with you...'

'May well be the best way of resolving the important things you speak about,' he suggested.

'No-o-o...' She shook her head vehemently as her feet backed further away. 'That's not how I conduct my life. I don't go in for using people.'

'There is nothing wrong with fair trading. If each person gives and receives something equitable...if mutual pleasure is reached...'

'I don't believe in poaching on other people's territory!' she hurled at him, fiercely defensive, her eyes flaring an accusation of unfair play.

Zageo frowned, puzzled by the offence she clearly felt. 'You gave me to understand that no man had any current claim on you,' he reminded her. 'Naturally I would have respected...'

Anger erupted. 'What about respecting the relationship you have with Veronique?'

Enlightenment dawned.

Gossip in the women's quarters.

Emily forgot about retreating further and took a belligerent stance, hands planted on her hips as she delivered a blast of scorn. 'Just because she couldn't come with you doesn't give you the right to play fast and loose with any woman who crosses your path.'

'Veronique is in Paris because being there is more attractive to her than being with me,' he drily informed.

'Our relationship has come to an end. So I am completely free, Emily, to be with any woman I choose.'

He could see her mentally floundering over the news that he had no moral obligation to Veronique. Having a strong defensive line demolished at one stroke was not easy to absorb. He wondered if her sense of morality was as sharp as she'd just indicated or had she snatched at Veronique as an excuse to evade the truth of her own desire for him?

But why did she *wish* to evade it?

'*You* choose,' she repeated, picking up the words with the air of grabbing new weapons for a further fight between them. She flung her hands up in the air. 'All the choice is yours. *I'm* not getting any choice in what's going on here. You have me kept in the women's quarters of your family palace, brought out to this boat...'

'I did not imagine your willingness to be in my embrace, Emily,' he cut in with unshakeable authority. 'As to the rest, is it not better to be under my personal protection than to be locked up in a public prison while the local authorities sort out the situation that has evolved from *your* choices?'

'At least it would have been in the process of being sorted,' she threw at him, apparently undeterred by the prospect of being forced into the company of more criminals.

'Believe me, Emily, it is best left to me to do the sorting as I have a personal interest in getting answers. However, since a choice means so much to you, I offer you one. You can come with me to Pemba Island and demonstrate how proficient you are at diving or I can instruct the captain of this vessel to take us directly to Stone Town where you can be taken into custody by local officials and rot in jail while *they* get around to checking your story in their own good time, dependent on how much paperwork is already on their desks.'

'You could just let me go,' she pressed, her whole body taut with exasperation at the limitations he was imposing on her.

'That is not an option,' Zageo answered, ruthlessly intent on keeping her with him.

'Why not?'

'I would not be doing my civic duty to release a potentially dangerous drug-runner into the community.'

'But you don't mind kissing a potentially dangerous drug-runner,' she mocked.

'It was not doing any public harm and I was prepared to take the personal risk,' he mocked straight back.

'You're not risking anything.'

'Do not speak for me, Emily. Speak for yourself. Make your choice. Do you wish me to call the captain and change our destination or do you wish to dive with me at Pemba Island? I might add that your professional referees are out of contact so there is no quick way of checking your story today. That has already been tried.'

Her long lashes dropped but not before he glimpsed a look of helpless confusion in her eyes. She heaved a long ragged sigh. 'Okay,' she finally said in a tone of reluctant resignation. 'I'll need a wetsuit. And I'll want to check the diving equipment.'

'There is a Diving Centre at Fundu Lagoon where we will drop anchor. I have directed that a diving special-ist be on hand to outfit us correctly and guide us to the best viewing places around the reef.'

She nodded distractedly, her gaze flitting around the saloon and fastening on the staircase. 'Does that lead down to a…a powder room?'

'To the staterooms, each of which has an ensuite bathroom.' Aware that she was emitting frantic vibra-tions in a pressing need to escape him, he waved her off on her own. 'Just go down and open the first door you come to, Emily.'

'Thank you.'

She shot him a look of almost anguished relief which Zageo pondered as she hurried to the staircase and dis-appeared below deck.

Was it a desperate call of nature that had to be an-swered or a desperate need to get away by herself to re-assess her position?

Zageo had to concede feeling a considerable amount of confusion himself. He'd kissed and been kissed by many women in his time. None had ever transmitted the sense of being inexperienced, innocent, virginal. It had been strangely fascinating to feel Emily Ross focusing an intense awareness on the touch and taste of his mouth, as though she'd never been kissed before, or it had been so long since she'd had the experience, she'd forgotten what it was like.

Needing to clear his own head of that tantalising im-pression, Zageo left the saloon and moved out to the

rear deck where he could feel the sea breeze in his hair
and the light spray from the boat's wake on his face. It
was good to cool off. He hadn't anticipated the swift fu-
elling of his own desire for her. Giving in to temptation
often proved a disappointment—the experience not living up to the promise. But Emily Ross…the way she'd
responded…it had been *without any artfulness*!

Unless she was an unbelievably good actress, so
steeped in deception it came naturally to her, Zageo
could not see her fitting the frame of a belly-dancer with
patrons on the side. It was far more likely that she had
only known one lover—a young husband who had not
been well skilled in the erotic arts. How else could those
quite electric moments of stillness from her be explained? Stillness followed by a flood of chaotic excitement. It was definitely not a *knowing* response to him,
more instinctive, primal, and so strong it frightened her.

It made her even more attractive.

More desirable.

Zageo decided he would pursue a relationship with
her, regardless of whether it was an appropriate move
for him or not. It had been a long time since he felt so
vibrantly *alive* with a woman.

CHAPTER EIGHT

EMILY clasped her cheeks, willing the heat in them to recede. She'd splashed cold water on her face over and over again, but still it burned, her blood temperature at an all-time high from a chaotic mix of anger and fear.

She was furious with herself for succumbing to the stupid urge to discover what it might be like to be kissed by such a total foreigner, who just happened to be powerfully charged with sex appeal. Now he'd think she *was* a belly-dancing bedhopper. Besides which, it hadn't just been a kiss!

That man had to have the most wickedly exciting tongue in the world, not to mention knowing how to incite such a flood of passionate need, her breasts were still aching from it, her thighs felt like jelly, and the moist heat still lingering at their apex demonstrated an appalling carnal desire for a more intimate connection with him. She'd never felt like this with Brian!

And that thought made her feel even more uncomfortable. Disloyal. Brian had been her mate in every sense. She'd loved him. There'd never been anyone else. She'd never wanted anyone else. The sex they'd had together had seemed natural, good, answering their emotional needs at the time. It felt wrong to look back now and think it hadn't really been a potent force between them, not a nerve-shaking, mind-bending, stomach-twisting, overwhelmingly dominant force!

Though exploring these feelings further with a man who was forcibly holding her *under his protection* went totally against her grain. It was all very well for him to claim he was saving her from a nasty situation by not handing her over to local authorities. She still had no real freedom of movement. No free choices, either. And knowing herself innocent of any wrong-doing, she hated being a victim of circumstances.

It wasn't fair.

Being hugely attracted to a man who was so completely outside her possible relationship zone wasn't fair, either.

So what was she to do now?

Emily doused her face in cold water once again, wiped it dry, took several deep breaths, rolled her shoulders, then concentrated her mind on making a plan.

Until more checks into her background yielded the information which would be consistent with her account of herself, she might as well resign herself to being Zageo's *guest*, so why not pretend to be one? A guest would be sociable. A guest would show pleasurable anticipation in the exploration of the pristine coral reef around Pemba Island. More importantly, a guest's wishes should be taken into consideration and she could certainly challenge Zageo on that point.

Emily mentally girded her *guest* loins and set off to not only face the devil and the deep blue sea, but smile at both of them!

Amazingly, once she had accepted the idea of being taken on a delightful adventure, she really did enjoy herself. Fundu Lagoon looked like a great holiday retreat with its beach lodge and bungalows built from mangrove poles and palm thatch, giving the place a sense of fitting perfectly into the beautiful island environment, while still providing every modern convenience and equipment for all watersports.

The reefs around the island were fantastic; great, plunging walls of coral with all the colourful Indian Ocean marine life swimming and hunting in the wondrous playground. Distractions were plentiful, making Emily less conscious of how Zageo looked in a sleek black wetsuit and less sensitive about how she herself looked in the second-skin garment.

The sexual tension which she'd found so difficult to set aside while still on the boat, dissipated while they were underwater, sharing the pleasure of what they found and watched. It also helped that she had plenty to chat about after the dive, recalling what they'd seen, comparing it to experiences in other places.

They lunched at the beach lodge, sitting on a balcony overlooking the turquoise waters of the bay, hungrily demolishing servings of superb grilled fish, several different tasty salads and a platter of freshly sliced fruit.

Emily was thinking that now was the perfect time for a siesta when Zageo spoke, shattering any sense of safety her *guest* role had given her.

'We could retire to one of the bungalows.'

'What?' Her whole body jerked in shock at the suggestion which immediately conjured up images of sex in the afternoon.

'You looked sleepy,' he observed, watching her through his own lazily lowered lashes.

'Just feeling replete after such a lovely meal,' she quickly trotted out. 'Are we going to dive again this afternoon?'

'Do you want to?'

'I guess the question is…are you satisfied?'

He cocked one eyebrow as though considering which area of satisfaction she was referring to, and the sensual little curl of his lips was very suggestive of much more satisfaction being desired on many levels.

Emily's heart skipped a beat then rushed into beating so fast she suffered a dizzying rush of blood to the head. Words spilled into erratic speech. 'I meant your test. About me being a professional diver. You wanted to know if it was true. That's why we came here, wasn't it? For me to prove I wasn't lying?'

'It was one of the reasons.' The glimmer in his eyes suggested others were of more interest to him. 'I no longer have any doubt that you are comfortable with being underwater. But as to satisfaction…'

He *was* talking sex. She could hear it in the sensual purr of his voice, feel it in the prickling wash of it over her skin. Her stomach contracted with anxiety. It was difficult to fight her own ambivalent feelings. With Zageo feeding the tempting desire to simply give in and tangle intimately with him, she could barely remember why it would be stupid to do it.

Hannah…

Real life…

Shedding complications and getting directly to where she should be…

'Stone Town,' she said emphatically, cutting off whatever else Zageo might have put to her because all her instincts were quivering with the very real possibility of her becoming enmeshed in something she might never escape from. She pasted a brightly appealing smile on her face. 'Could we go to Stone Town now?'

He viewed her quizzically. 'You sister is not there, Emily.'

'You just spoke of satisfaction, Zageo,' she picked up pointedly. 'I've been aiming to get to Stone Town ever since I stepped foot on Jacques Arnault's yacht. That trip carried a load of unexpected stress and last night's swim and trek through the mangrove swamp wasn't a picnic, either. Now here I am, close to where I started out to be, and feeling really frustrated that you're holding me back from it.'

She heaved a feeling sigh and poured what she hoped was an eloquent plea into her eyes. 'If I could just have the satisfaction of going to The Salamander Inn myself…'

His mouth quirked into a sardonic smile. 'You don't believe me, Emily?'

'No more than you believe me, Zageo,' she shot back at him.

He shrugged, his dark eyes dancing with amusement. 'What reason would I have to lie?'

'I think you find me a novelty and since you have the power to play with me, that's what you're doing,' she stated unequivocally.

'A novelty…' He mused over the word, nodding as he spoke his thoughts. 'Something new…or is it something as old as time? Certainly you are not like other women I've known. Which I find intriguing. But *playing* with you…'

His eyes narrowed to glittering slits as though harnessing their penetrating power into intensely probing beams. Emily felt as though she was pinned inside his mental force-field and her heart was under attack. She couldn't think, couldn't move. She had to wait for him to release her from this eerily hypnotic connection.

'This is not a game, Emily,' he said quietly. 'It is a journey where the signposts are not clear, where the turnings are yet to be decided, where the destination is still obscure, yet…I will take it. And you will take it with me.'

Emily was swamped with a sense of inevitability. Her mind thumped with the certainty that whatever he willed was going to happen. She fought to assert her own individuality, to gain at least one foothold on the life she'd had before meeting *him*.

'Well, one signpost is very clear to me and that's Stone Town,' she insisted wildly. 'So why don't we go there right now before our journey takes us somewhere else?'

He laughed, tipping his head back in sheer uninhibited joy in the moment, making her pulse dance in a weird mixture of relief in the normality of laughter and a bubbling happiness at his pleasure in her.

'Are you sure you would not prefer to idle some time away in one of these bungalows first?' he teased, his eyes flirting with the promise of more physical pleasures. 'Indulge ourselves with some rest and relaxation under the cooling whirl of a fan…'

'With the air-conditioning in the saloon, we'll be cooler on the boat,' she quickly argued.

One black eyebrow arched wickedly. 'You do not wish to enjoy some heat?'

'It will still be hot in Zanzibar when we return there.'

'Why choose one satisfaction over another when you could have both?'

'It's as you said, Zageo. I don't have a clear signpost on anything but Stone Town.'

'Then we shall get Stone Town out of the way so we can progress beyond it.'

He rose purposefully to his feet and rounded the table to hold back her chair as she stood up, ready to leave. The zing of triumph at having won this concession from him was short-lived. He took firm possession of her hand for the walk through the beach lodge to the wharf which led back to the boat, and when she wriggled her fingers in a bid for freedom, his interlocked with hers, strengthening the hold.

Still a captive to his will, Emily thought, though he had ceded to her wishes on the destination issue. It was probably an indulgence he could well afford, letting her see the meeting place nominated by her sister. An unimportant sidetrack. The journey he wanted them to take revolved around physical contact and the insidiously distracting heat his hand generated was already beginning to erode her sense of purpose.

What was she going to achieve in Stone Town?

'How old were you when you met Brian, Emily?' Zageo asked as they reached the wharf and began the long stroll to the end of it where an outboard motorboat was waiting to transport them back to the cruiser.

Her mind gratefully seized on the reference to the man who had been the love of her life, hauling out the memory of their first meeting and blowing it up to blot out her current confusion. 'I was fourteen. His parents had just moved up to Cairns from the central coast of New South Wales and he came to my school that year.'

'School? How old was *he*?'

She smiled at the surprise in Zageo's voice. 'Sixteen. Tall and blond and very hunky. All the girls instantly developed crushes on him.'

'Did he play the field before choosing you?'

'No. Brian played it very cool, not linking up with anyone, just chatting around, but every so often I'd catch him watching me and I knew I was the one he liked.'

'The one he *wanted*,' came the sardonic correction.

Emily bridled at Zageo's personal slant on something he knew absolutely nothing about. 'It wasn't just the sex thing,' she flashed at him resentfully. 'Brian *liked* lots of things about me.'

'What's not to like?'

The slightly derisive retort was accompanied by a long sideways head to foot appraisal that shot Emily's temperature sky-high.

'I'm talking about the person I am inside,' she declared fiercely. 'Brian took the time to get to know me. He didn't take one look and decide what I was, as you've done!'

The accusation raised one mocking black eyebrow. 'On the contrary, despite what I'd call damning circumstances, I have continued to look at you, Emily, many times. And I am still gathering evidence as to your character.'

'But you don't care about it. You don't really care,' she hotly countered. 'You would have taken me to bed in one of those bungalows back there if I'd said yes.'

'You are not sixteen anymore, and sexual attraction does not wait upon niceties.'

'But I do have a choice over whether to give into it or not.'

The look he gave her ruthlessly blasted any hope she might be nursing about holding out on that score. Emily shrivelled inside herself, wishing she hadn't challenged him on it since they were on their way back to where a number of staterooms were readily available for intimate privacy. Not that he would stoop to raping her. He would disdain using force with a woman. But if he somehow trapped her into another kiss…

Extremely conscious of her vulnerability to his sexual magnetism, Emily kept her mouth firmly shut and her gaze averted from his as they rode in the outboard motorboat the island wharf to the air-conditioned cruiser. Zageo also remained silent but it was not a restful silence. The sense of purposeful power emanating from him had her nerves jangling and her mind skittering along wildly defensive lines.

At least he had agreed to take her to Stone Town.

Maybe Hannah would arrive any minute now.

Some action was needed to save her from this man and the sooner it came, the better.

CHAPTER NINE

ZAGEO maintained his darkly brooding silence until after they were served coffee in the saloon. Anxious to separate herself from any physical connection to the man who was now dominating her consciousness, Emily had seated herself in an armchair on one side of the low coffee table, but he sat opposite her, granting the relief of distance although there was no relief from the direct focus of his attention.

She listened to the powerful motors taking them back to Zanzibar, mentally urging them to make the trip as fast as possible. She was so wound up in willing the cruiser to speed them over the water, it came as a jolt when Zageo spoke.

'So…tell me the history of your relationship with the man you married,' he tersely invited.

The edge to his voice sounded suspiciously like jealousy, though Emily reasoned he simply didn't like coming off poorly in any comparison. Regardless of his motivation for seeking more knowledge of Brian, she was only too eager to fill this dangerous time talking about her one and only love, recalling shared experiences which had nothing to do with *sex*.

Words tumbled out, describing how from being school sweethearts, she'd followed Brian into a career in the tourist industry which was a huge part of the economy in far north Queensland. They'd worked on dive boats, been proficient in all water sports, crewed on cruise ships that worked the coastline around the top end of Australia, sailed yachts from one place to another for the convenience of owners to walk onto at any given time.

'When did you marry?' Zageo asked somewhat critically, as though the timing of the wedding had some relevance to him.

'When I was twenty-one and Brian twenty-three.'

'A very young man,' he muttered deprecatingly.

'It was right for us!' she insisted.

'Marriage is about acquiring and sharing property, having children. What do you have to show for the five years you had together?'

'Marriage is also about commitment to each other. We had a life of adventure…'

'And that's what you're left with? Adventure? Falling into the company of a man like Jacques Arnault?' Zageo remarked contemptuously. 'Your husband made no provision for your future, no—'

'He didn't know he was going to die!' she cut in, hating the criticism. 'The plan was to wait until we were in our thirties before starting a family. After we'd been everywhere we wanted to go.'

'Did it occur to you there is always another horizon?'

'What do you mean?'

He shrugged. 'Your Brian acted like a grown-up boy, still playing boys' games with the convenience of a committed companion. What if it was not in his psyche to ever settle down and provide a family home?'

'It's people who make a family, not a place,' she argued.

'You would have dragged your children around the world with him?'

'Why not? Experiencing the world is not a bad thing.'

'You have no attachment to your home country? Your home city?'

'Of course I do. It's always good to go back there. It's where my parents live. But Brian was my partner and wherever he went, I would have gone with him.'

Her vehemence on that point apparently gave Zageo pause for some reconsideration. His eyes narrowed and when he eventually made comment, it was laced with cynicism.

'Such devotion is remarkable. From my own experience of women in western society, I gathered that the old biblical attitude of—*whither thou goest, there goest I*—was no longer in play.'

'Then I'd say your experience was askew. I think it's still the natural thing for most women to go with the man they love. Certainly my sister did. When she married Malcolm, there was no question about her going to live with him on his farm in Zimbabwe. She just went.'

'Where exactly in Zimbabwe is this farm?'

'On what's called The High Veld,' Emily answered quickly, relieved to be moving onto a less sensitive subject. 'Malcolm is the third generation working this family owned land and although so much has changed in Zimbabwe he wants to hang onto it.'

Zageo shook his head. 'I doubt he will be able to. The process of reclaiming their country from foreign settlement is a priority with that government.'

Emily heaved a fretful sigh. 'Hannah is worried about the future. Especially for the children.'

'The two daughters.'

'Yes. Jenny is getting to school age and the local school has been closed down. Sally is only three.'

'Will both these young children be accompanying your sister to Zanzibar?'

Emily nodded. 'That was the plan.'

'How was this plan communicated to you?'

'Through a contact address I'd set up on the Internet.' The cloud of confusion that had made any clear path of action impossible suddenly lifted. 'That's what I have to do in Stone Town! Find an Internet Café!'

Zageo frowned at her. 'If you had told me this last night, Emily, there are Internet facilities at the palace. All you had to do—'

'I didn't think of it,' she cut in, throwing her hands out in helpless appeal. 'It was quite a shock being hauled into a place that conjured up thoughts of fairy-tale Arabian Nights, not to mention being confronted and cross-examined by a…a sheikh.'

A tide of heat rushed up her neck, telegraphing her acute embarrassment at being so fixated on him she couldn't even think sensibly, let alone logically. Horribly conscious of the scarlet flags burning in her cheeks, she swivelled in her chair to look out the saloon windows, ostensibly intent on watching their approach to Stone Town. The public harbour was coming into view and her whole body twitched with eagerness to get off the boat.

'Excuse me while I arrange for a car to meet us at the dock,' Zageo said.

'A car?' The pained protest burst from her lips and her gaze swung back to his, pleading for more freedom of movement. 'Couldn't we walk through the town to the inn? I've heard that the markets here are amazing. Besides, unless you know where an Internet café is…'

'There is no need to find a café. I offer you the Internet facilities at The Salamander Inn. We can go directly there so you can check for some communication from your sister.' He paused to underline the point before adding, 'Is it not your top priority?'

'Oh! Right! Thank you,' she rattled out, knowing she was cornered again and telling herself there was no point in fighting his arrangements.

Nevertheless, having to get into the black Mercedes which was waiting for them at the dock made her feel even more like a prisoner, trapped in an enclosed space with her captor and being forcibly taken to the place of his choice. Never mind that she did want to check out The Salamander Inn and she did want to get onto the Internet, doing both of them under Zageo's watchful eyes automatically held constraints she didn't like.

Common sense argued to simply accept being *his guest*—just sit back and enjoy being driven around in a luxury car. Except *he* was sitting beside her, dominating her every thought and feeling, making her intensely aware that he was sharing this journey and was intent on sharing a much longer and more intimate one with her. Apparently she had no choice about that, either.

Emily's nerves were so twitchy about the overwhelming nature of his current presence in her life, she evaded even glancing his way, staring fixedly out the tinted side-window, forcing her brain to register the images she saw in a desperate bid to wipe out the tormenting image of Sheikh Zageo bin Sultan Al Farrahn.

The problem was in its being far too attractive for any peace of mind; ridiculously attractive because he no more belonged in her world than she did in his; dangerously attractive because just the mental image of him was powerful enough to make her forget things she should be remembering.

'Pyramids,' she muttered, focusing fiercely on the market stalls lining both sides of the street on which they were travelling.

'I beg your pardon?'

She heaved a sigh at having broken a silence that probably should have been kept if she was to succeed in keeping Zageo at a distance. 'The stall keepers have stacked their fruit and vegetables into pyramids. I've never seen that before. I guess it must be some Egyptian influence. The people here seem to be such a melting pot of races,' she babbled, not looking at him, keeping her attention fastened *outside* the car. 'So far I've seen a Hindu temple, a mosque minaret and a Christian church spire, all in the space of a few hundred metres.'

'Egyptians, Phoenicians, Persians, Indians, even Chinese visited Zanzibar and settled here, along with the East Africans and traders from South Arabia,' Zageo informed her in a perfectly relaxed manner. 'Then, of course, the Portuguese took control of the island for two centuries. They've all left their influence on the native life and culture, including religion.'

Emily's mind seized on the Portuguese bit. She had thought Zageo looked Spanish but maybe his bloodline came from a neighbouring Latin country. 'Are you part Portuguese?' she asked, curiosity trapping her into looking directly at him.

He smiled, blitzing at least half her mind into registering that and nothing else, making her heart flip into a faster beat, causing her stomach to contract as though she had received a body-blow.

'My great-grandfather on my mother's side was Portuguese,' he finally replied, having done maximum damage with his smile. 'My great-grandmother was half-Indian, half-British. It makes for an interesting mix of races, does it not?'

'Your father is an Arab?' The half of her mind that was still working insisted that a sheikh couldn't get to be a sheikh without having a father who was pure Arab.

He nodded. 'Mostly. His grandmother was French. We are a very international family.'

'A very *wealthy* international family,' Emily said, deciding sheikhdom probably had more to do with who owned the oil wells.

He shrugged. 'Wealth that has benefited our people. And we keep investing to consolidate the wealth we have, ensuring that the future will have no backward steps. There is nothing wrong with wealth, Emily.'

'I didn't say there was. It just happens to form a huge gap between your circumstances and mine. And while you take all this for granted—' she waved wildly at their uniformed chauffeur and the plush interior of the Mercedes '—I hate not being able to pay my own way.' A passionate need for independence from him fired up other resentments. 'I hate not having my own money, my own credit card, my own…'

'Freedom to do whatever you want?'

'Yes!'

'Then why not feel free to be with me, Emily? It *is* what you want,' he claimed in that insidiously silky voice that slid straight under her skin and made all her nerve ends tingle.

His eyes mocked any attempt at denial. She struggled to come up with one that sounded sensible enough to refute his certainty. 'What we want is not always right for us, Zageo. Even you, with all the freedom your wealth gives you, must have been hit with that truth somewhere down the line.'

'Ah, but not at least to try it…to satisfy the wanting…how is one to make an informed judgment without embracing the experience?'

'I don't have to put my hand in a fire to know it will get burnt,' she slung at him and tore her gaze from the sizzling desire in his.

'You prefer to stay cold than hold out your hand to it, Emily? What of the warmth it promises? The sense of physical well-being, the pleasure…'

Her stomach contracted at the thought of the sexual pleasure he might give her. Panicked by how much she did want to try it, Emily seized the first distraction her gaze hit as the Mercedes started through a narrow alley.

'The doors…' Even on these poorer houses in the old part of Stone Town, they were elaborately carved and studded with very nasty looking iron or brass protrusions. 'Why are they made to look so intimidating?'

'The studs were designed to stop elephants from barging inside.'

'Elephants!' Emily was startled into looking incredulously at him. 'Are you telling me there are elephants rampaging around Zanzibar, even in the town?'

'No.' He grinned at having drawn her interest again. 'There have never been elephants on Zanzibar. The doors were originally made by Indian craftsmen who brought the design from their home country centuries ago. The style of them apparently appealed and has endured to the present day.'

She frowned, not liking them despite their elaborate craftsmanship. 'They give the sense of a heavily guarded fortress.'

'Very popular with tourists,' he drily informed her. 'They form one of Zanzibar's main exports.'

'What about spice? Isn't this island famous for its spice trade?'

'Unfortunately Zanzibar no longer has the monopoly on growing and selling cloves. Indonesia, Brazil, even China are now major producers. The island still has its plantations, of course, but they are not the economic force they once were.'

'That's rather sad, losing what made it unique,' Emily commented.

'The golden years of Zanzibar were not only based on the trade in cloves, but also in ivory and slaves, neither of which you would wish to revive,' he said, his eyes boring intently into hers. 'The past is the past, Emily. One has to move on.'

The words thudded into her heart—words she had recited to herself many times since being widowed. Zageo was making a pointedly personal message of them. But any journey with him would have to reach a dead end, forcing her *to move on* again. On the other hand, she certainly didn't regret her marriage. She might not regret a sexual dalliance with this sheikh, either.

She stared down at her hands which were tightly clasped in her lap, the fingers of her right hand automatically dragging at the ringless state of her left. What did she fear? The world famous model, Veronique, had taken Zageo as a lover. Why couldn't she? It wasn't a betrayal of her love for Brian. It was just something else. A different life experience.

Except she couldn't forget how out of control she'd been when he'd kissed her. To hand him that kind of power required an enormous amount of trust, and how could she give that trust to a man she hadn't even met before yesterday? To blithely act upon sheer attraction did not feel right, regardless of how strong the attraction was and no matter what Zageo argued.

She sucked in a deep breath, lifted her gaze and once more focused on the outside world. 'How much further is it to The Salamander Inn?' she asked, looking out at a veritable jumble of buildings, many of which were crumbling from sheer age.

'Not far. Perhaps another five minutes.'

'Why build an expensive hotel in this location?'

'It's the most historic part of Stone Town and tourists like local colour. They come to Zanzibar because of its exotic past and because its very name conjures up a romantic sense of the east, just like Mandalay and Kathmandu.' He smiled, his eyes wickedly teasing as he added, 'Sultans and slaves and spice…it's a potent combination.'

'For attracting the tourist dollar.'

'Yes,' he conceded, amused by her sidestep away from anything personal. 'And thereby boosting the economy of the island, generating more employment.'

'So this hotel is a benevolent enterprise on your part?' she half-mocked, wanting to get under *his* skin.

'I am, by nature, benevolent, Emily. Have I not kept you out of the local lock-up, giving you the benefit of the doubt, sympathising with your concern over your sister's whereabouts, offering you a free means of communication with her?' His eyes simmered with provocative promises as he purred, 'I wish you only what is good. And what will be good.'

It was futile trying to get the better of him. He was the kind of man who'd always be on top of any game he cared to play.

The car pulled up outside *his* hotel.

No doubt he could claim any suite he liked for his personal use.

Emily desperately tried telling herself she was only here to use a computer, but a wild sense of walking into the lion's den gripped her as Zageo escorted her into the foyer.

And came to a dead halt.

Right in front of them, impatiently directing a bellboy on how to handle her luggage, was the stunningly beautiful and uniquely glamorous French-Moroccan model—Veronique!

CHAPTER TEN

EMILY could not help staring at the woman; the long glossy mane of black hair, flawless milk-coffee coloured skin, exotically tilted and thickly lashed chocolate-velvet eyes, a perfectly straight aristocratic nose, full pouty lips, and a cleanly sculptured chin that lifted haughtily at the sight of Zageo holding another woman's arm.

As well it might, Emily thought, suddenly feeling like a very common overcurvy peasant in her cotton skirt, casual little top, and very plain walking sandals. Apart from which, her own long hair was not exactly beautifully groomed after an underwater swim and her make-up was nonexistent.

Veronique's entire appearance was superbly put together. Her model-thin figure was wrapped in a fabulously elegant and sexy dark brown and cream polka-dot silk dress which screamed designer wear, and the high-heeled strappy sandals on her feet were so brilliantly stylish, anyone with a shoe fetish would have lusted for them. Her magnificent facial structure was highlighted with subtly toning make-up, her nails varnished a pearly cream, and just looking at the glossy black hair made Emily's feel like rats' tails.

'Veronique...this is a surprise,' Zageo said in his silky dangerous voice. Clearly it was not a surprise that pleased him.

'Your call last night felt like a call to arms, *cheri*,' she lilted, her tone warmly inviting him to take pleasure in her presence.

He'd called her last night?

Emily shot him a sharply inquiring look. Had he lied about having ended his relationship with Veronique?

'Then you were not listening to me,' he stated coldly.

Anger flashed from the supermodel's gorgeous dark eyes, flicked to Emily, then back to Zageo, having gathered a fierce determination to fight. 'You were mistaken in thinking I didn't want to be with you. I came to correct that misunderstanding.'

They were drawing attention from other people in the foyer. 'A private conversation should remain private,' Zageo cautioned sternly, signalling to the man behind the reception desk.

Instant action. A key was grabbed. The man ushered them to a door on the other side of the foyer. It opened to what was obviously the manager's domain, an office combined with a sitting area for conversations with guests.

Veronique stalked ahead, using the arrogant catwalk style of motion that automatically drew everyone's gaze after her. She was a star, intent on playing the star to the hilt, perhaps reminding Zageo of *who* she was, the kind of status she commanded.

'I can wait out here,' Emily suggested, pulling back from being witness to a lovers' quarrel and grasping what felt like the opportune moment to slip away entirely, extracting herself from a very sticky situation.

'*Oui,*' Veronique snapped over her shoulder.

'*Non!*' came Zageo's emphatic retort, forcibly steering Emily inside. 'Miss Ross is my guest and I will not do her the discourtesy of abandoning her for you, Veronique.'

It wasn't a discourtesy, Emily thought wildly, but again she was given no choice. *His* decision was punctuated by the door closing behind them.

Veronique wheeled to face them, jealous fury spitting from her eyes. 'You prefer *this woman* to me?'

On the surface of it, the preference seemed utter madness even to Emily's mind, so she didn't take offence, although a strong streak of female pride whispered that for a relationship to last—as her own with Brian had—there had to be more than surface stuff driving it. Two years, she reflected, was the usual timeframe for passion to wear thin.

Zageo ignored the question, blandly inquiring, 'How did you get from Paris to Zanzibar so quickly?'

The mane of hair was expertly tossed. 'You are not the only man I know who owns a private jet.'

If it was an attempt to make him jealous, it was a miserable failure, evoking only a curt, disdainful reply. '*Bien!* Then you'll have no problem with flying back tomorrow.'

Veronique scissored her hands in exasperated dismissal. 'This is absurd!'

'Yes, it is,' he agreed. 'I informed you of my position in no uncertain terms. Your coming will not change it.'

'But you misread my choice not to accompany you, Zageo.' She gestured an eloquent appeal. 'I wanted you to miss me. I wanted you to realise how good we are together. I wanted you to think about marrying me.'

'What?' Sharp incredulity in his voice. 'There was never any suggestion of a marriage being possible between us,' he thundered, hands lifting in such angry exasperation, Emily was able to slide out of his hold, quickly stepping over to the sofa against the wall, out of the firing line between the two antagonists.

'That doesn't mean it couldn't be,' Veronique argued.

'At no time did I lead you to think it. What we had was an arrangement, Veronique, an arrangement that suited both of us. You know it was so. Perhaps it does not suit you to have it ended, but I assure you, this attempt to push it further is futile.'

'Because of *her*?' A contemptuous wave and a venomous look were directed at Emily.

It was a good question, Emily thought, curious to know the answer herself since the ruction between Veronique and the sheikh had only occurred last night. She tore her gaze from the glittering double fangs of Veronique's eyes to look at Zageo, and was instantly shafted by two laser beams burning into her brain.

'Because its time was over,' he answered, speaking directly to Emily, his eyes hotly impressing the point.

'I had decided that before Miss Ross walked into my life.'

Curiously enough, it was a relief to hear this. Being the source of breaking up a long-standing relationship would not have sat easily with her, although she had done absolutely nothing to effect such an outcome.

'But you've let her sweeten the decision, haven't you?' came the furious accusation. '*She* is why you won't take me back. So what has *she* got that I have not, Zageo? What does *she* give you that I did not?'

Emily's cheeks burned.

Nothing, she thought, hating being dragged into what was definitely not her business.

But Zageo was still looking at her and the heat in his eyes simmered with needs and desires that were focused on her, making her heart catapult around her chest, flipping her stomach, shooting her mind into chaos as it tried to deal with responses that were scattering her wits.

'How does one compare a hothouse carnation to a wild water-lily?' he rolled out in a softer tone that somehow caused goose-bumps to erupt all over Emily's skin. 'It is foolish to try to measure the differences. Each has its own unique appeal.'

A wild water-lily?

Emily wasn't used to hearing such flowery language from a man, though her heart was thumping its own wanton appreciation of it even as she tried to force her mind into reasoning that this was definitely Arabian Nights stuff, totally surreal, and she *must not* let herself get caught up in it.

Zageo's riveting gaze finally released hers, turning back to the woman who had so recently been his intimate companion. 'Please...do not lower yourself with these indignities,' he urged, appealing for a cessation of personal hostilities. 'Our time together is over. Yesterday is yesterday, Veronique. Tomorrow is tomorrow.'

'You see how it is?' she shot at Emily, highly incensed by the comparison she had forced by her own angry diatribe. 'No doubt you have been as swept away by him as I was. But it will only last for as long as the arrangement suits his convenience. He might not look like an Arab but he is one at heart.'

'An Arab whose generosity is being severely tested.' The warning was delivered with a hard look of ruthless intent. 'Do you want to continue this spiteful scene or do you want the Paris apartment?'

Veronique delivered another expert toss of her hair as she disdainfully returned her attention to him. 'I was doing Miss Ross a kindness, Zageo, informing her of the bottom line so she's not completely blinded by your beauty.'

'You are intent on poisoning something you do not understand,' he whipped at her. 'Make your decision now, Veronique.'

The threat whirling in the air forced the supermodel to take stock. She was not winning. And regardless of her star status, Sheikh Zageo bin Sultan Al Farrahn was by far the more influential person here in Zanzibar, with the power to make her visit very unpleasant. The bottom line was she hadn't been welcomed and had worn out his patience with making herself even less welcome.

She inhaled a deep breath, calming herself, pulling a mask of pride over her more volatile emotions. 'I could not bring myself to believe what you said last night,' she offered in a more considered appeal. 'I came to mend fences.'

It made no difference. He simply replied, 'I'm sorry you put yourself to that trouble.'

She tried a rueful sigh. Her hands fluttered an apologetic appeal. 'Okay, I took our relationship for granted. I won't do it again.'

He gave no sign of softening, implacably stating, 'If you had truly valued it, you would have made different decisions.'

'I do have modelling assignments lined up throughout the next three months,' she quickly excused.

'I offered you my private jet to get to them.'

He was giving her no room to manoeuvre, not so much as a millimetre. Veronique had no choice but to accept their affair was over. Emily felt a stab of sympathy for her, having been subjected to no choice herself at this man's hands.

'I will take the apartment, *cheri*,' came the final decision, bitter irony lacing her voice as she added, 'I've grown fond of it.'

He nodded. 'Consider it settled. I shall inform the manager here that you are my guest at the inn until you return to Paris. Tomorrow?'

'*Oui*. Tomorrow I shall put all this behind me.'

'*Bien!*' Zageo strode to the desk, proceeding to call the manager on the in-house telephone system.

Veronique subjected Emily to a glare that seethed

with malevolence, belying the resigned acceptance of the kiss-off apartment and suggesting that if the model could do her supposed replacement an injury on the sly, she would not hesitate to uproot the wild water-lily and take huge satisfaction in tearing it to pieces.

Emily was glad the supermodel would be flying away from Zanzibar tomorrow. She had enough trouble on her hands without having to deal with the fury of a scorned woman. Besides, the fault behind this situation did not lie at her door. Zageo had made that very clear. On the other hand, it would have been much clearer if he hadn't made the break-up call last night.

The manager of the inn knocked and entered the tension-packed room, warily closing the door behind him as he awaited more instructions from the sheikh. Zageo waved to the computer on the desk, requesting the password for Internet access to be written down for his use. This jolted Emily into remembering the purpose which had brought them here. It amazed her that Zageo had not been distracted from it. She certainly had.

The manager quickly complied. He was then asked to escort Veronique to a guest suite and ensure her needs were met. The main current of tension in the room swept out with the supermodel's exit, leaving Emily feeling like a very limp water-lily, trapped into waiting for the strong flow that would inevitably come from Zageo.

He beckoned her to the desk where he was already tapping away on the computer keyboard. Emily took a deep breath and pushed her feet forward, trying desperately to put the thought of contact with her sister in a more important slot than contact with Zageo. Hannah was her reason for being here. She could not let a totally unsuitable attraction to this man cloud that issue.

She took the chair he invited her to take in front of the computer. Her fingers automatically performed the functions necessary to access her e-mail. The tightness in her chest eased slightly as Zageo moved away, choosing not to intrude on her private correspondence.

Whether this meant he did finally believe her story or whether it was simply ingrained courtesy on his part, Emily didn't know and didn't let it concern her. A message from Hannah was on the screen. It was dated the same day Emily had woken up from a drugged sleep on Jacques's yacht to find he didn't have a wife onboard and she was the only member of his crew and they were already at sea.

Emily—I hope this reaches you before you set sail for Zanzibar. I won't make it there. Can't. We didn't get very far before running into an army patrol and it didn't matter what I pleaded, the men confiscated everything and called Malcolm to come and get me and the girls. We're all under house arrest now. Not allowed to leave the farm to go anywhere. I'm half expecting the phone lines to be cut, as well, so if you don't receive another message from me, they will have stopped all outside communication.

I'm scared, Emily. I've never been so scared. I don't mind standing by Malcolm but I wish I'd managed to get the girls out. You could have taken them home

to Mum and Dad in Australia. There is so much unrest in this country and I just don't know if these
troubles will pass or get worse.

Anyhow, I'm sorry we won't be meeting up. And
please don't think you can come here and do something because you can't. So stay away. It won't help.
Understand? I'll let you know what's happening if I
can. Lots of love, Emily. I couldn't have had a better
little sister. Bye for now. Hannah.

Emily didn't realise she'd stopped breathing as she
took in the words on the screen. Shock and fear chased
around her mind. This was the last message from her sister. The last one. It was a week old. Seven days of silence.

'Emily? Is something wrong?'

She looked up to find Zageo watching her, his brow
lowered in concern. The trapped air in her lungs
whooshed out as she mentally grappled with Hannah's
situation. Her mouth was too dry to speak. She had to
work some moisture into it.

'Hannah is a prisoner in her own home,' she finally
managed to blurt out, silently but savagely mocking
herself for railing against being Zageo's prisoner. That
was a joke compared to what her sister was going
through—her sister and nieces and brother-in-law.

'They might be dead now, for all I know,' she muttered despairingly.

'Dead?'

'Read it for yourself!' she hurled at him as she

erupted from the chair, driven by a frantic energy to pace around the room, to find some action that might help Hannah. 'You wanted proof of my story?' Her arm swept out in a derisive dismissal of his disbelief. 'There it is on the screen!'

He moved over to the desk, accepting the invitation to inform himself.

Emily kept pacing, her mind travelling in wild circles around the pivotal point of somehow getting Hannah and her family to safety, right out of Zimbabwe if possible. She did not have the power or the resources to achieve such an outcome herself, but what of the Australian Embassy? Would someone there help or would diplomatic channels choke any direct action?

She needed someone strong who could act...would act...

'This is not good news,' Zageo muttered.

Understatement of the year, Emily thought caustically, but the comment drew her attention to the man who arranged his world precisely how he wanted it, wielding power over her without regard to any authority but his own. She stopped pacing and gave him a long hard look, seeing what had previously been a very negative aspect of him as something that could become a marvellous positive!

Maybe...just maybe...Sheikh Zageo bin Sultan Al Farrahn could achieve what she couldn't.

Veronique had said he owned a private jet. Almost certainly a helicopter, too, Emily reasoned. With pilots on standby to fly them.

Building his hotel chain throughout Africa must have given him powerful political contacts in the countries where he'd invested big money. Apart from which, his enormous wealth could probably bribe a way to anywhere. And out of anywhere.

Zageo wanted her in bed with him.

Emily had no doubt about that.

He'd also once wanted Veronique in bed with him—and for the satisfaction of that desire he'd been prepared to give away what was surely a multimillion dollar apartment in Paris.

A hysterical little laugh bubbled across Emily's brain. Jacques had tried to trade her to the sheikh in return for his freedom, and here she was, planning to trade herself to him for her sister's freedom.

Which would turn her into the whore he'd first thought her.

Emily decided she didn't care.

She'd do anything to secure the safety of Hannah and her family.

She'd try the trade.

CHAPTER ELEVEN

ZAGEO parted from Emily as soon as they returned to the palace. He wanted to alleviate her distress, if possible, by finding out if the Coleman family had survived this past week. He had instructed Abdul to pursue inquiries in Zimbabwe, so some useful information might have already been acquired.

Zageo no longer had any doubt that Emily had spoken the truth all along, and everything he'd learnt about her made her a more fascinating and desirable woman, certainly not one he'd want to dismiss from his life at this early juncture.

They would meet for dinner, he'd told her, hoping to give her news that would clear the worry from her eyes. He wanted her to see that having his favour was good. He wanted her to look at him with the same deep and compulsive desire he felt for her. And he wanted her to give into it.

Abdul was in his office, as usual, more at home with his communications centre than anywhere else. He was amazingly efficient at keeping track of all Zageo's business and personal interests. If he didn't have the information required at his fingertips, it was relentlessly pursued until it was acquired.

'The Coleman family…' Zageo prompted once the appropriate courtesies had been exchanged.

Abdul leaned back in the chair behind his desk, steepling his hands over his chest in a prayerful manner, indicating that he'd decided this issue was very much in the diplomatic arena. 'The M written in the register at The Salamander Inn stands for Malcolm. His wife's name is Hannah. They have two young daughters—'

'Yes, yes, I know this,' Zageo cut in, quickly recounting the e-mail he'd read at the inn to bring Abdul up-to-date on where the situation stood to his knowledge. 'The critical question is…are they still alive?'

'As of today, yes,' Abdul answered, much to Zageo's relief.

He could not have expected Emily to be receptive to him if she was in a state of grief over the deaths of people he had never met. She would want to go home to her parents in Australia, and in all decency, he would have had to let her go.

'However…' Abdul went on ominously, 'I would call their position perilous. Malcolm Coleman has been too active in protesting the policies of the current regime. His name is on a list of public antagonists who should be silenced.'

'Is the danger immediate?'

'If you are concerned for their safety, I think there is time to manoeuvre, should you wish to do so.'

'I wish it,' Zageo answered emphatically.

There was a long pause while Abdul interpreted his sheikh's reply. 'Do I understand that Miss Ross will be staying with us beyond Monday, Your Excellency?'

'Given that her sister's family can be rescued, yes, I have decided Miss Ross's companionship will add immeasurably to my pleasure in this trip around our African properties.'

'Ah!' Abdul nodded a few times and heaved a sigh before bringing himself to address the problem posed by Emily's family. 'Quick action will be needed. The pressure is on for Malcolm Coleman to give up his farm and leave the country but he is persisting in resisting it. Defying it.'

'Intent on fighting for what he considers his,' Zageo interpreted.

Abdul spread his hands in an equitable gesture. 'It is a large and very profitable farm that has been in his family for three generations. It is only natural for a man to wish to hold onto his home.'

'There will be no home with himself and his family dead,' Zageo commented grimly. 'He must be persuaded to accept that reality.'

'Precisely. Even so, to walk away with no recompense…'

'See if we can buy his farm. It will allow him to leave with his pride intact, giving him the financial stake he might need to start over in another country and still be successful in the eyes of his wife and children.'

'You want to acquire property in Zimbabwe?' Abdul queried somewhat incredulously.

'Very briefly. Perhaps it can be used as barter for the Colemans's safe passage out of the country. Find a recipient in the regime who understands favours, Abdul. The idea of acquiring a profitable farm without paying a cent might appeal. Delivery on delivery.'

'Ah! A diplomatic resolution.'

'Behind doors.'

'Of course, Your Excellency.'

Zageo relaxed, reasonably confident that his plan could be effected. Tonight he would tell Emily that not only was her sister's family still amongst the living, he had also set in motion the steps to extract them from their dangerous situation.

She would want to stay with him then.

She would want to know firsthand the outcome of his rescue plan.

It might not be bending to his will but…Zageo decided that winning her favour was the best way to gaining her submission. In fact, it would give him much satisfaction to arrange a meeting between Emily and her sister. This could not be held in Stone Town. He had to move on. Nevertheless, he would give Emily Ross what she had come for.

Delivery…for delivery.

CHAPTER TWELVE

BACK in the women's quarters of the palace, Emily wasted no time in organizing what she wanted done. Zageo had said they would meet for dinner. With the image of Veronique still vividly in her mind, the presentation of herself with the view of becoming his mistress definitely required perfect grooming, artful make-up and sexy clothes. Since her own luggage contained nothing that could be described as seductively tempting…

'The trunk of belly-dancing costumes…do you still have it, Heba?'

'Yes. Will I have it brought to you?' she offered obligingly.

Emily nodded. 'Let's see if we can find something really erotic in it.'

That was certainly what Zageo had expected of her last night so let him have it tonight, Emily reasoned, deciding that an in-your-face statement of her intention was more telling than a thousand words.

She chose a hot-pink costume with beaded bands in black and silver. The bra was designed to show optimum cleavage. The skirt was slinky, clinging to hips, bottom and upper thighs where it was slit for freedom of leg movement. The edges of the slits were beaded as well, making them very eye-catching.

'It is a bold costume,' Heba commented somewhat critically.

'I have to be bold tonight,' Emily muttered, beyond caring what the women who were attending to her needs thought.

Only one thing was important.

Getting the sheikh *to do something* about Hannah and her family.

She had her mind steeled to deliver her part of the trade, yet when the summons to dinner came, a nervous quivering attacked her entire body. What she was setting out to do wasn't *her*. Yet she had to pull it off. If something terrible happened to Hannah and she hadn't done anything to help, she would never forgive herself.

Besides, it wasn't as though she was unattracted to Zageo. It could well be a fantastic experience, having sex with him. She couldn't imagine he'd want a long relationship with her. The stunningly beautiful and glamorous Veronique, who shared his jet set class, had only held his interest for two years. Emily figured on only being a brief novelty, possibly lasting for the duration of his tour of the Al Farrahn hotels. Once he returned to his normal social life, she'd be a fish out of water—one he would undoubtedly release.

So, what were a few months out of her own life compared to the lives of Hannah and her family? She had no commitments. There was nothing to stop her from offering herself as a bed companion to a man who might or might not take up some time which was of no particular use to her anyway.

The costume trunk had also yielded a black silk cloak which Emily employed to cover herself while being escorted to the sheikh's private apartment. She was ushered into the same opulent sitting room where Zageo had commanded her presence last night. He was back in his sheikh clothes, the long white tunic and richly embroidered over-robe in purple and gold, making her feel even more nervous about his foreignness.

However, she was not about to baulk at doing what she had to do. The moment the door closed behind the men on escort duty, she whipped off the cloak, determined on getting straight to business. However, instead of exciting speculative interest in Zageo, her appearance in the provocative belly-dancing costume evoked an angry frown.

'What is this?' he demanded, the harsh tone making her heart skitter in apprehension. His eyes locked onto hers with piercing intensity. 'You claimed the costumes did not belong to you.'

'They don't! I just thought…' She swallowed hard, fighting to prevent her throat from seizing up. 'I thought it would please you to see me dressed like this.'

'Please me…' He spoke the words as though this was a strange concept to be examined for what it meant. His gaze narrowed, then skated down over the bared curves of her body, seemingly suspicious of their sexual promise.

Emily's heart was thundering in her ears, making it difficult to think over its chaotic drumming. She told herself she should be moving forward, swaying her hips like a belly-dancer, showing herself willing to invite him to touch, to kiss, to take whatever gave him pleasure. A sexy woman would slide her arms around his neck, press her body to his, use her eyes flirtatiously. It was stupid, stupid, stupid to stand rooted to the spot, barely able to breathe let alone shift her feet.

'Why would you suddenly set out to please me, Emily?'

She trembled. His voice was laced with *dis*pleasure. She was hit with such deep confusion she didn't know what to do or say. Her hands lifted in helpless appeal, needing to reach out to him yet frightened now of being rebuffed, spurned, sent away.

'For the past twenty-four hours you have been determined on putting distance between us,' he mockingly reminded her.

The heat of shame scorched her cheeks. What she planned was the act of a whore. There was no denying it. The trade was too blatant. She hadn't thought it would matter to him as long as she gave him the satisfaction of having what he wanted. But as he strolled towards her, the sardonic little smile curling his mouth made her feel she had lost whatever respect she had won with him.

'Now what could have inspired this change of attitude?' he queried, his brilliant dark eyes deriding any

attempt at evasion. 'Was it the proof that my relationship with Veronique is over?'

'That…that does help,' she choked out, realising that
the break-up arrangement had contributed a great deal
to her thinking. Though it didn't excuse it. No, it was
desperation driving this deal and Emily was suddenly
afraid Zageo would find that offensive.

He moved around behind her, lifting her long hair back
over her shoulder to purr in her ear, 'So…you are now
ready to take this journey with me. You *want* to take it.
You *want* to feel my touch on your skin.' He ran soft fingertips down the curve of her spine. 'You *want* me to taste
all of you.' He trailed his mouth down her throat, pressing hot sensual kisses. 'Let me hear you say that, Emily.'

Her hands had fallen to her sides. They were clenching and unclenching as waves of tension rolled through
her. She sucked in a quick breath and started pushing
out the necessary words. 'You can do…you can do…
whatever you like with me—'

'No, no, that sounds far too passive,' he cut in before
she could complete spelling out the deal. 'Though now
that you have given me permission…'

He unclipped the bra and slid the straps off her shoulders. As the beaded garment started to fall from her
breasts, the sheer shock of being so swiftly bared, jolted
Emily into defensive action. Her hands whipped up,
catching the cups and plastering them back into place.

'Did you mean to tease me, Emily? Have I spoilt
your game?' he asked in the silky dangerous tone that
shot fearful quivers through her heart. Even as he spoke,

his hands glided up from around her waist and covered her own, his fingers extending further than the bra cups to fan the upper swell of her breasts. 'No matter,' he assured her. 'I'm on fire for you anyway.'

'Stop,' she finally found voice enough to gasp out. 'Please...stop.'

'This does not please you?'

'No...yes...no...I mean...'

'What do you mean, Emily?'

His voice was now like a sharp-edged knife, slicing into her. Tears of confusion welled into her eyes. This scene was going—had gone—all wrong. She simply wasn't sophisticated enough to bring off the subtle sexual bartering that went on in his world.

'I'll take this journey with you if you'll help my sister,' she blurted out in wild desperation.

'And you will withhold yourself if I do not agree? You will push me away, refasten your bra, and scorn my desire for you?' The whiplike edge to his voice gathered more intensity as he added, 'Not to mention your desire for me.'

It sounded horrible. Everything decent in Emily recoiled from using sex as a bargaining tool. It eliminated any good feelings that might have eventuated from being intimate with this man. She shook her head in hopeless shame and humiliation.

'I'm sorry...sorry...I didn't know what else to do.'

'Little fool,' he growled. 'Playing a game that is not in your nature.'

His hands dropped to her waist and spun her around

to face him. He cupped her face, his fingers gently sweeping the trickle of tears from her cheeks. The tender gesture was in perverse contrast to the glittering anger in his eyes.

'Did you imagine I was not aware of your distress over your sister and her family?'

'They are nothing to you,' she choked out in a ragged plea for his understanding.

'*You* are not nothing to me, Emily.'

'I was counting on that,' she confessed.

'Yet you did not credit me with caring enough to do whatever I could to ease your distress?'

His words seethed with deep offence. Emily frantically seized on what she thought were mitigating circumstances. 'I don't know you,' she pleaded. 'All I know is you've kept me here to…to play with me.'

'Play with you,' he repeated in a scoffing tone that stirred Emily's blood, triggering a flood of volatile feelings that instantly threatened to burst out of control.

She wrenched her head out of his hold, stepping back to let fly at him with her own tirade of deep offence. 'You've had me jumping through hoops ever since I was forced into your company. First, you play the grand inquisitor, deliberately choosing not to believe a word I said. After which, you left me no alternative but to dress up as a belly-dancer for you…'

'Which you have no problem doing tonight,' he sliced at her.

'Because you made it your game, Zageo,' she asserted vehemently. 'I was only trying to fit into it.'

'Fine! Then fit!'

Before Emily could even draw breath to utter another word, he swooped on her, swept her off her feet, and in a dizzying whirl of movement, carried her through the sitting room and beyond it to another lamp-lit room where he tipped her onto a pile of exotic silk and satin cushions spread across a massive, four-poster bed. Her arms flew out to stop herself from rolling. The bra became dislodged again and Zageo whipped it off, leaving her naked from head to hips.

'No backtracking now, Emily,' he fired at her. 'We have a deal. In return for my services in rescuing your family, you've agreed to let me do whatever I like with you. Right?'

The violence of his feelings made her pulse beat faster, increasing the wild agitation racing through her. 'How do I know you'll help?' she cried, alarmed by the thought he would just do what he wanted anyway.

'Because I am a man of honour who always delivers on a deal,' he stated savagely.

He was shedding his robe, hurling it away. She scrambled to sit up, acutely aware of her full breasts swinging as she did so and realising her nipples had tightened in some instinctive response to the raking heat in his eyes.

'Are you a woman of your word, Emily?' he challenged, discarding his tunic and underpants with swift and arrogant carelessness while fiercely warning her, 'Leave that bed and you leave with nothing from me.'

She sat utterly still, staring at him, not because of the

threat but because he looked so stunningly magnificent. She had seen many almost naked men, especially guys who excelled in water sports, and they invariably had well-honed physiques—broad shoulders, flat stomachs, lean hips, powerfully muscled thighs. Zageo had all that but somehow his body was far more pleasingly proportioned.

It emanated an aura of indomitable male strength without the overdelineated musculature that came from excessive weight lifting at a gym. And his dark olive skin gleamed with a taut smoothness that incited an almost compelling desire to touch. Emily was not an expert on judging men's sexual equipment, but the sight of Zageo's certainly set up flutters of nervous excitement.

He stepped forward, his hands virtually spanning her waist as he lifted her into standing on the bed. 'Unfasten the skirt,' he commanded. 'Show me how willing you are to do whatever I want.'

Impossible to back down now, she told herself. The challenge blazing from his eyes seared her own sense of honour, forcing her past the point of no return. He'd taken the deal. She had to deliver.

As she reached around to the zipper at the pit of her back, he released her waist and lifted his hands to her naked breasts, rotating his palms over the taut peaks, making them acutely sensitive to his touch, driving arcs of piercing pleasure from her nipples to below her belly and causing Emily to gasp at the intensity of the feeling.

The unfastened skirt slithered down to pool around her feet. Her gasp turned to a moan of yearning as the almost torturous caress of her breasts ceased. Her hands curled urgently around Zageo's shoulders, unconsciously kneading them in a blind desire for continuity. He bent his head, his mouth swiftly ministering the sweetest balm to her need, licking and sucking as he hooked his thumbs into her panties and drew this last piece of clothing down her legs.

She stepped out of the restricting garment without a moment's hesitation, her previous inhibitions erased by the excitement coursing through her. He stroked her inner thighs, making them quiver, making her stomach contract in wild anticipation as he moved a hand into the slickened folds of her sex, fingers sliding over the moist heat that had been building and building from the erotic ministration of his mouth on her breasts.

Every one of her internal muscles tensed, waiting for a more intimately knowing touch, wanting it, craving it. Slowly his fingers slid inside, moving as deeply as they could, undoubtedly feeling the pulsing welcome her body gave instinctively. They withdrew to circle the entrance tantalisingly while his thumb found and caressed her clitoris, increasing an erotic pressure on it as his fingers pushed in again. And again. And again.

Emily's whole body bent like a bow, driven to an exquisite tension, blinding pleasure consuming every cell and needing to burst into some further place, reaching for it…reaching…the momentum escalating, then breaking past a barrier that was almost pain to shatter into a flood of melting sweetness, her knees buckling at the intensity of the waves sweeping through her.

Zageo caught her as her hands lost their purchase on his shoulders, carrying her with him as he plunged onto the bed, lying her flat on her back amongst the cushions and hovering over her, his eyes glittering fierce satisfaction in her helpless response to him.

He lifted her arms above her head, pinning them there with his own. They were simply too limp to resist the action though she knew intuitively this was a deliberate expression of domination over her and at another time and place she would have fought it. He clearly exulted in what he saw as submission to his will.

Emily smiled. Right here and now she didn't care what he thought. Her body was humming its own exultation. His gaze fastened on her smile. His mouth quirked into a cruel little twist and swooped on it, his lips hard and hungry, forcing hers apart, his tongue driving deep, intent on stirring another storm of sensation. *Her* blissful contentment was irrelevant. This was all about him taking his pleasure and he was the one who had to feel satisfied.

Some primitive streak inside her insisted on contesting the ruthless ravishment of his kiss. Her tongue duelled with his, sparking a passionate fight for possession. He might have the use of her body for a while but she hadn't traded any of her spirit. If he'd imagined getting a tame sex-slave, he could think again.

So consumed was Emily with the need to hold her own in this kiss, when Zageo released her arms she grabbed his head, instinctively moving to wrest back some control over what was happening. She was so caught up in trying to match his wildly erotic plunder, the lifting of her lower body took her by surprise. The shock of him entering her caused a total lack of focus on anything other than the sensation of his hard flesh moving past the soft convulsions of her own, tunnelling to her innermost depths, filling what had remained empty for a long, long time.

The jolt of that intensely satisfying fullness took Emily straight to the edge of climax again. Everything within her pulsed to the rhythmic beat of his smooth and powerful thrusts—each withdrawal setting up a drum-roll of exquisite anticipation, each plunge sending her hurtling into a tumultuous sea of ecstasy.

She heard herself moaning, crying out—totally involuntary sounds issuing from her throat. She was barely conscious of her hands squeezing his buttocks, instinctively goading, wanting the rocking to be harder, faster, wilder, until the waves turned into one continuously rolling crest, the explosive spasms of his climax driving it, and she floated off into a space where she was only anchored by him, his arms wound securely around her as she lay on his chest—a heaving chest that felt like the gentle swell of calmer waters after riding through a tempest.

Emily didn't move, didn't attempt to say anything. Not only was she in a daze of sensory overload, she had no idea what should or would come next. Besides, her whole experience of this man was that he took the lead in any activity to be shared with him. Moreover, the bargain she'd made put him in charge of her life. There was no point in even stirring until he showed some desire for it.

He stroked her back, making her skin tingle with pleasure. He certainly knew how to touch a woman, Emily thought, silently marvelling at the incredibly fantastic sexual experience he had just given her. If this was a sample of what she'd have to *endure* at his hands to keep her side of the trade, it was absolutely no hardship.

In fact, she understood why Veronique had come flying to Zanzibar to get him back. It was not going to be easy to say goodbye and walk away from what he gave. Not even an apartment in Paris would make up for having lost a lover of his calibre. Emily had a sneaking suspicion that the memory of what Zageo had just done to her would be a pinnacle of pleasure she might never reach with anyone else. Not even with Brian…

She clamped down on that thought. It was wrong to make comparisons. This relationship—if it could be called that—was something very different to her marriage. It was a slice of life she hadn't been looking for, eventuating from circumstances over which she'd had no control.

Anxiety welled up as she thought of Hannah, fraying the langour she had succumbed to in Zageo's soothing embrace. He was playing with her hair, lifting up the long tresses and letting them trail around his fingers, and as though he sensed her change of mood, he suddenly bunched her hair in his hand, slightly tugging to grab her attention.

'They are alive,' he said.

'What?' His statement seemed surreal, as though he had just read her mind.

'Your sister, her husband and daughters…they are alive. Do not be imagining them dead because it is not so,' he gruffly declared.

Adrenaline shot through Emily's sluggish veins. She bolted up to scan his eyes for truth, breaking his embrace and planting her own arms on either side of his head to lean over him in his current supine position. 'How do you know?' she demanded.

One black eyebrow arched in mocking challenge. 'You question my knowledge?'

She huffed with impatience. 'Not your knowledge, Zageo. I'm asking how you came by it.'

'Given that your sister had not arrived at the inn, as you had expected, I left instructions that her whereabouts be traced while we were out today,' he answered matter-of-factly. 'When we returned from Stone Town…'

'Are they under house arrest as Hannah feared?' Emily pressed, filled with an urgency to know what problems her sister was facing.

'Yes. But the point I am making, my dear Emily, is—' he ran a finger over her lips to silence any further intemperate outburst '—they are alive. And I shall now take every step I can to guarantee their future safety.'

Relief poured through her. Trading herself for this outcome had been worthwhile. No matter how big a sacrifice of her own self it might become, she would not regret making it. Some positive action would be taken to help Hannah.

'What do you plan to do?' she queried eagerly.

'Enough!' He surged up, catching her off-guard and rolling her onto her back, swiftly reestablishing his domination. The fingers that had been teasing her lips now stroked her jawline as though testing it for defiance. His dark eyes gleamed with a ruthless desire to re-acquaint her with the trade she'd made. 'You will trust me to negotiate your sister's freedom as best I can. How I do it is not your business. It is your business to please me, is it not?'

Had she?

Doubts whirled, attacking her natural self-confidence.

Was he satisfied with what he'd had of her so far?

Before tonight her sexual experience had been limited to one man—a man who'd had no other woman but herself. Her heart stampeded into thumping with panic as she thought of the high-living, sophisticated Veronique. She didn't know how to compete.

'You'll have to tell me what you want me to do,' she pleaded, frightened of being inadequate.

'Oh, I will,' he promised, smiling some deeply sensual and private satisfaction.

And he did.

Emily didn't mind doing any of it.

The happy knowledge that Hannah and her family were alive bubbled at the back of her mind, but in the forefront of it was the amazing truth that being intimately entangled with Sheikh Zageo bin Sultan Al Farrahn was making her feel more vibrantly alive than *she* had ever felt in her life.

CHAPTER THIRTEEN

ON MONDAY they flew to Kenya.

'But it's in the opposite direction to Zimbabwe,' Emily had protested.

An instant flash of anger had answered her. 'Do you doubt that I will deliver on my promise?'

'It just doesn't seem logical to travel there,' she had temporised warily. 'If you'd explain…'

'The negotiations to secure the safety of your sister's family will take time. We must move through diplomatic channels. While this is proceeding, there is little point in my not keeping to my own schedule. And you will accompany me—' his eyes had stabbed a challenge to her commitment '—as agreed.'

Again there was no choice but to go his way.

And as usual, it turned out that *his* way gave Emily an immense amount of amazing pleasure and it wasn't all exclusively connected to the intense sexual passion he could and did repeatedly stir.

The hotel he was checking on in Kenya was unlike

any hotel she had ever seen. It was, in fact, a safari resort, and the rooms were designed to look like a series of mud huts nestled cunningly around a hillside overlooking the Serengetti Plain. Inside they provided every luxury a traveller might want while the decor made fascinating use of the brightly colourful beading and fabrics much loved by the Masai tribe.

Best of all was the magnificent vista from every window—great herds of wildebeest grazing their way across the vast rolling plain which was dotted here and there by the highly distinctive acacia trees with their wide flat tops. It was also a surprising delight to see so many species of wild animals just roaming free, totally ignoring the intrusion by mankind.

When she and Zageo were taken out in one of the special safari vans, they might have been in an invisible spaceship for all the notice the animals took of them. A pride of lions, resting in the long grass by one of the tracks, didn't even turn their heads to look at the vehicle. In another place, a cheetah was teaching her three young cubs to hunt with absolutely no distraction from her mission, despite a number of vans circling to give their passengers a view of the action. Real life in Africa, Emily kept thinking, feeling very privileged to see it firsthand.

It had far more impact than viewing a film, though it wasn't always a pleasant one. It gave Emily the shudders seeing a flock of vultures waiting to feed on a fresh kill—horrible birds with their big bloated bodies and vicious looking beaks. On the other side of the spectrum were the giraffes—fascinating to watch a group of them amble along with a slow, stately grace, automatically evoking a smile.

On each of their trips out—different vehicles, different drivers—Emily was seated in the body of the van where a large section of the roof was lifted so passengers could stand up and take photographs. Zageo sat beside the driver, chatting to him about his life and work, observing how the safari session was handled—radio communication between the vans giving information about sightings so the drivers could change course, if necessary, to get to the scene as fast as they could.

Emily came to realise he didn't just check on the top-level management of his hotels. Nothing escaped his attention. He even stopped to talk to the employees who swept the paths to the rooms and it was not done in an autocratic manner. He accorded each person the same respect, none higher than another, and was clearly regarded with respect in return.

There was no shrugging or grimacing or rolling of eyes behind his back. He was liked, all the way down the line, and Emily couldn't help liking him, too, for the way he dealt with *his* people. It forced a revision of opinion on how he'd dealt with her.

In all honesty, she had to concede her story had probably sounded unbelievable. Zageo could well have been justified in not even listening to her, just handing her over to the police as an associate of Jacques Arnault. Instead of which, he'd given her the benefit of the doubt, proceeding to check the facts she'd given him while extending his highly generous and luxurious hospitality. Looked at objectively, this was more than fair treatment.

Except somehow none of it had been objective.

From the first moment of meeting it had been personal. Very, very personal. And it hadn't been all on his side, either. She'd been reacting against an attraction, an unwelcome one in both its strength and unsuitability, although when it came to a point of physical connection, she hadn't stopped him from kissing her. Now it was totally impossible to deny how much she wanted him to keep wanting her.

It even frightened her when he asked if she'd prefer to relax by the resort swimming pool, not accompany him on yet another safari trip. 'I thought you wanted me with you,' she answered anxiously, wondering if she had displeased him in some way.

He frowned, looking both exasperated and frustrated. 'You do not have to be a slave to me for your sister's sake,' he said tersely. 'I am here to carry out my responsibilities. I do not wish you to be bored, to put on a face of interest when you would rather be…'

'Bored?' Emily cried in astonishment. 'I'm not the least bit bored, Zageo.'

His dark intense eyes lasered hers for the truth. 'You have had day after day of rough travel. Perhaps you would like a long session of relaxing massages…'

'And miss out on seeing what I may never have the chance to see again? No way!' she asserted emphatically. 'I'm with you!'

A smile twitched at his lips. 'So. The adventure appeals.'

'I've always loved the world of nature. There's nothing in the animal kingdom I find boring,' Emily assured him.

One eyebrow arched. 'Including me?'

Him least of all, she thought, but looked askance at him, unwilling to give away too much. 'For me, *you* are an adventure, too, as I'm sure you're perfectly aware.'

Yes, he was, Zageo silently conceded.

And so was she for him—totally unlike any other woman he'd been with. Her lack of sexual sophistication had challenged him into making each new experience in the bedroom not only a titillating surprise for her but a sensual delight to be savoured over and over again. Her response was always intensely gratifying, sometimes quite intoxicating.

She also had a natural joy in life that revived his own. Gone was the jaded feeling with which he had left France to begin this trip. In fact, he was conscious of feeling a deeper pleasure in Emily Ross than any of the women who had preceded her. Which made it all the more vexing that she had come to him on such frustrating terms, denying him the satisfaction of winning her to his side.

She was happy enough to be there.

No doubt about that.

She didn't have enough artifice in her to pretend.

But would she have ever submitted to his will, given

there had been no problem with her sister, pushing a choice that might resolve it?

He hated this trade—hated it with a vengeance. He wanted done with it as fast as possible.

But Africa was Africa and very little moved at a fast pace. The days wore on with no progress towards an agreeable settlement between Malcolm Coleman and the hostile elements responsible for holding his family under house arrest.

Abdul was working overtime on pressing acceptable negotiations. The stumbling block was Coleman himself, not trusting anything he was offered and refusing to give up ownership of his farm. Abdul finally advised that direct confrontation would probably be required to gain an effective outcome.

'So a way to Coleman's farm must be cleared,' Zageo decided. 'Best to go in by helicopter.'

'But how not to get shot down?' Abdul muttered worriedly. 'I don't like this, Your Excellency. Why not explain to Miss Ross that her brother-in-law will not co-operate with the rescue plan? Perhaps she...'

'No!' Zageo flicked him a scornful look. 'Failure is unacceptable. The conference scheduled at our hotel in Zambia...find out what officials are coming from Zimbabwe and ensure that one of them has the power to grant me access with immunity. If you can also get some idea of what inducement would be welcome...'

Abdul nodded, looking relieved to be directed back into familiar territory.

Zageo reflected that this mission could end up costing him far more than he had anticipated. Endangering his own life was certainly going too far just to please a woman, yet there was no question in his mind that if it had to be done for Emily Ross, it had to be done. There had been no quarter asked in her giving to him, no excusing herself from anything he'd demanded of her, no protest at his leading her where she had not gone before. It was as though he had bought a slave. Which went against his every grain.

He *needed* this business finished.

Only after the trade had been honoured by him would he know if Emily Ross desired to stay at his side for reasons other than her sister's safety.

Emily couldn't help fretting over not knowing how things were for Hannah. She wished she could ask Zageo but he interpreted her need for information as a lack of trust in him. Having been sternly rebuffed for showing an impatience about getting results from his side of the bargain, she was wary of bringing up the subject again. However, his announcement that they would be flying on to Zambia instantly loosened her tongue.

They were in bed, relaxed after another exhilarating peak of intimacy, and Emily's mind leapt to a very different connection. 'Zambia and Zimbabwe share a border. Does this mean—?'

'It means we are going to Zambia,' he stated tersely, cutting off the spill of words from her.

Emily gritted her teeth as a wave of rebellion surged through her. She had been obedient to his wishes. She had been patient over the time he needed to clinch his side of the deal. But she was not going to be fobbed off as though she had no right to know what was happening with Hannah.

She heaved herself up, planting her hands on either side of his head, positioning herself directly above him for a very determined face-to-face encounter. 'What for?' she demanded.

His eyes glinted a deliberate challenge as he answered, 'One of our hotels is sited on the Zambezi River, just above Victoria Falls. It is on my itinerary.'

'So this move has nothing to do with my sister?'

'I will be meeting with people who may help.'

'May? *May?*' Her uncertainties coalesced into a shaft of anger. '*May* I remind you, Zageo, that you've had a very comprehensive downpayment on my side of our agreed trade and I have yet to receive any solid indication that you are doing anything productive on your side.'

'A downpayment!' he scoffed. 'Is that what you call doing what you want to do? Where's the cost to you, Emily? What have you paid?'

The counterattack was so swift and deadly, it threw her mind into chaos. Had it cost her anything to be with him? Not really. Which meant the trade wasn't equitable. And that left her without a reasonable argument. Panic whirled, wildly prompting action that might set the balance right again. She flung herself away from him, rolling off the bed, landing on her feet and backing away out of easy reach.

'So you think I would have said yes to you anyway.

Is that it, Zageo?' she fired at him. 'You think I find you irresistible?'

He propped himself up on his side, observing her with narrowed eyes. 'If there had been any resistance on your part, Emily, I would have been aware of it,' he mocked.

'Well, how about resistance now?'

'Don't be absurd.'

Emily steeled her backbone. Her eyes defied his arrogant confidence. He might be the most beautiful, sexiest man on earth but... 'I can say no to you,' she declared with enough ferocity to warn him she was serious.

His heavy-lidded gaze raked her naked body, reminding her of how intimately he knew it and how deeply he had pleasured it, sending her temperature sky-high in a rush of self-conscious guilt over her ready compliance to whatever pleased him.

'Why would you want to frustrate both of us?' he asked, his mouth curving into a sardonic little smile that derided such obvious foolishness.

Emily struggled to rise above the sexual pull of the man. If she didn't fight him now she would lose any bargaining power she had.

'You withhold information from me,' she swiftly accused. 'Why shouldn't I withhold myself from you until you share what I need to know?'

'So...we are back to bartering, are we?' Anger tightened his face and flashed from his eyes. 'There has been no progression in our relationship?'

'A relationship can only grow from sharing,' she hotly argued.

'Have I not shared much with you?'

'Yes,' she had to concede. 'But I want you to share what you're doing about Hannah and her family.'

Steely pride looked back at her. 'I have said I shall move them from harm's way and I will. That is all you need to know.'

'*Will!* And just how far in the future is that, Zageo?' She was on a roll now and nothing was going to stop her from pinning him down. Her pride was at stake, too. She had given herself to him in good faith and she was not going to be taken for a ride. '*Will* some action be taken from your hotel in Zambia?'

'Enough!'

He swung himself off the bed, rising to his feet with an autocratic hauteur that squeezed her heart and sent flutters through her stomach. His eyes blazed shrivelling scorn at her as he donned a robe, tying the belt with a snappy action—signal enough that the intimacy they had shared earlier was at a decisive end. He waved a dismissive hand over the bed.

'Consider it yours. I will not require any more *payment* from you…'

His tone was so savage it took Emily's breath away.

'…until you have received satisfaction from me,' he concluded bitingly, as though she had dismissed all the sexual satisfaction he'd given her as nothing worth having.

Emily sucked in some air, needing a blast of oxygen

to clear the shocked fog in her brain. 'I just want some news of Hannah!' she cried. 'Is that so unreasonable? Too much to ask when I'm so frightened for my sister?'

He ignored her, striding for the door which he clearly intended to put between them.

'I don't know where you're coming from, Zageo,' she hurled at his back. 'But where I come from we have a saying that every Australian understands and respects. *Fair go!* It's an intrinsic part of our culture—what we live by. And to me it's not fair of you to brush off my concern when I have tried my utmost to please you in every respect.'

He halted, his shoulders squaring with bunched tension. They rose and fell as he drew in and exhaled a very deep breath. His head did not turn. She could feel violence emanating from him as though it was a tangible thing, attacking her nerves and making them leap in a wild frenzy.

'No harm comes to the source of a lucrative deal while the deal is still pending,' he stated coldly. 'At this point in time, you need have no fear for your sister's life. Nor the lives of her husband and children.' He cast one hard glance at her as he added, 'We fly to Zambia in the morning. Be ready.'

Then he was gone.

CHAPTER FOURTEEN

I WILL be meeting with people who may help.

This must be it, Emily kept thinking, observing the preparations for a special dinner being set up on the perfectly manicured and very green lawn, which ran smoothly from the long line of white buildings comprising the hotel, right to the edge of the water. It was a fantastic site, overlooking the vast spread of the Zambezi River just before it plunged down a massive chasm, the spume from Victoria Falls sending up clouds of mist.

Government dignitaries from various African nations had been arriving all afternoon and the paths around the numerous units of accommodation were being patrolled by their security guards. A stage had been constructed under one of the large shade trees, facing the carefully arranged tables and chairs. Three African tenors were checking out the sound system, rehearsing some of the same operatic arias Emily had heard sung by the famous three—Pavarotti, Domingo and Carrera.

She had barely seen Zageo since they had arrived at this unbelievably beautiful place. He had appointed a hotel staff member to see to her every need and arrange whatever Emily wished to do. It felt as though he was divorcing himself from her.

Accommodation was designed in four suite units, two up, two down, each with a balcony or verandah with a direct view of the river. Emily was installed in an upstairs suite and she knew Zageo was in the adjoining one but he had made no attempt to visit her.

Everything inside the suite was designed for two people; a king-size bed, two large lounging chairs with matching footstools, a very long vanity bench with two wash bowls in the spacious bathroom, plus a huge shower recess with a shower-head as large as a bread plate spraying out so much volume it gave one the sense of standing under a waterfall. So much luxury for one person felt very lonely.

Maybe after tonight—if he had a fruitful meeting— Zageo might deign to give her some news of what he was doing about Hannah's family. Emily could only hope so. Confronting him again would not elicit anything but another rebuff.

All along she had known there was a chasm of cultural differences between them, yet she had wanted him to deal with her as though he understood and shared her *Australian* attitudes. Big mistake! His way was *his* way and she had no choice but to accept that, especially with helping Hannah because she had no one else to turn to.

It was almost sunset. Drinks and canapés were being served from the bar at the back of the large wooden deck built around a large shade tree and extending over the edge of the river. Emily sat on a cushioned lounger, sipping a tropical fruit drink, listening to other guests commenting on the fantastic scenery.

The sky was streaked with vivid colour. About twenty metres away in the water was a raft of hippos, most of them submerged enough to look like a clump of rounded rocks. Much further away and silhouetted by the setting sun, a string of elephants started crossing the river from one island to another. Emily counted seven of them.

The splendour of Africa…

She fiercely wished Zageo was beside her, sharing it as they'd done in Kenya. She missed his company, his knowledge and experience, the excitement of his presence, the fine sexual tension that was constantly between them, promising more intimate pleasure to come as soon as they were alone together.

After two years of being single, with no inclination to join up with anyone, Emily realised that Zageo had well and truly revived her memory of what it was like to be in a relationship with a man—the physical, mental and emotional links that somehow made life more exhilarating. Even though common sense insisted this relationship could only be a temporary one, Emily had to acknowledge she didn't want it to end here.

It didn't matter how *foreign* Zageo was, in so many respects he was a marvellous person who lived an extraordinary life. She felt privileged to share just some of it with him. If he cast her off once he'd achieved his side of the trade…a sense of wretchedness clutched her heart.

She deeply regretted having reduced the sex they'd had to a form of prostitution, holding out for payment. The frustration of having no news of her sister's situation had driven her stance, not a lack of trust in Zageo's integrity. However, he'd clearly felt a strong sense of insult on two counts—her rejection of a natural outcome for their mutual attraction and her apparent disbelief in the keeping of his word.

Mistakes… Emily brooded over them, making herself more and more miserable as the evening wore on. She ordered a light dinner from room service but had no appetite for it. In her anguish over what was happening at the special outdoors dinner Zageo was attending, she switched off the lights in her suite and sat on the darkened balcony, watching the VIP guests below and trying to gauge if the meetings taking place were convivial or strained.

The three African tenors took turns in entertaining their audience, only coming together for a grand finale after coffee had been served. They were enthusiastically applauded, deservedly so, each one of them in marvellous voice. Once their concert was over, Emily trailed off to bed, having learnt nothing except for the firsthand observation that powerful people were royally entertained and probably expected it as their due.

Bed was the loneliest place of all. Her body yearned

to be once more intimately entangled with Zageo's, to feel all the intense and blissful sensual pleasure he had introduced her to. She tossed and turned for what seemed like hours. She didn't know when sleep finally overtook her restlessness, didn't know how long she had slept, didn't know what woke her.

There was no slow arousal from slumber, nothing pricking at her consciousness. It was as though a charge of electricity had thrown a switch to activate her. Her eyes snapped open. Her mind leapt to full alert.

The figure of a man was standing by the bed. The room was too dark to see his face but her heart did not flutter with fear. She knew instantly who it was. A surge of relief, hope and pleasure lilted through her voice.

'Zageo…' She pushed up from the pillow, propping herself on her elbows. 'I'm so glad you're here.'

Her gladness ran smack into a wall of tension, which seemed to suck it in and become even stronger, keeping him resolutely separate from her. It sparked a swift awareness that he had not meant to wake her, that he had come in the dead of night to look at her for some private reason and did not like being caught doing it.

Did he miss her, too?

Did he still want her as much as she wanted him?

Was pride forbidding him to admit it?

'Glad?' he fired back at her. 'Because you want news of your sister?'

His voice was clipped, angry, *hating* how his involvement with her now turned on the welfare of people he didn't even know.

Emily sat up, *hating* having dealt with him as she had. 'No,' she answered quietly, seriously. 'I'm sorry for…for making it sound as though being with you was only for the help you might give.'

There was a taut silence as he considered her apology. 'So…you admit this is not true?' His tone was more haughty this time, delivering scorn for the lie.

She heaved a rueful sigh. 'You know it's not true, Zageo.'

'Do not think I am deceived by this meek and mild act, Emily. If you imagine it might gain you more to butter me up than to demand…'

'No!' she cried in horror at his interpretation of her apology. 'I have really enjoyed your company and…and you're a fabulous lover, Zageo. I'll remember this time with you for the rest of my life, the pleasure you gave me…'

'Are you saying you no longer wish to withhold yourself from me?'

Emily took a deep breath, anxious to right the wrongs she'd done him and not caring how brazen she was about it. 'Yes,' she declared emphatically. 'I'd like you to come to bed with me right now.'

There! She couldn't be more positive than that! Her heart galloped as she waited for some response from him, frightened by his chilling stillness and frantically hoping for the desire he'd shown her to return in full force.

After an interminable few moments he spoke. 'You want me.'

Emily wasn't sure if it was a question or an ironic comment, but she answered without hesitation, 'Yes, I do.'

'Then show me how much, Emily.' No doubt about his tone now. It was hard and ruthless, challenging her mind, heart and soul. 'Show me that what I do tomorrow will not be done for nothing.'

Tomorrow…Hannah…the link burst through her brain, and on its heels came the red alert warning *not to ask*! If she brought her sister into this moment which was charged with explosive elements relating to only Zageo and herself, it would blow apart everything that could be good between them. Every instinct she had urged her to seize this night and make it theirs.

She swung her legs off the bed. He made no move towards her. His silence screamed of waiting…waiting to see how far *she* would go for *him*. Her eyes had become accustomed to the darkness, allowing her to see he was wearing the light cotton robe supplied by the hotel. No need for him to dress properly when the doors to their suites faced each other across the upstairs porch. Emily had no doubt he was naked underneath the robe.

She'd worn nothing to bed herself, hoping he might come. Any inhibitions about her body were long gone with Zageo. She was only too eager for him to touch it, caress it, pleasure it. But he didn't reach for her as she stepped close. He maintained an aloof stillness. Waiting…

Emily thought of how much he had *shown* her. Without the slightest hesitation she started undoing his tie belt. 'Were you lying in bed, thinking of what you could be doing with me?' she asked huskily, determined to seduce him out of this stand-off.

No reply.

'I was, for hours and hours,' she confessed, drawing his robe apart, sliding her hands up his chest, lightly rubbing her palms over his nipples. 'I wanted to feel you as I'm feeling you now.'

His chest lifted as his nipples hardened under her touch. The swift intake of breath was inaudible but his body revealed the signs of excitement. Emily moved around behind him and slid the robe down his arms, getting rid of the garment. Her hands went to work on the taut muscles of his neck and shoulders—a soft, sensual massage.

'Relax, Zageo,' she murmured. 'I don't want to fight you. I want to make love to you.'

He didn't relax. If anything, his muscles tightened even more.

She ran featherlight fingers down his back in soft whirling patterns, revelling in the satin smoothness of his skin as she gradually worked her way to his waist. Then she moved in, pressing her breasts against his sensitised back, gliding her hands around to the erotic zones on either side of his groin, caressing them, silently rejoicing in the tremors she raised with her touch.

'You've brought me back to life again,' she confided, trailing kisses down the curve of his spine. 'I've just been going through the motions for the past two years. Meeting you, knowing you…it came as a shock. I didn't know how to handle it, Zageo. But I do want you.' She pressed her cheek into the hollow between his shoulder blades, fervently murmuring, 'I do.'

His diaphram lifted with the quick refilling of his lungs with air. Emily moved her fingers lower, reaching for him, hoping she had aroused the desire he'd always *shown* her. Elation zinged through her as she felt his strong erection, the soft velvety skin stretched to contain the surge of his excitement.

Just the most delicate touch on the tip…and Zageo exploded into action, whirling around, seizing her waist, lifting her, carrying her headlong onto the bed with him, pinning her down, his eyes stabbing into hers with fierce intensity.

'Do not play with me, Emily. This has gone beyond games,' he stated harshly. 'Beyond anything civilised.'

'I wasn't playing with you,' she cried breathlessly.

'Then give me the new sense of life I gave you. I need it now. Now…'

He kissed her with a devouring passion that fired a tumultuous response from her. She wasn't trying to prove anything. Her own wild surge of need met his, fiercely demanding expression, craving satisfaction. His arms burrowed under her. She eagerly arched her body, wanting fierce collision, a swift primitive mating, the ecstatic sense of him driving into her.

It came and her body seemed to sing with exultation in his possession of her, her possession of him. It was marvellous, beautiful, glorious. She was hungry for the wonderfully intense feelings it generated, greedy for them. Her arms grasped him tightly. Her legs wound around him, urging him on, goading him on.

Zageo filled her with his power, lifted her onto wings of ecstasy that had her flying high, then swooping into delightful dips before soaring again, higher and higher until she simply floated in a delirium of pleasure, waiting for the ultimate fusion of his climax, the final fulfillment of their becoming one again.

When it came, to Emily it was sweeter than ever before. She hoped he felt as deeply moved by this special intimacy as she did. His forehead pressed briefly against hers, mind to mind, she thought, body to body. Then he heaved his weight off her, rolling, scooping her along with him, pressing her head over his heart, his fingers thrust into her hair, not stroking as he usually did, but grasping her scalp, holding her possessively against the thud of his life-beat.

He didn't speak.

Neither did she.

Emily was happy to have her head nestled precisely where it was. Her own heart kept time with his, giving her a blissful sense of harmony, the soft drumming gradually soothing her into a deep and peaceful sleep, cocooned securely in his embrace.

When he removed that embrace and left her, she had no idea. It was morning when she woke again and where he had lain in the bed was cold. For a few minutes she fretted over why he would have returned to his own suite instead of staying with her. Perhaps she hadn't answered his need. Perhaps…

Then she remembered.

Hannah!

Zageo had some action planned for tomorrow and now it was tomorrow. Last night she'd been certain it related to the trade they'd made. If that assumption was right, did he feel it was worth doing this morning? Was that why he was missing from her bed? He'd already gone about the business he had prearranged?

Emily rushed to the bathroom, anxious to be showered, dressed and ready for anything.

Today was important.

On how many counts she couldn't begin to guess.

CHAPTER FIFTEEN

EMILY braved knocking on the door to Zageo's suite, arguing to herself that last night's intimacy gave her the right to at least say hello. There was no response—disappointing, but to be expected, since it was almost nine o'clock and he was probably already attending to whatever he had planned for today.

A tense anticipation was jiggling her heart as she took the path to the central complex of the hotel. She wanted news of Hannah's situation but was frightened of what it might be. Something pertinent had transpired at last night's dinner or Zageo would not have come to her. From his attitude—from what he'd said—Emily sensed the news was not good. *The trade* was giving him more trouble than he'd bargained for.

Guests were breakfasting on the terrace and in the main restaurant. Neither Zageo nor his aide-de-camp, Abdul Haji, was amongst them. Emily walked on to the grand reception area—built like a pavilion with its splendid columns and open-air sides. She found Leila, the employee Zageo had appointed to look after her needs.

'Have you seen the sheikh this morning, Leila?'

'Yes. He left the hotel very early with Mr Haji.'

'How early?'

'At sunrise.'

'And they haven't returned,' Emily muttered, wondering if Zageo had left a message for her at reception.

'Mr Haji has,' came the helpful reply. 'I saw him walking by the river a little while ago. Would you like me to find him for you, Miss Ross?'

'No. No, thank you,' Emily answered quickly, acutely aware that Zageo's right hand man was not at her beck and call and would be affronted by such a move on her part. However, if she ran into him accidentally…

'Is there anything else I can do for you?' Leila inquired.

Emily flashed her a smile and shook her head. 'I think I'll just idle away this morning. Thanks again, Leila.'

Where would Zageo have gone by himself? The question teased her mind as she left the reception area, passing by the Livingstone Lounge—honouring the explorer, David Livingstone, who'd discovered and named Victoria Falls after the then Queen of England. It was furnished like a British colonial club room with many groups of leather chairs and sofas, card tables, chess tables, mahjong tables, plus a bar at the end—all designed to cater for every recreational taste. A glance at the few occupants assured her the black bearded Abdul Haji was not present.

She stood on the terrace, looking from left to right, hoping to spot the man. To the left, the view along the river was unobscured. Everything from last night's dinner and entertainment had been cleared away, leaving nothing but pristine green lawn and the magnificent shade trees. She saw no one taking a stroll in that direction.

To the right there were more trees, plus the cabana providing service to the swimming pool, and closer to the river bank two white marquees where various types of massages were on offer. If Abdul Haji was still walking, Emily decided it had to be somewhere beyond the marquees.

Five minutes later, Emily spotted him, leaning on the railing of a small jetty, apparently watching the swirl of the water as it rushed towards the fall. He caught sight of her approach and straightened up, focusing his attention on her with what felt like a hostile intensity, which was highly disquieting. She hesitated on the bank beside the jetty, torn between her need to know about Zageo and the sense of being distinctly unwelcome.

Abdul Haji frowned, made an impatient gesture and tersely said, 'There is no news. We must wait.'

It seemed that Abdul thought she knew more than she did. Hoping to elicit some information, she prompted, 'Zageo left at sunrise.'

Hands were thrown up in disgust. 'It is madness, this adventure—' his eyes flashed black resentment at her '—flying directly to the farm over the heads of Zimbabwe officialdom. What if your brother-in-law persists in not seeing reason, even when your passport is shown to him? So much risk for nothing.'

Shock rolled through Emily's mind and gripped her heart. Zageo was putting his own life at hazard to keep his word to her. It was too much. She would never have asked it of him. Never!

Diplomatic connections...bribery...deals under tables...big money talking as it always did...all these things she had imagined happening, but no real personal risk. However, the comment about Malcolm not seeing reason suggested that Hannah's husband hadn't cooperated with what had been initiated to help the family's situation. And Emily realised her own attitude about *payment* had virtually forced Zageo to deliver.

'I'm sorry,' she blurted out, her own anxiety for his safety rising. 'I didn't mean for it to go this far.'

Abdul glared a dismissal of her influence. 'His Excellency, the sheikh, does as he wishes.'

'Yes, of course,' she agreed, not about to argue against male supremacy in this instance. 'It's just that if we hadn't met...'

'It is futile to rail against Fate.'

Emily took a deep breath as she tried to stop floundering and gather her wits. 'I didn't realise Malcolm would cause problems.'

'A man does not easily give up what is his. This I understand. But Malcolm Coleman must be made to understand that the loss is inevitable. There is no choice,' Abdul said fiercely. 'That was made very clear last night.'

The meeting...Zageo coming to her afterward...deciding what had to be done to honour his side of their trade.

Emily felt sick. 'I shouldn't have asked him to help.'

Abdul frowned at her. 'You made a request?'

'Yes,' she confessed miserably. 'After I'd received the e-mail from my sister…when we met for dinner that evening—'

'The decision was already made,' Abdul cut in, waving a dismissal of her part in promoting this action.

Flutters attacked her stomach. 'What do you mean…*already made*?'

'On his return to the palace from your visit to The Salamander Inn, His Excellency sought me out and ordered a preliminary investigation into ways to secure the safety of your sister and her family,' Abdul curtly informed her.

'Before dinner?' Emily queried incredulously.

'It was late afternoon. His Excellency wished to alleviate your distress, Miss Ross. Surely he told you so when you met that evening.'

She'd rushed straight into the trade!

It hadn't even occurred to her that Zageo might care enough—on such short acquaintance—to initiate action which might give her some peace of mind about her sister. No wonder he'd been angry at her assumption that he'd only do it to have sex with her.

'Yes, he did say he'd help,' she muttered weakly.

'These are difficult times in Zimbabwe. Our negotiations kept breaking down. It has been very frustrating,' Abdul muttered in return.

And on their last night in Kenya she had more or less accused Zageo of doing nothing!

She'd been so wrong. So terribly, terribly wrong.

Feeling totally shattered by these revelations, Emily almost staggered over to a nearby bench seat and sank onto it, her legs having become too rubbery to keep standing.

'He took my passport to identify himself as a friend to Hannah and Malcolm?' she asked.

'It is to be hoped it will satisfy.' Abdul frowned at her again. 'You did not know this?'

'Zageo said he had something planned for today but he gave no precise details.'

'All going well, he intends to fly them out.'

'Without…' She swallowed hard. 'Without permission from the authorities?'

'A blind eye may be turned but I have no reason to trust these people.' The signature tune of a mobile telephone alerted him to a call. 'Please excuse me, Miss Ross,' he said, whipping the small communicator out of his shirt pocket and striding to the end of the jetty to ensure a private conversation.

Emily waited in tense silence, hoping—fearing—this was news of Zageo's rescue mission being transmitted. Abdul had his back turned to her so she could neither hear him speak or see his expression. Her heart jumped as he wheeled around, tucking the telephone back in his pocket.

'We go,' he called, waving her to join him as he strode back to the river bank, clearly galvanised into action.

Adrenaline surged through Emily as she leapt to her feet. 'Go where?'

'To the landing pad. Your presence is required there.'

'Landing pad?'

'For the helicopter,' he explained impatiently, probably thinking her dim-witted.

Emily had imagined Zageo was using his private aeroplane, but a helicopter definitely made more sense in the circumstances—a much quicker in and out. *If* Malcolm and Hannah had co-operated in leaving the farm with Zageo.

She half-ran to keep up with Abdul as he headed up to the hotel. 'So Zageo is on his way back?' she asked breathlessly.

'Yes. But not yet out of danger. He is using one of the helicopters that normally flies tourists around and over Victoria Falls. It allows some leeway over Zimbabwe airspace but not as much as this flight has taken.'

Could it be shot down?

Emily couldn't bring herself to raise that question, though she felt compelled to ask, 'Is my sister...?'

'They are all in the helicopter,' came the curt reply. 'It will be reassuring for the Coleman family to see you, Miss Ross.'

'Right!' she muttered, thinking what black irony it was that *they* didn't completely trust Zageo's word, either.

Guilt and shame wormed through her. She had not credited Zageo with compassionate caring nor with the kind of integrity that went beyond any normal expectation. He was not only a man of great character, but the most generous person she had ever known. Given another chance, she would show him an appreciation that went far beyond the bedroom.

At the hotel entrance a driver and minibus were waiting to transport them to the helicopter base. This was only a fifteen-minute trip from the hotel and neither Abdul nor Emily spoke on the way. Once there, they were met by the base manager and escorted straight through the waiting lounge where groups of tourists were gathered for their sightseeing flights.

As soon as they were outside again and taking the path to the landing pad, their escort pointed to a black dot in the sky. 'That's it coming in now.'

'No problems?' Abdul asked.

The base manager shrugged. 'Not in the air. Our best pilot is at the controls.'

The limited answer worried Emily. 'Are any of the passengers injured?'

'Not to my knowledge. There was no call for medical aid,' came the reassuring reply.

They waited near the end of the path, watching the black dot grow larger and larger. Emily felt a churning mixture of excitement and apprehension. While she desperately wanted to see Hannah and her family safe and sound, would they thank her for interfering in their lives? Zageo had acted on her behalf, probably being very forceful, intent on *showing* her he did deliver on his word. She could only hope this dramatic rescue had been the right action to take.

The wind from the whirling helicopter blades plastered her clothes against her body and blew her hair into wild disarray but Emily maintained her stance, facing the landing so she was immediately recognisable to her sister. She could now see Hannah in the cabin, directly behind Zageo who was seated beside the pilot.

At last the helicopter settled on the ground. The base manager moved forward to open the door and assist the passengers in disembarking. Zageo was out first. He gave Emily a searing look that burnt the message into her brain—*payment made in full*! Then he turned to help Hannah out, delivering the sister who had not made it to Zanzibar—the sister who had inadvertantly brought Emily into his life.

But would he want her to stay in it?

CHAPTER SIXTEEN

EMILY had found it a strangely fraught day. While there had been joy in the reunion with her sister and relief that the rescue had been very timely according to Malcolm, who was immensely grateful to have his family brought to a safe place, she was wracked with uncertainty over where she stood with Zageo.

He had bowed out of any further involvement with her family once they had been brought to the hotel and given accommodation. 'I'm sure you'll want some private time together,' he'd said, making no appointment with Emily for some time alone with him.

Naturally the moment he had excused himself from their presence, Hannah had pounced with a million questions about *the sheikh* and Emily's involvement with such an unlikely person, given her usual circle of acquaintances.

Where had she met him?

How long had she known him?

What was their relationship?

Why would he do so much for her?

The worst one was—You didn't sell yourself to him, did you, Em?—spoken jokingly, though with a wondering look in her eyes.

She had shrugged it off, saying, 'Zageo is just very generous by nature.'

'And drop-dead gorgeous.' Hannah's eyes had rolled knowingly over what she rightfully assumed was a sexual connection. 'Quite a package you've got there. Are you planning on hanging onto him?'

'For as long as I can,' she'd answered, acutely aware that her time with Zageo might well have already ended.

A big grin bestowed approval. 'Good for you! Not, I imagine, a forever thing, but certainly an experience to chalk up—being with a real life sheikh!'

Not a forever thing... Her sister's comment kept jangling in her mind. Having said good-night to Hannah and Malcolm and their beautiful little daughters, Emily walked slowly along the path to her own accommodation, reflecting on how she had believed her marriage to Brian was to be forever. The words—*Till death do us part*—in the marriage service had meant fifty or sixty years down the track, not a fleeting few.

It was impossible to know what the future held. Life happened. Death happened. It seemed to her there were so many random factors involved, it was probably foolish to count on anything staying in place for long. With today's technology, the world had become smaller, its pace much faster, its boundaries less formidable. Even culture gaps were not as wide. Or maybe she just wanted to believe that because the thought of being separated from Zageo hurt.

She wanted more of him.

A lot more.

On every level.

Having arrived on the porch outside the doors to both Zageo's suite and hers, she decided to knock on his, hoping to have some direct communication with him about today's events. Disappointment dragged at her heart when there was no response.

She tried arguing to herself that he had come into her suite last night and would come again if he wanted to. There was no point in chasing after him. It hadn't worked for Veronique and Emily had no doubt it wouldn't work for her, either. When Zageo decided it was time up on a relationship, that was it.

Tomorrow his private jet was to fly Hannah and Malcolm and the girls to Johannesburg, from where they would catch a commercial flight to Australia. For all Emily knew, she might be expected to go with them. With the depressing thought that this could be her last night anywhere near Zageo, she turned to her own door, unlocked it and entered the suite which she knew was bound to feel even more lonely tonight…unless he came.

He didn't come.

He was already there.

As Emily stepped past the small foyer and into the bed-sitting room, Zageo entered it from the balcony where she had sat watching last night's special dinner. She wanted to run to him, fling her arms around his neck and plaster his face with wildly grateful kisses for his extraordinary kindnesses to her family. It would have been the natural thing to do if everything had been natural between them. But it wasn't. Because of the trade *she* had initiated. So she stood with her feet rooted to the floor, waiting to hear her fate from him.

He didn't move towards her, either, standing stiffly proud and tall just inside the room, his brilliant dark eyes watching her with an intensity that played havoc with every nerve in her body. If he still felt desire for her, it was comprehensively guarded.

'Is all well with your sister and her family?' he asked, his tone coolly polite.

'Thanks to you, Zageo, as well as it can be, given such a traumatic upheaval to their lives,' she answered quietly.

'In the end there was no choice but to accept the upheaval,' he stated unequivocally. 'Your brother-in-law was a marked man, Emily.'

'Yes. So I understand. And while I will be eternally grateful you did go in and get them out, when I made the…the deal…with you, I didn't expect you to endanger your own life, Zageo. I thought—' she gestured a sense of helplessness over his decision to act himself '—I thought something more impersonal would be worked.'

His eyes blazed a fierce challenge. 'Was it impersonal…your joining your body to mine?'

'No! I…'

'Then why would you expect me to do less than you?'

'I didn't mean…' She stopped, took a deep breath, and desperately not wanting to argue with him, simply said, 'I was frightened for you.'

His head tilted to one side consideringly. 'You cared for my safety?'

'Of course I did!'

'As, no doubt you would for anyone in danger,' he concluded dismissively.

It wiped out what she'd been trying to get across to him. How could she build bridges if Zageo was intent on smashing them? Before she could come up with some winning approach he spoke with a chilling finality.

'Nevertheless, all is well that ends well. You no longer have anything to fear, Emily.'

Except losing him from her life.

He gestured towards the writing desk. 'There is your passport. Now that our trade is complete, you are free to go wherever you like. Perhaps to Johannesburg with your sister tomorrow.'

Her inner anguish spilled out, needing to hear the truth from him. 'You don't want me with you anymore?'

A blaze of anger answered her. 'Do not turn this onto me. You have said over and over again I give you no choice.' He flung out an arm as though releasing her from all bondage to him. 'Go where you will. I free you of any sense of obligation to me.'

She lifted her own arms in an impassioned plea. 'I want to go with you, Zageo. Wherever you go.'

He gave her a savage look. 'For as long as it suits

you, Emily? To see more of Africa and do it in the style I can provide?'

'I wouldn't care if we were doing it on a shoestring budget. I want more of you, Zageo,' she cried recklessly.

'Ah! So it is the sex you want more of,' he mocked. 'The pleasures of the flesh are enticing, are they not?'

'Yes,' she flung back at him, seizing on his mocking statement to fight his stand-off position. 'That was what enticed you into keeping hold of me in the first place, and it didn't seem to me you were tired of what I could provide for you last night.'

His eyes narrowed. 'Most men facing possible death would want to have sex beforehand.'

She burned, hating the humiliating minimalisation of what they'd shared. 'You were just using me? Is that what you're saying, Zageo?'

'You do not care to be used, Emily?'

The message was scorchingly clear.

He'd hated being used by her.

The heat in her cheeks was painful, but she would not drop her gaze from his, determined on resolving the issues between them. 'I'm sorry. Mr Haji told me this morning you had intended to help with Hannah's situation anyway. Believe me, I already feel wretched over misjudging the kind of person you are. My only excuse is…I thought the way you dealt with Veronique meant dealing with me in the same way would not be unusual for you.'

He gave a derisive snort. 'I knew what I was buying into with Veronique. You, my dear Emily, did not fit any mould I was familiar with.'

'Well, if I surprised you, multiply that surprise by about a million and you might approach how big a surprise you've been to me,' she retorted with feeling. 'Talk about being in foreign territory with a foreigner…'

'Yes!' His eyes fiercely raked her up and down. 'Extremely foreign territory with a foreigner!'

'But we have found a lot of mutual ground, haven't we?' she quickly appealed. 'And we might find even more pleasure in everything if we stay together. And I don't mean only in bed, so if you think I want to tag along with you just for the sex…'

She ran out of breath. The tension in the room seemed to have a stranglehold on any free flow of oxygen. In fact, Emily felt hopelessly choked up and couldn't think what else to say anyway.

'Do I understand you now wish to accompany me on this journey without fear or favour?' Zageo asked, cocking an eyebrow as though merely ascertaining her position, certainly not giving away his own.

Emily swallowed hard and managed to produce a reply. 'I'd like to try it.'

'Being companions and lovers.'

'Yes.'

'No more bartering.'

'No. Complete freedom of choice.'

Let this woman go, Zageo fiercely berated himself. *No more talk. No more delay. Let her go now*!

'Emily, freedom of choice is a myth. There is no such thing, not in your culture nor mine. We are bound into attitudes and values by our upbringing and we think and act accordingly.'

Her beautiful blue eyes begged a stay of judgment. 'But we can learn more about each other, try to understand where we're both coming from, be willing to make compromises…'

She was still tugging on him, getting under his skin. 'No,' he said emphatically. Abdul was right. His mind was barely his own around this woman. She drove him into excesses. He had to put a stop to it, regain control, make sensible decisions. 'What we came together for… it is done, Emily.'

Her shoulders slumped. There was a flash of anguish on her face before her head bowed in defeat. 'So this is goodbye,' she said in a desolate little voice.

'Yes,' he said firmly, hating seeing her like this. She was a fighter, strong, resilient, resourceful. She had challenged him to the limit and beyond. Whatever she was feeling right now, she would get over it and move on.

As he must.

Zageo propelled his feet forward, determined on walking out of this suite, walking out of her life. It was better that the power she had exerted over him was brought to a close. Though he couldn't help thinking there was a bitter irony in her surrendering to his will at the end. He didn't like it. He liked it even less when a glance at her in passing showed tears trickling through her lowered lashes and down her cheeks.

Silent tears.

She had dignity.

Dignity that pulled hard on him.

Emily Ross was not just sexually desirable. She was a very special woman, unique in his experience. When she gave of herself, she gave everything.

He reached the door.

There was no sound behind him. No movement.

Did he really want to give up what he'd found in Emily? Did such a decision make him master of his life or did it make him less of a man for not meeting the challenge of keeping her at his side?

He sucked in a deep breath, needing the blast of oxygen to clear the feverish thoughts attacking what had seemed so clear to him all day. His hand was on the doorknob, ready to turn it. A few more seconds and his exit would be effected. No going back.

'I forgot to say thank you,' she jerked out huskily. 'Not for my sister and her family. For me. All you did for me. Thank you, Zageo.'

The emotion in her voice curled around his heart, squeezing it unmercifully. His brain closed down, instinct taking over, driving his legs back to where she still stood with her head bent in hopeless resignation. He grabbed her waist, spun her around, clamped her to him with one arm, cupped her chin with his hand.

'Look at me!' he commanded.

She raised startled, tear-washed eyes.

'I have decided our journey should not end here. We shall continue to be companions and lovers if you find this arrangement agreeable.'

Sparkles of joyful relief shone back at him. Her arms flew up around his neck, hooking it tightly. The soft lushness of her breasts heaved against his chest, reminding him how very delectable they were, as was the rest of her.

'Sounds good to me,' she whispered seductively, no hesitation at all about surrendering to his will, which Zageo liked very much this time. Very much indeed.

It drew his mouth to hers, the desire to taste and savour her giving was totally overwhelming, obliterating any possible second thoughts about having changed his mind.

It was a kiss worth having.

Emily Ross was a woman worth having.

And have her he would, regardless of where it led.

At least until this passion had spent itself and he was free and in control of himself again.

CHAPTER SEVENTEEN

THE last hotel, Emily thought, looking out the tall windows of their suite, taking in the sparkling view of Cape Town's waterfront. Their journey through Africa had been amazing—so many different facets of the country from wonderful wildlife to highly cultivated wineries— but it was coming to an end now. Once Zageo was satisfied that all was well with this perfectly sited boutique hotel, the next stop would be Dubai.

Emily didn't know how their relationship was going to work in Zageo's home territory. Perhaps he would decide to house her in Paris or London, avoiding too big a cultural clash. Emily didn't mind what he arranged as long as they remained lovers. The thought of having no part of his life was unbearable.

'I see Veronique wasted little time in mourning my departure,' Zageo drawled sardonically.

The mention of his former mistress sent a frisson of shock down Emily's spine. She'd just been thinking of Paris and now she was reminded that the model had been with Zageo for two years. Would her own relationship with him last that long?

Behind her came the rustle of the English newspaper he'd been reading over his after breakfast coffee. 'According to this report, she's about to marry the German industrialist, Claus Eisenberg. It will be his third trophy wife but I don't imagine Veronique is looking for lasting love so they will probably suit each other well.'

His mocking tone goaded her into asking, 'Do you believe that love can last, Zageo?'

The impulsive question was driven by her deep sense of vulnerability about her future with him and she hoped for a serious reply, needing some guide to where they were heading together.

'Yes,' he asserted strongly. 'I do believe it can. My mother and father are still devoted to each other.'

While this statement did not relate to her in any way, it lifted Emily's heart and she turned around, smiling at him. 'That's really nice.'

He smiled back. 'We do have that in common since your own parents are content with their marriage. And speaking of them—' he waved towards the computer notepad he'd acquired for her use '—you haven't checked your mail this morning.'

'I'll do it now.'

She crossed to the writing desk where the small slimline computer was set up, ready for her to connect with the Internet. As she switched on and started keying in her password, she was very conscious that this was yet another example of Zageo's generosity and his caring consideration for her needs, ensuring she had electronic access to her family at any time of the day or night.

She hadn't asked for it. She hadn't asked Zageo for any of the things he'd bought for her along the way. He'd taken her shopping for clothes whenever he'd considered her own outfits unsuitable for *his* companion and Emily had argued to herself she was indulging his pleasure in her, not taking him for all she could get. The clothes were unreturnable but this computer could be passed to Abdul Haji if and when Zageo said her time with him was over.

She wasn't like Veronique.

She had come to love Zageo with all her heart.

'There's a message from Hannah,' she said, wanting to share everything with him.

'Any news?'

'Malcolm is happy to get into the sugar industry, managing Dad's cane farm. Jenny and Sally have started at a playschool to get them used to being with other children and they've both found best friends to play with. And Hannah…oh, how wonderful!' She clapped her hands in delight and swung around, beaming a big grin at Zageo. 'Hannah's pregnant!'

'That's good?' he quizzed with a bemused air.

'She wanted to try for a boy, but Malcolm was worried about her going through another pregnancy when the situation in Zimbabwe was so unstable. Besides, he insisted he was perfectly happy with his girls and didn't need a boy.'

'All children are precious,' Zageo commented.

'Yes, but having been just two sisters ourselves, Hannah and I always fancied having mixed families. I do hope it's a boy for her this time.'

'You wouldn't mind having three children yourself?'

'Actually I think four is the perfect number. Two of each.'

'Four has always been a very significant number,' Zageo mused. 'Did you know it resonates through all the religions of mankind?'

'No, I didn't.'

'Even in your Christian religion, it comes up over and over again—forty days and forty nights in the desert, the four horsemen of the apocalypse…'

Emily's interest was captivated as he went on, spelling out the commonality that underpinned so much of what the people of the world believed in. Zageo was far more broadly educated than herself and he often expounded on fascinating pieces of knowledge. She couldn't help thinking he would be a marvellous father and fiercely wished she could be the mother of his children.

He suddenly stopped theorising and smiled at her, bestowing a sense of warm approval that made Emily tingle with pleasure. 'There's a place I'd like to show you today. Let's get ready to go, once you've replied to Hannah. And please send my congratulations to her and Malcolm.'

'Will do.'

She turned back to the computer notepad, happy to write her own congratulations as well as his and eager to go wherever Zageo wanted to take her.

When they emerged from the hotel, a gorgeous yellow Mercedes convertible with blue and black leather upholstery was waiting for them. 'Wow!' Emily cried excitedly as the doorman led the way to it. 'Is this for us?'

Zageo laughed at her burst of pleasure. 'It's a beautiful day, we will be driving down the coast, and I thought we should have a happy sunshine car to make it a more exhilarating trip,' he said.

'What a great idea! I love it!' Emily enthused, having long given up protesting Zageo's extravagance over anything he did with her. Over the past three months of being with him, she'd learnt that what gave him pleasure invariably gave her pleasure so it made no sense to fight it.

It was, indeed, an exhilarating trip, all the way to Cape Point which offered a spectacular view over the Cape of Good Hope, the southernmost point of Africa. The peninsula ended in a high cliff, on top of which stood a lighthouse. It was clearly a popular tourist spot. Numerous flights of steps led up to it and there was a funicular to transport those who didn't want to do the long climb.

'Would you like to ride or walk?' Zageo asked.

'Walk,' Emily decided. 'We can take our time enjoying the view from all the rest stops along the way.'

He took her hand, encasing it firmly with his. Emily loved the physical link with him. Somehow it was more than just companionable. It felt as though he was laying claim to her in a much deeper sense. Or maybe she was reading into it what she wanted to.

Just savour this time with him, she told herself, and make the most of each day as it comes. Hadn't she learnt from losing Brian so young that it was important to live the moment, not spend it counting her tomorrows?

Yet even as she enthused over the spectacular vista of cliffs and ocean, she couldn't help commenting, 'You really should visit Australia, Zageo. It has the most brilliant coastline in the world. Just north of Cairns we have the Forty Mile Beach, all clean white sand. The Great Ocean Road down in Victoria with the fantastic rock formations called the Twelve Apostles rising out of the sea, is just breathtaking. Not to mention…'

She ran off at the mouth, encouraged by the warm pleasure that danced over her from his twinkling eyes. 'If you would be happy to show me, I would be happy to come,' he said when she'd finished her tourist spiel, making her heart swell with joy. It was clear proof that he saw no end for their relationship in the near future.

Emily's delight in the day increased a hundredfold. Having been assured that this last tip of the African continent had no personal relevance as far as she Zageo were concerned, she could barely stop her feet from galloping up the last flight of steps to the top viewing area around the lighthouse.

They moved to the furthermost point and she stood against the stone safety wall, cocooned from the other tourists by Zageo who stood closely behind her, his arms encircling her waist, making her feel they were on top of the world together.

'Here we are at the Cape of Good Hope and you are looking down at where two great oceans meet, Emily,' he murmured, his head lowered to rub his cheek against her hair, his soft breath making her ear tingle.

'There should be some sign of it,' she mused. 'Waves clashing or different water colours mingling.'

'Instead there is a harmonious flow, a union that does not break because of coming from different places. This is how nature ordains it. It is only people who make demarcations.'

Emily sighed at this truth. Why couldn't the stream of humanity recognise its natural commonality instead of dividing itself into hostile camps?

'Are you brave enough to merge your life with mine, Emily?'

Her heart leapt. Her mind frantically quizzed what he meant. Hadn't she already merged her life with his?

'I'm brave enough to do anything with you, Zageo,' she answered, her stomach fluttering nervously over whether this was what he wanted to hear. She had the frightening sense that something critical was coming.

His arms tightened around her, pulling her body back into full contact with his. He kissed the lobe of her ear and whispered, 'Regardless of the differences that have shaped our lives, we have that natural flow, Emily. So I ask…will you marry me and be the mother of my children? Stand with me, no matter what we face in the future? Stand together as we are now.'

The shock of hearing a proposal she had never expected completely robbed Emily of any breath to answer. Her body whipped around in his embrace, her arms lifting to fly around his neck, instinctively grabbing for every linkage to him. Her eyes drank in the blaze of love and desire in his, taking all the fierce courage and determination she needed from it.

'Yes, I can do that, Zageo,' she said with absolute assurance. 'I will do it,' she promised him. 'I love you with all that I am.'

Sheikh Zageo bin Sultan Al Farrahn looked into the shining blue eyes of the woman who had made it impossible for him to choose any other woman to share his life. He remembered arrogantly determining to put her in her place, not realising at the time that her place would be at his side. He had decided to find a *suitable* wife, and he had found in Emily Ross a true compatibility in everything he really valued.

He lifted a hand to stroke her cheek in a tender caress, wanting to impart how very precious she was to him. 'And I love you with all that I am,' he replied, cherishing her words to him, repeating them because they carried a truth which should be spoken and always acknowledged between them.

A lasting love…

A love that no force could touch because they willed it so…together.

At the Sheikh's
Command

KATE WALKER

Kate Walker was born in Nottinghamshire, but as she grew up in Yorkshire she has always felt that her roots are there. She met her husband at university, and originally worked as a children's librarian, but after the birth of her son she returned to her old childhood love of writing. When she's not working, she divides her time between her family, their three cats, and her interests of embroidery, antiques, film and theatre, and, of course, reading.

You can visit Kate at www.kate-walker.com

For The Hoods and everyone in the
Writing Round Robin who made
those weeks such fun.

CHAPTER ONE

It was the outriders that Abbie saw first. Big powerful men on big powerful motorbikes, engines purring, chrome and black gleaming in the sunlight. In spite of the heat, their muscled bodies were encased snugly in supple black leather, their heads concealed in helmets. But then of course these men were the bodyguards of a man who ruled a country far away. A desert country where the sun beat down day after day, building to temperatures far higher than the moderate heat of an English summer's afternoon.

The man who was in the car behind them.

The convoy swept down the drive in a roar of engines, swirling to a halt outside the main door and waiting, body-guards sitting taut and tense on their machines, unseen eyes clearly darting everywhere, watching, observing. Their job was to protect the occupant of the vehicle that followed them. That big, sleek car with smoked glass windows behind which she could just detect the form of Sheikh Malik bin Rashid Al'Qaim. The car also had a small flag on the bonnet.

The flag of Barakhara.

Abbie drew in a deep breath and felt it tremble all the way into her lungs.

So he was here. It was really happening. This was not a dream. It was absolutely, totally real. And that reality turned it into the biggest nightmare she had ever known. Her grey eyes blurred briefly with tears and she blinked them away hurriedly, pushing trembling hands over the blonde smoothness of her hair as she fought for control.

He was early. They hadn't been expecting him for another half an hour or so. That was why she was still tidying the room, her white blouse and neat skirt covered by the ridiculous cotton apron, splashed all over with big colourful flowers, borrowed from the housekeeper to keep herself clean.

'Dad!' she called, her voice as shaken as her breathing. 'They're here.'

But her father was already aware, already heading out of the room, hurrying into the hall, pulling open the big front door. Abbie saw him pause to draw breath for a moment, brush his hands down his sides to ease their dampness and her heart constricted in fear.

If her father, a man who had always seemed able to handle anything, felt nervous then the worries that had kept her awake at night ever since the news had broken were even more justified than she had feared.

'Good luck!' she called, knowing he would need more than luck.

The whole family would do everything—anything they could—to help Andy. But when her younger brother's fate was in the hands of an absolute ruler of a foreign land, the sheikh of an Arabian country… She had no idea at all what he might demand of them.

He might listen to pleas for leniency, they had been told. Then again, he might refuse to do any such thing. No one, it seemed, could predict the way he might jump. But today, after three weeks of careful negotiation and diplomacy, somehow they had prevailed on this man, this sheikh, at least to discuss the matter with them.

And he was the man inside the car.

The man who…

Abbie's thoughts stopped dead as the uniformed chauffeur now came to the rear car door, opening it smoothly and stepping back, head up, spine stiffened as if at attention. He didn't actually salute, but his whole stance was one of respect and formality as he held the door so that the occupant of the limousine could emerge.

'Oh…'

It was all she could manage. The single syllable escaped from her on a long breathy sigh, pushed out on a wave of shock and pure disbelief. If a sleek black panther had uncoiled itself from a sitting position and prowled out of the car and on to the gravel driveway leading to the house, she couldn't have been more stunned.

Or more afraid.

This man was every bit as big and dark and sleek and powerful as a hunting cat. His long body held a controlled strength that was belied by his easy stride, every lithe movement smooth and relaxed.

But his face was anything but relaxed.

Just looking at his expression sent a cold shiver of dread slipping down Abbie's spine. It was not a pretty face, nor even one that she could describe as handsome. It was too strongly carved for that, all angles and hollows. High, slanting cheekbones defined the forceful lines of his features, emphasising the lean planes of his cheeks, the power of his jaw. There was an aquiline slash of a nose and under straight black brows were the deepest, darkest eyes that Abbie had ever seen.

It was a strong face—a harsh and imposing face. And it was very definitely an unyielding sort of face. Which wasn't something that held out any chance of hope for the help that they needed right now. He was younger than she had anticipated too—closer to thirty than the fifty she had somehow expected. Though whether that was good or bad—a point in their favour or against it—she had no way of guessing.

'I thought he was a sheikh!' a young voice said from close

at hand and looking down, she saw that her youngest brother, George, had come to stand beside her, staring out of the window at the important arrival.

'He is, love. The Sheikh of Barakhara.'

'But he's not wearing the right sort of clothes!'

'No…'

A faint smile touched Abbie's mouth, warming and easing a little of the anxiety from her grey eyes. At just twelve, George was still young enough to think in the simplest terms. Their imposing visitor was a sheikh and, as such, he should be wearing the flowing robes that were the traditional dress of men from his country. Instead, this sheikh was dressed in an immaculate steel-grey silk suit, superbly tailored, hugging the width of straight shoulders that had no need of extra padding to make them, or the chest beneath them, look broad and strong. The fine material slid over the powerful muscles of long, long legs, clung to the lean line of his hips, as he moved forward to where her father now stood on the doorstep, waiting to greet him. Under the afternoon sun, hair black as a raven's wing gleamed glossily sleek and the hand that he lifted to brush it back from his wide forehead had the same smoothly golden bronzed tone as the skin on that devastating face.

'So he's not a real sheikh?'

'Yes—yes, he is, sweetheart. But I think he only wears those robes in his own country.'

'In the desert—when he's riding on his camel?'

'Yes, I expect so.'

Another wider smile curved her lips at her young brother's innocent questions.

'So he is a real sheikh—and he can help Andy?'

Abbie's smile vanished, evaporating rapidly at this reminder of just why the Sheikh was here, and the seriousness of the situation that had brought about his visit.

'Yes, George. I hope so. I really hope so.'

'Daddy will talk to him,' George asserted.

'Daddy will talk to him,' Abbie echoed.

But her voice didn't have the conviction she wished for. Her shadowed eyes were watching the scene beyond the window, seeing the way that the Sheikh strolled towards the door, handsome head held arrogantly high, keen dark eyes scanning his surroundings assessingly.

He held out his hand to her father courteously enough and the clasp seemed firm and sure. But watching James Cavanaugh intently, sensitive to every move, every change of expression, Abbie saw the way the older man almost bowed, instinctively inclining his head in respect for his royal visitor. The gesture worried her. It made her fear that her father had been overawed by this much younger man. She didn't want to think about the possible implications of that.

They needed her father to be fully in control of the situation. He had to be able to cope, to discuss the matter calmly and confidently. Andy's future depended on it.

The thought of her brother, only just nineteen, alone and afraid, locked away in one of Barakhara's darkest, most secure jails made her shiver in fear, her nerves tying themselves into tight, cruel knots in her stomach. Andy had been foolish, stupid, totally irresponsible—but he wasn't *bad*. He'd made a mistake—a very serious one, admittedly, but a mistake was all it was. And if he was given a second chance...

He *had* to be given a second chance! After all, that was why the Sheikh was here.

Surely he wouldn't have travelled all this way just to tell them that he wasn't prepared to show her brother any leniency?

Leaning forward a little, she tugged slightly at the fall of the elderly lace curtain that shielded the window, twitching it aside so that she could see more clearly. Then froze as the small movement caught the corner of the Sheikh's eye, causing him to turn his head sharply, narrowed eyes hunting the source of the distraction. In a heart-stopping second the black, black gaze locked with silver-grey—and held.

'Oh, help!' Abbie couldn't hold back the exclamation of something close to horror.

If she had been a small scurrying mouse that had suddenly looked up and found itself the centre of the concentrated attention of some hunting hawk the shiver of apprehension that raced through her couldn't have been any more fearful. Abbie felt her throat close on a spasm of pure panic and her nerveless fingers let the curtain drop as she stepped back sharply, dodging out of the firing line of that laser-like scrutiny as quickly as she could.

But even so she felt the burn of his gaze hot on her skin, the sense of shock and bewilderment lingering as the net curtain fell back into place, shielding her once again from those sharp, assessing eyes.

Dear God, please let these negotiations be over and done with soon, she prayed silently. For no logical reason whatsoever, she was suddenly assailed by the feeling that she would not be safe while this man was in the house.

She just wanted him to go—be on his way—and out of her life for good.

And yet…she admitted as she stepped back as far out of sight as possible.

And yet she had never seen a man like him in her life. In spite of her fears, she knew that she would find it impossible to erase the image of his stunning features that was etched onto her mind.

If only they could have met some other time, in some other way.

Who the devil was that?

Sheikh Malik bin Rashid Al'Qaim wasn't a man easily distracted from his purpose. If an issue demanded his attention, it got it—wholeheartedly. And the subject he had to discuss with James Cavanaugh was one that needed whole-sale concentration. But, just for a moment, the sudden flash of movement, the twitch of a net curtain over to his left had caught his eye. He had turned...

And found himself transfixed, his gaze caught and held by the blonde who was staring at him in open curiosity from the ground floor window.

A stunning blonde. Tall and slim, with sleek, smooth hair and a figure shapely enough to distract his attention even further just for a moment. Even the ridiculously old-fash-ioned and unflattering cotton apron wrapped around her and tied tightly at her slender waist couldn't disguise the very sensual appeal of the feminine curves it covered.

Curves he would like a closer look at. Very much closer.

But even as the thought crossed his mind the blonde's eyes widened in something like embarrassment and she stepped back hastily, letting the lace curtain drop between them once again, concealing her from him.

No matter.

Malik crushed down the sudden twist of disappointment, the murmur of protest from senses that had been woken by the swift glimpse of the unknown blonde. He had more im-portant matters on his mind. The woman—clearly a maid or some other home help that the Cavanaughs employed—would keep.

'Would you care for something to drink—some refresh-ment after your journey?'

Swiftly Malik turned his attention back to what James Cavanaugh—Sir James Cavanaugh, he reminded himself—was saying.

'That would be very welcome,' he acknowledged and allowed himself to be escorted into the cool shade of the big oak-panelled hall, their footsteps echoing on the ornately tiled floor, his bodyguards following behind him.

He would much rather state his business and get the whole

thing out into the open so that they each knew where they stood, he reflected as he followed the older man through a door on the left and into a large bay-windowed room. A room that had obviously once been elegant and luxurious, but which now showed every sign of the sort of neglect and decay into shabbiness that came from a lack of ready cash to put things right.

He had spotted these indications of disrepair everywhere on the approach to this house. The ornate wrought iron gates had not had a coat of paint in years and were rusting and falling into decay, the fountain in the courtyard was coated in green moss and the flower beds were obviously unweeded and uncultivated.

The house itself might be huge and elegant, showing the way that this family had once held power and status in English society, but clearly the upkeep of their stately home was now beyond the means of the very limited income they possessed.

Which would make his task easier, he decided, watching his host fuss over his comfort in a way that did little to conceal the way that James was clearly a bundle of nerves. They would have little choice but to accept the offer he was here to make, and be grateful for it.

Malik just wished they didn't have to go though this pantomime of welcome and polite small talk first. The friendliness his host was now displaying would vanish soon enough. James Cavanaugh was not going to like what he had to say—not one little bit.

But if James wanted to see his son again this side of young Andrew's fortieth birthday then he would have no alternative but to agree to the conditions he was being offered.

Whether his daughter would go along with them was quite another matter.

CHAPTER TWO

IT WAS like waiting for the countdown to an explosion, Abbie told herself as she headed up the stairs to change, moving as quietly as possible past the library in the hope of hearing what was being said behind the closed door. But the only sound that came through the thick wood was the muffled murmur of voices, too blurred to make out any words, let alone decide how things were going.

She could tell which was her father's voice and which their visitor's but that was all. The rich, accented tones of the Sheikh's words carried even if their meaning didn't—and it appeared that he was doing all the talking.

Which seemed terribly ominous, she admitted, the thought draining all the strength from her legs so that she had to force herself to keep moving, holding on to the carved wooden banister for support. Had her father run out of things to say already? Or had the Sheikh rejected every suggestion put to him and was now laying down the terms on which he would help them?

Or, worse, was he making it plain that he had no mercy to offer? That her brother must serve out the sentence that had been passed on him, without any hope of remission?

'Oh, Andy!'

Bitter tears of despair burned in Abbie's eyes and, as she reached the half-landing, she sagged against the wall, covering her face with her hands.

Her brother had been a delicate child. He suffered badly from asthma and had often been in hospital or just sick at home. As a result he'd missed a lot of schooling so that he was young for his age and very naive. The trip to Barakhara had been his first experience of being abroad on his own. Now he was locked in some foreign prison and in the single brief phone call they had had from him, arranged with a lot of difficulty by the British Ambassador, he had quite obviously been terrified, begging them to get him out—to let him come home.

Frantic diplomatic efforts had followed and the Sheikh's visit was the result of that. It was their only chance. It couldn't fail. It just couldn't!

The sound of movement in the room below jolted her upright in haste. Someone was coming to the door—opening it.

Her father appeared in the hall below. He paused, looked back at the man inside.

The Sheikh, Abbie reminded herself. The man of power who held the future happiness of their family in the palm of his hand.

In the palm of his arrogant hand, a spark of defiance added, recalling the way that the man had turned to look at her in the moment of his arrival. The assessing way those dark eyes had scanned her.

'I'm sorry, but I must take this call.'

It was her father who spoke, his voice floating up to where she stood.

'I won't be long…'

He hurried off in the direction of the kitchen and Abbie watched him go. From her position here, higher up on the landing, even her father's powerful figure looked shortened, smaller somehow and reduced. The sight of him wrenched at Abbie's heart, making her bite her lip hard against the distress that threatened to choke her.

'Oh, Andy...' she began again, then caught herself up sharply.

It wasn't all Andy's fault! Okay, so her brother had been silly—downright stupid—but surely what he'd done hadn't been all that bad! Other boys his age had done as much, worse even! In England, pocketing some items from the archaeological dig he was working on would just be petty theft—wouldn't it? So what right did this sheikh have to lock her brother up and throw away the key?

Anger made her heart swell. A sense of bitter injustice made it beat at twice the speed as before, sending the blood coursing through her veins so fast that it made her head spin.

Who did he think he was? How dared he...?

She hadn't even realised that she was moving until she found herself halfway down the stairs again—heading in the direction of the hallway and the room her father had just left. She didn't know what was going to happen, had no idea what she was going to say. She only knew that she was going to say *something*.

The library door was still partly open, just as her father had left it. There was nothing there to make her stop, or even pause to think. The impetus that had taken her down the stairs had built up into almost a run, taking the last couple of steps two at a time, and sending her hurtling into the room before she had a chance for second thoughts.

Or before she had a chance to think of anything to say.

So there she was, suddenly face to face with the man—the *sheikh*—who had come to make demands of her family. Who was, in most respects, holding her younger brother to ransom, and was now letting them know just how they would have to pay.

Here she was, face to *gorgeous* face...

Oh, no, heaven help her, she didn't want to think of how stunning he was close up. How devastatingly dark and sexy. Just seeing him scrambled her thoughts until she had to fight against the urge to say something that was the complete opposite of the anger that had brought her in here.

He was lounging comfortably at his ease, damn him, in one of the big, well worn, soft leather armchairs that flanked the big open fireplace. His handsome head leaned comfortably against the studded leather back, soft blue-black hair brushing equally soft chestnut leather. His long, long legs were stretched out in front of him, crossed at the ankles, revealing superbly crafted handmade boots. One hand held a teacup, the finest bone china looking absurdly small and delicate, impossibly white, against the burnished bronze strength of his broad palm, the powerful fingers of the other hand resting negligently on the arm of his chair, totally relaxed.

Unlike Abbie, who was fizzing with rage, bristling with defiance.

'You can't do this!'

The words burst from her before she had time to consider them or even try to decide if she would be wiser to hold them back. And she didn't know whether to feel a sense of near panic or intense satisfaction as she saw the way that his head went even further back, forceful jaw tightening, gleaming jet-black eyes narrowing sharply as he looked up into her face.

'I beg your pardon?'

It was a shock to realise that these were the first words she had ever heard him speak clearly. She had been intensely aware of him, of his presence in the house, ever since that moment that he had stepped out of his car and into the sunlit courtyard. It was as if he had always been in her life, not just newly arrived in her experience.

'What did you say?'

The rich, dark, lyrically accented voice had sharpened, developing a razor's edge that made her wince inside to hear it. And there was a new tension in the long muscular body that no longer lounged easily in the chair but had developed the tightness of a coiled spring, like that hunting cat she had imagined earlier waiting and watching for just the right moment to pounce.

He hadn't actually moved but still there was enough of a threat of danger in him, in the tautly drawn jaw, the sharply narrowed eyes, that made her insides quail at the thought of that coldly reined-in anger turned on her. And yet somehow the new sense of risk added a sharper edge to the harsh male beauty of his face, the brilliance of those glittering jet eyes.

But not enough to curb her tongue.

'You can't do this! You can't treat people this way!'

'And what way would that be?'

'You know only too well!'

'I think not.'

To her nervous horror, he was leaning forward to replace the cup and its saucer on the table, uncoiling his long body with a slow and indolent grace as he got to his feet. Standing at his full height, he towered over her, big and overpowering, sending her throat into a spasm of shock and freezing her runaway tongue into silence. She swallowed hard and fought for the control not to turn and run straight for the door—fast!

'I don't believe I know what you're accusing me of—or why,' he went on, the beautiful voice shockingly soft and warm. Deceptively so because there was no way that the tone of his words matched the fierce, cold assessment to which those black, black eyes were subjecting her. 'So perhaps you'd like to explain.'

He'd wanted to meet the sexy blonde from the moment he'd seen her watching him from the window, Malik reminded himself. In fact, he'd agreed to James Cavanaugh's suggestion of tea largely in the hope that the maid would be the one who would bring it. He'd been disappointed when James himself was the one to go and fetch the tray. But then his host had been called away to an important phone call and now here was the blonde, appearing unexpectedly in the library without warning.

He would have sworn that, in the moment their eyes had met earlier, he had seen the same sudden flare of interest, of attraction, that he had felt for her. In fact, he had been so sure of it that he had been content to wait, believing it was only a matter of time before they came together. And her sudden appearance seemed to have proved him right.

She was even more stunning close up than he had imagined from the quick glimpse he had had of her through the window. She was tall, with rich, full breasts, a neat waist and curving hips. That ridiculous apron with its multicoloured flower print should have made her look anything but glamorous but the way it fastened around the slenderness of her waist emphasised the swell of her breasts, the flare of her hips. A real woman, unlike the almost boyish figures of so many of the females he had seen around London.

The sudden clutch of sexual hunger he experienced, just looking at her, was so primitive it was shocking. It was a long time since his rather jaded appetite had been stirred so strongly.

But her mood was not at all as he had anticipated. This hissing, spitting cat had little in common with the image of a warm, willing temptress he had built in his mind, letting himself consider that perhaps this trip to England might not be the boring diplomatic duty and family responsibility it had promised to be.

Instead he was faced with an aggressive, fiery creature who had marched up to him in a way that no woman in Barakhara would ever dare to do, confronting him with her hands on her hips and a blaze in her cool grey eyes.

'I don't need to explain! You know why you're here!'

'My business here is with Sir James—'

The attempt to squash her, silence her, failed as she drew in a sharp breath, then launched into a further attack, dismissing his intervention with an audacious wave of her hand.

'Your business here is to decide Andy's—Andrew's—fate!' she flung at him. 'I don't know who you think you are, dicing with people's lives like that! Just what gives you the right…'

'The law gives me the right,' Malik broke in on her with a snap. 'The law of—Barakhara. The same law that young Andrew chose to flout when he decided to pocket some of the items he found at that archaeological dig he was working on.'

Andy, his mind had noted, grabbing at the single word and working on the meaning behind it. She'd changed it pretty hastily to Andrew, but *Andy* was what she'd said at first, before she'd corrected herself.

And *Andy* meant a familiarity, a closeness that was more than servant to a member of the family she worked for.

'A few paltry items!' she scorned. 'What? A coin or two? A fossil? And for that you'd lock him up for life!'

'A few paltry *religious* items,' Malik corrected coldly. 'Items of deep significance to the history of Barakhara and its rulers. Items that in just the last century would have meant death for any non-Barakharanian to touch…'

He watched the colour ebb from her face with grim satisfaction. The ashen shade of her cheeks told him all he needed to know.

'You didn't know that?'

She could only shake her head, sending the pale gold of her hair flying as she did so.

Andy. Malik's mind went back to the word in the way that he might worry at a sore tooth with his tongue. *Andy*… So what was the relationship between these two? Did they have something going between them? Was *Andy* perhaps her lover? The sting of jealousy that thought brought was as jagged as it was unexpected, making him move sharply, uncomfortably.

'So he omitted to tell you the full facts about why he was arrested?'

Or was it the father who had done that? Was it the truth of the matter that James Cavanaugh—*Sir* James Cavanaugh—didn't want the world to know just what his stupid elder son had been up to?

Malik's mouth curled in distaste. The Honourable Andrew Cavanaugh was what the son called himself—what he had insisted on being called, Jalil had said. And the *Honourable* Andrew Cavanaugh lived in a house like this, with maids to clean and fetch and carry for him, and still he stole to line his own pockets. There was little that was *honourable* about that.

'So now perhaps you'll admit that I have a reason for what I'm doing. That I am not quite the spawn of the devil you think me?'

'I…'

She didn't seem able to find an answer for him. Her soft pink lips opened, but no words would come out. And clouds of confusion dulled the silvery grey of her eyes.

Suddenly Malik felt a sense of rage at the fate that had brought him here, the job he had to do. Why couldn't Jalil do his own dirty work?

There were times when he wished he could just let his young fool of a half-brother go to damnation in his own way. But if Jalil fell, then the whole of his country would go to rack and ruin too, and he had sworn an oath to his mother—Jalil's mother too—that he would never let that happen. A vow made within the family was sacrosanct, and he couldn't live with himself if he didn't keep it—no matter what it took.

He had hoped that a little dalliance with the blonde maid would at least provide some entertainment, some relaxation after the delicate negotiations he was going to have to handle. But from the stubborn, mulish expression on her face, he was going to have to work harder at winning her over than he had ever thought.

The unwanted and uncomfortable thought suddenly hit

him that if she knew the son—this *Andy*—so well, then maybe she was close to the daughter as well.

That was a complication he could do without. He had seen no sign yet of the Gail that Jalil had talked about, but if she and this girl were friends...

'No—he didn't tell me,' she managed now, stumbling over the words faintly and a raw colour washed those pale cheeks, betraying her embarrassment...

And making her look damnably sexy. It might be mortification that had put the blush on her skin but it made her look as if she had just got out of bed after a long, passionate session of sexual indulgence. It might have been the way that she had bitten down hard on her lower lip that had made it so pink, with all the blood rushing to the surface, but in his mind he knew that her mouth would look like that when she had been kissed senseless, taken to ecstasy and beyond.

'What's your name?' he demanded suddenly, his voice rough with the effort of trying to distract himself from the heated blood that seemed to be pooling low in his body, hardening and tightening so that it was a struggle to think straight—to think at all.

'I'm Abbie,' she told him, looking a little startled that he should ask.

Not Gail, Malik thought on a rush of relief. Just for one uncomfortable moment he had wondered...

'And what should I call you?'

She'd pulled back some of her confidence now, some of the strength there had been in her in the moment of her arrival in the room. There was a definite edge of sarcasm to her tone on the question. One that tugged a smile at the corner of his mouth, one that was impossible to hold back.

'You can call me Malik.'

'Malik...' Abbie's tongue curled around the exotic sound of the word as if she were tasting it.

It sounded rich and exotic, strong and firm—just right. Just like him.

'Is that all?'

Her voice was softly husky, dragged from a throat that was too dry, too tight, to speak naturally. She swallowed hard and slicked a moist pink tongue over suddenly parched lips, watching his black gaze drop just for a moment to follow the tiny revealing gesture. And when his eyes lifted again, burning straight into hers, she knew that she was lost. She had fallen into sensual slavery without knowing why or how it had happened. But she was in and tumbling head over heels into an endless chasm of awareness, one from which she already knew she had no hope of escape.

Not that she wanted to. That smile had rocked her world. It had only been a small curl at the corners of his sexy mouth but it had made her shiver in instant reaction, heated pinpricks of awareness tormenting her sensitised skin.

'Shouldn't I add something else?'

Her question brought those brilliant eyes swiftly back up to her face, locking with her own bemused gaze, holding it fixed.

'Add something?' he asked, the musical sound of his voice coiling round her senses like warmed silk. 'Like what?'

Like what? Abbie asked herself, scrabbling through the disorder of her thoughts, trying to find the original track they had been running on, the one she had meant them to follow.

'Like—like *sir*,' she managed hesitatingly.

He was a sheikh, wasn't he? A ruler. Of the royal house of Al'Qaim. Surely he must have some official title that she had to use.

'Or—or *Your Majesty*—or…*Highness*—'

The words broke off, her voice cracking as he moved suddenly, coming so very close. In spite of the heat, she found that she was once again shivering as if a cold draught had blown over her skin.

Having looked into the dark depths of his eyes, she found she couldn't look away again but was held frozen, mesmerised, captive. She couldn't have moved away if she'd tried. But she didn't try—couldn't try—didn't *want* to try.

Instead she knew that the saving grace of all that anger was deserting her, evaporating in the warmth of that smile. And when she saw the faint golden glow of amusement that lit those amazing eyes then she was lost. All the resistance in her melted like ice before a fire.

'Just Malik...' he murmured. Somehow he had moved closer so that the heat of his breath on the words brushed along her cheek, stirring a tendril of hair at the lobe of her ear.

She inhaled deeply, breathing in the scent of him, the warm musk of his skin, and let her breath out again on a sigh.

'Malik...' she said softly, her tongue savouring the exotic sound of his name. The frantic beat of her heart had slowed, become heavy, indolently sensual, and the honeyed warmth of arousal was uncoiling low down in her body, all that was most feminine in her reaching out to all that was masculine in him.

'Malik...' she said again, wanting to say so much more but not having the courage to do so.

Touch me! she wanted to say. *Let me feel the heat of your skin on mine, the strength of your hand, the stroke of your caress...*

But the words died on her lips; she couldn't make her tongue form the words even though she felt as if they were screaming inside her head. She had never felt this way before in her life.

No—the truth was that she had never known that it was possible to feel this way. To know this hunger, this desire for a man she had only just met. A man who made her heart thud, her pulse race, who made her aware of him in every part of her body so that her breasts stung and heat pooled in the most intimate spot between her thighs.

She'd had boyfriends in the past, but no one—*no one*—had ever affected her like this.

'You're beautiful…'

Malik moved slightly, coming even nearer, and once again the scent of his skin, the faintest hint of the perfume of cedar wood, reached out to surround her, tormenting her senses. She couldn't take it any more. Couldn't bear just to stand here and know he was so close—and yet not close enough.

She *had* to touch.

Throwing caution to the wind and giving in to the primal need that made her skin burn, her bones ache with need, she reached out a hand at last…

And encountered *his* hand reaching for her at the same time.

Their fingers met, touched, and it seemed to Abbie that sparks flew in the air, fizzing between them like fireworks. But then those long bronzed fingers tangled with hers, twisting together, holding tightly, drawing her closer to him with an irresistible strength. Abbie knew she had to give in to the need that swamped her, dark waves of sensuality breaking over her head as she almost fell against him and his mouth came down to claim hers.

The kiss that Malik had been imagining since the moment he had first seen her was far more in reality than it had ever been in his mind. The soft feel of Abbie's lips against his own was like setting a match to the tinder-dry brushwood of the hunger that was just waiting to burst into flames, flaring savagely through the whole of his body, making him burn with need. The taste of her on his own mouth, his tongue, was like the most potent aphrodisiac, driving him to plunder the soft interior as she opened to him, yielding in the same moment that she demanded more.

And he would give her more. He wanted this woman so much it was like a thunder in his head, pounding at his thoughts, obliterating all sense of reality. He forgot where he was and why he had come here, the mission he had set out to achieve. All he could focus on was the soft, feminine body in his arms, the tender mouth that opened under his, the hands that clung...

'You're beautiful...'

Her fingers were making a path up his arms, stroking their way over his shoulders, tangling in his hair. The faint scrape of her nails over the sensitive skin of his scalp made him drag in a raw, shaken breath before crushing her closer, taking her mouth yet again. His own hands had found the elastic band that fastened her long blonde hair back and tugged it loose, tangling hard in the silken strands, holding her just so—so that he could kiss her exactly the way he wanted to.

And *she* wanted it too.

There was no resistance in her supple body, no stiffening or drawing away; instead, she pressed closer than ever, the fine bones of her pelvis cradling the heat and hardness of his erection. Each tiny movement she made stoked the fire of need, making it flare higher and hotter and fiercer than ever before.

'I want you...'

He barely recognised his own voice, barely understood the language he spoke, it was so hard and thick and rough with the hunger that tortured him. His accent was harsher than ever before and for a moment it crossed his mind that she might not be able to make out a single word he had spoken.

But the woman in his arms simply sighed and muttered something against his mouth, something so muffled and in-distinct that he was forced to wrench his lips away from hers. He tugged her head back with his imprisoning grip on the blonde length of her hair to look down into her passion-flushed face, seeing the sensually glazed eyes, the swollen mouth.

'What?' he demanded, needing to hear the words in spite of the evidence his eyes were giving him. 'What did you say?'

'I said…'

But she didn't even trouble to finish the sentence, reaching up instead to fasten one arm tight around his neck and drag his head down to her again.

'Yes…'

It was a sigh against his mouth again—or a moan. A sound of surrender? A sound of demand?

He didn't know and he didn't care. This wasn't a time for words, for talking, but for action. And the action that his hotly aroused body demanded was that he take this willing and wanton woman hard and fast—and *now!*

With his mouth still on hers, his hands locked in her hair, he half walked, half carried her backwards, moving awkwardly, stiff-legged, supporting her in his arms, dodging furniture by instinct rather than sight until they came hard up against the wall with a thump that drove the breath from her body on a gasp that went straight into his mouth.

Swallowing down the shaken breath, Malik cupped her face in both his hands, tilting it again to get just the right angle to kiss her hard and long, taking the sweetness from her mouth and feeling it intoxicate his already fizzing senses, heat his blood even higher.

'Yes!' he muttered against her lips. 'Yes! You're mine. I knew that from the first moment—'

The words broke off, raw breath rasping in his throat as he felt her hands push between them, tugging at his tie, pulling it loose at his neck, her fingers seeking the warm flesh beneath, raking it hungrily.

'Abbie…' Her name was just a rasp, a sound, barely a real syllable of a word.

'Malik…' Her voice was no better. It shook on his name, coming and going like an untuned radio. 'Malik…'

He crushed her against the wall, unable to get close enough, to feel her warmth and softness against every part of his body. He wanted to spread her out beneath him, to tear her clothes from her body, to feel her heat and tightness enclose his aching sex. But at the same time he didn't want to move away from her for even those few seconds it would take to get them both into that position.

Moving would mean ending that delicious pressure of body against body, heat against heat. It would mean breaking away from the hungry, demanding caress of her hands, the way that her fingers fumbled and snatched at the buttons of his shirt, seeking out the flesh beneath, tugging lightly, tormentingly at the curls of dark hair she found there.

But *he* had to touch *her*. Just the caress of her mouth, the feel of her body beneath the thin cotton blouse, was nowhere near enough. He needed—yearned for—the sensation of skin on skin. Of hot flesh burning into flesh, the heady perfume of arousal reaching into the air and stimulating already strained senses to breaking point.

'Abbie…'

With a rough movement he jerked her into a slightly different position, holding her captive against the wall as he brought his hands down over her thighs, reaching out and grabbing the hem of her skirt, pulling it roughly upwards, rucking it over her hips, exposing the soft skin of her legs.

The soft *bare* skin, he noted on a sound of surprised satisfaction, feeling the silky smoothness beneath his greedy fingertips. Just skin, not the appalling synthetic scratch of tights—just skin, soft as heated velvet, enticing as hell. Just *Abbie*.

And *just Abbie* was all that he wanted.

Her hands had found his skin, buttons were wrenched open, his shirt pulled out of the way until it was skin on skin at last and a sigh broke from her on a gasp of contentment. Her fingers smoothed over his chest, tangling for a brief moment in the curls of body hair before that wandering touch curved over his shoulders, finding the tension in his muscles, then slid down his back, along each vertebrae as far as she could reach.

And Malik needed to touch too. The pressure and heat of body against body just weren't enough. A pressure and heat was building inside him too, rising to boiling point, creating a sensation inwardly that was like some violent volcano that was about to blow. And he would explode if he didn't touch her.

Muttering thick-tongued endearments in his native language, he pushed the clinging skirt even higher. The feel of his fingertips on her hot flesh sent sensations like the shock of a bolt of lightning right through him and he felt the shudder that shook her. The same shudder that tormented his own hungry body.

He heard her moan softly—or was it his own voice he heard? He had no idea but the next moment his mouth captured hers, plundered deep, but then was wrenched fiercely away when just to kiss no longer satisfied. He needed to go further, explore deeper, taste more of her. And she understood totally, arching her neck into his caress, mutely inviting him to take what he wanted.

'Yes…'

It was a sound of yearning, of encouragement, of pure need. One that made an answering need kick hard at him low down in his body.

The ridiculous apron was always in the way. Fastened tight around her waist, about her neck, it hindered every move he tried to make. But by throwing it upwards from below, he had access to the heated core of her. To the lilac-coloured, flimsy bit of nothing that guarded the centre of her femininity. The frivolous bit of silk was such a contrast to the severely practical and sensible outerwear that it brought a shaken laugh into his throat, making him catch his breath in shocked response.

'So this is what you have hidden away under this absurd uniform. This is what the real woman wears. I like it—more than like it.'

He could feel the heat of her even from this distance, feel the moisture that betrayed her hunger. The scent of her aroused body filled his nostrils, obliterating all thought, driving him wild.

And her kisses drove him wilder. Fierce, urgent, demanding little kisses that pecked at his cheek and neck like an insistent, hungry bird. Her hands didn't seem to know where they most wanted to be—in his hair or over his shoulders or down his arms. The jacket he wore was skimmed off, dropped to the floor, discarded carelessly. More buttons were wrenched undone, his shirt was tugged from his waistband, her fingers...

Oh, by Allah, her fingers were unstoppable, probing lower, seeking, touching, caressing...

'Abbie,' he groaned, but whether in encouragement or in protest at the impossibility of actually doing anything *here* and now, he didn't know. 'We can't. We must— We—'

But a wild shake of her head denied his words, not giving him the chance to continue.

'Kiss me,' she demanded. *'Kiss me!'*

He would do more than *kiss* her! So much more!

Her breasts were tight against his chest, the hard points of her nipples communicating the sharpness of the arousal she made no attempt to hide. He wanted to get his hands on those richly curved mounds, to touch—to feel—to taste...

But first he had to get past the bib of that damned apron. The appalling flowered cotton was there between him and what he wanted so much—but not for long! With a muttered curse he wrenched at it, pulling hard at each shoulder. The thin cotton straps snapped without much difficulty, ripping apart the worn seams.

At last!

Hands shaking with hunger, with the urgency of need, Malik tugged at the buttons halfway down the prim white blouse, pulling them open roughly. The small opening he made was just enough to let him push his fingers in and touch the warm, swelling softness of one exposed breast. At the feel of his caress Abbie choked some incoherent, wordless sound of response, her eyes closing ecstatically, her mouth blindly seeking his.

Another button popped free from its restraint and now he could get his whole hand underneath her blouse. He cupped the softness of one breast, feeling its heat through the silk and lace confection of her bra. The nub of her nipple pushed into his palm in wanton demand and the ache of desire between his legs was almost unbearable.

He had to have her. Had to…

But, even as he closed his hand around her heated softness, his ears caught the sound outside the room that broke into and shattered the sensual delirium that had him in its possession.

CHAPTER THREE

'I'LL leave that with you then…'

The voice sounded out in the hallway, coming clearly through the barely closed door. Calm and decisive and totally shattering to the heated mood that gripped the pair of them.

'We'll sort it out later.'

A male voice.

James Cavanaugh's voice.

His *host's* voice.

The voice of the man he had come here to negotiate with.

What the hell was he doing?

Dazed, shaken, blinking like a man dealing with the aftermath of a blow to his head, Malik lifted his eyes to lock with Abbie's silver gaze. He found that she too had frozen into immobility, her eyes wide and staring straight at him. She looked glazed, unfocused, not seeing anything, and her head was tilted slightly to one side as if she was straining to hear.

'Cavanaugh…' he managed, his voice croaking roughly. 'My—'

She swallowed hard, unable to continue to form the words. 'Your boss.'

Malik nodded, understanding the embarrassment she would feel at being caught like this—especially with the important visitor that the family must want to impress and please as much as possible.

Your boss?

It took the space of a couple of uneven breaths for the words to penetrate the buzzing haze of shock that filled Abbie's mind, and even when they did finally hit home they made no sense at all.

Your *boss!*

He thought that she worked for…

But then the sound of movement from behind the door, the sound of footsteps in the hallway, froze the thought in her mind, leaving instead room for her to grasp at a realisation that was far more stunning, more shocking.

Her *father* was outside in the hall.

And he was coming back.

Her father was crossing the hall, coming back, heading for the library, coming back to his guest…

He would open the door, would look across the room and he would find…

He would find her *here*, like…

With the instinct of panic her hand went to the gaping front of her blouse, fingers spread wide to cover the exposed white skin, the delicate flesh still slightly reddened by the touch of Malik's hard fingers.

'Here…'

Already Malik was moving, acting—taking charge. Already his behaviour was totally back under control—the control she had completely, abjectly lost without a hope of finding again.

He was tugging down her skirt, smoothing it over her hips, along her thighs, his movements brusque and—that damn word again!—controlled. He didn't seem aware of the way that his touch, so cool and calm, distant as a doctor's, made her want to cry out in shock and loss as it came so close to the spot where the throbbing tension of need even now held her in its grip. The sting of arousal still pricked at her breasts, demanding appeasement. The whole of her body felt like a long moan of protest at the way that the pleasure it had been seeking had been so brutally snatched away, leaving her lost and desolate.

'Fasten yourself up.'

Malik's tone was brusque, his curt words a cold command. His eyes were hard as jet without any trace of the burn of warmth that had been in them before. The man who had called himself 'just Malik' was gone and the person that Abbie thought of as *The Sheikh* was back and wholly in control.

He was busy tidying himself as he spoke, quickly and efficiently fastening the buttons her fingers had tugged open, tucking his shirt back into his trousers, smoothing his hand over his tousled hair.

'I said, fasten yourself up!'

It was an order and a sound of reproof all in one and the cold disapproval in the black gaze that swept over her cut straight to her heart.

She had been lost, adrift on a sea of passion so intense that it had taken over her mind and driven all rational thought from it. The sensation had been so devastating that she was having trouble focusing on anything else. But Malik was icily, unemotionally back in control in the space of a heartbeat, and it was obvious that nothing at all had touched him in the way that it had affected her.

'Do you want Cavanaugh to find you here like this?'

'N-no…'

She could only manage a whisper, her voice refusing to obey her. So were her fingers as she fumbled with her disordered clothing, the sense of panic at the thought of her father finding her like this making matters worse.

'Abbie!'

Her name hissed through Malik's teeth in a sound of total exasperation and he reached for her again. Perhaps his intention was only to help; perhaps he meant to do what she couldn't manage and pull things back together again, but that wasn't the thought that crossed Abbie's mind.

'No!'

Remembering only the burning pleasure that those hands had brought her just seconds before and not knowing whether she most longed for a repetition of it or feared it utterly, she reacted on total instinct. An instinct that was even closer to the panic she had barely been able to control.

'*No*—I—I have to go!'

There was one way she could avoid any confrontation with her father, ensure that he didn't know what had been happening in his absence. There was a side door on the far wall of the library, one that led out of the room in the opposite direction to that in which her father was approaching.

True, it also led to the conservatory from which the only way back into the house, without retracing her steps, was to go out into the garden and come in again by the kitchen door. But at least she would have a few moments in which to draw breath. Everyone was inside so she would have time in which to pull herself together, both mentally and physically.

How could she have let this happen? How could she have lost all control, all sense of self-preservation so completely as to forget just who this man was and why he was here?

She couldn't even look him in the face, couldn't meet his eyes. And yet just seconds ago…

'Your boss,' Malik had said. He had thought that she was employed by her father—by the Cavanaugh family. She could only suppose that the appalling apron and her scruffy clothes had given him that impression.

He thought that she was only a servant and so fair game for him to waste time with, to flirt with heartlessly. To use for his pleasure and then discard when he felt like it.

'I have to go,' she muttered again, hoping it sounded more convincing this time. With her head down, her eyes burning with bitter humiliation, she turned for the door, moving as quickly as she could, just wanting to get away—get out of there.

She made it to the door, had turned the handle—opened it—when, to her shock and horror, he came after her. One strong bronze-skinned hand closed over her arm, imprisoning her wrist, holding her.

'Wait!' he said, his voice low and thick. 'Wait!'

'Wait for what?'

For further humiliation? For him to tell her that she wasn't worth his time? That she had simply been an amusement with which to fill the minutes while he had been waiting for her father to return? Wasn't that what men like him—sheikhs like him—had harems for? So that they could pick any woman they chose. Any woman who happened to catch his eye. Any woman he fancied mauling.

'So that you can maul me again?'

'Maul?'

He actually looked shocked. His proud dark head went back, brilliant eyes narrowing sharply.

'Maul!' he repeated on a deeper note. 'You dare to call that mauling! Let me remind you, *sukkar*, that you wanted it every bit as much as I did—you still do.'

His cruel gaze dropped to where her breasts were still exposed. To where the tight, hungry points of her nipples betrayed the need she might try to deny with words—an unconvincing denial when her body spoke so eloquently against her.

'And I still do.'

Malik's voice was rough and thick. So he wasn't quite as much in control as he pretended, Abbie realised. There was still a lingering rawness in his eyes and the hand that imprisoned hers was not quite as steady as she had first thought.

The realisation made her hesitate. She couldn't move, either in or out of the open door. She could only stare up into the glittering darkness of his eyes and wait...

But then the footsteps—her father's footsteps paused outside the door. She saw the handle turn…

And suddenly Malik's hand came up to touch her face. He cupped her cheek in one hard palm, looked deep into her eyes as if determined to hypnotise her into total obedience.

'Come to me tonight,' he whispered softly, huskily. 'Come to me at my hotel and we can finish what we started.'

She didn't answer. She couldn't answer. But she knew from his faint smile how he saw the change in her face, the one she couldn't disguise. The one that meant acquiescence, whether it was wise or not.

He saw her face change and knew he didn't have to say anything more.

'The Europa,' he said, the total confidence in his tone that of a man who knew he had won and there was nothing more to say. 'The Europa at eight. I'll be waiting.'

His mouth took hers for a hot, brief moment and then was gone.

Abbie didn't know if she moved herself or if Malik pushed her, but either way it was only just in time. Somehow she was on the other side of the door, and with it firmly closed behind her. And in the library she heard the other door open and her father's voice apologising for being so long.

'Not at all…'

This time, Malik's accented voice came clearly through the heavy wood that separated them. Cool and clear and totally unperturbed as if nothing had happened and he had simply been standing there, waiting for his host's return.

'I had plenty to think about. Plenty to occupy me while I waited. I never noticed the time at all.'

It was already turning dusk outside. Under cover of the gathering darkness, Abbie swiftly tidied herself up, adjusted her appearance. The wretched apron was ruined, torn beyond repair, so she pulled it off, crumpling it into a bundle and stuffing it out of sight behind a couple of plant pots. She would come back and retrieve it later tonight, when no one was likely to see her.

Later tonight. Tonight. The word hit home to her as she hurried along the shadowy path, heading for the kitchen door.

Tonight. Come to me tonight...and we can finish what we started.

He had been so sure, so confident that she would not refuse him. He would be waiting for her at eight, just as he had said.

Would she be there?

Even as the question entered her head, Abbie knew that the answer would push it straight out again, giving her no time to think. Not that she needed any.

Of course she would be there. She had no other choice. No alternative.

It was dangerous. It was crazy. It was probably the most stupid thing she would ever do—but how could she ever live with herself if she didn't do it? How could she leave this stunning man, this devastating meeting, only half known, his lovemaking only half completed? The ache in her body, an ache that felt like a bruise right into her soul, told her that she couldn't. She just couldn't leave things like this.

The Europa at eight...

Malik's confident voice rang inside her head.

He was so sure that she would be there.

Her footsteps slowed, coming to a halt in the darkness, and her fingers crept up to her mouth, pressing against her lips, thinking back, remembering how it had felt to have Malik's kiss on her mouth. His caresses on her yearning body.

The Europa at eight...

And she would be there. Of course she would be there. How could she ever live with herself if she wasn't?

CHAPTER FOUR

THE huge gilt clock in the foyer of the Europa hotel was striking the half hour as Abbie made her way to the reception desk.

She was exactly half an hour late—deliberately so. She had fully intended that Malik should have to wait for her. Or at least she had once she had finally decided that she was coming here tonight. Because the confidence of that first decision hadn't lasted. She had barely got inside the house, closing the kitchen door and leaning back against it, before the doubts had assailed her.

How could she have ever been so stupid? she had asked herself. What was she thinking of, planning to go to him—to take him up on his invitation?

His invitation to seduction.

No, it hadn't been an invitation. It was an order—a command from a man used to giving commands to everyone every day. Giving them and having people jump to obey them as soon as he spoke. He probably didn't even have to ask most of the time, just click his fingers and he would be obeyed.

And was she going to jump to do his bidding too?

Not on her life!

No, she told herself as she made her way through to the hall again. His Royal High and Mightiness the Arrogant

Sheikh Malik bin Rashid Al'Qaim could snap his fingers all he liked. She wasn't going to be at his beck and call just because...

Just because he was the most devastatingly attractive, the most shockingly sexy man she had ever met in her life.

Her footsteps slowed, turned, drawn by some invisible force, some powerful magnetism, taking her towards the library in spite of the resistance she tried to impose on them. The door was tightly shut, the sounds of the voices inside the room muffled, their words impossible to make out. But she knew when Malik was speaking She had only heard a few hundred words from that erotic voice but already it seemed to be imprinted on her mind so that she recognised it instantly.

And wanted to hear it again.

And again.

She wanted to hear it tell her to call him 'Just Malik'. To hear him say that she was beautiful, that he wanted her... She wanted to hear that glorious voice whisper to her in the darkness, giving her words of love, of caring, of hunger.

Tonight. Come to me tonight...and we can finish what we started.

Oh, dear God, she just wanted to listen to that voice all night—every night—for the rest of her life.

But was that enough to base her future on? Surely she was totally unwise—crazy!—to go to him.

But, oh! How she *wanted* to.

'Can I help you, madam?'

The receptionist's question broke into her thoughts and dragged her back to the present. To the moment she had been worrying about from the point she had set out on this wild assignation.

'Come to me,' Malik had said, and he'd told her the name of the hotel, but he hadn't given her any further information than that. She had never visited someone so important, someone royal before. Surely there would be security checks at the very least.

'My name is Abbie…' she began hesitantly and was intensely relieved to see the woman's face break into a smile.

'Of course. We are expecting you. Would you please come this way?'

A few moments later, whizzing upwards in the express lift that went only to Malik's suite, Abbie couldn't believe how easy it had been. She had merely given her name and everyone had jumped into action, informing the penthouse suite that she was here, checking her identity, escorting her to the lift. There she had been handed over to the care of a tall, dark and deeply polite security guard who now stood, strong legs planted firmly on the floor, deep-set eyes alert and watchful, on the opposite side of the lift.

Just at that moment it slowed to a halt and the doors slid open silently. Her companion gave a small bow.

'After you, madam,' he said as he stood back to allow her to precede him.

This must be what it was like all the time if you were a sheikh, Abbie reflected as she stepped out on to thick, soft pile carpeting in a rich royal blue. To have people whose only job was to follow your instructions, to do as they were told, to do as you asked. Once again Sheikh Malik had snapped his fingers and everyone had jumped to do his bidding.

If she had been nervous before, then now her stomach felt as if a million desperate butterflies were beating frantic wings against her ribcage, sending waves of unease up into her throat. She struggled for breath as she headed into the small foyer where a smooth, pale wooden door barred her way. Another security guard stood beside it, firmly at attention, arms by his sides, the smooth fitting of his tailored jacket very slightly marred by an ominous-looking bulge at his waistband.

Abbie swallowed hard at just the thought of being this

close to a gun, forcing herself to smile nervously into the guard's dark, set face. But her attempt at a polite greeting was ignored as, with another of those small, stiff bows, he reached to open the door and hold it for her.

'Th-thank you!'

Her legs seeming to have only the strength of cotton wool, Abbie stumbled into the room, her personal security guard following close behind her. From behind, she heard the man say something in Arabic, obviously announcing her. As she blinked to clear eyes that had blurred with tension, she saw Malik's tall, elegant figure uncoil smoothly from the soft black leather-covered settee set in the middle of the huge luxurious room.

'You came!' he said, the impact of that rich honeyed voice hitting her senses hard all over again. 'Welcome!'

Had he really questioned that she would appear? Privately, Abbie took the liberty of doubting that he had thought any such thing. Men like Malik never even considered that there was any likelihood that they would not be obeyed, and obeyed without question.

But then she remembered the stunning news that her father had given her over dinner. The news that had totally changed her mind when it had been set against coming here at all.

She had decided that she was going to be sensible. That she couldn't take the risk of doing as Malik had asked, no matter how much her foolish heart had pleaded with her. And then her father had said that he had something to discuss with her.

'It's Andy, isn't it?' she'd said apprehensively, seeing the way his face was set into lines of strain, his blue eyes shadowed with concern.

'The Sheikh has told you something—what has he said? Will they let him go?'

'There is a chance,' James Cavanaugh had responded. 'But it's going to be difficult.'

'However difficult it is, you have to do it!' Abbie had declared. 'You *have* to. You can't leave him there in that jail, locked up for…'

Her words had faltered nervously, dying on her lips as her father shook his head, his expression sombre.

'Why are you looking at me like that?' she'd asked. 'What does he want? What is it you're not saying?'

'It isn't a question of my doing something,' her father had told her solemnly. 'The only person who can help your brother is you. You're the one who has it in your power to help him, but I don't know if you can possibly agree to what's been asked…'

'Come and sit down…'

Malik was moving towards her, his hand outstretched. Without even really knowing that she was doing it, Abbie pushed her own hands into the pockets of the blue-and-white dress she wore, putting them securely out of reach. If he was to touch her, she didn't know what her reaction would be. Just being in the room with him was bad enough.

She had told herself that she hadn't been thinking straight. That she had been so desperately on edge all day—all week!—worrying about her brother, fearful of the moment that the all-powerful sheikh would arrive, dreading the thought of the demands he might make to free Andy. She must have exaggerated the stunning impact this man had had on her.

She had to have exaggerated it. No man could have launched such an assault on her senses, driven her so out of her mind that it had left her shaking with reaction long after she had left him.

But Malik had. And she hadn't overstated a thing! Even now, when he was still several metres away from her, she could feel her senses start to react, like a flower unfurling in the sun, turning towards the heat and the light, drawn irresistibly to what it needed most.

Her heartbeat had already quickened and her pulse was throbbing. The clean masculine scent of his body was in her nostrils, making her quiver in response.

At some point he had changed his clothes and now here, in the privacy of this huge suite, he was surprisingly casually dressed in jeans and a clinging T-shirt, black as his hair and eyes. And seeing him like that seemed to dispel the thought that he was a sheikh, a prince, the ruler of his desert country. Instead he was just a man. A devastatingly attractive man. An incredibly, hotly sexy man.

And a man who had made it plain how much he wanted her.

'Abbie?'

He had reached her side and his hand touching her shoulder to draw her attention startled her into new awareness. The heat of his hand seemed to burn through the material of her dress, scorching the skin beneath so much that she didn't know whether she most wanted to lean into it or pull away sharply.

Hot colour flared in her cheeks and she swallowed hard to relieve the uncomfortable pressure in her throat.

'Thank you…'

There was a sense of release in walking away from him. Release from the heated tension that had tightened every muscle, release from the stinging sensitivity to everything about him. But as soon as she moved she knew that she wanted it back again, longed for him to come close once more.

It wasn't easy; it wasn't comfortable. It didn't feel safe or relaxing. The truth was that it knotted her nerves tight with tension and uncertainty. It made her stomach twist just to think of it—but at the same time it was thrilling and exciting. It was the most wonderful thing that had happened to her. It brought her *alive* in a fizzing, crackling way. So alive that it was as if she had only been sleepwalking through her life before.

And on top of that it made her feel so completely, gloriously feminine. She had never felt so much of a woman as she had in the few short hours she had known this man and he had made his desire for her so obvious.

And more than his desire, if what her father had told her was right.

'Can I get you a drink?'

Malik stood beside her as she sank down into the soft comfort of the leather-covered settee, his height and strength so much more imposing from this lower position.

'Please...'

She had to find some way of speaking in more than monosyllables! Abbie reproved herself. But simply being in this man's presence seemed to have tied her tongue into knots and scrambled her brain so that she couldn't think straight.

'Wine? Or mineral water—or something stronger?'

'Mineral water, please.'

She would do well to keep a clear head and not muddle her thoughts even further with alcohol.

Or perhaps some alcohol would relax her.

'No—wine, please—red. Anything, really. I don't mind. Whatever you've got will be fine.'

Well, at least she was talking in sentences of a sort, but now there was the risk of her tongue running away with her. Clamping her lips shut, Abbie tried again for control, only to find that any hope of it eluded her as she saw the small, almost unconscious hand gesture that Malik made, the automatic inclination of his head towards a dresser on which a selection of bottles and glasses stood.

And the immediate move into action that was the result.

She had barely even noticed the man who had been standing at the far side of the room. He had been so still and silent that he had almost blended in with his surroundings, his navy blue shirt and jacket toning with the dark velvet of the ceiling to floor curtains. But now he moved forward, a result of Malik's brief, almost imperceptible summons.

Silent and smooth, he moved to the tray of drinks, opening bottles and pouring without another word needing to be said, then handing them to his prince with a bow.

This was what it would be like all day every day for Malik, Abbie thought on a wave of shock. This was what he was used to, what was normal to him. He was accustomed to be waited on hand and foot, his slightest whim attended to, almost before he had even realised it.

And this would be her life too if…

No, she couldn't think of that now! It would destroy the little composure she had managed to gather together.

But of course it was totally impossible that she could *not* think of it! It was all that had been spinning round and round in her thoughts ever since the moment that her father had told her the conditions that had been offered to enable Andy's release.

'The Sheikh of Barakhara needs a wife. He has chosen you to be that wife. If you say yes, then he will drop all charges against Andy and free him as soon as it can possibly be managed.'

Her father had believed that she couldn't possibly agree to the demands he was making. He had assumed that she would refuse to have anything to do with the idea. That she would declare she would rather die or face prison herself. But then, of course, her father had no idea that she had ever met the Sheikh—met Malik in person.

And he had definitely no suspicion at all of the effect that Malik had had on her.

Something had happened in the time they had been apart, Malik told himself as he took the two glasses—one of wine and one of water—from Ahmed and carried them over to the coffee table before which Abbie was sitting. She had changed—or at least her mood was very different from the sparky, vibrant young woman he had met earlier that day.

There was a stiffness about the way that she held herself,

a wariness in those enormous eyes and she looked as skittish as one of his thoroughbred Arabian mares, as if she might turn and run from him at the slightest suggestion of anything that might spook her. As he put the glasses down her eyes flicked up to his face, very quickly, and then away again, twice as fast. And her 'Thank you,' was so faint as to be almost inaudible.

Well, he knew how to handle an uncertain woman. He was almost as much of an expert in it as he was in soothing a nervous horse. It needed patience, consideration, but the end result was worth it. He would get what he wanted in the end.

And what he wanted out of Abbie was a long night's pleasure. She was to be his relaxation after a day from hell. From the way that she had responded to him earlier, he had anticipated that it would be a lot easier than it now seemed likely. But he could wait. He had all night.

But first he needed to work on the atmosphere a little— make things easier, more comfortable for both of them.

'Leave us.'

A wave of his hand gestured towards the door, indicating that Ahmed and the security guard should leave. Abbie would relax much more if they were alone. The bodyguard would have to remain at the door but at least they would be spared his inhibiting presence in the room.

'So now,' he said, coming to sit opposite her as the door closed behind the other two men, 'we can be alone together.'

Abbie reached for the water, gulped some of it down, setting the glass back on the table with an unsteady crash.

'He—they—walked backwards,' she managed on a raw shaken note.

'Hmm? Oh, Ahmed and Ishaq?'

The truth was that he had barely noticed the other two men leaving the room. His attention had been solely focused on the woman in the blue-and-white dress. The woman whose

blonde hair was too tightly fastened back for his liking.
Whose huge grey eyes, fringed with lush thick lashes, still
had that startled, apprehensive look about them, like a rabbit
caught in car's headlight.

'It is the custom in Barakhara.'

'They always have to do that?'

Malik's only response was a curt nod. His half-brother
stuck strictly to the old-fashioned rituals expected of servants
and here in England he was acting as Jalil's representative
so he was accorded the same deference, no matter that he had
dispensed with such nonsense in his own kingdom. But he
saw that it must seem stunning and almost shocking to her.
Of course, it would be that that had put her on edge.

'Don't worry, I won't expect it of you.'

Now what had he done to bring that expression to her
eyes? This time she lifted her gaze to his and studied his face
searchingly for a moment. And when she reached for her
glass it was the wine she drank. Uncertainty or relaxation?
He didn't know but he knew which one suited his purposes
best.

He didn't want her to sit perched on the edge of the settee
like that, her mouth strictly controlled, her hands fastened
around her glass as if she feared she might drop it. What he
wanted was the woman he had met that afternoon. The woman
who had heated his blood so fast it had felt like an explosion in
his head. The woman who had melted into his arms like a
candle before the blaze of the fire. The dress she had on might
be so much more flattering and feminine than the elderly blouse
and skirt uniform—and that ridiculous ugly apron—but just the
fact that she was wearing it meant that she was wearing too
much.

What he wanted was to skip the formalities and get
straight to the intimacy she had all but promised him this afternoon. He wanted her out of that dress and whatever little
bits of lace she was wearing underneath it. He wanted her

naked and responsive, warm, willing and open to him, lying underneath him either here or in the big luxurious bed in the next room—he didn't care where.

And she wanted the same. She wouldn't be here otherwise. He had asked her to come to him, to finish what they had started, and here she was, ready to do just that. It was too late for second thoughts.

And the first thing that had to happen was that appallingly controlled and unappealing hairstyle had to go.

'But I do want this changed…'

Leaning forward, he put his hands around the back of her head, finding the elastic band that restrained the blonde hair. A couple of swift, efficient tugs soon had it sliding down and off the silken ponytail before he tossed it carelessly on the floor, not looking where it fell.

Instead his attention was fixed on her face. On those widening grey eyes, the way that the soft rose mouth had opened on a gasp of surprise. The wineglass she still held remained frozen, the movement to replace it on the table stilled completely.

'That's better…'

With his fingers he combed through the loosened strands, freeing them even more, ruffling them around her face, over her shoulders. At first he was simply acting to ease away the restriction of the severe style but as soon as he felt the slide of the silky hair against his fingers he lost sight of what his original intention had been.

All he knew was that he wanted to stroke, to smooth, to caress…just to touch. He wanted to tangle his fingers in the silken slide of it, to inhale the scent of some floral shampoo that blended with the warmth of the skin on her scalp to create an aroma so potently intoxicating that it made his senses swim just to breathe.

'Much better,' he said on a very different tone, his voice suddenly deeper, husky and thickened by the need that was already gnawing at him deep inside. '*Much* better.'

Abbie made some faint inarticulate sound that might have been agreement then abandoned it on a faint sigh.

She slicked a soft pink tongue over her upper lip as if to ease some dryness there then froze in shock as she caught him watching the tiny betraying movement.

'Malik…' she managed and her voice sounded so much like his, hoarse and fraying at the edges, that he laughed out loud, the sound catching deep in his throat, emerging more as an uneven sigh than the chuckle he had aimed for.

The caress of his hands moved from her hair to her scalp, shaping the fine bones of her skull against his palms, feeling the warmth of her skin. Twisting his fingers in her hair so that he held her gently prisoner, he drew her face towards his.

'Much, much better.'

Her eyes never blinked, never flickered. Their wide grey gaze remained fixed on his until it blurred as their lips met. The kiss was slow, gentle, lingering. It was a greeting, an exploration, an invitation, and it couldn't have been more different from the fierce, passionate kisses they had shared in the library earlier in the afternoon.

But the fierceness, the passion was still there. Malik could sense it hidden just below the surface of the kiss. He could taste it on her mouth, on the moistness of her tongue as it tangled with his so briefly, then slipped away again. Her head fell back against the support of his hands and at last her eyes closed and he felt the warmth of her sigh on his skin.

Malik lifted a finger and traced it down the side of her face, tracing the shape of her cheek, the line of her jaw

'I'm glad you came,' he muttered, kissing those closed eyelids softly.

They fluttered open again, grey eyes looking straight into his, so close that he could see the soft lilac colour that flecked them here and there, in contrast to the black pupil at their heart.

'Did you doubt that I would?' Abbie asked, knowing the answer even before the question.

One corner of his sexy mouth curled up into a wicked, knowing smile.

'Not for a moment,' he told her huskily.

Of course not. Of course he hadn't doubted for a moment that his command that she come here tonight would be obeyed. That she would do exactly as he said. That he had only to crook his little finger and she would jump to obey him, just as his servants had when he snapped his fingers to order drinks or waved a hand to dismiss them.

He'd expected instant obedience and got it from them.

And from her?

Suddenly Abbie needed the fortifying effect of the wine and, tilting her glass, she swallowed down a gulp of the rich ruby liquid. Its warmth flooded her veins, potent and intoxicating, but no more effective than the scent of Malik's skin, the heat of his hand on her face.

'You knew I'd come?'

'I knew you'd come.'

'You're very sure of yourself!'

Malik shook his dark head slowly, denying her accusation.

'I was very sure of you.'

That wandering finger had moved down from her face. Now it was trailing a path under her ear, along the side of her neck, down to her shoulder. Slowly, lazily, Malik hooked it into the loose neckline of her dress and pulled the silky material back, exposing the soft skin.

Just for a moment, he let his strong, tanned fingers rest against the spot where her pulse beat under the skin, the intensity of his glittering black eyes belying the relaxed ease of his movements.

For a couple of seconds he concentrated on the beat of her blood just underneath his fingertips and the knowing, arrogant smile grew by several degrees.

'I knew you wanted me just as much as I wanted you…'

'I…' Abbie began but he leaned even further forward and laid a long finger over her mouth to silence her.

'No protests—no pretence,' he told her softly. 'We both know how it is between us. That's why I knew you would come.'

Glancing down at the wineglass she still held, he reached for it, taking it from her unsure, nerveless fingers and lifting it slightly as if making a toast; he deliberately turned it so that the exact spot where she had drunk from was facing him. Placing his mouth over it he drank from the glass too, the gesture seeming like a pledge of feeling, of togetherness…

…and commitment?

Just for a second her father's unbelievable words floated into her head.

The Sheikh of Barakhara needs a wife. He has chosen you to be that wife.

Yes, she was here because of the way she had felt, the way she had responded to Malik earlier that afternoon. She had always known, even when she'd protested that she would not, that she *would* come to him. She *had* to. But what about that stunning proposal of marriage? Why had Malik not said anything about it? When would he tell her…?

Abbie's thoughts went back to the moment when her father had told her that the price of her brother's freedom was that she should become the Sheikh's bride. She knew he had been stunned when she had actually considered the ultimatum. He had been amazed that she hadn't turned it down flat.

But then he didn't know where she had been planning to go tonight, and who would be waiting for her when she got there. He didn't know that she was already Malik's, heart and soul, and had been from the moment he had first kissed her.

He was right, she admitted to herself. Of course he was right. She would be here anyway, there was no way on earth she could have stayed away.

She would be here, had to be here without any thought of

commitment or a future with him. She just had to know Malik, be with Malik, *love* Malik for as long as he gave her.

So it had seemed impossible, a dream come true, to know that he wanted her so much that he had actually told her father he wanted to marry her.

Okay, so he had muddied the issue by making marriage to him the condition he placed on Andy's release, rather than making any emotional statement, but she thought she understood that. If she felt confused and shaken by the speed and force of her own feelings for him, then how much more so would a man like Malik—coming from a country where men didn't show their feelings openly—and as the ruler of it, no less—hesitate to express his feelings openly? He wanted her and for now that was enough. He wanted her enough to marry her—what more could she ask? It was too early to talk of love, at least for Malik. But when they were together then surely that love would come.

But then Malik moved to sit down beside her on the big black leather settee. His arms came round her tightly and his mouth took hers in a long, sensuous kiss that had her senses swooning in a second.

She dropped her head back against his chest, feeling its strength support her, hearing the heavy pounding of his heart beneath her ear. His scent was all around her, swamping her, invading her. Breathing it in was like inhaling some powerful drug, one that drove all thought from her head and left her intoxicated with need, delirious with hunger. The hunger that this man had woken with his touch on her skin as he had crushed her against the wall in the library that afternoon.

She had fallen into his arms without thinking then, and she fell into them again without a second's hesitation now. Her own arms went up around his neck, her fingers lacing frantically in his hair, clutching at the crisp black strands, pulling his head down so that his lips crushed hers even harder than before. Her mouth opened under his, her tongue teasing, provoking, inviting the intimate invasion that echoed the deeper, more primitive union her body screamed for.

She wanted to hold him there, like that for ever, never letting go, but at last Malik had to lift his head, wrench his mouth away from hers, if only to drag in a raw, much needed, uneven breath.

'So now...' he muttered roughly against her lips, his voice heavy and thick with the same powerful hunger that poured through her veins, pounded at her thoughts. 'I think we should continue from where we had to leave off this afternoon.'

CHAPTER FIVE

IT WAS happening all over again, Abbie sighed inwardly as she surrendered to the sensual power of that kiss, going limp in Malik's arms and giving herself up wholeheartedly to the caress.

She had no hope of wondering, of questioning, of even thinking, when her senses were being besieged in this way. And the truth was that she didn't *want* to think or ask any questions; she just wanted to feel, to melt into the heat of the sensations that were flooding through her and give herself up to them, totally and completely.

Malik held her tight, pulling her up against him as he lay back on the soft cushions, stretching out long legs along the length of the settee. Abbie had just time to feel the heat of him and the force of the thick ridge of his erection against her back before he twisted her around, rolling her over until she lay at his side, her head pillowed on his arm, her body half imprisoned by his.

His hands were in her hair again, tilting her head and positioning it just so that he could reach it with ease, exert the most sexual mastery over her mouth, torment her already fizzing nerves with yet more excitement.

At the same time his hands were exploring her hungry body. They traced out every line of muscle, every curve of flesh, making her shiver in involuntary response under his heated caress.

And when those hard, hot fingers spread over her breast, stroking along one side, cupping the swollen shape through the linen of her dress, she couldn't hold back the low whimper of response that broke from her throat, feeling Malik's sexy mouth curl into a smile against her own.

'You like that?' he murmured, his accented voice rich and warm as a tiger's purr, the pressure of his hand increasing, moulding, shaping her so that she moaned in delight.

'And you'll like this too…'

The feel of the caress changed, lightening, trailing tormenting fingers over her sensitised skin, moving up to where the tight bud of her aroused nipple pushed at the restriction of her clothes, seeking his touch. She heard Malik's laughter deep down in his throat as she felt the response she couldn't hide and he closed his fingers around the pouting nub, tugging, teasing, playing with it until she writhed against him.

'And this…'

Pushing her on to her back, he bent his head, nuzzling at her breast. His mouth closed over the distended nipple, his tongue moistening the fine material until she felt its dampness against her skin. And then, seeming to judge the perfect moment with a faultless instinct, he suckled hard, the combination of heat and moisture, the abrasiveness of her clothing against her sensitised skin making her cry aloud, her head falling back, her eyes closing.

'More… Malik—more!'

It was choked from her, impossible to hold back. All her inhibitions seemed to have burned up in the blazing flames inside her head, melting in the boiling heat that seared her blood. And once more she felt the warm breath that his laughter pushed against the skin at the neckline of her dress.

'Oh, I have a lot more in mind,' he promised darkly. 'But I think we would be much more comfortable in my bed…'

With her eyes closed, she felt him swing his legs to the floor, gathering her into his arms and getting to his feet in one smooth movement. Instinctively she flung her arms around his neck, burying her face against the bronzed column of his throat, suddenly afraid that even a glimpse of reality in the form of the room they were crossing might bring her out of the heated dream in which she was lost.

And wanted to stay lost.

Some sort of strange, exotic magic seemed to have taken over her world from the moment Malik had appeared in it. One moment she had been ordinary—lonely and afraid for her brother trapped in a prison far away. The next, this amazing, stunning man had swept into her life, literally sweeping her off her feet.

Men like Malik, men who had the power of imprisonment, of freedom, over her brother, didn't want girls like her. He could have his pick of any one of a thousand society beauties, beauties from every country in the world, so why should he even look twice at her?

But he had. He'd not only looked, he'd liked what he'd seen. More than liked—he wanted her. More than wanted. He had told her father that he wanted to marry her…

And that thought was too much to take in. Too much to believe. It made her draw in her breath so sharply, so deeply that the scent of Malik's skin overwhelmed her again, making her head spin.

Still with her eyes closed, she let her face press closer to the source of the musky erotic perfume, pressed her lips against the side of his neck where his pulse throbbed underneath her mouth. She let her tongue slide out to taste the faintly salty tang of his skin and felt his heartbeat kick up a pace. He muttered something thick and rough in his native language and, quickening his pace, crossed the lounge in several long, fierce strides. The bedroom beyond took even less time and then she was tumbled on to the crisp white cotton of the bed, almost buried in the softness of the duvet, crushed even further by the weight of Malik's body as he came down beside her.

'Beautiful, beautiful Abbie…'

Her name was a soft crooning sound as he spread her out on the bed, kissing her face, her still-closed eyelids, her hair. Once more, that tormenting mouth pressed against her own but when she would have responded, lifting her head from the pillows to kiss him back, he was already gone, moving over her body, unable to stay still, kissing every spot her could find, making her nerves sing in yearning response.

Those wicked hands were busy with the fastening of her dress, finding the long zip at the back and easing down, pulling the soft material away from her body and pressing yet more kisses on the exposed flesh revealed to him. Her bra was dealt with in the same speedy, efficient way, no uncomfortable or embarrassing fumbling dragging her from the burning golden haze that made her whole body glow in hot excitement.

The heat seemed to have pooled between her legs so that even the finest soft tights she wore seemed desperately restricting, the delicate, barely-there silk of her underwear clinging and tight. She moved restlessly, urgently, tossing her head on the pillows, burying her heated cheeks in the cool of the covers.

'Easy, *sukkar*, easy,' Malik soothed, stroking a calming hand over her burning face and taking her mouth again in a slow, drugging kiss. 'Let's not rush things—not this first time.'

'No…' Abbie didn't know how she managed to form the word. When she let it out in a long moaning sigh she had no idea at all whether she was agreeing with him that they should take their time or trying to voice a protest at the delay in the appeasement of the hungry demands of her body.

Malik was kissing his way down the length of her now, making her writhe with delight as his hot mouth moved over the soft flesh he had exposed. His kisses marked out a burning path along her shoulders, down her ribcage and under the swell of her breasts. She wished he would take the aching tip of one of them in that sensual mouth, but instead he continued on his way down over the softness of her belly, teasing her navel with a wicked slide of his tongue.

'Malik…' she sighed, reaching down restless hands to close over his shoulders, wanting to drag him up to her hungry mouth again.

But her mood changed very slightly as her fingers tangled in the black cotton of his T-shirt, reminding her that, although she was almost naked, he was still fully dressed.

'You're wearing too many clothes.' She pouted.

'I agree.' Malik's response was muffled against her skin. 'But it's a matter that's easily remedied.'

He proved his point by tugging off the T-shirt so quickly that Abbie barely noticed his lips had left her body before they were back again, kissing her so seductively that her toes curled, her lower body twisting up against his. The potent force of his arousal rubbed against her pelvis, making her burn hotter and hungrier than ever before.

'And *you* have more on than I like,' Malik muttered roughly.

He hooked his thumbs in her remaining flimsy garments and wrenched them down along her thighs. His movements were so forceful that Abbie heard the fine tights rip and hole, her knickers not faring any better. But she didn't care and a moment later she was incapable of considering *anything* when Malik's mouth kissed its way through the light curls at the top of her legs, his tongue seeking the tight bud of her clitoris and teasing it into yearning life.

His breath was hot against the soft folds of her sex, adding an extra dimension to the need that made her toss restlessly against the pillow. She wanted him to go on—and on—but at the same time she needed so much more. She needed the reality of his possession, the sense of his heat and hardness filling her, taking her…

'M-Malik…'

This time her hands tangled in his hair, tugging softly, trying to bring his handsome head and that tormenting mouth towards her. Her mouth needed his; her breasts burned for the touch of his tongue, the tug of his mouth. And deep inside her she wanted that most forcefully male part of him, the hunger the most fiercely primitive she had ever known.

At first he resisted her, using his tongue to torment her still further, both adding to the delight he had been creating and yet making her so hungry for more that the pleasure was as cruel as a pain.

'Malik!' she protested, fingers twisting the black strands, pulling harder. This time he let himself be moved, giving in to her urging and sliding back over her body, but deliberately taking his time, delivering yet more kisses to her already burning skin.

'What is it you want, *habibti*?'

She could feel the smile on his mouth against her zinging nerves.

'Is it this…?'

His mouth caressed the curve of her right breast, making her cry aloud in fierce delight.

'Or this…?'

This time he sealed her lips with his own, catching the moaning cry in his own mouth and swallowing it down as his tongue tangled with hers, his hands pushed into her hair at the side of her head, holding her face so that she couldn't move away from him.

'Or perhaps what you want is this…'

She was still tasting him on her tongue, on her lips, but already he had slipped away, his mouth taking one breast so suddenly, so fiercely that she screamed aloud with the stinging torment of delight he inflicted on her, hot tears of joy springing to her eyes, spilling out on to her cheeks.

'Yes…yes…yes…'

It was a chant of wildly erotic delight, her voice soaring

up into a near shout of ecstasy, then fading back again to a whimper of pure pleasure as that tormenting mouth first suckled hard and then softly soothed the stinging nipple with his tongue.

'Oh, yes—' she sighed '—oh yes…'

But, wonderful as it was, it still wasn't quite enough. Each movement of his long, hard body on hers reminded her that, while she might be naked, Malik still wore his jeans, the rough denim abrading her skin and coming as a barrier between the throbbing heat at the centre of her and the fierce pulse of his erection.

And she wanted to know the full force of that demand. To feel it probe the female core of her body, to know the swollen fullness deep inside her.

'Malik—I want you—need you…'

'Soon, *sukkar*, soon,' Malik crooned against her breasts, punctuating the words with devastating little slicks of his tongue over her swollen and hot nipple. 'You must learn patience—to wait…'

'I don't want to wait! I want you now!'

'But I told you, we have all the time we need. We have all night.'

All night. It had a wonderful, wonderful sound. So wonderful that she couldn't hold back the swift, flashing smile of pure delight, pure happiness.

All night—tonight. And then…

'All night and every other night.' Abbie sighed. 'Every night of our married lives.'

'*What?*'

If the silence after that one single explosive word was devastating, then his sudden appalling stillness was even worse. It seemed as if Malik had frozen completely, every limb taut and stiff with rejection, every kiss and caress ceasing in a second.

With the moisture from his tongue drying, cooling, stinging on her aroused nipple, the thunder of need pounding at her nerves, throbbing in her body, sending a hungry pulse into her brain, Abbie felt as if she had suddenly dropped from a great height and was falling, falling, spinning and tumbling sickeningly. She was blinded by shock, deaf and breathless with it too. Every word she might have managed was snatched away from her, broken off in her throat, impossible to find in the devastation that was her thoughts. She had fallen out of the world she knew, out of the warmth and sensual delight of the bedroom, out of the comfort of the bed and Malik's lovemaking. Had fallen into a cold, dark, bleak alien world in which nothing fitted any more, nothing made sense and she had no idea where or even quite who she was and what had happened to shatter the existence she had once known.

'What did you say?'

If the first sense of shock at what Abbie had said had hit Malik like a toss of cold water in his face, freezing him in confusion, then the second, full realisation of just what she'd meant went through him like a burning electrical shock. It rocked his sense of reality and made him reel back in an explosive combination of disbelief and horror at what might be involved.

Every night of our married lives.

Had he really been so damn stupid that he hadn't seen what was coming? Had he let his desire for this woman trick him into an area where he was usually much too wily and aware to be caught? Had he in fact not spotted a honey trap when it was baited with such luscious sensuality and had only woken up to find that a spider had him in its sticky imprisoning web when it was almost too late?

A beautiful, sexy, shockingly appealing spider, it was true, but a spider nevertheless. A spider who now stared up at him with wide dazed-looking grey eyes, her soft pink lips, still swollen from his ardent kisses, slightly apart in shock at his reaction.

'I...' she began but the sound of her voice was enough to

jolt him out of the stillness into which he had frozen. His long body jacknifing away from her, he flung himself off the bed and partly across the room.

Only then did he feel he had himself under control enough to turn back and confront her.

'*What* did you say?' he demanded, the brutal control he was having to impose on his feelings, the hard, hungry—*hurting*—protests that his awakened senses were making at the vicious way he had stamped on the pleasure they had anticipated, making his voice harsher than even he had ever heard it before.

Cold-eyed, he watched her wince, flinch back against the pillows, but he squashed down the flicker of remorse that struggled against his anger. He had said nothing about marriage, had promised her nothing. Visions of the possible repercussions if she let her story out flashed into his head. The tabloid press would have a field day. He could see the headlines now—

Sexy Sheikh bedded me then betrayed me.

He promised me marriage but left me wandering in a loveless desert.

'Tell me!' he roared, using the black fury to drive away the temptation to let himself be distracted by the sight of her. She lay there, still spread-eagled on the bed, her delicious body openly displayed, pink-tipped breasts tilted towards him, seeming still to demand—to plead for—his attention.

Damn her! She looked so appealing—so damnably tempting and it was all that he could do not to go straight back to her and finish what he'd started.

It was what his body wanted to do. His heart was thudding, making his blood pound inside his head, and his hotly swollen penis throbbed with hunger and the cruel frustration it was enduring. It was impossible to think straight—and yet he had to if he was to salvage something from this appalling mess—and fast!

'Tell me…' This time he injected his words with a deadly poison and at last that seemed to get through to her. She stirred faintly, blinked her eyes, licked her lips.

Lips that still bore the imprint of his kisses, that must taste of his mouth when she slicked her tongue over them. He could still taste *her* on his own mouth, the lingering flavour of her tongue making desire kick him hard where he already ached with it, making his anger twist a notch higher as a result.

'Our—our married life,' she stammered. 'The life we'll have together when we—we're married…'

So he hadn't been hearing things. He hadn't let passion drive him so completely out of his mind that he hadn't caught what she was actually saying and instead had misinterpreted it, putting in its place something so wild and crazy that it could only be the result of the heat of his blood making his brain cells fuse in need and invent something that was the result of his wild imagination.

'"Our married life",' he repeated, lacing each word with the darkest, most savage sarcasm he could find. No woman had ever heard that tone from him before—and no man in Edhan could have borne it without flinching, trembling at the thought that he had angered his ruler so badly. 'I don't remember offering you marriage. In fact, I don't recall the word ever even being used. So will you kindly tell me just what put the thought into your mind?'

CHAPTER SIX

'What put...'

She was a great little actress, he would give her that. She actually looked as if he had slapped her in the face, opening and closing her mouth as if in shock.

Shock that her little trick hadn't worked, more likely. That her scam to blackmail him—to get as much out of him as she could—had failed.

That had to be the reason for it, surely. She couldn't possibly ever have imagined that he was really going to *marry* her.

'What...' Abbie tried again and the pretence at being stunned, the way she was clearly trying to play on his sensibilities, on his conscience, only infuriated him further. Where gold-diggers were concerned he had no conscience, none at all.

'In your own time,' he snarled, tossing the sarcasm at her like a blow.

'I'd answer if you let me get a word in!'

Oh, now she was showing her true colours! The change of mood revealed what the sweet, innocent female act had hidden all the time. And behind the mask was a snapping vixen. A beautiful little bright-eyed, neat-featured female fox, but one whose sharp white teeth could administer a deadly wound if he let her.

She was a fool to let the mask slip this easily. He was fore-warned and would be much more on his guard than before.

Privately Malik cursed himself for not being fully on his guard from the start. He should have known that his wealth and position would always make him a potential target for the gold-diggers of this world, but, damn it, he had been so attracted to Abbie from the start that stupidly all such thoughts had gone out of the window.

Of course, he'd forgotten the attack she had launched at him in the first moments of their meeting, when they had been alone in the library at the Cavanaughs' house. He should have taken that as a warning. She had been determined to accuse him of cruelty, of ill-treating her precious Andy, and all he'd been able to think about was how beautiful she was, how sexy, how infinitely desirable.

He couldn't believe how damn stupid he had been. He had let basic lust, his body's most primitive needs blind him to what was really happening. How the hell had he let her get past his guard like that? He had enough experience not to take risks. He would have sworn he was not so easily conned.

But she had managed to deceive him well and truly and now all he could do was to practise careful damage limitation to make sure that matters went no further.

'Then speak!' he flung at her.

But it seemed that that only incensed her further.

'Don't take that tone with me, *Your Highness!*'

The spin she put on the title turned it into something that was light years away from the respect he was used to. No woman had ever spoken to him in that way in his life. And no woman had ever pulled herself up on the bed where he had left her and spat fury into his face as she was doing. Every woman he had taken to bed had shown him a proper respect and they had known that marriage was the last thing on his mind. When he married he would not just be looking for a wife, but also for a queen.

'I'm trying to answer if you would only let me!'

'Be my guest…'

He accompanied the words with a mocking little bow.

One that Abbie felt like a cold-blooded slap in the face. She wished so much that she'd not let him pressure her into snapping. She could have bitten her tongue as soon as the words were out. But she hadn't been able to think straight as it was. Malik's reaction had rocked her sense of reality, leaving her thoughts spinning sickeningly. He'd behaved as if she had suddenly turned into a hissing, spitting snake, and then he'd bombarded her with demands, flinging the hard words into her face before she'd had a chance to draw breath and try to think.

So had her father got it all totally wrong? Had he made an appalling error and misheard—misinterpreted—what Malik had said? But he had been so sure! So definite!

The Sheikh of Barakhara needs a wife. He has chosen you to be that wife.

What was there to mistake about that?

But perhaps he'd wanted to tell her about it himself—to propose in his own time and his own way. After all he was a sheikh—a ruler—a king. He wouldn't be at all pleased to find that someone had pre-empted him and revealed his wishes before he was ready.

Or perhaps he'd rethought the whole idea? Had had second thoughts about everything? Had finally decided not to demand marriage? Oh, dear God, had he decided not to show mercy to Andy at all?

Oh, she'd been *stupid* to reveal the fact that she knew about his plans, foolish to have let the heat of passion push the declaration from her lips at just the wrong moment. But she hadn't expected the ferocity of his reaction, the sheer black fury in which he'd rounded on her as if she had suggested that he sell his soul to the devil—or worse.

In the end she'd reacted in pure self-defence. Though

she'd known the hot words were a mistake as soon as she'd
said them.

'At least let me put some clothes on first!'

She felt so dreadfully exposed like this, naked in front of
those pitch-black, accusing eyes, that furious glare.

'Why?' Malik tossed back at her. 'I'm enjoying the view.'

'I'm sure you are, but I don't intend to provide a strip show
for you!'

'You were happy enough to do so a moment or two ago.'

'But that was…'

She couldn't find the strength to finish her sentence, her
voice dying away to a whisper as she met the full blaze of his
furious glare. Standing there so tall and proud, handsome
head flung back, looking down his long aquiline nose at her,
he was pure arrogant Arab chieftain from head to toe. And he
didn't have to worry about the embarrassment of being suddenly abandoned without a stitch to cover him. He still had
his jeans on, the waistband and the zip unfastened as a result
of her urgent, seeking hands, making her face heat fierily to
remember. The wide expanse of his chest, the bronze skin
lightly hazed with black hair, only added to the wild, primitive impression, making him look too untamed, too elemen-
tal to belong in the luxurious surroundings of the hotel suite.

'That was when…'

Abbie couldn't help recalling how, when she had first
seen him, she had been stunned by how sleek and sophisticated he had looked. How urbane and—and civilised.

Civilised! She almost laughed out loud at the irony of the
thought but the sudden fear that he would take it completely
the wrong way had her clamping her mouth shut on the revealing reaction. Which only made matters so much worse
by turning it into a sort of a weak, smothered whimper.

'That was when what?' Malik prompted harshly, what little
patience he had exhausted by even the brief time it took her
to struggle to squash down the unwanted nervous laughter.

'When you thought that I wanted to marry you? That I would pay for my pleasure with a circle of gold that bound you to me for life? Was that what made your *strip show* respectable? What justified you coming to my bed without a second's hesitation?'

'No…'

She was starting to shiver inside, as much from the effect of his cold, cutting words as from the fact that she was stark naked sitting on his bed.

But the truth was that her skin was warm, both the central heating in the room and the rush of mortified blood through her veins making her burn in desperate humiliation. It was the way that Malik had changed. The way that the ardent, passionate lover had suddenly become this brutal-toned, set-faced monster whose icy words lashed at her exposed flesh like a whip, making her insides quiver in apprehension and her nerves twist into tight painful knots.

'Because I don't recall you holding out for a ring on your finger then.'

'No…'

It was all that Abbie could manage. All that she could force past her trembling lips.

What was the point in trying to deny it? She *couldn't* deny it! She had been his for the taking from that first kiss, that first touch—from before then. Perhaps she had been his from the first moment she had seen him. From the second that he had turned those fierce black eyes on her as she'd stood in the window watching his arrival.

He had looked at her and she had become his just as surely as if the brilliant black gaze had been like a fiery brand of old. Marking her out as his—his servant—his *slave* to do with as he pleased.

So she had come here tonight knowing she had no option, no other choice. She was his and there was no way she could deny it.

'Come to me tonight,' he had said, '...and we can finish what we started.'

And she had obeyed his command.

But because of what her father had told her, she had come here tonight with a whole new sense of excitement and happiness. She would never have dared to allow herself to hope—to dream that Malik might care for her, that he might do more than just want her. She had been prepared to settle for that. So when she had been informed that he wanted to marry her, she had been fizzing with delight and excitement, unable to believe that this might be possible.

She had fallen into Malik's arms—into his bed—without a heartbeat of hesitation. This was the man she wanted and he wanted her—for a lifetime, it seemed.

So how had it all turned so sour? How had her father got it so terribly, terribly wrong?

'No...' She sighed again.

'No,' Malik echoed in cruel satisfaction. 'No—because then you were too hot for me—too damn lustful to care. So tell me, *habibti*, just when did this wild idea that I wanted to marry you slip into your pretty head? When you saw the suite—the number of my attendants? Or did you have the whole idea planned in your scheming mind from the start?'

'Planned?'

Abbie wished she could think more clearly, manage to say something—*anything*—other than just stupidly parroting his words back at him.

How could she have planned anything when it was he...?

'Did you come here tonight to get into my bed for two reasons? For your own obvious enjoyment—and then the idea of making a fine profit from it either by blackmailing me into marrying you or...'

'No!'

Abbie had had enough. She still didn't know just what had happened. She had no idea how the terrible mistake had been made—who it had come from. She only knew that her weak, foolish dreams, dreams that had really only just begun to form, had been totally ruined and thrown back in her face by Malik, so that they now lay around her in splinters, shattered beyond repair.

'No, there was nothing like that in my head at all!'

The much needed protection of her clothes was too far away to reach. Even to get hold of her dress would mean going almost to Malik's feet—Malik's still booted feet! she noted on a shudder of reaction—and stooping to snatch up the discarded item from the navy-blue carpet. And that would put her almost in the position of *bowing* and scraping to the horrible man. Which was something she had no intention of doing—ever!

But there was one of those heavy towelling robes that hotels provided for their first class visitors lying on the chair under the window.

'How could I even have thought of that?'

Forcing herself from the bed, she grabbed at the white robe, hauling it up against her, unable yet to face the struggle to find the sleeves, push her arms into them. But at least it served as some sort of protective shield from the fiercely accusing black eyes that seared over her trembling form.

'How could you?' Malik echoed, cold as a hissing snake. 'Oh, somehow I suspect that it was all too easy! You made it plain from the start that you thought I was the evil villain for the way that *Andy* is being treated. What more simple idea than to further your sweetheart's cause by seducing me and blackmailing me afterwards?'

'I did not *blackmail* you.'

There was something very wrong with what Malik had said—some word, some phrases that grated against her desperately raw nerves, telling her that this was why he had got hold of completely the wrong end of the stick. But her thoughts were still buzzing too frantically to let her get a grip on just what it was.

'But only because you didn't get the chance.'

Malik turned unexpectedly and strolled over to the window, where he stood for a few moments staring down at the illuminated city below. Grateful for the brief reprieve, Abbie snatched at the opportunity to pull on the towelling robe. Her hands shook as she pushed them into the sleeves, nerveless fingers fumbling clumsily with the tie belt, but at least it was on and she was covered...

The sudden appalling realisation that Malik had obviously been wearing the robe before her and that it still bore the scent of his skin made her close her eyes on a shudder of purely physical reaction. It was only a few minutes since she had inhaled that musky, intensely personal scent as she lay underneath him, there, on that bed, with her body responding to his, opening to him, just as she had opened her heart...

Immediately she forced her eyes open again. She couldn't let such thoughts into her mind. They would weaken her still more—destroy her if she let them.

As she shifted uneasily on the carpet she felt something soft and light tangle itself around her right ankle and, glancing down, saw to her horror that the lavender-coloured knickers that Malik had pulled down her thighs only moments before were still coiled round one slender ankle. In a flurry of hot embarrassment she kicked herself free, sending the flimsy garment spinning away from her.

'You didn't blackmail me because you didn't play your cards right.'

Malik had turned away from the window and was leaning back against the sill, lean hips propped on the white-painted wood. And once more those burning black eyes were fixed on her pale face in a way that made her tug the robe closer around her, tightening the belt around her waist as much as she could.

'You opened your mouth before you had enough evidence to use against me. What is that saying about putting your foot where your mouth is?'

'Foot *in* your mouth!' Abbie snapped automatically, feeling that little bit safer and more confident with the thickness of the white towelling between her and the glittering glare of those fierce black eyes. 'And why should I want any evidence to use against you?'

'To uphold your crazy story—your fantasy—your lies!'

'My *lies!*'

Abbie's fury almost choked her, making her voice crack on the exclamation.

'I'm no liar!'

'No?'

Malik's stunning face was a mask of contempt as his cold hard gaze seared over her from the top of her head to where her toes curled into the softness of the carpet.

'Then where the hell did you get the idea that marriage was on the cards?'

'Where do you think? My father told me!'

She flung the words at him, wanting to discomfit him, wishing they were actual hard slaps on that handsome, sneering face.

'Your father told you what?'

To her horror Malik didn't appear in the last bit discomfited. If anything, his expression was colder and harder than ever.

'What do you think—Your *Highness*? Isn't it obvious? He told me that you wanted to marry me.'

'He did what?'

Malik's dark head went back, his eyes narrowing until they were just slits above his high, carved cheekbones.

'Then your father is the liar because I said no such thing.'

CHAPTER SEVEN

HER father had told her that he had proposed marriage?

Malik couldn't believe what he was hearing. He wanted to shake his head, slam his hand against the hardness of the window sill, anything to bring himself out of the delusion into which he seemed to have fallen.

Was the woman mad? Or was he dreaming? What sort of a nightmare had he tumbled into without knowing how?

'My father is no liar!'

Did she know what it did to him when she stood up so tall and straight? When she flung back her head and lifted that small stubborn chin so high and proud, silver eyes blazing into his? Did she know how the defiance in her gaze went straight to his groin like a bolt of white-hot lightning, threatening to destroy his ability to think straight—to think at all?

His body still burned with the thwarted passion that had seared through him, melting his bones in its scorching pulse. He didn't dare to fasten the zip of his jeans over the still swollen throb of his sex because just the brush of the loosened material was an agony he could barely endure. And even now the most primitive urgings of his senses were fighting against the cooler warnings of rational thought, demanding that he give in to the needs of his body and fling caution to the winds.

What he wanted most in all the world was to grab this

Abbie, snatch her off her soft little feet and fling her on the bed in front of him. He wanted to rip the stupid oversize robe from her sexy body, strip her naked in seconds and feast his mouth on the satin softness of her skin, know again the taste of her on his lips. He longed to pull her underneath him, bury his hungry body in the welcoming warmth of hers. And she *would* welcome him; he knew that without any doubt.

The blazing fire they had lit between them, the storm of need, could not just be doused in a second, stilled in the space of a heartbeat. His whole body still throbbed with the yearning for fulfilment that had gripped him and hers must feel the same. She must know the nag of frustration, the ache of emptiness that had tortured him ever since the moment he had flung himself from her—know it and want to end it, just as he did now.

If only cold reason didn't warn him of the dangers of taking that sensual path.

Crushing down the erotic thoughts that plagued him, Malik forced himself to face Abbie, to look into her eyes and see not the flashing sexual invitation that she had been offering him just minutes before, but to find instead the cold defiance, the deliberate provocation, the calculated scheming that had brought her here tonight. She had come here to ruin his reputation, to blackmail him for everything she could get and he was not going to let her get away without being punished for that.

'I tell you that your father lied. Or worse. In fact, he made the whole story up. You probably hatched the whole thing between you.'

Once more those eyes flashed, but this time in total rejection of everything he'd said, and she tossed her blonde head in wild defiance.

'I—we did no such thing! There is no plot—no story. Nothing! My father said...'

'"My father said..."' Malik echoed, the burn of dark cynicism in his words. 'Forget it, *sukkar*, drop your lying story now—it will go better for you in the end. Your father can't have spoken of any such thing because the truth of the matter is that I don't know the man—have never spoken to him.'

He'd caught her on the raw there all right, shocking her into silence with the cold dismissal of her lying tale. Her silver gaze lost its sharpness, looked dazed and unfocused. Her soft mouth opened, once, twice, tried to form a retort and failed, closing again slowly as if in despair.

Ruthlessly he pressed home his advantage, hammering home the final nail in the coffin of her lying fiction.

'How could I when your father and I have never met?'

But this time her reaction was the exact opposite of what he had anticipated. Instead of going down under the final blow—giving in and admitting defeat—it was as if something he'd said had stirred her senses again, renewing her conviction, giving her new strength.

The look she turned on him was blazing ice, searing him from head to foot with calculated disdain and cold derision.

'Oh, come on, Your Magnificence!' she scorned contemptuously. 'You are going to have to do better than that! For a moment there you had me worried, but now... Now you might as well give in and admit that *you're* the one who's been trying to lie his way out of this—and not succeeding. You see I *know* you're not telling me the truth now.'

'You know?' Malik questioned, cold and hard as a blade. 'And how...?'

'I'll tell you how.' This time her anger swept her voice right across his coldly phrased question, cutting him off completely. 'I'll tell you how I know. You can't have forgotten that I saw you there—you can't deny that I saw you in the house—in the library.'

'Of course you did.'

Malik's angry gesture dismissed her words, brushing them aside with an impatient flick of his wrist.

'Of course you saw me there. Just as I saw you. It was where we met. Why should I want to deny that I was there? I was waiting for—'

'Waiting for my father,' Abbie put in sharply, harshly, her voice breaking rawly on the last word.

'What did you say?'

Malik's eyes narrowed sharply, a dangerous frown drawing his black brows together.

'Where you were waiting for my father.'

This time the words had a whole new strength about them. A strength that gave them a power of conviction that stopped him dead. Made his head reel.

'When I met you in the library, then you were there because you had come to meet my father. He took you into the library and then later went to speak on the telephone. That's when I came into the room. When I met…'

'When you met me.'

If Malik's thoughts were reeling before, now his head felt as if it was about to explode.

'In the library, I was waiting for James Cavanaugh…'

He caught the slight movement of her head in a faint nod, met the silent accusation of those eyes.

'Damnation, woman—just who is your father? And who the hell are you?'

It couldn't be the way he suspected—could it? Fate couldn't be so malign.

'My name is Abbie Cavanaugh. My father is James Cavanaugh.'

They were the words he had most dreaded hearing. The words that held the power to ruin everything. To shatter his plans and force him to break his vow to his mother. He heard them but he didn't want to accept them, shaking his head in violent rejection.

'No. I don't believe you.'

'Yes!'

Abbie actually stamped her foot to emphasise the word, wishing that it had more effect than the soft thud on the thickness of the carpet.

'Yes—believe it!'

'But they said his daughter was called Gail and she—'

'But I am Gail—Abigail—and...'

She lost her train of thought as the full impact of what he had said hit home.

'Who said that? And what else did they tell you?'

But if Malik had looked hard to reach before, now he was totally closed off from her. His expression was as blank as if it was carved from stone, his eyes opaque as if steel shutters had slammed shut behind them.

'Get dressed!' he snapped, waving an imperious hand towards the bathroom door. 'Put your clothes on—cover yourself up!'

'I'm perfectly well covered up, damn you!' Abbie protested in spite of the fact that just a few minutes before she had longed for the concealment of her clothes, wanting only to protect herself from the cruel burn of his furious glare.

But now she wanted the answers to some questions. Wanted—needed to know just what was going on here. What was happening? Who had said what? And why?

'And you can stop ordering me around! You might be able to dictate to everyone else, and your servants and subjects might have to do as you say—to bow and scrape to you because they have to, and it's off with their heads if they don't—but I've no intention of doing as you command. I want some answers and I want them now. I want to know...' she began again, but Malik wasn't listening.

'Get dressed,' he said again, grabbing her by the arm and bundling her across the room and through the bathroom door. 'Then we talk.'

A hand in the small of her back propelled her into the spacious room. A moment later her clothes were bundled up and tossed in behind her, flying through the air to land in a crumpled heap on the cream tiled floor.

'But…'

Abbie whirled round to protest, only to find the door slammed in her face.

'Get dressed!'

Even through the thickness of the door she could hear the danger in Malik's tone, the way his accent had thickened on the words, warning her of the vicious mood he was in. *Don't mess with me!* that tone declared. *Don't mess with me unless you're prepared to take your chance and risk the consequences.*

Just for a second she was tempted. But then the foolish impulse gave way to a rush of common sense and she silently conceded defeat. Better to be safe than sorry and right at this moment discretion was definitely the better part of valour. And at least at the moment she had the protection of the door between them.

'All right,' she flung at him from behind it, slamming home the bolt just to make extra sure. 'All right, you bully— I'll get dressed! But after that you owe me an explanation!'

Malik's response from behind the door made no sense at all and it took her a couple of moments to realise that he had flung something harsh and violent—and probably very, very rude—at her in his native language. But there was no mistaking the meaning of his next remark.

'Where explanations are concerned, the shoe is very definitely on the other foot. You're the one who owes me the explanation!'

'I think not!'

Security made Abbie feel brave and she edged closer to the door to fling her defiance from behind its shield.

'You're the one who seems to know what's going on—the one who called my father a liar and now me. And, by the way, it's boot! The boot is very definitely on the other foot…'

The words broke off on a yelp of panic as she heard his snarl of fury and saw the door handle move with sudden violence. Nervously, she backed away but the bolt held at least enough to make Malik reconsider his actions.

'Get dressed!' he commanded again, the handle still held taut from the other side. 'Or else I'll come in there and do the job for you!'

'You'd have to break the door down first. And the hotel would want compensation for that.'

'And you think I give a damn?'

Even through the thickness of the wood Malik's tone showed how little he cared about that. Hastily Abbie decided that she had provoked him quite enough, her earlier foolhardy defiance evaporating in a rush to be replaced by a shiver of uncertainty.

'All right! I'll get dressed! Just leave me in peace to do it!'

The tension in her spine and shoulders only eased just the slightest bit when she saw the door handle click back into place. He'd gone along with what she wanted—for now. But how long would his patience last? How soon would it be before he got frustrated and then what would happen?

With a sigh, Abbie stooped to snatch up her clothes from the floor, struggling for the control she had lost so spectacularly just moments before. There had to be some explanation for this—there just had to. She was going to take a few moments to catch her breath, take stock, and then she was going out there to tackle his High and Mighty Sheikhness and find out just what was going on.

She wished she had time to take a shower. She felt grubby and used, the memory of her pleasure in Malik's touch, his kisses, tainted by the realisation that everything had not been as she had foolishly imagined. How she wished she could wash the feeling, the memory of Malik's caress from her skin.

But there wasn't enough breathing space for a shower.

Malik was already impatient enough; she could hear him prowling about in the bedroom, restless as a caged tiger. She didn't dare to provoke him any further than she had done already. She'd have to make do with splashing water on her face to freshen herself.

It was as she was doing just that that her numbed brain finally unfroze and jolted back into action, slamming home a realisation that made her thoughts swim.

She had forgotten about Andy!

In all the uproar that had followed the shock of Malik's reaction to her foolish words, she had forgotten perhaps the most important point of all. She'd lost track of the real reason why Malik was here in the first place—why he had ever come to England. She'd blotted from her mind the negotiations that had brought him to her family home to talk to her father.

But now she had remembered and she had to keep on remembering.

Lifting her head from the washbasin, she stared into her wet, pale face, seeing the shadows that darkened her eyes, making them cloudy and dull. Whatever else had happened, one terrible fact was true. For good or evil, Malik was still in control where Andy was concerned. He held her brother's future in the palm of his hand, to save or to destroy as he willed. She couldn't risk angering him too much or her brother would suffer the consequences.

Her fingers trembled as she pulled on her clothes, fumbling with the fastening of her bra, the zip at the back of her dress. It was impossible to forget the burn of needy passion that had seared through her as Malik had taken it from her, the way her body had trembled in need as he'd peeled the fine silk and lace from her aching breasts, exposing them to his hungry mouth and hands.

'Stop it!' she muttered to herself as she tried to comb through her hair with her fingers. 'Stop it now!'

She mustn't think that way or it would destroy her. It would crush her totally to remember just how much Malik had seemed to want her and how quickly he had thrown off all sign of any such thing. So how had he been able to totally switch off the passion that had had them both in its grip? Even now she still trembled from head to toe simply *remembering* how she had felt, her body a screaming mass of tormented nerves, while he was icy cold and in absolute control of every gesture, every action.

'Abigail…'

As if to prove her point, Malik's voice interrupted her thoughts, sounding a note of warning that once more what patience he had was wearing thin.

And she was Abigail now, was she? The warmth of 'Abbie' had gone, for ever it seemed, and her full name sounded harsh and alien in that exotically accented voice.

'Coming!' she called hastily, torn between wanting to stay hidden inside the bathroom for as long as she possibly could and the fear of the possible consequences if she challenged him by doing so.

Once again discretion won out over rebellion, the thought of Andy's plight sounding an extra warning note of caution not to make matters worse. She should be mending bridges instead of burning them—her brother's future depended on her.

Besides, there was little more she could do to make herself look respectable. The face that looked back at her from the mirror was white as a ghost's, with shadows forming like bruising under wide, dazed-looking eyes. Without the brush that was still in her handbag in the suite's sitting room she could do little to restore the tangled mass of her hair to any sort of order and had to resort to combing it through with her fingers, smoothing her palms over the blonde strands as a last resort.

'Abigail!'

The note of warning was back again. Any further delay was too dangerous. Wiping hands that were sweaty with nerves on the soft white towel, Abbie took a long deep breath, straightened her shoulders, lifted her chin. Swallowed hard and pulled back the bolt.

She fully expected that Malik would be waiting for her in the bedroom and so was surprised to find the room was totally empty. Not only empty, but the ruffled bedclothes had been pulled back over the bed to erase all sign of the wantonly sensual activity that had been played out there such a short time before. The whole of the room had been restored to such order that it seemed impossible that anything had happened there. It almost seemed like some sort of dream to remember just how hotly aroused both she and Malik had been.

If only it *had* been such a dream! If only it had all been in her imagination and now she could wake up and face the world again, shake off the last clinging remnants of the nightmare that had tormented her sleeping hours, put it to the back of her mind, knowing the monsters and the horrors had been only figments of her wild imagination.

But of course she couldn't. It had been real. And there in the sitting room was the dark physical evidence of just how real.

Malik was sitting in one of the big leather armchairs, his long legs stretched out in front of him, crossed at the ankles. He had fastened up his jeans and pulled on the black T-shirt that had been discarded only a brief time before, under conditions that made Abbie's skin burn to remember.

His elbows were resting on the arms of his chair, hands clasped together, his firm chin resting on them. He was staring into the distance as if his mind was miles away, his concentration on his inner thoughts intense.

And it was the consideration of what those thoughts might be that made Abbie shiver inside as she walked, silent on bare feet, through the bedroom and out into the sitting room to join him.

At first she thought that he hadn't heard her approach but then he flicked a swift, burning glance in her direction, black eyes glittering, his dark head not moving an inch. And the expression in those hooded eyes made her legs tremble so much that she was afraid they would give way beneath her.

'I'm here.' To her horror her voice shook disastrously as well.

That gleaming dark gaze swept over her once more, cold as black ice.

'So I see.'

One strong hand gestured towards the settee.

'Sit down,' he commanded.

He was too damn ready to issue orders and expect her to jump to obey them. Brief rebellion flared in Abbie, only to fizzle out again almost at once. For one thing she wasn't at all sure that her legs would support her if she tried to stay where she was. So she made her way to the chair opposite Malik's, carefully avoiding the settee he had indicated. The memories of the time she had spent on there, with him, and the feeling those moments had created in her were still too agonisingly raw, too terrible to remember. Just to think of them would destroy her ability to handle this talk and she strongly suspected that the next few minutes were going to be bad enough without adding any extra emotional pressures.

'Have a drink.'

Once more he gestured with his hand, indicating the glass of red wine that stood on the table to hand.

'Thank you.'

Abbie had to force herself to say it, not caring that she sounded gruff and hostile. She *felt* gruff and hostile, her skin prickling all over, her mind buzzing with nervous uncertainty.

It was impossible not to feel as if she had suddenly entered a time warp and that in a way they were replaying the whole evening, starting where they had begun tonight, with her arrival at the hotel and his offer of a drink.

Where they should have begun.

Perhaps if they'd started with a cool drink and even cooler words then the wholesale fiasco that tonight had turned into might have been avoided. If they'd actually *talked* before launching into a headlong rush for the bed then maybe this whole mess—whatever this whole mess actually was— would have been cleared up and she wouldn't have made such an appalling fool of herself.

Sitting down wasn't just that simple either. She had to remember that she was sitting opposite him and arrange herself and her clothing to create the right sort of impression—from his point of view. Not easy when the skirt of her dress was short and revealing and no matter how much she tugged it down it wouldn't go anywhere near covering her knees. Add to that the way that her tights had been ripped to shreds when he had tugged them from her legs and the fact that her knickers had not been in the bundle of clothing that Malik had tossed into the bathroom after her. They had to be still in the bedroom where she had kicked them off earlier after finding them hooked around her ankle, but she hadn't been able to spot them as she'd walked through. She couldn't cross her legs without Malik knowing that she was naked under the dress…

Shifting uneasily on the soft leather, Abbie took just as much of Malik's stony silence as she could bear. Then, nerves stretched to snapping point, her skin feeling raw as a result of that dark, intent stare that was fixed on her face, she gave up trying to be patient.

'You said you wanted to talk! So talk!'

Something dangerous flashed in the black depths of his eyes. Clearly Sheikh Malik bin Rashid Al'Qaim might be used to giving orders but he wasn't at all used to being on the receiving end of them. And equally obviously he didn't like it one bit.

But, whatever explosion threatened, he swallowed it down with the sip of his own drink and turned on her a face that, if not at all warm, then at least was not as furious as she had feared.

'Your name is Abigail Cavanaugh?'

'Yes.'

It sounded a bit spare and stark just like that and an imp of mischief fuelled by a strengthening swallow of wine pushed at her to add quellingly, 'The Honourable Abigail Cavanaugh, to be strictly correct.'

Of course Malik appeared neither quelled nor impressed, which annoyed her even more as she was left feeling foolish as well as edgy, irritated and vulnerable. All of which combined into a volatile mix of emotions that made her feel as if she was sitting on the rim of a powder keg, watching the fuse burn slowly towards her.

'You told me your name was Abbie, but in the past you have sometimes used the name Gail?'

'Yes.'

What was this, an interrogation?

'Abbie—Gail—they're both shortened forms of my given name. What's the shortened form of Malik? Mal?'

'No one shortens my name. I go by Malik and only Malik.'

He dismissed her flippant question with a cold-eyed glare, one that Abbie was sure had reproved courtiers, diplomats and any arrogant aristocrat who had tried to get above himself in the past. It left her feeling like a small child that had been soundly ticked off by an irritated parent and it was another uncomfortable feeling to add to the roiling mix.

'And you used to dye your hair black?'

That surprised her. More than surprised. It was a shock to discover that he knew anything about that. That he knew so much about her past. Why had he bothered to find out so much about her? And, on an even more uncomfortable thought, just who had been his source of information?

'Well?'

Her few seconds' hesitation had tested his non-existent patience again and the single word question had a real bite to it.

'Yes.'

She wanted to leave it at that but a sense that it wouldn't satisfy him pushed her into embroidering a little.

'When I was at school—boarding school—in the last year—the sixth form—I went through a Goth phase.'

She expected—and got—a frown of incomprehension at that comment but Malik clearly wasn't interested in the minor fashion details. Instead, he was intent on following whatever line of thought was running inside his handsome head and not deviating from it in the slightest.

'And in that year you had a friend—a male friend?'

But Abbie had had enough of being interrogated—of questions—when what she wanted was explanations.

'Just where are you going with this?'

'I'll tell you where I'm going.'

Malik reached for a jacket that was hanging on the back of a nearby chair and pulled a black leather wallet from the inside pocket. Opening it, he pulled out a piece of paper that he tossed towards her, watching as it fluttered on to the top of the table near her wineglass.

Abbie glanced at it, then stared in blank confusion. Finally, she picked it up and studied it intently, trying to make sure that she had actually seen what she thought she'd seen.

The photograph was six years old but she remembered when it had been taken. The last evening of the year at St Richard's boarding school. Exams had been over, the courses finished, and everyone in the sixth form had got together at a party to round off the year and to say goodbye. She and several of her friends had posed for the camera, all in a line, arms round each other's waists.

'Yes, that's me,' she said slowly, not really quite believing it herself. If she hadn't known then she wouldn't have recognised the girl who was in the middle of the group. Why had no one told her just how badly the dyed black hair had suited her? She looked totally dreadful, like some grotesque vampire from an ancient horror film. Gothic all right.

If this was the photograph that Malik had been using, then it was no wonder he hadn't recognised her from the image of her eighteen-year-old self.

'So what...'

A dawning memory stopped her in the middle of her question and she glanced back at the photograph to check.

Yes, she'd been right. There next to her, with his arm around her shoulders, hers around his waist, was Jalil. A wealthy young Arab, he had been sent to the exclusive private boarding school for the last year, to study and improve his English. Even though she had lost touch with him since, Jalil and she had become friends in the time they had spent together.

So was this what Malik was talking about? Was Jalil the male friend he had meant? She hadn't thought about him in years.

'Do you mean Jalil?'

'So what did your father tell you?'

Abbie's puzzled question clashed with Malik's cold demand and then they both fell silent. But when the look that Malik turned on her made it plain that he expected her to answer, not him, she made herself swallow down her pride and respond.

'He said that—that you had offered a way out of the mess that we—that Andy has found himself in. Is that not true?'

The horror of what that would mean, the way that Andy would have to stay in prison in Barakhara, made her shiver inside. It would be terrible if it was so—but clearly her father had got something very wrong.

But, to her amazed relief, Malik was nodding his dark head in agreement.

'It is?'

'I did offer your family a choice.'

Malik was measuring each of his words carefully. He was clearly back in the role of diplomat, well used to discussing matters of national and international importance.

'So then…'

'But not the one you appear to believe,' he continued ruthlessly, cutting across her stumbling attempt to speak. 'I have no intention of marrying you—and never had.'

CHAPTER EIGHT

So THAT told her.

Totally clearly, brutally honest, with no chance of any possible mistake. And how did it make her feel? Reluctantly, miserably, Abbie forced herself to face the truth.

She was relieved that Andy's fate didn't rest in her hands—but also worried that there had been no offer of hope for him. Shocked to think that her father might have misheard so badly and come to the conclusions that he had.

And cut right to the heart by Malik's reaction to even the idea that he might want to marry her.

Oh, admit it, Abbie, you weren't looking for marriage when you decided to come here!

Well, no, she hadn't been looking for anything—only for what Malik had openly offered. The wild sensual passion that had swept her off her feet and into his arms. But once she'd let her father put that thought into her head—for whatever mistaken reasons, he had thought it was the truth—she had come up hard against the sudden realisation of just how much she really wanted it, even though she had never allowed herself even to *dream* of the possibility.

In the deepest, most emotional part of her she had been singing, her blood bubbling with excitement. In her heart of hearts, she had acknowledged the disturbing, the almost shocking, the frankly terrifying truth that she had fallen headlong into love with this dark, proud, devastating stranger and her life would never be the same again.

But he had never suggested marriage, didn't want it. At least if he did want it then it was not with her. His reaction to just the word, the way he had flung himself from her and the careful, icy cold distance he had kept between them ever since didn't just tell her that, it slapped her right in the face with it.

He didn't want marriage.

He didn't want her.

At least not to marry. He had wanted her hotly enough when the idea had just been that she should warm his bed. But the idea of *marriage* to her had made him behave as if all the devils in hell were after him. She didn't need to be hit over the head with that more than once for it to sink in. The humiliation the first time had been bad enough.

'Who did you think I was—if you didn't realise that I was Abigail…?'

She'd made a wrong move there somewhere, taken a turning in the direction he didn't want to go and the flashing glare he turned on her told her that without any room for doubt. But, to her amazement, he followed her just for the moment, though his obvious reluctance warned that he was going to come back to whatever he had planned to say.

The terrible suspicion that she was going to like it even less than what had already gone before twisted the nerves in her stomach into a tight, painful knot that made it difficult to breathe.

'I thought you were the maid—or the housekeeper.'

Just for a moment a slow, wicked smile of memory curled the corners of his beautiful mouth, adding an extra twist of torment to the way that Abbie was feeling. Once, for a few brief shining moments, that had been the face she had seen, the expression that had been on his stunning features when he had turned to her.

She hadn't been deceiving herself. She'd seen that smile when he'd greeted her on her arrival and later, when that autocratic wave of his hand had cleared the room and they had been left alone together. For the space of a heartbeat he had shown her another side to him. One that was gone now, hidden under the cold, withdrawn mask that made him look as if his proud head was carved from marble.

'It was the apron that did it.'

The smile widened suddenly and Abbie couldn't stop herself from responding to it.

'It was a stylish piece of clothing, wasn't it? I'd borrowed it. I think it was the housekeeper's once—the previous housekeeper's—or the one before that.'

'I've never seen anyone but a servant wearing such a thing. So naturally—'

'Naturally—' Abbie put in sharply, her tone hardening, all amusement fading from her mind.

'Never seen anyone but a servant' he had said. Well, that put her in her place. No wonder he had flung himself away from her and from the thought that she might expect him to marry her! He was a sheikh—a desert prince—a ruler. And he would never lower himself to marry someone so far beneath him as a *servant*.

Taking a servant to bed for his pleasure, though, that was a very different matter. That was what harems had been created for, so that the king could take his pick.

So Malik had decided he could take his pick of the servants in the Cavanaugh household. And his choice had fallen on her.

But what would he feel now that he knew she wasn't the lowly maid he'd believed but in fact the daughter of the house?

Don't go down that road! she warned herself. Don't even risk it! What was she going to do? Hand him another knife and ask him to plunge it right into her already wounded heart?

'But if I had known who you were, I would never have touched you.'

And that answered the question without her having to ask it.

The burn of misery was so savage that she almost cried aloud with it. Hastily she reached for her glass and swallowed down another mouthful of the wine, wishing it would drown some of the pain she was feeling. But in fact it had the opposite effect. In her present, already emotional state the alcohol only heightened every sense to the presence of the man opposite. It stripped away the fragile, shaky defences she had built up, leaving every nerve suddenly raw and exposed.

It was as if she had been desperately short-sighted and suddenly someone had handed her a pair of spectacles so that her fight *not* to look straight at Malik, to blur the impact of his long, powerful body lounging at his ease in the chair opposite, was lost in a second. She became aware all over again of the strength of his lean form, the tightness of muscle in the arms exposed by the short sleeves of his black T-shirt. She couldn't miss the way that the light above his head gleamed on the blue-black silk of his hair, the polished jet brilliance of those deep-set eyes from behind their fringe of lush, thick lashes.

She followed every movement of his hands as if hypnotised, watched the way his mouth moved as he spoke and heard that voice as if in a dream.

'So my father had everything wrong? He's made a terrible mistake and...'

The words shrivelled on her tongue as she saw his expression change. Saw every last trace of the smile fade, the light of amusement die from his eyes. And knew a terrible sense of loss for the fact that they had gone.

'Are you hearing a word I've said?'

The anger in Malik's tone was like a slap in the face. She could only stare at him in confusion and doubt, blinking in shock.

He had said something while she was lost in thought and she had watched the movement of his lips but not heard anything of what had come from his mouth.

'I don't need to, do I? You've said all I want to hear—made everything perfectly clear!'

She'd got this far on a rush of panic, needing to get the words out. But now, to her dismay, her strength started to fail her and she could feel the shake forming on the last words as she forced herself to say them.

'It's okay. I understand.'

'No! You don't understand—not a single thing! You wouldn't be talking this way if you did.'

'But I do! My father got it completely wrong. There was no marriage suggested—ever.'

'No!'

In violent movement Malik flung himself from his chair and whirled to pace around the room for a couple of uncomfortable seconds, only coming back to stand facing her again when it seemed that he had got his uncertain temper a little more under control.

'In the name of Allah, Abbie! Listen!'

Something in the darkness of those eyes was deeper than ever before and the way that a muscle worked in his cheek gave away the fact that his jaw was clenched tight, which sent a rush of apprehension through her, her stomach twisting tighter in panic.

'I—I'm listening,' she managed weakly.

Her hand was clenched around the stem of her glass, clutching so hard that her knuckles showed white. She didn't want to listen. What she really wanted was to say, No—stop this now—I don't want to know...

But she didn't dare. If she feared what was coming, then she feared even more Malik's reaction if she tried to make him stop. It was like setting off to ski down the highest, steepest mountain she had ever known. She had already launched herself off and the movement couldn't be stopped, even if she suddenly spotted a terrible line of cruelly jagged rocks lying in her path. She was heading towards the inevitable and she could no more stop and turn round, back up the mountain, than she could tell her heart to stop beating, her breath to leave her lungs.

'Go on…' It was no more than a whisper. One that she doubted he heard, though he watched her lips move. 'I'm listening.'

'What *exactly* did your father say to you?'

Abbie didn't have to think, didn't have to hesitate. The words were etched on her brain in letters of fire. She couldn't forget them if she tried.

'He said—he said—"The Sheikh of Barakhara needs a wife." He has chosen me to be that wife. If I say yes, then the Sheikh will drop all charges against Andy and free him as soon as it can possibly be managed.'

'And you assumed that that meant that I wanted to marry you?'

'I—well, yes—it's obvious, isn't it? But of course it's not, now that I know you didn't say it and that Dad got things wrong, but…'

She was babbling stupidly and just the fact that he let her tongue run on with the nonsense, not saying anything, not correcting but simply watching her face, fixing her with the black intent gaze of a waiting predator, made her hand tighten even more on her glass, her throat drying painfully.

'But it seemed so, didn't it?' she croaked. 'After all, you're the—the Sheikh of Barakhara and you've come here to—'

'But I'm not.'

Malik spoke at last, his words cold and clear and deadly, dropping into the tumble of her answer like blocks of ice, bringing it to a stumbling halt.

'What?' Abbie managed, knowing she was gaping stupidly. 'What did you say? You're…'

'I'm not the Sheikh of Barakhara. My country is Edhan. Barakhara's borders adjoin those of my country and it is ruled by a member of my family—my brother. He is the one who wants a wife.'

'He…'

There was a nasty little crack and the bowl of the glass that had held the wine separated from the stem and crashed to the floor. The strength of her grip had snapped it and she winced as she felt the sharp point of the broken edge slice into her finger. But she couldn't react—couldn't move, couldn't think…couldn't believe. He couldn't be saying what she thought he was saying—he just couldn't!

And yet what else *could* he be telling her?

Her father had broached the subject of the Sheikh's proposal, not knowing that she had ever met Malik—and not knowing that she would immediately assume that *he* was the Sheikh who wanted to marry her. So he had been stunned, amazed but clearly overjoyed when she had answered his hesitating words with a wide, brilliant smile of pure delight and the declaration that…

Abbie's mind blew a fuse at that point, refusing to go any further, to think, even to consider what other horror Malik was trying to tell her now.

'Your brother?'

Her voice came and went in the most embarrassing way but Malik ignored the peculiarities of her delivery and simply nodded.

'My brother,' he confirmed. 'Half-brother to be exact. My father died when I was three and my mother married again. This time to the Sheikh of Barakhara.'

That brilliant black gaze dropped from her shocked, stunned face to the photograph that still lay on the table, a splash of wine spreading over its surface. And the way he looked at it told Abbie all that she wanted—no—all that she needed but had no *want* at all to know.

'My brother is now the one who rules Barakhara. He is the one who has the power over the laws of Barakhara and can say yes or no to the prison sentences they impose. He is the one who has your brother's future in his hands. He can show no mercy or the greatest leniency. And *he* is the one who wants you as his bride.'

'I don't believe you!'

The shrug of Malik's broad shoulders dismissed her protest. But it was the cold-eyed indifference in his eyes that shook her to her soul.

'Why do you think I asked you about Jalil?'

'Jalil!'

The ruined glass fell from Abbie's nerveless hands to land on the floor where the wine soaked into the carpet in a darkening puddle.

'You've hurt your hand.'

Malik's sharp eyes had caught the well of blood from the cut on her thumb and he was moving forward suddenly.

But Abbie couldn't take the thought that he might touch her. Her body was still stinging from the arousal that had flooded it. She felt barely under control, shaken to the core, brittle as ice. If he laid a finger on her she would go up in flames, splintering in the heat like the glass that lay on the carpet at her feet.

'Don't touch me!'

Whirling up on to her feet, she spun away from him, needing only to put as much space between them as possible.

'I was only going to…'

Malik flung the immaculate white handkerchief he had pulled from the pocket of his jeans in her direction, watching silently as it fell on to the arm of the chair she had just vacated.

'I wanted to help,' he muttered darkly as she snatched it up and wound it tightly around her wounded thumb, covering the thin line of the cut.

'Then help by explaining this situation to me.'

Abbie's chin came up, her mouth firming against the unwanted and far too revealing tendency to wobble betrayingly.

'My old school friend Jalil is the Sheikh… And he's the one who wants to marry me?'

'He's the one who put that condition on your brother's release.'

Malik's nod was curt and cold. The impulse to help had clearly died and he was once more the icily distant stranger he had become from the moment she had let slip those foolish words.

Jalil wanted to marry her? But he hadn't been in touch with her for years. And they had only been *friends*. She had never felt anything more for him. Certainly nothing like the fierce burning hunger she had felt for Malik.

But then she was forgetting that at one point Jalil had made a pass, had made it obvious that he had a major crush on her. She had thought that she'd let him down gently, but he'd acted as if she'd been callous and cruel.

'A condition I thought you had accepted. Your father phoned me earlier—before you arrived here. Perhaps before you even set out. He said that he'd spoken to his daughter about Jalil's proposal. That he'd sounded her out.'

'But that was…'

That was when I thought the marriage proposal had come from you, she had been about to say, but she couldn't let herself finish the sentence. How could she when it meant letting Malik know just how delighted she had been by his proposal? How much she had wanted to say yes.

How she had fallen head over heels, heart and soul in love with him.

She could only be so deeply grateful that she had never said a word about love to this distant, cruel-tongued man in front of her, his black eyes cold as ice. Letting slip the fact that she had actually thought of marriage was bad enough, to have admitted to love would have been the worst possible mistake. It was quite clear that Malik wanted no such thing from her and that she would only be fooling herself if she ever dreamed of him feeling anything at all for her.

If she could only find some way of covering her tracks, of hiding her stupid mistake, make him believe that she was as emotionally indifferent to this whole thing as he obviously was. That way at least she might emerge with some sort of pride intact.

But perhaps, just perhaps, Malik had given her just such an escape route with his talk of Jalil.

'And what if I say no?'

'You don't have the luxury of that choice.'

Malik's tone was flat, unemotional, as detached as his poker-faced expression.

'Your father rang to say that his daughter had said yes. My brother rang soon afterwards to know what was happening. Your agreement to marry has already been given to him. He is expecting you as his bride at the end of the fortnight. And I'm afraid that things will go badly for your brother if you are not there.'

Abbie's blonde head went back, her grey eyes widening even more as she absorbed this fact. She looked as if someone had slapped her hard in the face and Malik felt his conscience give an uncomfortable twist.

It was one thing keeping to his vow to their mother, quite another to go along with the crazy scheme the boy had come up with to use that vow for his own advantage. He had been assured that Gail Cavanaugh wouldn't give a damn about being used in this way—that she had always hated the way that her family had an elite name but not the money that went with it—death duties had seen to that.

Gail would do this, Jalil had assured him. She'd do it for the position she'd acquire, for the chance to save her baby brother from rotting away in one of Barakhara's jails. But most of all she'd do it for the money.

Gail would do anything for money.

But that was Gail. The woman in the photograph—the one with the dyed hair and the attitude.

This woman was different. This was Abbie—blonde-haired, grey-eyed Abbie. And Abbie seemed genuinely shocked at the idea.

'I'm sorry...' he began, but her laughter cut into what he had been about to say, stopping him dead.

She was shaking her head, sending that glorious blonde mane swirling about her face, one strand of it catching on the moistness of her lower lip and sticking there, making his fingers itch to reach out and brush it away. But he knew that, if he did, it wouldn't stop there.

If he so much as touched her then he wouldn't be able to stop. If he felt the softness of that lush mouth under his finger-tips then he would have to go further. He would have to trace its yielding contours with his hand, feel its warmth, slip into the welcoming heat beyond her lips, feel it close around his fingers.

He would have to give in to the urge to kiss her...

But then she laughed again, the sound even more jarring this time.

'You're sorry— Oh, don't say that, Malik! There's no need for that—no need at all to be *sorry!* Everything's worked out just fine. Exactly as I wanted it.'

'It has?'

He could hardly believe that he was speaking to the same woman. It was as if that laughter had transformed her face, wiping away the softer, more approachable mask that she had worn until now.

And what was under the mask was as hard as nails. The fine jawline tightened, her chin tilting in open defiance. Those delicate grey eyes sharpened, turning from mist into ice in one slow sweep of the long brown lashes. And the look she turned on him was pure ice too—a slow scathing survey that swept from his head down to his feet and back up again, her expression one of open disdain.

The woman he had known as Abbie had disappeared and in her place was a cold, arrogant individual he detested on sight. Abbie had vanished and in her place was the woman Jalil had called Gail.

'Oh, yes, it's quite, quite perfect,' she drawled now, giving him a smile that turned his blood to stone in his veins. 'Couldn't be better. You see, I only came here tonight because I thought that I'd managed to get a sheikh to agree to marry me. That was what my father had told me—and, quite frankly, I couldn't wait.'

She paused for a moment there, tossing back her hair and tilting her head to one side, as if she was waiting for him to speak.

But Malik had nothing to say. The bitter taste of acid on his tongue had burned away any words he might have managed, even the insults he could have flung in her face, to express the contempt he was feeling inside.

Surprisingly, the movement still hadn't dislodged the strand of hair from her mouth, but it didn't matter now. The impulse to move it, to touch her, had died completely. He would rather have picked up a live sand viper with his bare hands than touch any part of her now. If the truth were told, his own skin crawled to think of the way she had almost enticed him to take her to bed, to…

'But then I played my cards a little clumsily and you…'

A tight, dismissive little shrug of those narrow shoulders brushed aside what had obviously been the momentary disappointment of his reaction earlier.

'But now it seems that I can get just what I want anyway. I came here tonight, determined to get a proposal of marriage from a sheikh—and I wasn't going to leave until I got what I wanted. So don't feel sorry for me, Your High and Mightiness Lord Malik—on the contrary, you should be congratulating me. And you can thank your brother Jalil very kindly for his gracious proposal—and tell him I'll be only too happy to accept.'

Once more she paused, obviously for deliberate effect, and once more Malik knew that he couldn't find the words to express the way he was feeling. But he knew that his face must be saying that for him. His jaw was clenched so tight that it ached and his skin felt as if it was stretched across his cheekbones, pulled taut at his mouth and temples.

'I'll tell him,' he managed, forcing the words from lips that seemed to have become formed from granite. 'I'm sure he'll be very pleased.'

Jalil would be pleased. It would get him out of the mess he was in, maybe save his throne—even his life. He and this Abigail deserved each other. They were a perfect pair.

'You do that,' Abbie purred, turning a limpid grey gaze, a mock flirtatious smile, on his shuttered face. 'And do one other thing for me, dear Malik…'

Leaning forward, she touched a teasing fingertip to the corner of his clamped mouth, tugging it up into a suggestion of a curve.

'Smile for me, darling! Go on—try it! I'm sure you can manage it if you make the effort.'

But that was just too much. He couldn't take any more.

With a muttered curse in his native language, Malik grabbed at that tormenting hand, snatching it away from his face. Eyes blazing with disgust and fury, he glared straight into her taunting face.

'And why in hell's name should I do that? Why should I want to smile at you?'

'Why?' Abbie echoed, amusement ringing through her voice, her own smile growing as she did. 'Isn't it obvious, my darling? It's only polite to smile at your relations—and that's what we're going to be in the very near future. I'm going to marry your brother—and that means that from now on you and I will be very closely related.'

CHAPTER NINE

THIS couldn't be happening.

Try as she might, Abbie couldn't get her head around her situation. She found it impossible to believe that she was actually here, in the luxurious cabin of this sumptuous private jet, flying out to Barakhara.

'Flying out to Barakhara, to meet the Sheikh who wants me to be his wife.'

She had to say the words out loud to convince herself of the reality of them. But even then they had no real impact on her battered and numbed brain. They simply sounded like the most ridiculous gibberish, bearing no relation to reality at all.

'The Sheikh…'

She tried again and only succeeded in attracting the attention of the young female attendant who hurried forwards at once, a puzzled frown creasing her smooth brow, to ask if there was something that Madam wanted.

'No… Nothing, thank you! I'm fine.'

Physically, at least, that was the case. Since the car that had been sent to collect her had arrived at her home she hadn't wanted for a thing. She had never known such luxury—but it came at a price that meant she had also never known such total unease. She hadn't had a decent night's sleep since the truth about the Sheikh's proposal had become clear to her.

'Madam—we are about to land. If you would fasten your seat belt, please.'

The attendant would even have done that for her. She was already bending forward when Abbie stopped her with a softly raised hand. She had to do something for herself. Had to keep her independence for as long as possible.

But what would happen once they had landed and she was with Jalil—in his court—as his proposed bride?

Was she really going to do this?

Could she do this?

Abbie laid her head against the back of her seat, closing her eyes, listening to the change in the sound of the plane's engines as they circled around the airport, banked, flew lower and lower.

Did she have any choice? Jalil had been all charm and friendliness on the phone—but he had made one thing very plain. Either she came to Barakhara, prepared to be his wife, or Andy rotted in the country's prison for most of the rest of his life.

It might help if she remembered anything much about Jalil. But all she could recall was that he had been a smallish, very exotically good-looking boy—almost pretty, if the truth were told. They had been friends through circumstances, rather than through any real affection. Of the people in that final year of school, Jalil had been one of the ones she had got on well with at the time. But they hadn't really had a lot in common. And she had changed so much since then. The Goth phase, and with it the appalling dyed hair, had gone long ago.

She was going to meet a stranger.

She was going to *marry* a stranger.

And she didn't know how she could go through with this.

Oh, how different it would be if the Sheikh she had been forced to marry had actually been Malik. Malik, who had once been every bit as much of a stranger as Jalil now was to her, but who had so quickly become something else. Someone else.

'Malik…'

It was a sigh of longing as the image of Malik as she had last seen him floated in the darkness behind her closed eyes. Malik—tall, dark and devastating. Malik's mouth kissing her, Malik's long tanned hands caressing her body, removing her clothing with passionate haste.

'No!'

With a struggle Abbie forced her eyes open, staring into the shadowy cabin where the lights had been dimmed ready for landing.

She mustn't think of Malik! Couldn't think of Malik or it would destroy her. She had fallen head over heels for Malik in the first moment that she had seen him. Had fallen straight into his arms and into his bed—had fallen headfirst, hopelessly, desperately in love with him.

There, now she had admitted it to herself. She had let in the word that she had been fighting to avoid ever since that night in Malik's hotel when she had been putty in his hands, too hungry, too desperate for him to think of denying him anything.

She had already been in love with him then. Already totally given over to him heart and soul. When she had been with him she'd felt as if she had no mind of her own, nothing except what was his.

It was scary—it was frankly terrifying to realise how quickly and how completely she had fallen under his spell. She had never believed in love at first sight but she had no choice but to do so now. If Malik had reached into her chest and snatched her heart out of it he couldn't have taken control of her any more completely. She was his and there was no room for anyone else in her life.

But Malik didn't want her.

Malik felt nothing for her except the hot desire that had

ared between them. Desire that had ended so abruptly and
ad no chance of ever reviving after that one night that had
one nowhere in his hotel suite two weeks ago. The hope of
ove and a future that she had dreamed of had proved to be
st that—a dream. And that was why she was here.

Malik didn't want her and so, with her heart feeling dead
side her, her thoughts too bruised and numb to fight, she
ad said yes to Jalil's proposal. At least this way she was
scuing her brother and Andy would have a future even if
he didn't.

The sound of the engines changed again dramatically and
moment later Abbie was jolted in her seat as the plane
nded with a bump, the screech of brakes and the rumble of
eavy tyres over the runway.

They had arrived. The land outside the window, obscured
y the darkness of the night, was Barakhara. The country
here Malik's brother Jalil ruled, where Andy was still in-
arcerated in prison—and where she was soon to meet her
rospective bridegroom. The man she had agreed to marry
ithout even seeing him again.

'If Madam will come with me, the car will be brought to
e plane.'

It was Sahir, the male attendant and bodyguard who had been
king care of her from the moment she had set out on her
ourney. He had been sent to her by Jalil with instructions not
 let her out of his sight until he handed her over to her pro-
pective bridegroom in the palace in Barakhara city. Abbie
ouldn't fault him for sticking to his job, but she was already
eginning to find his constant presence oppressive and unnerv-
g.

At least when she reached the palace she would be free
f him. Free of Sahir, but handed over to a new sort of im-
risonment... Oh, how different this might all have been if
e had been coming here to be with Malik—to become
alik's wife.

Biting her bottom lip hard to fight back the sudden burning tears that stung at the back of her eyes, Abbie followed her escort out of the plane.

The heat hit her like a baking hot wall as she made her way down the metal steps to the waiting limousine and it was hard to catch her breath when even the air seemed to burn in her lungs. The space for the Sheikh's private plane had been cordoned off from the main part of the buildings, the formalities on arrival already conducted on board the plane, and so they were still some distance from the low building of the main part of the airport.

'Madam…'

The back door of the car was open, Sahir standing back with a faint bow. She would have to get used to this sort of treatment, Abbie supposed, the thought distracting her so that she slid into her place and leaned back, closing her eyes as the door slammed into place. It had barely done so before the car's motor roared, the powerful machine moving immediately, swinging away from…

There was something wrong! Very wrong.

Realisation and a terrible sense of dread struck at Abbie at exactly the same second. Instinctively, intuitively, she knew that this should not be happening.

Sahir had not had time to get into the car after her and, besides, she had not heard another door open and close or felt the change in the air-conditioned temperature in the back of the car.

Something…

'Sahir!' her voice was sharp with panic and concern as she sat up straighter. 'Sahir!'

'I'm afraid Sahir will not be joining us on this stage of the journey. He—has been relieved of his duties.'

'He…'

Abbie found it impossible to get any other words past the burning knot of fear that closed her throat.

She knew that voice. Knew it and had feared ever hearing

again. Or did she mean that she had feared *never* hearing again? She didn't know and there was no room in the hirling red haze of panic that was her thoughts to allow her think.

She was only aware of the fact that the voice—*that ice—Malik's* voice—had come from just next to her, unding in her right ear.

Whirling in her seat, she confronted the man who sat side her.

Malik—and yet not Malik.

The forceful, strongly carved features were the same, such she could see them in the shadowy darkness of the car. She uld only snatch quick glimpses of his stunning face as the r sped onwards, allowing her just moments of light as they ssed a window or some other form of illumination on their ay past the airport buildings.

The brilliant glitter of those black eyes was the same, the me lean powerful form so close to her that the faint scent his skin and the tang of some citrus cologne tantalised her strils. But this was no longer the sleek, sophisticated Malik ho had come to her father's home. Nor was he the more ca- ally dressed but equally westernised male who had been aiting for her in his hotel suite on the one night she had me to him there.

Now, clothed more traditionally in a white *thobe* topped a loose black robe, his dark hair covered by the traditional *tra*, the male headdress, bound round by the cord *igal*, he peared much more foreign and dangerous, so outrageously otic and arrogantly masculine that his presence seemed to l the car and overpower her.

'M-Malik…' she managed, her tongue stuttering over the und of his name, her heart thudding high up in her throat that it was impossible to breathe.

'What—why…?'

The questions tumbled out on a rising note of hysteria.

'Oh, my…'

But her voice died there, crushed by the large powerf
hand that was clamped across her mouth, strong finge
shutting off any sound she tried to make. She was hauled u
against the strength of his body, her head supported on th
hard bones of his shoulder, and burning jet eyes glared dow
into her widely fearful grey ones.

'No!' Malik hissed the word into her face, the ferocity b
hind them freezing her into panicked stillness, barely eve
able to breathe. 'Not a word! You will not say a thing—is th
understood?'

It was almost too much to take in.

The beat of his heart under her ear, the purr of the car
engine, combined with the husky ferocity of his tone to i
tensify the effect of his accent and make the words almo
incomprehensible. But she recognised the force behind th
words and knew there was nothing she could do but give in
for now.

She had been going to scream. Malik had seen it in h
face, in her eyes. She had been going to scream and th
would have ruined everything.

There were still too many people around—too many pe
ple who might hear her. Or people who might recognise hi
or the car, in spite of the way that he had insisted that the fl
and any other identifying marks should be removed from
If they were spotted now then they might not get away
safety.

And so he had had to act. Which meant that he now ha
her head crammed against his chest, his hand across h
mouth, and the wide, shocked grey eyes staring up at hi
above the pressure of his fingers.

And it was pure torment.

He had thought that after two weeks apart from her l
might have recovered from the madness that had gripp
him when he had first met her. That he would realise that l

ad exaggerated the sexual allure of her body and the way it
poke to his own. He couldn't have been so knocked off
alance by this woman. He'd known many women in his
fe—beautiful, stunning, glamorous women and they had en-
hanted him for a time—but only for a time. He had wined
nd dined them, enjoyed them, and had been able to walk
way in the end without a single backward glance.

So why hadn't he been able to forget this one woman?
Vhy had his days been haunted by memories, his nights by
ot, erotic dreams from which he woke sweating and
haking, his whole body aching in frustration?

And it had only taken a single split second to have all those
celings rushing back.

So now, with the silky feel of her hair against his cheek
nd the scent of her body rising up around him, he knew that
he two weeks they had been apart had not been enough—
ould never be enough. In the space of a heartbeat he was
ack under her sensual spell, with no hope of escaping if he
ied.

And the hellish thing was that he didn't want to try.

That knowledge made his voice rough, his tone harsh as
e crushed his hand against her mouth to stop her from be-
aying them both.

'Not a word—not a sound! You understand?'

Was that a nod or had she simply tried to free herself from
is restraining grip? He saw the flicker of something in her
yes—fear or defiance?—and knew that neither of them
ould stay like this.

'If I let you go—you must promise…'

He didn't know which of them was more relieved when he
ased his grip on her, allowing her to sit up. But the release
as only temporary as she pushed herself away from him,
rned her head in a swirl of blonde hair and opened her
houth…

It was impossible to get his hand back over her lips. She

was too far away, had turned too much towards the window
There was only one way he could hope to silence her.

He clamped his hands around her shoulders, hauled he
back against him and brought his mouth down hard on hers

And went up in flames in a split second.

Heat melted his thoughts, turned his blood molten in hi
veins. His head swam, his heart pounded and all sense of wher
he was or why he was there evaporated. He was hard an
hungry, instantly wanting her with a ferocity that made
nonsense of his earlier beliefs that he could ever forget thi
woman or free himself from the sexual spell she had cast ove
him.

'Abbie...'

He sighed her name into her mouth as she melted unde
him. Her lips had parted under the onslaught of his, he
tongue touching his, seeming to dodge away, but then, as i
unable to stop herself, she met his intimate caress, teasing
inviting, tasting, taking...

His hands twisted in her hair, coiling the silky strand
around his fingers to hold her head at just the right angle t
increase the pressure of his mouth, his palms curving ove
the fine bones of her skull.

Her arms had folded around his neck, holding him close..
so close. The soft swell of her breasts was crushed agains
his chest, her legs entangled with his as she lay half unde
him, almost full length on the back seat of the car, the ach
and heat of his erection cradled in the tilt of her pelvis.

The lights of the airport flashed by unnoticed, the sight
and sounds of the streets outside not reaching them as the
lost themselves in each other, swamped by the primitive hun
ger that simply being together created.

He hadn't been alive for weeks, hadn't *felt* anything fo
days. His skin seemed hot and tight, his eyes were blind, hi
brain was lost in a wild explosion of electrical sparks. H
didn't know if it was day or night, only that the woman wh

KATE WALKER 113

ad haunted his dreams, tormented his days, driven him crazy
with frustration and denial, was here now, with him, under
him, her mouth on his, her fingers in his hair...

But then the car suddenly swung around an unexpectedly
sharp bend, the driver lost control for a second, regained it
almost immediately. But not before the rough, jolting movement had flung his passengers to one side and then back
again, wrenching them apart, throwing them against the
opposite doors.

'What the...?'

Malik bit off the furious outburst, clamping his mouth
tight shut on the savage curse that almost escaped him. Or
clamping his mouth shut against the temptation to reach for
Abbie, to kiss her again—his whirling brain couldn't even
begin to decide which.

This must not happen! He couldn't let it happen. His life
was complicated enough as it was without getting entangled
with some cheap little gold-digger who was already committed to his brother. He had come here tonight with the aim of
helping Jalil—again—not making matters worse for him.

'I'm sorry...' Somehow he forced himself to say it. 'That
should not have happened.'

'You're damn right it shouldn't have happened.'

Abbie had taken herself as far away as she possibly could.
Which in reality meant just as far as the end of the seat, crammed
up against the door. She had twisted in her place as well so that
her back was to the window, her legs in their loose grey trousers
forming a protective barrier between the two of them. Her hair
was savagely tangled, her lips looked swollen from his kisses
and her grey eyes spat defiance and rejection at him.

'It shouldn't have happened and it's not going to happen
again!'

'Well, at least there's something we're both agreed on.'

'Both!' Her voice rose sharply in indignation. 'Both! I
don't remember having anything to do with it. You pounced!'

'Only in order to shut you up!' Malik pointed out coldly 'Admit it,' he went on, his voice softening slightly. 'You wer going to scream.'

'And what if I was? Of course I was going to scream— think I'm perfectly entitled to scream. I got in here expect ing—expecting Jalil at least. And instead I find—I find…'

'You found me.'

It was a struggle not to let the amusement that was sneak ing into his mind show at all. He knew that she thought she was aiming for the defiance and rejection she had shown earlier, but only wished she knew just how far short of it she was falling. She might think she was being fierce and strong and as bold as could be when in fact she looked like nothing so much as a small cornered kitten, hissing and spitting a some marauding tom cat several times as big as herself.

'I found you—and you immediately started mauling me!

'I did not maul!' Indignation and pride drove any hint o amusement from his mind. 'You accused me of that once before, but let me assure you, I have never mauled a woma in my life!'

'Whatever you like to call it, it was not what I wanted! So let's be absolutely clear on this—I don't want you to touch me ever again without my express permission. I don't like you—I don't want you—and you're the last person on earth I want to be with right now…'

'Tough.'

Malik had total control of himself again. She might look like a hissing kitten but the reality was that she was much more of a problem than she ever realised. And she was in a danger that she couldn't even begin to imagine.

'I'm afraid you're going to have to put up with me for a while.'

'But why—why you? Why couldn't Jalil come to mee me? Why did he send you?'

Her voice stopped dead and Malik knew the moment tha

he thought hit home. He saw it in the way the colour drained
from her face, leaving it white and ghostlike in the dim light
of the car. Her eyes opened even wider, staring at him in
shock and fear.

'*If* he sent you,' she managed on a gasp. 'Is that what's
happened? Where is Jalil? Does he even know you're here?'

CHAPTER TEN

'THERE'S been a slight problem.'

Malik's voice came from the darkness of his corner of the car, coldly calm and unemotional. His face was hidden by the folds of the *gutra*, concealing any expression from her, and his fingers were loosely linked in his lap, totally still. The very opposite of those ardent, caressing hands that had driven her to a frenzy of response only moments before.

'What sort of a problem?'

Abbie couldn't manage the same sort of control. Her voice went up and down in a most embarrassing way, echoing the erratic and fearful beat of her heart.

'What's happened? Has Jalil changed his mind? Does he not want to marry me after all?'

And if that was the case, then what would happen to Andy? After nerving herself to get this far, she couldn't bear it if anything went wrong now.

'The marriage deal is still on.'

If Malik's tone was meant to be reassuring, then it didn't work. In fact, it had exactly the opposite effect, sounding darkly ominous in a way that sent a miserable shiver running right down her spine. She wished she could move even further away from Malik's dark, malign presence but she'd edged just as far as she could go. The door handles were sticking into her back and her head was against the coolness of the window.

'Then why isn't he here?'

'He'd be here if he could.'

'If he could… What does that mean? What's going on?'

Panic rose in her throat. She had no idea what was happening; she only knew that she didn't like it one bit. Jalil must have had a good reason for providing her with a bodyguard but now Sahir was gone. What if he had been meant to protect her from just such a situation as this—from a man like Malik?

Twisting round in her seat, she grabbed at the door handle, yanking it hard, wrenching at it in desperation. And she didn't know whether to feel despair of relief when it didn't move.

'It's locked,' said that calm, controlled voice from behind her. 'They all are. Which is perhaps just as well. I hate to think what might have happened if you'd managed to open that just now. You'd have been dumped on a country road in the middle of Barakhara, without any idea of where you were or where to go.'

'Which right now would be preferable to being stuck in here with you!' Abbie flung at him, lying through her teeth and knowing it.

She suspected that Malik knew it too, though he didn't actually say it. But the way that one coal-black brow arched in mocking question and the cynical twist to his beautiful mouth made it plain that he was thinking along the same lines as she was.

'We're both stuck with each other,' he pointed out with a gentle tolerance that made her teeth snap together at the way it was so obviously faked. 'So we might as well make the best of it.'

'The best being what?' Abbie began but her sarcastic comment was broken into by a crackle of sound on the radio and a sudden sharp comment in thick Arabic from the driver.

The effect on Malik was dramatic. Leaning forward, he pushed aside the glass panel that separated him from the

driver and snapped out curt questions—or commands—
Abbie had no way of knowing—in the same language.

'What is it?' she asked sharply. 'What's happening now?'

It seemed an age before Malik answered her but in fact it
was probably only a few moments. But those moments were
long enough to twist her pulse rate up higher, making her
breath catch hard in her throat.

'Malik—what's going on?'

The expression on the face he turned to her was more
frightening than anything he might say. His jaw was held so
tight a muscle jerked at one side and the deep-set black eyes
were hooded and withdrawn.

'We need to get out of here. Can you ride?'

'Ride?' It was the last thing that Abbie was expecting and
she had nodded before she had time to consider just why he
might have asked.

'Yes, I can ride, but...'

She caught hold of Malik's loose sleeve, dragging his attention back from the sharp-toned discussion he was having
with the driver.

'But why should I? And don't tell me because you say so.
You might be king in your own country, but here...'

Her voice faltered suddenly as she realised that she didn't
really know where 'here' was. She had flown into an airport,
that was all she knew. Quite where Malik had taken her was
another matter.

'You don't rule me!' She managed to force a little more
strength into the words. 'You have to give me some explanation for what's going on. Some reason to go with you—
and it has to be better than "There's been a slight problem"
or I'm not going anywhere.'

Malik's sigh was a masterpiece of resigned exasperation.

'Do you ever do anything without arguing?'

'Not where you're concerned—no.'

To her amazement her rebellion earned her not the savage

reproof she was expecting but a smile. It was only a small smile, barely there in the curve of that sensuous mouth, scarcely lighting the darkness of his eyes. But it was at least a smile and not the frown and the flare of fury she had been dreading.

'I could order you to do as I say.'

'You could try!'

It was pure defiance, and she knew it. And so, she suspected, did Malik.

He could order her to do as he said and she would have to obey. It was either that or take her chances in a country she'd never visited before, where she didn't speak the language and had no idea at all where she was. If she looked out of the car window all she could see was darkness. Endless, impenetrable darkness. She didn't have a hope of finding her way anywhere in that. Even Malik was a safer bet than taking that sort of a risk.

'But you're right.'

'I am?'

She couldn't hold back the exclamation of surprise and disbelief, earning herself another wry smile and a nod of his proud head.

'I do owe you an explanation—'

He had to tell her some time, Malik admitted to himself. The situation was messy enough as it was.

'You do?'

Her astonishment was even more evident this time and, in spite of himself, Malik felt the corners of his mouth twitch again.

'I do. Believe it or not, I am not in the habit of abducting young women.'

'You mean you don't have plans to kidnap me and take me away with you to your desert lair to have your wicked way with me?'

In spite of the shadows in the car, he could see the way that her soft mouth quirked upwards and the big grey eyes opened wide, the flash of teasing mockery showing in them threatening his fight for composure.

'You've been reading too many novels.'

The vision her words put into his head had created erotic images that fired the carnal thoughts he had been clamping down on since that kiss. He could tell himself as often as he could that it had simply been meant to silence her—but his fiercely aroused libido knew different as the ache in his hungry body proved. It was torment sitting this close to her, inhaling the scent of her skin and not being able to indulge the need she woke in him.

'I've not been reading any novels!' Abbie retorted. 'There was nothing fictitious about that kiss.'

The realisation that she had been thinking on exactly the same lines as he had, remembering the heated potency of that kiss, did nothing to ease Malik's already uncomfortable state of mind—and body.

'I told you that was a mistake,' he growled. 'It isn't going to happen again.'

'No.'

Just for a moment he made the mistake of looking straight at her, looking into her eyes. Their gazes clashed, locked... clung.

This time a fine strand of blonde hair had caught on the long curving lashes of her right eye, moving, catching when she blinked.

This time he couldn't hold back. His hand moved on pure instinct, reaching out, touching the softness of the hair, her lashes.

He saw her eyes widen as she watched his finger come closer. She watched every movement, her mouth slightly parted, her breath snatching in and then stopping. Holding.

With infinite gentleness he eased the hair away, freeing it from her eyelashes and saw her throat move as she suddenly swallowed hard. Her breath snagged again, in the same moment that his heart thudded hard, just once, and he saw the pink tip of her tongue slip out to slick over her dry bottom lip.

Abbie...

Her name was a thought in his head, not spoken out loud.

What he did say out loud, clashing with exactly the same word from her mouth was:

'No.'

'No,' Abbie said again, reinforcing it with a shake of her head that broke the spell her eyes had had on him. *'No!'*

'You were going to give me an explanation,' she said a few minutes later, dropping the words into the silence that had fallen around them, broken only by the hum of the car's tyres on the road. 'And it had better be a good one.'

'There is trouble in the city—a riot. It was thought better—safer—to have you out of the way until things had settled down.'

'So Jalil sent you to fetch me?'

'Jalil has his hands full dealing with things there.'

He was deliberately avoiding the truth in his answer, and he suspected she knew that. Jalil hadn't spared her a thought. His mind had been only on himself—as always.

But it seemed that Abbie too was thinking along different lines.

'This—trouble... What will it mean for Andy? Will my brother be safe?'

'At the moment your brother is in the safest place possible.'

It wasn't the prisoners who were in trouble but the man who had put them under lock and key. Jalil's petty tyrannies, his greed and self-indulgence had always put him at risk of rebellion in Barakhara. Now it seemed that tensions had boiled over.

'So where are we going—why did you ask if I could ride?'

'Right now, the safest place is in the desert—the car will not take us where we're going.'

'You expect me to come with you just like this? To trust you—put myself in your hands...'

Abbie couldn't help it. The shiver that ran through her at the thought of being literally in his hands made her voice shudder too.

But not with fear. Never with fear.

She wasn't afraid of what he might do to her physically. That had never even entered the equation. But the emotional cost of simply being with him was something that made her heart clench in pain.

She'd hoped for more time to get over the vivid, violent response she had had to Malik from the start. It would take years, not days, to blur the memory of the way it had felt to be in his arms, to ease the sense of loss at his rejection. Whether she would ever get over the love she had felt for him was something she had to doubt.

And being here with him like this was only going to make matters so much worse. Already she had had to fight against the powerful pull of attraction. That kiss had made all the feelings she had tried to crush down reawaken. They had swamped her, destroying her ability to think, leaving her only able to feel, and her wild, foolish, stupidly passionate response had been the result.

So what was Malik's excuse?

He probably didn't think he needed one. She was just a gold-digger in his eyes and she only had herself to blame for that. She'd certainly dug herself right into that particular hole so that she couldn't get out.

'Or is it just that you snap your fingers and expect me to obey? I think you should remember that I'm not yours to command.'

'You're not mine...'

Malik let the sentence trail off without completing it, giving it a completely different meaning. One that added to the shivering sense of awareness so that she felt as if icy little footprints had been marked out all over her body.

'You're not mine, but if you were I would make it my aim

to make sure that you were protected and kept safe at this troubled time. So, for this time, I will treat you as if you were mine. I will do all that I can to make sure that not a hair on your head will meet with any harm.'

'You—you'd do that…?'

She could hardly breathe well enough to get the words out. Her heart was thudding high up in her throat, cutting off her air supply and making her feel light-headed, her thoughts spinning as a result.

Those words, spoken in a voice that sounded so deep and heartfelt, the beautiful accent adding an extra note of sincerity to the declaration until it sounded almost like the vows one might make in church, made Abbie feel shaky all over in a very new and different way. This time she no longer felt cold. Instead she felt warm and safe, as if strong, protective arms had folded around her, holding her close, keeping her safe. She could almost hear those same husky tones declaring the age-old promises, To have and to hold…in sickness and in health…from this day forward…*Till death us do part*.

'You'd do that for me?'

The darkness in the car was almost complete, so that if it hadn't been for the whiteness of Malik's headdress she might have missed the way that his proud head inclined in a brief gesture of agreement.

'You are promised to a member of my family and so, as the representative of that family, it is my duty to ensure your safety.'

It is my duty…

Abbie could only be thankful that the lack of light hid every trace of her reaction. Otherwise Malik might have seen the way that the blood drained from her face, the sharp dig of her teeth into the softness of her lower lip and the betraying sheen of painful tears that filled her eyes.

Every last trace of that wonderful protected glow evaporated from her, leaving her cold and miserable, as if she had been caught in a sudden shower of icy rain. If he had actually lifted a hand and slapped her hard across her cheek he couldn't have set her back in her seat with any more cold-blooded force, knocking all fight, all sense of hope, right out of her.

It is my duty...

Of course she was only a duty to him. Her own words, her defiant declaration that she had determined to marry a sheikh and she didn't care which one—Malik or his brother—had convinced him that she was nothing but a gold-digger and so unworthy of his concern or his respect. It was only because she was, as he had said, 'promised to a member of my family' that he was taking this trouble to care for her.

And she would be just creating a fantasy to even imagine otherwise.

The stinging pain made her want to lash out, putting a bitter note into her voice when she spoke again.

'So tell me, why do you spend so much time at your brother's beck and call?'

She caught Malik's brief frown that indicated that his normally near perfect English couldn't quite cope with the phrase.

'Why do you act as his messenger—his advocate? I wouldn't have thought of you as his servant—'

'I am no man's servant,' Malik cut in, the bite in the words showing how her comment had caught him on the raw. 'But I made a vow to Jalil's mother—*my* mother—that I would care for my brother. His father died when he was only eighteen—just after he left the school you were both at—and our mother only lived a couple of years longer.'

He hadn't ever suspected that looking after his half-brother would be such a full-time occupation, Malik reflected as the car came to a halt at the place they had arranged to meet the horses.

Indulged from the start, Jalil had been a cosseted baby, a spoilt child, and he had grown into a weak and selfish young man. His grip on the reins of his country had always been loose but this latest bout of trouble was the worst he'd provoked. The young fool just didn't know the meaning of restraint—and he was incapable of listening to advice.

Abigail Cavanaugh might think that she had got the best of a bargain in winning Jalil's ring on her finger, but he doubted if the marriage would bring her any sort of happiness. But it seemed that she believed that immeasurable wealth would more than compensate for any lack of affection she had to put up with.

And of course there was the question of her brother's safety. Certainly, that had seemed the subject uppermost in her thoughts when she had heard about the rioting in the city. Was it possible that…

A sudden movement at his side distracted him from his thoughts as he turned just in time to see Abbie reaching for the door handle. Asif, the driver, had got out to talk to the men who had brought the horses to the rendezvous, and he had left the door unlocked.

'Oh, no, you don't…'

Reaching across hurriedly, Malik grabbed hold of Abbie's arm and hauled her back inside the car, earning himself a savage glare of fury as he did so.

'Just what do you think you're doing?' she snapped, twisting her arm this way and that in an attempt to break free. But all she managed was to get herself breathless and frustrated and rub her imprisoned wrist sore with her exertions.

The sight of the bruised redness on the delicate white skin was shocking enough to hit home like a kick in the guts. He couldn't control the roughness in his tone when he retorted, 'It's more a matter of what you think you are doing! Who gave you permission to leave the car?'

That brought her up short, her eyes flashing wild defiance, her breath snatched in on such a heaving gasp that the lifting and swelling effect on the rich curves of her breasts was dangerously erotic. Malik felt his lower body heat and harden in the space of a second, and the resulting fight with himself for control almost made him lose his grip on Abbie's wrist.

Almost.

The situation was risky enough as it was. If word ever got out that Sheikh Malik Al'Qaim had been seen with an unchaperoned western woman—and worse, his half-brother's betrothed—Jalil's future wife—there would be the sort of repercussions that Abbie could barely imagine. They had to take careful precautions—the sort of precautions that he strongly suspected she was not going to like at all.

He was right.

When, still holding her firmly by the hand to make sure she didn't leap out of the car in some wild attempt at escape, he reached with his other hand into the side glove pocket and pulled out a package, she watched him closely, eyes narrowed in suspicion.

'Here, put this on…'

As he tossed it towards her, the parcel opened and the contents tumbled out, falling to land in a swirl of black muslin over Abbie's knees and lap.

'What—is that what I think it is?'

Her opinion was made plain in her voice, the cold fury, the disgust in the words, but Malik chose to ignore the implied rebellion and instead answered her question quite literally.

'If you think that the robe is an *abaya* with a *hijab*—a headscarf—and veil, then yes, that is exactly what they are. I suggest you put them on now, before you set foot outside this car.'

'Put them on—you have to be joking!' Abbie's fingers stirred the fall of muslin with reluctance, as if she feared just to touch it would contaminate her. 'How dare you ask it of me? It's an insult—'

'Only if you *see* the *abaya* and veil through Western

eyes—as an imposition and a curb.' Malik cut across her outraged protest. 'It can also be a form of protection. You are not in London or any western city now, Miss Cavanaugh. The men outside are not sophisticated bankers or CEOs. They are desert tribesmen with a fierce pride in their way of life, their traditions. To them, the *abaya* is a form of protection—and for you it will be the same. If you have any sense you will do as you are told.'

Seeing the way she still hesitated, the spark of mutiny that still burned in her eyes, the set of her mouth, he let his breath hiss through his teeth in a sound of pure exasperation.

'We do not have time to waste in delaying.'

'Then…'

'And you are not leaving this car unless you are wearing that! So make up your mind, Abbie. Before I make it up for you.'

The look she shot him from under her lashes was filled with pure venom, but she lifted her hand to demonstrate the way he still held her imprisoned.

'You'll have to let me go first.'

Then, when he still looked doubtful, unsure whether this was the prelude to another rebellion, perhaps an attempt at escape, she sighed and lifted her other hand, palm up, in an appeasing gesture.

'I promise,' she said. 'I give you my word. I won't fight or argue any more—not over this.'

Malik's mouth quirked at the corners into a smile that he couldn't keep back.

'That would be a first.'

Slowly, reluctantly, he let her go, knowing deep inside that the reason for his reluctance was not that he doubted her word or believed she would take advantage of her freedom. It was at once more simple and much more complicated than that. He didn't *want* to let go of her hand. Didn't want to relinquish the feel of the warmth of her skin underneath his touch, the fine strength of her bones, the softness of her flesh.

The truth was that he wanted to hold on for much, much longer. He wanted to expose more of that white skin to his hungry gaze, feel its smoothness underneath his caressing hands, kiss...

But if he didn't let go then she would begin to suspect just what sort of carnal path his thoughts were following and he could just imagine her reaction to *that*. Or, rather, he couldn't imagine this time.

And so released her. He moved his hands away and kept them away. But he couldn't tear his eyes away. Couldn't stop them from watching the swift, elegant efficiency of her movements as she pulled on the *abaya*, fastened the *hijab* over the pale glory of her hair.

Then she turned to him, the concealing veil still dangling from her hands.

'Okay?' she questioned. 'Satisfied now?' and he inclined his head in agreement.

'Okay.'

'But this is only for now. Don't think that because I've agreed to this it means I'm going to be a pushover from now on.'

'The thought never crossed my mind,' he assured her gravely, though the effect he was aiming for was rather spoiled by his mouth's tendency to curve even further into a smile. One that, to his surprise, Abbie met and matched with a quick, flashing grin of her own.

'Well, at least we understand each other on that.'

'So what made you decide to do as I asked?'

Abbie considered the question for a moment before looking him straight in the eye and admitting honestly, 'The fact that I have no other choice. I need to keep you sweet because you're the one looking after me. The one I have to rely on to keep me safe and get me to Jalil in safety.'

Pulling on the veil, she turned and scrambled out of the car so that she didn't see the way that Malik's face changed, the way that the smile that had warmed his expression faded at her words.

Jalil would have insisted on the *abaya* well before this, he thought as he followed her out. His half-brother might be a self-indulgent libertine who flouted the rules he had grown up by when his own pleasures were concerned. But he was a narrow-minded and unliberated bigot with regard to the way he felt that women should behave.

He was going to have to do some straight talking with Abbie about her situation and the young man she was so determined to marry, just as soon as he got the chance.

CHAPTER ELEVEN

ABBIE woke very slowly, very reluctantly. Yawning and stretching lazily, she winced as muscles she wasn't accustomed to using protested at the movement. Her legs ached and so did her neck and shoulders and for a couple of dreamy seconds she couldn't begin to imagine why.

But then her memory woke up too and with it came the recollection of what had happened the previous night, the thought jolting her upright in her bed, grey eyes looking round the room she was in, searching for the man who had brought her here. Searching for Malik.

He wasn't there.

Nor, of course, was she in a room. She had only a haze of memories of her arrival here, but one thing stood out so clearly. After hours of riding, hours of darkness, total darkness, with sand swirling in the desert wind, stinging against her face even with the protection of the veil, at long last, when the rising sun had turned the sky a burning red at dawn, they had come to this oasis encampment.

She had been barely awake by then. In fact, she knew that she had spent some of the journey asleep, the long hours of travel and the stress of the fearful anticipation of what the day might bring finally getting the better of her so that she had swayed in her saddle, her eyes closing in weariness.

Malik had noticed.

He had seen how her head had drooped, her hands loosening on the reins. He had rapped out a command that had halted their small caravan and then he had brought his own horse alongside the mare that Abbie rode and had touched her arm softly.

'Are you all right?' he asked, the husky concern in his voice almost destroying her completely. She was exhausted, lost, alone in a foreign country. It was years since she had actually ridden this far or this hard, though she would have died rather than admit it, and she didn't think she could go an inch further.

Behind the concealing veil tears of fatigue burned at her eyes and she struggled to blink them away as she nodded her head in response to his question.

'Can you continue?'

She wanted to say yes. Anything other than admit to him the weakness she was feeling. But she didn't seem to be able to form even the single word.

And then in a moment there was no need for speech. She hadn't even opened her mouth before Malik edged his mount even closer and was reaching out to take hold of her. Strong arms closed round her; powerful muscles bunched as he lifted her bodily from the saddle and brought her over from her horse to his. He settled her on the saddle before him and enfolded her in a supportive, protective grip.

'You are safe now,' he murmured in her ear. 'You can sleep if you need to.'

And the problem was that she did feel safe. Supported by the strength of those arms, with her head resting against the hard bones of his shoulder, she could close her eyes and lean back and feel protected. She even dozed a little, sleeping fitfully and waking to know the strength of Malik's hold on her, the scent of his body surrounding her. But the truth was that he could never protect her from the cruellest blows that attacked her heart.

He could never protect her from himself.

But he had kept her safe on their journey. And he had brought her here, to where they could shelter from the elements and from whatever trouble was still brewing—or had boiled over—in Barakhara's capital. Abbie had managed one thankful glance at their destination and she had fallen into a sleep so deep that she had no recollection at all of even being lifted down from Malik's horse or carried into the black woven tent.

She certainly didn't have any memory of being placed on this low, sofa-like divan and...

Another stretch, the feel of the sheets against...against her *skin*...made her sit upright in sudden shock.

Someone had undressed her before they had put her to bed! Someone—Malik—because surely it could only be Malik—had taken off the white shirt and pale grey cotton trousers, leaving her in only the lacy bra and knickers she wore underneath. Abbie's blood ran cold and then flooded hotly under her exposed skin until she felt as if she was in the grip of a fever. What made matters so much worse was that in her mind she could almost hear Malik's cool, intriguingly accented voice saying that he didn't know what all the fuss was about. Hadn't he seen her in far less—in nothing at all—on that night at his hotel suite?

But that was...

Abbie couldn't finish the sentence even inside her own head because she could almost see Malik's scornful expression, see the way that one jet-black brow would lift cynically as he looked her up and down.

What made the difference? he would scorn. Why was she now embarrassed? Then she had been only too keen to help him remove her clothing, had actively encouraged it.

But that was when you thought that enticing me into bed was also trapping me into marriage.

She could hear the words as clearly as if he were actually in the room.

Now that you know you're not going to get your way, you're not so keen to provide a strip show for me, is that it, hmm?

And the worst thing was that she wouldn't be able to find a way to answer him.

How could she tell him the truth—that yes, in a way, because she had had the hope that he wanted to marry her the time she had spent in his bed had become so special? That hope had made her offer her body—and her heart—so willingly.

How could she ever admit that it was because she had been weak enough, foolish enough—*stupid* enough to dream that maybe, if they did enter into an arranged marriage, he might one day come, if not to love her, then at least to care for her? He had had no thought of any such thing, and he had been totally upfront about that.

And she could have accepted that too. In fact, the truth was that she wished she had.

Flinging back the bedclothes, Abbie swung her legs out of the bed. A shining ivory silk robe, glowing with embroidery, lay across another divan nearby, obviously meant for her use, and she pulled it on to cover her near nakedness.

'If only I hadn't said anything.'

She said the words aloud as she paced restlessly over the beautifully carpeted floor, unable to sit still because of the discomfort of her thoughts.

If she hadn't opened her mouth, if she hadn't let slip that stupid, blundering comment about 'Every night of our married lives,' then she would have spent that night—and maybe many more—in Malik's bed, as happy as she could ever have dreamed she could be. She would have known his lovemaking, would have experienced the full knowledge of his physical possession, and she would have given herself up to the fullest of pleasures that he could give her.

And she wouldn't have asked for more.

But instead she had opened her mouth without thinking and so she had ruined everything. She had made Malik think that it was an 'all or nothing' situation when it was nothing of the sort.

If only she could have her time again. If only she could have another chance then she would grab at it with both hands, but keeping her mouth clamped tight shut this time.

If Malik would only show her once again the passion he had felt for her that first night, then she would meet it with a passion of her own, a passion fired and fed by the love she felt for him as a man until it would more than match the fire in his soul. Because that fire was still there. She'd felt it when he'd kissed her in the car and she had been unable to resist responding to him.

And oh, how she would respond if she got a chance to make love with him. If she only got a second chance she would grab at it with both hands and not lose out this time.

If she got a second chance...

But there was no hope of that—none at all. Malik had made it clear that he considered her forbidden fruit. She was betrothed to his half-brother and, as such, untouchable in his eyes. He had only kissed her because she had been about to scream, had only taken the kiss further because she had responded to him, her hunger feeding his. But then he had broken away and held himself coldly distant ever afterward. Even on the journey here, when he had lifted her on to the saddle before him and put his arm around her to hold her safe, his touch had been as cool and distant as a stranger's, unemotional as a doctor's.

He would never touch her again, not willingly. She was only dreaming to consider it—and, by allowing herself to dream, she was keeping open the wounds he had inflicted on her that first night. But how could those wounds have a chance to heal when she was forced to spend time with Malik like this in this desert hideaway?

Besides, she couldn't want Malik's passion and still hope to rescue Andy. The only way to help her brother was to marry Jalil—even if it tore her heart to shreds to do so.

It was late evening before Malik returned to the tent. Late evening on what had been a long, worrying, lonely and unsettled day for Abbie. The attendants that Malik had instructed to look after her had been diligent in following his orders, attentive to any need she might have, but they couldn't—or wouldn't—answer any of the frantic questions that were pounding at the inside of her skull, tormenting her thoughts, demanding to know…

What was happening in Barakhara ?

What had happened to Jalil?

And what effect would that have on Andy's future? How would her brother be coping in this new upheaval—and were the effects of it potentially good or bad?

But, most importantly, most frequently running round and round in her head was the need to know just where *was* Malik? Where had he gone and why? And when—*when*—would he be back?

By evening she was almost in a state of despair and so when the tent flaps parted and Malik finally appeared in the opening she was beyond restraint, beyond making just a polite greeting. All the pent-up emotion and worry exploded from her like champagne erupting from a violently shaken bottle.

'So you've decided to come back at last! Where the hell have you been? Do you know what time it is? How long I've been left here—on my own…'

'And good evening to you!' Malik snapped back, kicking the tent flap closed behind him and striding across the carpet.

As he did so, he dragged the white *gutra* from his head and tossed it and the black cord *igal* vaguely in the direction of the nearest divan before raking both hands through the jet-black hair he had exposed… He was dressed in a simple white *thobe*, topped with a long black cloak, both of which were wrinkled and dust-stained. Clearly, wherever he had been, he had not been dressing for show or as befitted his royal rank.

'What sort of greeting is that…?'

'The only sort of greeting that you deserve after abandoning me here alone all day long! I didn't even know that you had gone—and when I woke…'

'I left you a note!' It was a snarl of exasperation, an ominous sound of warning. 'I explained everything in that.'

'Everything! *Everything!*'

Abbie knew she should be heeding that warning tone but she was past caring. The long, mostly silent hours of waiting and worrying had stretched out her already taut nerves until they were near breaking point and she had to let her feelings out somehow.

'You explained nothing!'

Abbie grabbed the crumpled note from where she had tossed it aside only a short time before after reading it for the hundredth time. She didn't care if the fact that it was so close that she could just reach out a hand for it revealed how she hadn't been able to let it out of her sight all day long. Or if the fact that it was so crumpled gave away just how many times she had gone back over its contents. She *wanted* him to know how worried she had been. Wanted him to know the sort of torture he had put her through.

'"I have to go and find out what is happening…"' she read out loud in a voice that made her opinion painfully clear. '"You will be perfectly safe here until I get back. If you need anything, then just ask…"'

'Well, you were perfectly safe, weren't you?'

Malik's black-eyed gaze swept round the tent where the oil lamps threw a shadowy light over the carpets and mattresses.

'I see no signs of rape or pillage—and Omar tells me that you asked…'

'Oh, I asked all right! I asked to know what was happening but no one would tell me. And I asked where you were but no one would say.'

'I told them not to.'

It was positively the last straw, shattering the little that remained of Abbie's control and bringing her to her feet in a rush.

'You told them! Do you know how long I've been here—'

'Not now, Abbie,' Malik broke in roughly, bringing up his hands in front of his face in a brusque, surprisingly defensive gesture, physically cutting off the communication between them. 'I don't want to talk about it.'

'You might not want to talk, but I do. I—'

'I said *not now*, Abbie!'

If his fury hadn't stopped her dead, then the look on his face would have had the required effect. The same blind anger that had thickened his voice, roughening it at the edges was there in the blaze of his eyes, in the taut set of the muscles in his jaw. But it wasn't that that stopped her. Instead, it was the realisation that she hadn't really been looking at him since the moment he had arrived in the tent. Not looking so that she could *see* him properly.

But now she was. And what she saw shocked her right to the core of her soul.

The beautiful golden skin was drawn over the strongly carved bones of his face, stretched so tight at the nose and mouth that at times it showed white with a strain that drained all the colour from his cheeks. There were deep shadows under his eyes—shadows that were created by more than just tiredness, but spoke of a draining exhaustion that was mental rather than physical. And that glittering polished jet gaze now seemed clouded and dull under heavily hooded lids.

'Not now, Abbie,' he said again but this time in a very different tone of voice. Low and worn and shockingly flat, with no emotion at all in its husky notes. 'I don't want to talk about it now.'

It had been a hell of a day and he didn't want to talk about *anything*. He didn't even want to think. He would have to do that soon enough. He would have to explain everything to Abbie, tell her what this meant for her and her brother. He rather suspected he knew how she would react and knew deep down that that was probably the main reason why he didn't want to talk. He just wanted to…

'Sit down.'

It was Abbie who spoke, but she sounded so different that for a moment he almost didn't recognise it.

'Sit down before you fall down. I'll get someone to bring you a drink.'

She was heading towards the tent entrance as she spoke but he put out a hand to stop her as she would have gone by.

'No. I'm sure you must have some water and that's all I need.'

'Of course.'

As she changed direction, Malik threw himself down on to one of the divans and rested his aching head thankfully against the soft cushions that were piled up around him. He closed his eyes and let himself be completely still and silent at last.

This was what he had dreamed of on the journey back to the oasis. The one thing that had kept him going had been the thought that, at the end of the long, tiring ride he would be here, in the peace and stillness of this tent. He had even allowed himself to imagine…

'Your water.'

Reluctantly he opened his eyes to see Abbie standing before him, holding a glass of water out to him.

'*Shokran*—Thank you…'

He took it, gulped down the cool liquid thankfully, but barely even noticed the clear taste of the water, the way it soothed his parched throat. Instead, his whole attention was focused on the woman who stood before him.

The woman he had been unable to get out of his mind all day long. The woman who had been at the forefront of his thoughts as he rode away from the oasis. The woman who had still been there as he rode back, with the news he had to tell her fretting at his brain. He had once, foolishly, allowed himself to imagine, to dream, how it would be if she was waiting for him to come back to her—to come home to her...

Malik's hand tightened convulsively around the glass until his knuckles showed white.

He'd actually allowed himself to picture how it might feel if he had a woman who loved him waiting for him—a woman he loved in return. And in his tiredness, the lowness of his mood, he'd let himself dream that Abbie might be that woman.

And now, here she was, standing before him, like his dream brought to life. She was looking more beautiful than he had ever seen her. The long blonde hair hung loose and flowed over her shoulders like gilded water. The ivory silk robe flowed too, skimming over the slender length of her body, clinging a little at the curves of her hips, the swell of her breasts in a way that made his mouth dry in spite of the water he had just drunk.

He had never wanted a woman in his life as much as he wanted Abigail Cavanaugh. He wanted her so much that his body ached with it—hell, his *soul* ached with the hunger she created in him.

If only she hadn't been who she was.

That night in his hotel suite, he had been on the edge of one of the greatest sexual experiences of his life. One of the greatest *experiences of his life*, with no qualification whatsoever. And then she had come out with those six shocking words: 'Every night of our married lives' and it had felt as if a grenade had exploded right in his face.

He couldn't touch this woman. She was the woman his brother had wanted as a wife and honour demanded that he walk away from her. He had tried, but he hadn't been able to get her out of his mind. He'd even used the fact that there was trouble in Barakhara as an excuse to come back into her life, to see her just one more time. Even though he'd known that it would put him through a torment of frustration just to be with her.

That and the fact that Jalil obviously hadn't cared whether his prospective bride could reach the capital in safety or not. Someone had had to ensure that she came to no harm between the airport and the palace.

At least that was what he had told himself. He knew that the truth was that he had just been hunting for an excuse to see her again.

But now…

Now everything was different. Or was it?

A lot had changed—changed irrevocably. Abbie was no longer forbidden to him. And he knew that he would do any-thing for another chance to spend even one night with her. To know the intimate delights offered by that glorious body, to bury himself in her, sate himself…

Hell, who was he trying to fool? How could he ever sate himself on this woman in one night?

'Why are you staring at me like that?'

Abbie was watching him warily, her grey eyes narrowed, a faint frown creasing the fine skin between her delicate brows.

'Was I staring? Forgive me.'

He could only pray that she would believe the huskiness of his voice, his struggle to compose himself and focus on the present and not his fantasies of a future, were the result of tiredness at the end of a long day.

'What has happened, Malik?'

Clearly he hadn't convinced her. Or did he mean that he

had managed to convince her only too well? If the truth was told, he didn't know the answer to that question and he didn't feel at all like trying to find it.

'Could I have some more water?'

He was dodging the issue and, to judge from the look she gave him, Abbie was only too well aware of the fact. But what was he to do? Blurt out the stark facts without any preparation?

But at least she took the glass he held out again and walked away from him to refill it without a word.

Malik had to smother the groan of response that rose to his lips as he watched the sensual sway of her hips, the way the ivory silk slid over the curves of her buttocks, and felt raw, brutal need claw at his guts. He wanted this woman so much that it was agony to sit here, watching her, and do nothing. And he wanted her more than ever today, wanted her as a way of asserting life in the face of...

Images flew up before his mind's eye, images he didn't want to see, couldn't bear to imagine, and he put his hands up to his face, covering his eyes, in an attempt to block them off.

'Are you ill?'

'Fine.'

Malik slid his hands up over his face and out at his temples, raking his fingers through his hair in an attempt to disguise the way he was feeling. The muscles at the back of his neck were tight and sore and he rubbed at them in an effort to ease the tension.

'You don't look fine. Do you have a headache?'

'*Naam.*' He was beyond finding even the simple English word as he nodded his head in agreement.

Why did she have to be this way now? Why did her voice have to be soft, concerned? Her eyes, when they met his as he raked both his hands through his hair, were shadowed with thought, a very different frown now showing between the pale brows. This Abbie awoke feelings, needs, that he was in no mood to struggle against.

Why couldn't she be the spiky-voiced woman who had greeted him with indignation on his arrival just a short time before? The woman whose sharp-eyed glare and even sharper tongue had made him long for silence and some time of peace in which to adjust. That woman...

Oh, who was he fooling? Not even himself!

This woman made him want to gather her close, hold her tight, but kiss her softly. Kiss away that look of anxiety, close the soft mouth against the words of concern that rose to her lips...

...And take her to bed.

The other woman, the other Abbie, made him want to grab at her, shake the anger from her face, crush the accusatory words from her lips and back down her throat. He wanted to kiss those blazing eyes closed against the burn of anger, smother her irritation under her closed eyelids...

...And take her to bed.

'I'd have something for that if I knew where my luggage had been taken.'

The sudden return of a touch of tartness to her tone made his mouth twist into a wry smile.

'The driver had orders to deliver it to the palace. It will be quite safe.'

'I'm sure it will, but in the meantime...'

She pushed the glass into his hand and then moved round the divan, coming up close behind him.

'What are you doing?' Malik demanded as soft fingers brushed the hair away from his neck, probed the muscles gently.

'Trying to help you with your headache. Hmm—your muscles are tight here... Sorry, did that hurt?'

'No.'

It came through gritted teeth. He'd not been able to hold

back the groan in response to the feel of her fingers on his skin, the warmth and softness of her touch. The scent of her body surrounded him, clean and sweetly feminine, setting his heart pounding as he inhaled.

Her touch was working magic. Under the massage, the tightness in his neck and shoulders was beginning to ease. If he admitted to the truth, then it was easing far too quickly so that his brain seemed to have melted along with it. If he leaned back just slightly then his head was resting against the warmth of her body, pillowed on her breasts, sinking into their lush contours. He could feel each breath she took, hear the beat of her heart, the pulse of her blood through her veins.

It was agony and ecstasy all at once. Ecstasy because of the almost sinful pleasure he felt, the sensual enticement that whispered to him to stop thinking, just feel, to abandon himself to the pleasure that the woman promised.

But the agony that slashed through that feeling was both physical and mental. Physical because he was hard and swollen, aching for release, mental because he knew he had to deny the bite of that need, and by denying make it so much more unbearable.

He couldn't relax until he had told her. Couldn't do anything for himself, indulge himself in any way—do *anything*—until she knew the truth.

She had to know.

'Careful.' Abbie's voice came from behind him, the lighter, almost teasing note shocking in contrast to the force of his thoughts. 'You almost relaxed then.'

'Abbie…' Malik began and knew that his tone had given away his mood in the space of a heartbeat.

The soothing fingers stumbled, paused, began again, but less confidently this time. The rhythm of her movements was less fluid, slightly awkward, in a way that showed how her mind was not on what she was doing.

'I have something to tell you.'

Was it easier to tell her when he couldn't see her face?

One part of him wanted—needed to see how she reacted. Another wanted to do anything but watch what happened to her face when he told her the news.

But already he'd hesitated too long. Her fingers might continue to move but their actions were mechanical, uninvolved, and he could feel the way she was holding herself, taut with apprehension and uncertainty, needing to know.

'What is it?' she asked when he couldn't find the words. 'What's happened?'

Find the words! Malik almost laughed out loud at the thought—except that this was no laughing matter at all. There were no words other than the ones that told it straight.

'Malik… What happened?'

He drew in a deep breath, forced it out.

'There was an accident—Jalil—Jalil's dead.'

CHAPTER TWELVE

JALIL'S dead.

The words hit like a blow in Abbie's face, stopping her fingers, stilling her breath.

Had Malik said…?

She couldn't have heard right, could she?

How could Jalil be dead?

'Abbie, did you hear what I said?'

Malik had moved on the divan, turning to face her, and the intent set of his face, the blaze of his black eyes told her that, whatever else had happened, he had most definitely meant what he had said.

'I heard—but…but I was going to marry him!'

A hundred thoughts ran through her head, thoughts she couldn't link together or make any sense of.

How could Jalil be dead?

When?

Had this terrible thing happened today?

And what did this mean for the future? For her? For Andy?

But then the shock cleared from her eyes and she looked into down into Malik's dark face, into those bleak black eyes, and her whole mood changed in a rush.

'He was your brother. I'm so sorry…'

Just for a second, Malik's proud head went back, his eyes closing briefly. When he opened them again it was as if he had brought shutters down behind them, so that his gaze was closed and opaque, impenetrable. Obviously she had over-stepped some line she hadn't been aware of, treading where she wasn't supposed to go.

'What—what happened?' she managed hesitantly, unsure if this too would be a step too far, one that might dramati-cally break his calm and bring down anger on her head.

But Malik answered evenly enough, though with a catch in his voice that tore at her vulnerable heart where he was concerned.

'Because of the mood in the city, Jalil decided to get out of there for a while and a helicopter seemed the easiest way to do that. My—he insisted on taking the controls himself and he is—was—never the best of pilots. Something went wrong and the helicopter crashed into the sea...'

'He might not have—died.'

Unable to bear the flat, desolate tone of his voice, Abbie rushed in to try and offer hope.

'They might have got out...'

Her voice, and the small hope, faded as she saw Malik shake his head sombrely.

'They found the bodies. He's gone.'

'Oh, no—'

And she had been nagging at him for leaving her alone! Jalil had been his brother—how would she feel if this had happened to Andy...?

Impulsively Abbie flung herself down on the divan beside Malik and caught hold of his hand. She didn't care that he had made it plain he didn't want her sympathy; she couldn't hold it back. She'd had to say this, but now, seeing the barriers he'd put up, she would have to accept that he didn't want to talk and that she needed to change the subject.

'I really am sorry.'

She sounded it too, Malik acknowledged. And there was

a softness in her eyes, in her face, that reached through the wall he had tried to build around himself. He had needed that wall because he knew she had only seen his brother as a sheikh—*the Sheikh* she had declared it was her ambition to marry. He hadn't expected any sort of sympathy at all, so he'd pulled away, mentally, when she'd offered it, taken aback when he'd been expecting something else. When he'd anticipated that her very first question would be...

'Where does this leave me?'

Okay, so it hadn't taken her too long to get round to it. And somehow the disappointment in knowing that she'd just been getting there was all the worse for the momentary belief that she might actually have cared.

'Well, the wedding's off.'

The grim humour worked where he couldn't find anything else to say. And Abbie actually flinched away from it, grey eyes reproachful.

'I meant where does it leave Andy?'

Of course. Her brother.

Well, he could understand that, couldn't he? Hadn't he always feared that one day Jalil would do something so stupid that there would be no turning back...? But if there had been a single chance that his brother could be helped, he would have moved heaven and earth to do so.

But what was Abbie prepared to do to rescue her brother? Were her actions solely selfless, or was she already looking for Jalil's replacement?

'There'll be a new sheikh in Barakhara—someone to take Jalil's place.'

As he had suspected, that brought a new spark to her eyes, her head lifting, expression lightening. The small smile that touched her mouth had the force of a double-edged sword slicing into his guts.

Was it a smile of relief—or triumph? Privately he cursed the fact that he hadn't seen her face when he had first told her about Jalil. If he had been watching her expression then, he would know more about the way her mind was working.

'Who is the new sheikh?'

Didn't she know? Couldn't she guess?

'Why do you want to know, *habibti*?'

'I need to know who to go to—who to talk to.'

He reached for her hand, stroked soft fingers down over her palm, watching her watching him, eyes wide, irises huge and black against a tiny rim of grey. And he knew the terrible temptation to test her, to find out just how far she really would go. The need to know was like a sore tooth, like a wound, that he just had to probe, to dig into, to scour right to its core. To root out and exorcise the corruption that was in it.

'Are you looking for another sheikh to marry, hmm? Will you throw yourself at his feet—into his bed? Into my bed?'

He slid the question in as if it was a stiletto slipping between her ribs, into her heart.

'Your...?'

She'd been looking down at their linked hands, long lashes lowered so that they lay like soft crescents on the fine slant of her cheekbones, but now her gaze flew upwards again to clash with his, lock—and hold.

'*Your* bed?'

'Of course my bed.'

Malik tightened his grip on her hand, exerting just enough pressure to warn her that he could hold her prisoner, that he could control her if he wanted. Not enough to hurt—but enough to caution her to be very careful in what she said next. And he saw the flicker in those grey eyes that told him she understood—on the very deepest level.

'Didn't you realise? That as Jalil's brother—as his one living relative—I am the only man who can inherit his throne? His country will unite with mine and I will rule them both.'

'Then you—you will have power over Andy?'

'I'll have control over everything in Barakhara.'

The hand he held jerked, just once, in his grasp, and her eyes were torn from his, her gaze dropping to stare down at the spot where their fingers linked together.

But not before he had caught the second, flashing smile that she couldn't control. And this was a smile that he recognised. He'd seen it before on that night in his hotel room—in his bed—when she had thought that she had him—that she had him caught snug and tight, wrapped in her beguiling spider's web.

It was a smile of pure feminine triumph. And suddenly he felt that he knew just what some poor misguided fly must feel to know that it was trapped and the female predator was bearing down on it, about to eat it alive.

He should leave right now. Back out—put an end to this before it had started. But everything that was male in him protested at the thought of never ever knowing this woman physically. Only a few moments ago he had told himself that he would do anything just to enjoy that glorious body once in his life.

And tonight, after all that had happened, he needed that release, that assertion of *life*, so much more than ever before.

'Then what can I do to persuade you to be merciful?'

'I would have thought that you would find that only too easy.'

He must be more tired than he had thought, Malik thought, cursing his unguarded tongue that had let the words slip out before he had had time to consider the wisdom of opening his mouth. But he had to know just how far she would go.

'And what do you mean by that?'

'Oh, I think you know, *sukkar*,' Malik drawled. 'After all, I have firsthand experience of just how…persuasive…you can be. So persuade me.'

'You want…'

Abbie couldn't believe what she was hearing. And she had

no idea at all just what she should feel. She had thought that she had lost her only chance to help Andy—and now she was being offered it all over again, but at what a cost!

'You want…'

'I want you.'

It was a flat, emotionless statement, one that stabbed right to Abbie's already wounded heart like the cruellest blade. She had always known he didn't care for her, but to hear it declared in this cold, blunt way was almost more than she could bear.

'I've always wanted you. More than any woman I've ever met. And I'm prepared to pay any price to have you in my bed.'

'Pay any price!' Abbie echoed, her voice sharp with incredulity. He wouldn't be *paying* anything! 'You mean, you'll set my brother free?'

'I'll do anything you ask, if you offer me what you were prepared to give Jalil. Come to my bed—'

'As—as your concubine—your mistress?'

She had to force the words out, her voice was shaking so badly and her tongue felt as if it had turned to solid ice.

Malik shook his dark head, refuting her words.

'No. As my wife.'

His *wife*. If he had taken hold of the invisible dagger that was in her heart and twisted it brutally, it couldn't have hurt her any more. He didn't know what he was asking. He *couldn't* know.

Loving him as she did, the thought of being his wife was like a dream come true—but not in a cold-blooded, cruel bargain like this!

'I—I can't…'

She wished she could make herself get up and move away but her mind seemed to have lost control over her limbs. They wouldn't move at all and she was sure that if she tried to stand up her legs wouldn't have the strength to support her. So she had to stay where she was, with her face so close to his, the black eyes burning into hers as he held her gaze with his.

'Why not ?' Malik demanded, low and hard. 'Surely one sheikh is as good as another. You wanted to marry a sheikh— I'm offering you marriage to one. Marriage, your brother's freedom—a life of luxury beyond your wildest imaginings— and every night of your life spent in my bed. How can you refuse?'

How *could* she refuse? Abbie could find no way even to answer herself as the question spun round and round inside her head. She'd vowed to do anything to help Andy, any-thing at all, but right now even her brother's future wasn't what was uppermost in her mind. It was her own deepest, most secret longing that was pushing her in the direction of the wildest, most impossible decision she had ever made.

...every night of your life spent in my bed.

She'd said she'd take one chance if it was offered—and here it was. Here Malik was offering the one thing that tempted her—the thought of really making love with him. And she couldn't walk away from that.

She had to take it. But she didn't dare to take it.

The risks were too great. It would hurt too much. But it would hurt far more to turn away.

'Abbie...' Malik prompted softly, drawing her eyes to him again.

The darkness that surrounded the tent was complete; there was no sound from the other men, the horses, the camels, outside the tent. They must all be asleep by now, it was already so late.

They might be alone out here in the desert, under the cool light of the moon. And here, in this tent, Malik was not the Sheikh of Edhan and Barakhara. Here he was just a man. A man who had endured a day from hell and bore the signs of it etched on his face, along with the shadows thrown over it by the guttering lamplight.

She longed for a kiss from that shockingly sensual mouth, and all she had to do was to bring her face just a little closer to his and she could take that kiss for herself—take it and see where that led her, what the consequences were.

She wanted to touch, and all she had to do was to ease her wrist from the loosened grasp of his fingers and reach out, touch his hair, touch his face…

But even as the thoughts slipped into her head they were sent flying right out again as Malik moved the hand that held her wrist and a sudden unexpected pain forced a small cry from her mouth.

'What?'

Malik turned her hand in his so that the lamplight fell directly on to her wrist and a rough curse in his own language escaped him at what he saw. The embroidered cuff of the robe had slipped back, exposing the pale flesh marred by a bruise that was already darkening to purple.

'Last night… In the car…'

Abbie blinked in shock at the change in the sound of his voice. It was as if another man had taken Malik's place, a man whose taunting, seductive tone had vanished and in its place was a tenderness that went straight to her vulnerable heart.

This time when his fingers touched the softness of her skin, they were infinitely gentle, meant to soothe rather than hurt. And the delicate path traced by those square, strong tips made her shiver in instant response.

'Forgive me,' he said huskily, lifting her bruised wrist to his mouth.

When he pressed his lips, warm and devastatingly soft, against the reddened skin, it was like setting a match to tinder-dry wood, starting a tiny electrical spark that raced along the lines of her nerves, heating the blood in her veins as it went, setting the whole of her body alight and alive with wanting.

As just as a few moments earlier she hadn't been able to hold back the quick smile of relief and delight at the thought that Malik was the one who had Andy's future in his hands, so now she couldn't rein in the yearning need that possessed her whole body simply at his touch.

'Malik…'

His name escaped her on the softness of a breath because even now she couldn't believe what she was going to say. She only knew that she had to say it. She could never live with herself if she didn't.

'This marriage that you're offering—with every night of my life spent in your bed… Show me what it would be like—and then I'll decide.'

His smile was like the sun coming up, the dawn of a brand new day, the start of something wonderful.

'Your wish is my command…'

And, leaning forward, he took her mouth in a slow, lingering kiss that seemed to draw her soul right out of her body and into his hands, to do with as he wanted. His lips were firm but gentle, the slow, provocative sweep of his tongue along the line of her mouth an invitation and a question all in one. And as soon as she knew the unique taste of him against her mouth it was as if she had taken a wild, abandoned gulp of the most potent spirit, with a fierce, intoxicating effect that flooded her veins with fire, seared her skin, turned her blood to white heat so that it felt as if her bones were melting in the burn of it.

But the wildest burn of all was between her thighs, at the very core of her femininity, where the heavy, honeyed pulse of primitive need throbbed, swamping every other sense, destroying any chance of thought. Her mouth softened under his, her tongue tangling with his, her sigh a sound of surrender and delight rolled into one.

'Is this what you were looking for, my lady?' Malik muttered against her yielding lips. 'Is this what you wanted?'

'Yes—oh, yes. It's everything I wanted…'

She could barely get the words out, she was so hungry for

his mouth, but even as she reached for him, lacing her arms up and around his strong neck, tangling her fingers in the sleekness of his hair, she heard his husky laughter, raw and deep, low down in his throat.

'Not *everything, sukkar,*' he reproved softly. 'This is very far from everything I can give you.'

And, with a low growl, he caught hold of her, twisted with an easy strength, flipping her over on to her back so that she landed with a soft exclamation on the softness of the cushions, sinking deep into the mattress as Malik came down on top of her, crushing her with his powerful weight.

'So, let's start again…'

He pushed his hands into her hair, holding each side of her head so that she was completely at his mercy, unable to move either to right or left.

'First—a kiss…'

'You've already kissed me…' Abbie tried to protest but Malik shook his head reprovingly.

'A real kiss—the sort of kiss I've been wanting to give you from the first moment that I saw you watching me from that window.'

Unexpectedly and without warning a bubble of laughter rose in Abbie's throat, making her smile up into his dark, intent face.

'In that appalling apron!' she gasped, only to receive a burning glance from those brilliant black eyes, one that told her there was no humour in Malik's mind now, only a primal male need, one that could allow for no resistance, brook no delay.

'In anything,' he told her huskily. 'In anything at all or—preferably—in *nothing* at all. This robe…'

His hands slid down the length of her body, over the silk of the robe, caressing every inch of her, stirring her hunger, building the need for him as the heat of his palms reached pleasure spots that longed for the reality of his touch.

'...is very beautiful, but the truth is that it is nothing like as beautiful as the body beneath it. The silk may be soft but t doesn't compare to the softness of your skin, the satin warmth of your flesh. It may cling to your breasts...'

His hands cupped the swell of her through the fine material, making Abbie gasp aloud in delight and shock at he intensity of the burn of need that shot through her at his ouch.

'To your hips...'

Strong fingers smoothed a burning path over her hips and down her thighs, his dark smile growing as he watched her face, felt her writhe in yearning response underneath his imprisoning body.

'And here...'

'Oh—Malik...'

His name broke from her control as one of those tormenting hands cupped the shape of the soft mound between her egs, pressing the fine silk against her sensitised skin, and she saw the burn of an answering need flare in his eyes, sear along he carved cheekbones as he aroused himself as well as her.

'But no silk can ever give me what I want from you. Nothing can compare to the feeling of you, naked and wanting, underneath me, welcoming me, opening to me...'

Those tormenting hands made the return journey back up her body, lingering in the same spots, caressing, tantalising, stirring... Until they were back on either side of her face again, but now they had to hold her still, control the way her head wanted to toss and twist against the silk pillows.

'So first the kiss—here...'

His mouth took hers, hard and strong, giving and demanding in the same moment, forcing her lips open, invading the soft moistness inside, tangling, tasting, teasing...

'And then here...'

This time the heat of his mouth fastened on the tip of one breast where the arousal-hardened nipple pushed against the ivory silk, as if demanding his attention. He suckled her softly through the fine material until the silk was moist and clinging to her skin and the scrape of his teeth sent a stinging arrow of awareness along every nerve, flooding the core of her with heat and hunger.

'Oh, please…please…'

Was she asking him for more—or asking him to stop? In the spinning heat of her mind, Abbie had no idea what she was trying to say, only that *please* was the only word that formed in her thoughts, that her tongue could manage.. Please…please…*please.*

'But you are wearing too much—far too much—so this…'

Tanned fingers flicked the crushed and crumpled silk traced the neckline from the point on her neck where her pulse raced in hungry demand, down to the embroidery-edged opening at the front.

'This has to go…'

And, before she was even aware of what he planned, those powerful hands had caught the two sides of the neckline gathering the silk up and wrenching it apart, ripping it right down the front until the two sides fell away from her body leaving her almost totally exposed.

'Malik!'

It was a choking cry of shock, of total disbelief, but he took it as a reproof and shook his head almost violently in rejection.

'It's only a robe,' he told her. 'I will give you another—I will give you a thousand other ones. So long as you're with me, you will never want for clothes—but you will also never want to wear them. Just as you will never want this…'

The scrap of lace that was her bra was swiftly unclipped and tossed aside, hot black eyes feasting on the exposed creamy flesh, the deep pink nipples that stood proud with yearning need.

'Or this…'

Another tug of his hands removed the last of her clothing
and he let out a deep, deep sigh of masculine satisfaction as
he surveyed her lying there, spread out on the bed, totally
naked.

'Now you're as I want you,' he declared, sitting up for a
moment to pull his own robe up and over his head, discarding his own underwear before he came back to her, proudly
nude, completely unself-conscious in his total male arousal.
'And now we can really begin.'

'B-begin!'

Abbie's mouth trembled on the word, her lips struggling
to form it at all. If this was just the beginning then she didn't
know how much she could take. But Malik clearly had every
intention of taking his time, subjecting her already quivering body to a sensual onslaught that was carefully designed
to take her as close to the edge as possible without ever
actually pushing her over.

'Do you like this?' he murmured, finding a hundred delicate sensitive spots and using his hands, his mouth, his tongue
on them until she was writhing in anguished delight, moaning
her pleasure aloud.

'Yes…' she groaned. 'Oh, yessss…'

But Malik shook his head and brought his powerful frame
up to straddle her yearning body, long hair-roughened legs
on either side of hers, the heated power of his erection
pushing into the nest of curls at the centre of her body.

Leaning over her, he took her face in both his hands again,
cupping her cheeks, holding her so that she had to look up
into his burning eyes.

'I do not understand,' he told her, just the faintest hint of
easing in his thickened voice. 'You have to speak to me in
my language—tell me *naam* for yes—*la* for no—then I will
be able to do as you want. So…do you like this?'

'N-*naam*…' Abbie sighed.

'And this?'

'*Naam…*'

'And…'

'*Naam…naam…*' Her voice rose until it was almost a scream of ecstasy as his knowing touch sought and found the most intimate, most sensitive place of all and teased it and her into stinging, yearning need. '*Naam!*'

She was clinging to him now, her fingers clenching on the hard, sweat-slicked muscles of his shoulders, nails digging into the bronzed skin. Her body was open to him, arcing towards his in urgent hunger, mutely inviting the fierce invasion that her tongue was incapable of describing in words.

Malik too was beyond speech, his black eyes glazed, his jaw set. But no words were needed, their touch, their kisses did all the communicating that was necessary and as he thrust himself into the moist core of her she gave herself up totally to the sensation of having him there, filling her, stretching her, possessing her.

For a moment the strong body above hers stilled, Malik drawing in a deep, ragged breath as he felt the soft tissues adjust around him. In the silence Abbie heard the air hiss in between his teeth as he struggled for control, for the strength to take the fullest pleasure from the moment, to absorb all it had to offer, to experience it totally. And then, just as she was beginning to fear she might come down from the heated heights to which he had taken her, whimpering in restless protest, he bent his head, kissed her, fierce and hard on her open mouth, and slowly, strongly, began to move.

And with that first moment all the powerful, almost brutal control that he had been exerting broke away from him and splintered irreparably. With a raw cry he gave in to the need he had been denying so long, thrusting in and out, hard and long, letting the wild, primal rhythm take him faster and faster. And Abbie clung to him, her body meeting his, taking his, giving back passion for passion. Together they climbed higher, fiercer, hotter, wilder, until it seemed as if they had broken free of the last threads that held them on the earth and were whirling out of existence and into another, more wonderful, more devastating universe where everything was pure sensation, pure delight. And in that other dimension Abbie lost control completely, dissolved, giving a wild keening cry of sheer fulfilment as she lost herself in a blinding explosion of stars that spun her out of consciousness and into total blank oblivion.

CHAPTER THIRTEEN

IN THE middle of the night Abbie woke suddenly, unsure of just what had disturbed her. The tent was dark, just one lamp burning in the blackness, and the silence of the desert outside was eerie, completely still.

Beside her, Malik too was still, his breathing soft, his long powerful body relaxed in sleep, the heat from it enclosing her as she lay curled up beside him. A faint smile touched her lips as she remembered the blaze of passion they had shared and she shifted slightly, moving closer so that she could feel his skin against hers, entangle her legs with the muscular strength of his.

And that was when she became aware of the fact that Malik was not actually asleep. He was lying completely still, totally silent, but when she turned her head she saw that he was wide awake and was lying with his head pillowed on his arms folded behind it and he was staring, blank-eyed and unblinking, up into the draped canopy above him.

And something about his very stillness and the way that those jet-dark eyes were unfocused told her that the thoughts that kept him from sleep were far from happy ones. Instinct led her in the probable direction of the cause.

'Are you thinking about Jalil?' she asked, keeping her voice as soft as possible so that he could act as if he hadn't heard her if that was what he wanted.

But Malik's dark head turned in her direction immediately, the deep-set eyes gleaming in the moonlight as he looked at her.

'I can't believe he's gone,' he said.

Under the covers, Abbie reached for his hand, folded her fingers around it and held tight.

'Would it help to talk? Tell me about him. I only knew the Jalil who was at school with me and then not very well. He was a bit arrogant…'

Malik's mouth twisted into a wry grin and a faint laugh escaped him.

'That's Jalil…that was Jalil,' he adjusted painfully. 'He was the only son—the only child of an elderly father and a doting mother who never denied him anything. Anything he wanted, it was his, and he always expected the rest of the world to treat him the same. He never learned discipline or control but was always lazy, self-indulgent and greedy. That's why he was never very popular with his people…'

His deep sigh made Abbie tighten her grip on the hand she held.

'And that was why he wanted—needed—a wife so much. If he married, had an heir, then things might have settled down a bit.'

'And you'd promised to help him?'

In the darkness Malik's nod was just a movement of the shadows.

'I made a vow to my mother that I would do everything in my power to keep him safe on his throne. In fact, I was the one who told him that marriage was his best hope of stability when there was unrest in Barakhara. At first he refused to listen but then, when things didn't quieten down, he conceded that maybe I had a point. Unfortunately for you, that was the time when your brother decided to help himself to some of the artefacts from the dig. Jalil remembered the crush he had had on you—and he became obsessed with the idea that you were the only bride for him.'

'And you were bound by your promise to help him.'

Under the covers Malik's hand tightened on her own and she felt the warmth of his lips brush her forehead in a gentle acknowledgement of her understanding.

'Bound by it but not in agreement with the way he went about enforcing his wishes. Though I thought it was "Gail" he was blackmailing into being his bride.'

'In Jalil's mind it probably was,' Abbie conceded. 'I was a very different person in those days—I've grown up a lot since.'

'Unfortunately, Jalil had not.'

Malik sighed, pushed his free hand through his hair and pressed it against his temple.

'He was a fool, a selfish, immature fool—but he was my brother.'

'And that bond is so strong that sometimes we have to do things we would never even think of because of it,' Abbie agreed, thinking of Andy. 'My own brother has made some major mistakes too. If he hadn't been so greedy for cash…

With a rustle of bedclothes, Malik turned towards her and planted another kiss on her mouth.

'Your brother had the misfortune to be *my* brother's means to an end. If Jalil hadn't wanted to have you as his wife, then he might well have been more prepared to listen to reason where Andy was concerned.'

In the concealing darkness the effect of that kiss was more than doubled, the taste of Malik's lips on hers intensified, the warm musky scent of his body reaching her as he stirred, the sound of his softly accented voice like music in the stillness of the night. Already the heat of need was lapping at her senses, making her far from satiated body come to life.

But there was something in the back of her mind that needed saying. Some question she still needed answering if she could just get her thoughts to work on it.

'How come Jalil needed an heir so badly and you don't? I mean, isn't it slightly hypocritical of you to have insisted

hat he did his duty by his country when you were still foot-
oose and fancy free? After all, you're so much older than him
ind there isn't even a sign of a wife in your life.'

*Except me…*a small voice whispered in reminder inside
ier head but she pushed it away hastily. She couldn't quite
pelieve that Malik had ever meant that sudden and impul-
,ive offer of marriage, and if she was honest just at this
noment she didn't even care. She had dreamed of being
with the man she loved for at least one night of her life,
ind that dream had been fulfilled. In fact, she was still
iving out that dream and she was wasting precious time
alking when they could be doing something much more
pleasurable.

Besides, she knew the answer to her own question. Malik
would never have let his country come close to rebellion be-
:ause of his own behaviour. He would always have had a far
stronger hold on the reins of power than his brother.

'Of course I need an heir,' Malik surprised her by answer-
ng. It was a shock to feel his breath on her face as he spoke.
And I need one more than ever now that I've inherited Jalil's
hrone and have two kingdoms to rule over.'

When had he come so much closer? She could feel the
ength of his body pressed up against hers and the heat and
strength of his obvious arousal pushed into the softness of
ier belly as a result.

'The fact is that I was once about to be married but it never
ictually happened—she had an unrecognised heart weakness
ind she died a few months before the wedding was to take
place.'

'I'm sorry…'

She could feel the rasp of his day's growth of beard as she
spoke, her lips almost pressed against the planes of his cheek,
he line of his strong jaw.

'Don't be—except for her. It was an arranged marriage. I
iardly knew her.'

But he would have married her, would have had children with her.

'You didn't love her?'

'Love didn't come into it. It wasn't important.'

And there she had her own fate declared in that flat, emotionless statement.

Even if he had meant the proposal he had flung at her—a proposal forced from him as much by the shocking events of the day as from any real belief in what he was offering—then he couldn't have made it any plainer that what he was looking for in a marriage was not emotional commitment.

Love…wasn't important.

So could she live with him—marry him—spend the rest of her life with him on those terms? Could she accept the little he would offer her emotionally and let it be enough?

'Marriage, your brother's freedom—a life of luxury beyond your wildest imaginings—and every night of your life spent in my bed…'

Malik's words, flung at her in the heat and despair of the moment, came back to torment her, echoing cruelly inside her head. He had thought that he was offering her so much but the truth was that for her it was far too little.

Malik might be able to offer her huge wealth, a life of luxury, but how could it ever be enough when she wanted, needed, longed for him to love her as she loved him?

'What is important?' she managed to whisper, fighting to wipe the tone of bitter disappointment from her words and hoping, praying, that he might just possibly say something more than what she already knew.

But her silent prayer went unanswered.

'What's important?' Malik murmured, coming even closer and enfolding her in the strength of his arms, 'Oh, *sukkar*, do you even have to ask? This is important…'

He drifted kisses over her hair, her forehead, over the closed lids of her eyes.

'And this…'

His hands began to move over her body, stroking, caressing, tantalising, finding the spots that were still needy, even after his attentions earlier in the night, stirring them, rousing them, making her writhe in growing response. Her mouth opened willingly to his, her tongue tangling in an intimate dance with his, and as the fire invaded her body she knew that, for now at least, she didn't, couldn't, care.

For now, Malik was right—this was important and she was not going to spoil it with thoughts about the future or worries about what might be.

For now, this was important—because it might be all she would ever have. This primal, fierce passion might be the only thing that Malik would ever feel for her, and right now that made it the most important and the most wonderful thing in all the world.

It was a long time before Malik's heart stopped racing, before his breathing eased. But as he slowly came back to himself he found himself wishing that he could have stayed in the mindless unconsciousness of the sexual force that had swamped him several times during the night.

At least there he had known what he was doing. He had known what he felt—and he had had a damn good idea of what Abbie was feeling too. Now, as the heated delirium ebbed from his mind and his body, he saw how little they had actually resolved. If anything.

'This marriage that you're offering…' Abbie had said. 'Show me what it would be like—and then I'll decide.'

And he'd shown her.

He'd shown himself too. He could hardly believe the experience he'd just had. Couldn't find the words to describe it, even to himself. He'd been taken out of this world and into another, a place he'd never known existed. And now that he was back in reality he knew that he would do anything—everything in his power to repeat that experience again and again.

Which meant keeping Abbie in his life.

A faint sound from the woman at his side made him turn, look down at her. She was still asleep, her long limbs relaxed and at ease, her breathing deep, her long tangled hair falling forward over her face. With a gentle hand he moved the blonde strands from her face and studied it silently.

Any minute now she would wake and tell him her decision. But there was only one decision he wanted to hear.

He had wanted this woman from the moment he had seen her. And last night had only added to that hunger, rather than doing anything to appease it. He no longer cared if she was only interested in him because of his wealth and power. She could be the worst gold-digger in the world and he would still want her. He couldn't lose her. Now that he had her, he would keep her whatever it took.

'Malik…?'

She was waking, stirring, stretching. Every movement of her body stirred his senses, made desire twist deep inside, setting his pulse racing again, his breathing becoming raw and uneven. All he wanted to do was to reach for, drag her into his arms, kiss her senseless…

But that was only a temporary solution. An immensely satisfying, intensely pleasurable temporary solution, but a shortlived, transient one all the same. He wanted more than that and so he was going to have to play this another way. So, in spite of the fact that it positively *hurt* to do it, he forced himself from the bed, snatched up his robe, and pulled it on just as Abbie stirred again, her heavy eyes opening slowly, blinking sleepily.

'Malik?'

Noticing his absence immediately, she pushed herself up on the cushions, turning her head sharply, blonde hair flying, looking for him in the grey light of dawn that was filtering into the tent.

'What are you doing? Where are you going?' she demanded when she saw that he was dressing.

'We're leaving.'

Was he fooling himself or had there been just the faintest reaction to that 'we'? Had she really thought that he would go without her? That he would leave her behind?

'Going where?'

'To Edhan—to my palace. We have a wedding—our wedding—to arrange.'

'Our wedding? But...'

She was obviously about to fling back the bedclothes and get out, coming to remonstrate with him, but an attack of second thoughts made her pause and decide to stay where she was.

'But I never said...'

'You didn't have to.'

Malik stamped his feet into soft leather boots, snatching up his cloak from the pile of cushions on to which he had tossed it the previous night.

'Your reaction last night said everything there was to say.'

Knowing it was coming, he watched the flare of indignation blaze in her eyes, saw the way that smooth, defiant chin came up, her soft mouth firming.

'I...' she began, but he had no intention of letting her finish.

'"This marriage that you're offering—with every night of my life spent in your bed,"' he quoted at her harshly, not wanting to give her an inch. '"Show me what it would be like—and then I'll decide." I showed you...' he added when she opened her mouth to argue. 'I showed you what it was— what it *is* going to be like, and now I see no point at all in wasting any time. We're going to Edhan and we're going to be married.'

She was about to argue again so he covered the space between them in a couple of swift, determined strides, taking that rebellious chin in his hand and holding it just where he wanted it as he planted a swift, silencing kiss on her partly open mouth.

'So I suggest you get up and get dressed, unless you plan on riding all the way to the capital dressed—or rather undressed—like that.'

And while she was still spluttering with indignation, still trying to find a way to answer him, he turned on his heel and marched out into the cool of early morning, letting the tent flap fall closed behind him, muffling her furious shout of his name.

CHAPTER FOURTEEN

MARRIAGE, your brother's freedom—a life of luxury beyond your wildest imaginings…

The words ran round and round on a never-ending loop inside Abbie's head all day, every day, from the moment that she woke up until the moment she fell asleep. And if she woke at any point in the night too, they were still there, still reminding her of how much Malik had promised her—and how little.

The luxury beyond her wildest imaginings was always there in the huge palace with its marble floors and walls, the decorations picked out in gold, the crystal chandeliers everywhere. There were miles and miles of corridors, huge ornately furnished rooms, and the suite allocated to her was enormous, bigger even than the flat she had once shared with three friends when she had been at university.

She had servants to attend to every possible need—and a few that she hadn't even realised she had. It seemed as if she had only to think of something and it was hers, sometimes without ever asking for it or raising her hand to indicate what she needed.

The cases that she had packed when she had thought that she was going to meet Jalil had been delivered and carefully unpacked and placed in the huge wardrobes where they had looked a little lost amongst all the hanging space. But then that space hadn't been there for long as Malik had ordered a vast wardrobe of new clothes for her, western designer outfits together with an endless range of traditional clothing, robes in the finest silks, in a hundred different colours, hand embroidered with beautiful designs. There were jewels too, necklaces and bracelets, ornate earrings in gold and set with the finest stones money could buy.

And in her wardrobe hung one very special gown with its matching robe, crafted from pure white silk, embroidered with silver and gold and with a matching scarf for her hair, so fine that it looked like a spider's web spun from pure gold.

Her wedding gown.

Because it was obvious that Malik was determined that the marriage was going ahead.

From the moment that he had walked out of their tent and started issuing orders to prepare for their journey back to Edhan, he had blithely ignored any attempt she had made to protest that she hadn't actually agreed to his proposal, that at no time had she ever said that she would be his bride.

'I showed you what it is going to be like,' he'd declared, 'and now I see no point at all in wasting any time. We're going to Edhan and we're going to be married.'

And here they were in the palace in Edhan, and preparations were well under way. No one could accuse him of wasting any time about it! The wedding was to be held at the end of the week—just five days from now—and less than a fortnight since she had left the oasis encampment and travelled back here to this city, this country where Malik was ruler of all he surveyed.

Privately Abbie wished they could still be in that oasis, in the small black tent under the desert stars where everything had seemed so simple and so possible. The single night she had spent there in Malik's arms held a magical memory for her as the one night when she had known the heat and the passion of his loving in a way that was wild enough and powerful enough to drive away all the fears and doubts that had clouded her mind. In that tent, Malik had just been a man and she had just been a woman and the sensual fires they had built between them had held the world at bay at least for the length of that glorious night.

Now they were back in the world and Malik was a different man. A sheikh. A ruler now of not one but two different countries. He had had to arrange Jalil's funeral, and then he had so many things to do and so little time to spare that she barely saw him, even at night.

If she could at least have shared his bed then she might have been able to talk to him, or try to burn away her doubts in the heat of the sexual desire they felt for each other. But she slept alone in the huge, softly comfortable bed in the private suite she had been given, too often lying awake, staring at the ornate patterns of arches and mosaics that formed the ceiling above her.

Marriage, your brother's freedom—a life of luxury beyond your wildest imaginings...

Your brother's freedom...

And there was one other reason why she didn't dare to go to Malik and tell him that she didn't think she could marry him after all.

Andy.

Malik had promised that he would free Andy and he had kept his word. In fact, he had acted far more quickly than she had ever anticipated. On the very same day that they arrived at the palace in Edhan, Abbie's brother had been freed from the jail where he was imprisoned and brought to the palace, where he was reunited with his sister. He was here now, along with her parents and a stunned, bug-eyed George who had seen as many camels as his heart desired, ready to attend the wedding ceremony when it took place.

When she had first seen him, Abbie had been appalled by Andy's thinness and pallor but after a few days of freedom, of relaxation and proper food, he was finally starting to fill out, to look more human. But that improvement was dependent on him being out of prison and being properly looked after.

And his freedom was dependent on her marrying Malik.

So, in spite of her fears, she had to go through with this.

She could do this, Abbie told herself. She had to do it. She had no choice.

She even managed to convince herself until Malik had stunned her by introducing her to his best friend's wife.

'Lucy has been through all this herself,' he told her when he announced that Sheikh Hakim bin Taimur Al Fulani and his English wife, the former Lucy Mannion, were coming to stay for a few days before the wedding ceremony. 'She and Hakim have only been married a year, so she knows all about the problems of adjusting—she'll help you with the problems and the possible pitfalls you might encounter. I also think you'll like her—you could become friends.'

Abbie had thought so too. Lucy, a petite blonde, very close to her own age, was a delightful person, someone she found it easy to get to know and even easier to like. Under any other circumstances, she would have enjoyed the other girl's company and welcomed her help with the complicated and stressful preparations for the approaching royal wedding.

But these weren't anything like normal circumstances. For one thing she, Abbie, was preparing for a wedding that she hadn't really ever said yes to. And for another, Lucy's presence and her obvious deeply loving relationship with her new husband, Hakim, threw the fake relationship that Abbie had with Malik into sharp relief, revealing it for the pretence that it was.

From the moment of Lucy's arrival at the palace, Abbie's doubts, already disturbing enough, took even deeper root, growing worse and worse with every day that passed. But the final straw was when Lucy, obviously bursting to tell someone, whispered a secret to her newfound friend.

'I'm pregnant, Abbie,' she said, barely able to get the words out for the width of her smile. 'I just found out I'm having Hakim's baby in seven months' time.'

'That's wonderful!' Abbie managed a genuine smile back. She was truly delighted for Lucy and her charming husband.

But her struggle for inward composure was shattered completely when Lucy added, 'You and Malik will have to hurry up and start a family too and then our little ones can grow up together.'

If anything was guaranteed to destroy Abbie's ability to think straight then that was it.

There was a long ceremonial banquet as part of the wedding celebrations and simply sitting through it was an endurance test for her. She had to sit beside Malik, devastatingly handsome in his traditional robes, and watch him receive the congratulations, the good wishes of what seemed like hundreds of guests. Never before had this man she loved seemed so outrageously exotic and arrogantly masculine. Never before had he looked so gloriously striking, so wonderfully attractive, and she found it impossible to do more than pick at her meal and swallow the smallest sips of her drink as she watched him with loving eyes.

Loving but lost eyes.

Because Lucy's words had reminded her of the part of this arrangement that she had been desperately trying to forget. Marriage was more than just two people living together, making love together. As far as Malik was concerned, that making love was for a purpose—and the purpose was to get himself an heir.

'Of course I need an heir,' he'd said. 'And I need one more than ever now that I've inherited Jalil's throne and have two kingdoms to rule over.'

Could she really go ahead with this marriage, knowing that Malik would expect a child from her to be his much-needed heir? It was one thing committing herself to a man who didn't love her when she felt she had no choice, but was it right to create a child from that marriage, knowing that the baby's father had never loved its mother?

Malik would see no wrong in it. He had been planning on an arranged marriage from the start, would have been married to his first chosen bride if she hadn't died so tragically. He would have no problem in going ahead with the marriage—and with fatherhood—this way.

But could she justify it to herself?

'Are you not well?'

Malik had noticed Abbie's silence, the way the colour had faded from her face. She had barely touched her meal, but had simply pushed the food around on her plate, putting very little of it near her mouth.

Her smile was swift, brief and a little wan, fading rapidly at the edges before it really had time to form.

'I'm just a little tired,' she murmured, her grey eyes dropping away from his concerned scrutiny. 'I—haven't been sleeping too well.'

'A strange bed and unaccustomed surroundings.' Malik nodded. 'And there has been so much to plan and prepare…'

Leaning forward, he took her hand, looking deeply into her cloudy eyes.

'And I have been neglectful of you lately.'

'You've had so much to do.'

'True—but that is no excuse. You are my betrothed—my bride-to-be. I should not be so inattentive to you. It is wrong.'

With a small, gentle tug on her hands he drew her even closer until he could rest his cheek against the softness of her skin and whisper right in her delicate ear.

'Shall I come to you tonight, *habibti*? Shall I share your bed—help you to sleep? I am sure that you would rest more easily in my arms.'

For a moment he thought she was actually going to refuse. Her eyes dropped to stare down at their linked hands and white teeth worried at the pink softness of her lower lip.

She couldn't say no! He would die if she held back now— if she said she wanted to sleep alone. Not that sleeping was what he was thinking of. He had found the nights' separation from her as difficult as she so obviously had. But he'd been working long days and long hours into the night and he had left her alone so as not to disturb her. The wedding day would come soon enough and when the ceremonies were over they would have all the rest of their lives together.

Tonight she looked lovelier than ever. Dressed in a silk gown that almost exactly matched her eyes and with her shimmering blonde hair piled up on the top of her head, diamonds at her ears and throat, she was incandescently beautiful, a pale ethereal vision of delight.

'Abbie…?' he prompted when she hesitated.

He'd missed her more than he could imagine and at this moment, with the scent of her body blended with some soft floral perfume tormenting his nostrils, he could barely control the hunger that was clutching at him. It was all he could do to stay in his seat and not leap to his feet, snatch her up and carry her off to his rooms, to his bed, right there and then.

'Yes…' she said at last and it was only when his breath hissed out between his teeth that he realised how much he had been holding it in and for how long. 'Yes, I'd like that.'

Like! In Malik's ears the word sounded too insipid, too restrained to match the way he was feeling. But then he was forgetting that Abbie was a fine-bred English woman and that restraint, in language at least, had probably been drummed into her from birth. But he knew from glorious experience that the one place his fine English wife-to-be entirely lost her grip on those reins of restraint was in bed.

In public now, with her cool colouring, her pale hair, her cool silver dress and the diamonds he had given her sparkling like ice around her neck and in her lobes, she might look like a water spirit, calm and clear as liquid. But when she was in bed with him, under him, opening to him, then she was all fire and air, as wild and wanton as any man's dream of a woman would be.

And tonight he would be with her again.

'Wait for me,' he told her softly, fighting to keep his voice level, his breathing even. The images his thoughts had thrown up at him were so powerfully erotic, so furiously arousing that he was going to have to struggle for control for the rest of the evening.

But that struggle would be all the more worthwhile when he finally joined this woman—his woman—in her bed. Then he would throw off all the constraints he had been fighting against and lose himself completely in her welcoming body.

The time couldn't come soon enough.

Somehow he managed to get through the hours that remained until he was free. He spoke with the right people, thanked the ones he needed to thank, accepted congratulations until his head was buzzing with them. And then, at long last, everyone had retired to bed, the palace was silent, the lights turned off in all but the most personal quarters, and he could go to Abbie.

To the woman who was soon to be his wife.

He hadn't felt this way since he had been an adolescent, escaping the confines of school, the palace, and saddling his favourite Arabian stallion, heading out into the wilds of the country, riding free with the desert wind in his hair. But tonight he didn't need to leave the palace to escape.

Tonight he had everything he needed right here.

He prayed she would still be waiting for him. She had never regained any of the colour in her face and had escaped the banquet at the earliest possible opportunity, pleading tiredness. Perhaps that tiredness would have overcome her and she had fallen asleep. Even just thinking of it made his body tense in anticipated frustration.

But then… As he had learned in one night, in a tent in the desert, there was a whole new sort of satisfaction to be found in just lying beside a woman, holding her close and watching her sleep.

At least there was that satisfaction with *this* woman. It was something he had never known with any other woman who had shared his bed. And the moment when she stirred, woke, opened her eyes and looked up into his face, with her silvery gaze still blurred from sleep, her expression soft, her mouth just the tiniest bit open…

Damn it! He was too hard, too hot already to even *think* about that. He couldn't even pause to discard the ornate ceremonial robes and change into something much more simple. He didn't want to waste a single second.

Let her be waiting for him… Please let her be waiting!

She was.

At the first glance into the room, where only a single bedside lamp burned to lighten the darkness, he thought that she had given him up. But then, as his eyes adjusted to the gloom, he saw that there was no sign of anyone in the bed, and in a faint pool of light he caught the gleam of her fair hair where she was sitting in a chair by the window.

She had discarded the gown she had worn for the banquet, pulling on a white silk robe that was wrapped around her slender form, knotted at the narrow waist. But her hair was still piled up on top of her head and the diamond necklace and earrings still glinted against her pale skin. She looked like an ice maiden—an ice queen.

An ice queen who would very soon turn to fire in his arms.

'Abbie!'

Barely pausing to kick the door to behind him, he crossed the room in half a dozen swift strides, his arms already reaching for her as he approached. And she rose to meet him, coming up out of her chair and almost throwing herself into those outstretched arms, with his name a cry of welcome on her lips. Their bodies met, mouths fused, hands grabbed and clung.

She was wearing nothing under the white robe. He could feel that from the way her breasts swung unfettered against his chest, the smooth sleek line of her hips and buttocks with not even the finest hint of lace to conceal, to mar the perfection of her skin.

And the robe itself was no barrier to his urgent hands. In seconds he had wrenched open the tie belt, ripped the silk from her body and, sweeping her off her feet and up into his arms, he carried her to the bed, flung her down. Discarding his own clothing with a violent haste, he came down beside her on the silken cover.

'I have been waiting for this so long.'

'Then you don't have to wait any longer.'

She was reaching for him even as she whispered the words, her soft hands closing over his arms, drawing her to him, her legs already parting underneath him, offering herself, giving herself, inviting him in. And she was already so soft, so wet, so obviously hungry for him too that he barely hesitated long enough to draw a heaving breath before he thrust into her, hearing her moan of sensual response as her yearning body lifted to meet his, her inner muscles closing round him.

It was hard, it was fierce, it was demanding. It was hot as hell. So hot that there was no chance at all of lingering, of delaying, of giving. It was all he could do not to let himself go in the first few glorious seconds. But Abbie didn't seem to want delay, or even finesse. Lying there beneath him like some wild tribal queen, naked except for the brilliant glitter of the jewels she wore, she urged him on with soft little groans and louder cries, her nails digging into the flesh on his back, her mouth nipping at his lips, his face, his chest. And when she gave a final, wicked little twist of her hips, taking all control from him as she slid herself up and down his throbbing shaft, he lost all control completely and gave himself up to the explosion that rocked his senses to their core.

'Abbie—my wife—my queen...'

It escaped him on a raw cry of rapture and somewhere in the shattered remnants of his mind he heard her answering whimper of delight, the keening moan of the moment of release as they both lost themselves in the blazing consummation of mindless ecstasy.

Malik thought that his heart had stopped completely. The next moment he believed that his pulse would never stop racing, that his breathing would never, ever settle down again. His head spun, his hands shook—his whole body shook. He had never known anything like it.

He had been taken out of the existence he knew, caught up in a whirlwind and a firestorm combined, hurled higher than he had ever been—and dropped back down to earth in a world that could never be the same again.

The one thing he knew was that Abbie was there with him—and Abbie was all he needed, all he wanted. All he had been looking for all his life.

'Abbie...'

He lifted his head from where it had fallen on to her shoulder as he'd collapsed on top of her, with his face crushed up against the hardness of the necklace, the jewels digging into his cheek.

'Abbie...' It was all he could manage as he pressed his lips against her face... And jolted upright, forced out of the sensual haze into which he had drifted by the taste of salt, the feel of moisture under his mouth.

'Tears? Abbie, habibti—why?'

Why? Oh, dear heaven, how did she ever answer that?

Released from the imprisoning pressure of Malik's long body, Abbie rolled over on to her side to curl in a miserable heap, her face and the betraying tears hidden in the cover.

She had never meant to dissolve into tears. She had been determined to be strong, to cope with this in the best way she could.

Waiting in the darkness for Malik to come to her, she had reached a decision, one that threatened to break her heart, but one that she knew was the only way forward for her.

She couldn't marry Malik, couldn't live with him for the rest of her life, loving him and knowing that he didn't love her. It would destroy her, take her heart and rip it to shreds. And when she added the thought that she might have a baby, a child who needed, deserved, two parents who loved each other, she had known that her decision had been made for her.

She had resolved that she would tell him tonight—but first she would allow herself the private personal indulgence of one more—one last chance to make love with him.

It would hurt, it would be a bitter-sweet experience, and she had been prepared for that. What she hadn't been ready for was the wild, fierce, totally overwhelming, all-consuming tidal wave of passion that had swamped her. The waves of love and need had broken over her head, swamping her, drowning her, taking her up and up into the greatest ecstasy she had ever known…

…And then she had been dropped right down on to the barren shore once more, knowing it was over and she would never experience such joy again.

And that was when the tears had come, flowing down her cheeks in rivulets of misery that she just couldn't even try to control.

'Abbie…'

Malik's hand on her shoulder was gentle, his voice soft, concerned.

'Why the tears? Why are you crying?'

Sniffing inelegantly, swiping at her face with the back of her hand, Abbie couldn't meet his searching gaze.

'I—we—Lucy's pregnant.'

'She is?'

It was clearly the last thing he had been expecting and his proud head went back in shock.

'She is? Hakim will be overjoyed. But…'

To Abbie's horror, he touched her again, turning her face towards him.

'Why is this a cause for sadness? Surely celebrations are—'

Tears flooded her eyes again so that his handsome face was just a blur.

'Celebrations for them perhaps—but what if we…?'

'You don't want children?' Malik jumped to the wrong conclusion when the words were choked off in her constricted throat, impossible to take any further. 'Abbie, if that's a problem then you only have to say. We don't have to have a baby if it's the last thing you want.'

The last thing… It was the thing she most wanted in all the world, if only it had been possible—if Malik only loved her.

'But—but you need an heir.'

She had to get a grip on herself or she would never be able to do this. Pushing herself up into a sitting position, she grabbed at a pillow and wiped her eyes on it, blinking hard to clear the stinging moisture from her vision. Then, pulling out a sheet from under her, she tugged it up, creating a fragile, partially protective wrap that at least concealed, even if it wasn't enough to act as any sort of armour against the pain.

'I need an heir,' Malik told her, looking deep into her tear-stained eyes. 'But if you don't—then when we marry—'

And this was when she had to say it. She had hoped that the moment wouldn't come so soon, that she would have a little time at least to prepare herself. To find the words she needed, but it seemed that the Fates were not going to be so kind.

And still, perhaps it was so much better this way. If she could just get it said and done and over with then maybe—

maybe—she might have the chance to get away and lick her wounds in private. Not to recover, because she was sure that she never would recover from this. Would never recover from loving Malik and knowing that she could have been his but he would never, ever be hers.

'We aren't going to marry,' she said as firmly as she could manage with her throat closing tight over the words, her breathing raw and agonising in her lungs. 'That's just the point, Malik. I can't do this. I won't marry you.'

'You won't…'

It was Malik's turn to rear back, his eyes narrowing in instant shock and disbelief. The movement freed the rest of the sheet that Abbie was wrapped in enough to let her off the bed, hauling the white linen with her and wrapping it around her further, toga-style. The concealing folds gave her a little more courage to go on.

'I won't marry you. I know you thought I was going to. You believed that I accepted your proposal—but I never did.'

'I offered you…'

'I know—I know about Andy. You freed him because of our arrangement, because I said I'd marry you, but please, please don't send him back to prison. I'll take his place—I'll serve his sentence…'

'You would rather go to prison than marry me? Don't be bloody stupid, woman!'

It was a wild, ferocious roar. The fury of a desert ruler thwarted by a mere commoner, and a woman at that.

'Your brother has nothing to do with this! Nothing! And he is most definitely not going back to prison—and nor are you. I was going to free him anyway—no matter what you said to my proposal of marriage.'

'He—you…'

Abbie couldn't get her breath back enough to speak.

'You were going to free him?'

'Of course. He's been a fool but, he assures me he didn't know the things he took had any religious significance and I believe him. Whatever he did, he certainly didn't deserve the sentence Jalil imposed on him.'

'But you said…'

'Your brother's freedom was part of what I was offering you in marriage—it wasn't there only *on condition* you married me. Andy is free—and he'll stay free, no matter what happens between us.'

'Thank you.'

It was all that she could manage.

'Thank you with all my heart,' she tried to go on, but Malik ignored her.

'So now that we have the suspicion of blackmailing you into marriage out of the way—will you please reconsider your decision not to marry me?'

That 'please' almost destroyed her but she had to hold strong.

'I can't.'

For a few terrible seconds she thought that he was going to argue. That he was going to refuse to accept her declaration. But then his face closed up, shutters coming down behind the black eyes, and he pushed himself off the bed, stalking across the room to snatch up the black robe he had discarded in such haste just a heartbreakingly few moments before. Slinging it on, he pulled the gaping front together over his chest, folding his arms to hold it secure, and the way that this man, normally so proud and totally unembarrassed by his nudity, had covered himself spoke volumes for the way he was feeling.

'You can't do this,' he said, cold and proud and totally autocratic. 'I won't allow it.'

'Oh, Malik—' Abbie sighed '—I have to. I've thought and thought about this and it's the only answer I can come up with—the only thing to do. I know all the reasons why you'll think that the wedding can't be cancelled, but I've thought them through and it can be done. It'll be inconvenient, but…'

'What reasons?' Malik demanded, shocking her with the savage ferocity of his tone. 'What reasons, Abbie? Tell me the reasons why it will be so *inconvenient* to cancel our marriage.'

'Why—well—the invitations have been sent out, the dignitaries are starting to arrive, the robes have been made…'

'The feasts are ordered, the decorations planned.' Malik took up the list in a tone so brutally cold that it made her toes curl in horror on the hard marble floor. 'I have your father's blessing, I've given you jewels—the bridal gift…'

'I know…'

With shaking hands, she reached up to unfasten the necklace, remove the dangling earrings from her lobes. Hurriedly she moved towards him, holding out the hand that held the jewellery.

'And now I'm giving them back to you. I don't want them—and you'll need these for the woman you marry—for your real bride.'

Malik glanced down at the sparkling handful, just once. Then, in a gesture of total disdain, he snatched at her fingers, folded them back over the brilliant jewels, thrust it back at her.

'Keep them,' he snarled. 'I gave them to you. I will never give them to any other woman, because if you do not marry me then I will never take another wife. There is no other woman I could ever meet who I'd want to marry after you.'

'Malik, please… I know how you—how we both feel—but sexual desire isn't the foundation to build a marriage upon.'

'Sexual desire?' Malik dismissed her protest with an arrogant wave of his hand. 'Desire isn't all of it. It isn't the only reason I want to marry you. The real reason is the one you've missed off your list of *inconveniences*. It's the reason you've forgotten, or perhaps that you didn't know—the most important reason of all.'

'And that is?'

She had no idea what he was going to say—didn't even dare begin to guess because the wild flames she saw in his eyes told her that it was more than important—that it was something so vital to Malik that he had no way of concealing how he felt.

'That I love you—that you are my dream, my soul mate, my life. I love you more than the world and that is why I want to marry you. That is why I can't cancel this wedding, because the truth is that I think I will die if I have to—that I can't go on if I'm forced to live without you.'

'Oh, Malik…'

Tears of joy slid from the corners of her eyes as she struggled to believe she had heard right, struggled to accept that all her dreams had come true. That this man she loved—adored—with all her heart loved her back with all the power and strength of which he was capable.

'Malik…'

She fought back the tears, blinking hard so that she could see his beloved face in this most important moment in her life.

'I love you too, but I thought you would never care for me—that's why I felt I couldn't go through with our marriage.'

'Not care for you?'

Malik's laugh had such a raw, shaken edge to it that it caught on her heart and tugged it painfully.

'Oh, Abbie, I once thought that I could accept an arranged marriage—a marriage that would bring me the heirs I needed, the security for my country. But as I got to know you I realised that I'd just been deceiving myself to think that I could live that way. I wanted you, needed you. Any woman in the world could give me the children I need—but only one woman on earth could be my true *wife*—the centre of my world. My reason for living.'

To Abbie's stunned amazement, he took her hand in his, then sank to one knee on the polished marble floor, looking up into her bemused face with intent jet-black eyes.

'Let's start again and do this right, this time. Abbie, my life, love, will you marry me and be my queen—the queen of my country—of my world—for the rest of our lives?'

Abbie had to swallow hard to relieve the tight constriction in her throat, to enable her to find the words to answer him. She could hardly believe that this was Malik, the Sheikh, the desert ruler. He'd swept into her room like the proud, arrogant king he was, dressed in ceremonial robes, his head high, black eyes filled with all the pride of his lineage. But now he was kneeling at her feet with all that pride, that arrogance, royalty stripped from him.

There was only Malik the man, laid bare for her as he would do for no other person in the world.

He was waiting for her answer.

And there was only one answer she could give him.

Folding her hand around his, she lowered herself to the floor beside him, kneeling as close to him as she could manage as she held his black, questioning gaze with her steady, glowing silver one.

'Yes, my darling Malik,' she told him softly but confidently, no trace of doubt putting even the hint of hesitation into her voice. 'Yes, my king. I will marry you and be your queen—and love you with all my heart.'

And, leaning forward into his waiting arms, she sealed her vow with a long, loving kiss.

Regency

HIGH-SOCIETY AFFAIRS

Rakes and rogues in the ballrooms – and the bedrooms – of Regency England!

6th March 2009
A Hasty Betrothal by Dorothy Elbury
A Scandalous Marriage by Mary Brendan

3rd April 2009
The Count's Charade by Elizabeth Bailey
The Rake and the Rebel by Mary Brendan

1st May 2009
Sparhawk's Lady by Miranda Jarrett
The Earl's Intended Wife by Louise Allen

5th June 2009
Lord Calthorpe's Promise by Sylvia Andrew
The Society Catch by Louise Allen

8 VOLUMES IN ALL TO COLLECT!

www.millsandboon.co.uk

FIVE fabulously sexy stories in the hottest beach read of the summer!

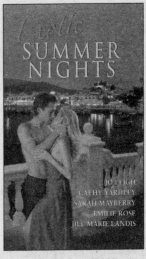

Start a fire in New York with a rugged cowboy...

Get down and dirty in California with a tempting playboy...

Steam up Sydney with an Australian tycoon...

Make some memories in Georgia with a sexy businessman...

Turn up the heat in Hawaii with a wealthy artist...

Available 3rd July 2009